Penguin Books

The State of the Art

Born in Nowra, New South Wales, Frank Moorhouse has lived for many years in the Sydney suburb of Balmain, a place he has affectionately fictionalized. He has worked as a journalist in Sydney and as an itinerant editor of country newspapers and was, for a time, editor of the *Australian Worker*. He has written fiction and commentary on politics and Australian life for the *National Times* and the *Bulletin* and has scripted the films *Between Wars, Conference-ville* and *The Disappearance of Azaria Chamberlain*. He has travelled in the United States, United Kingdom, parts of Europe, India and around Australia, reporting and giving readings of his work. His interests include bush-walking and night clubs. He has published six books of stories: *Futility and Other Animals, The Americans, Baby, The Electrical Experience, Conference-ville, Tales of Mystery and Romance* and *The Everlasting Secret Family and Other Secrets*; and one non-fiction book: *Days of Wine and Rage*.

The Mood of Contemporary Australia
in Short Stories

THE
STATE
OF
THE ART

Edited by Frank Moorhouse

Penguin Books
Published with the assistance of the Literature
Board of the Australia Council

Penguin Books Australia Ltd,
487 Maroondah Highway, P.O. Box 257
Ringwood, Victoria, 3134, Australia
Penguin Books Ltd,
Harmondsworth, Middlesex, England
Penguin Books,
40 West 23rd Street, New York, N.Y. 10010, U.S.A.
Penguin Books Canada Ltd,
2801 John Street, Markham, Ontario, Canada
Penguin Books (N.Z.) Ltd,
182-190 Wairau Road, Auckland 10, New Zealand

First published by Penguin Books Australia, 1983
Reprinted 1984 twice

This collection Copyright © Frank Moorhouse, 1983

Copyright in individual stories is retained by the author

Typeset in Century Old Style by Dovatype, Melbourne

Made and printed in Australia by
The Dominion Press-Hedges & Bell, Victoria

CIP

The State of the art.

ISBN 0 14 006598 9.

1. Short stories, Australian — 20th century.
1. Moorhouse, Frank, 1938-.

A823'.0108

CONTENTS

THE STATE OF THE ART
OF LIVING IN AUSTRALIA

Not only is this book a look at the art of story-telling in Australia, it also looks at the state of the art of living in Australia. This anthology is not a deliberate presentation of social concerns, styles or conventions. It isn't a newspaper. But it is something of a map of social concerns that are part of the background to these stories, mostly written in the 1980s.

Ten years ago I edited the last *Coast to Coast* anthology. I said then that I had not found an abundance of riches. This time I did. I could have confidently put together two books of stories. I found another thirty or so writers – for the most part unknown writers – who engrossed me as much as those I eventually included in the book.

I had to limit the boundaries to make selection less frustrating. I have, for instance, excluded the work of the master practitioners: Frank Hardy, Hal Porter, Dal Stivens, Peter Cowan, John Morrison, Amy Whiting, Alan Marshall, Peter Shrubb, Thea Astley and Marjorie Barnard. They are represented well in other anthologies. So the book evolved not as a selection of 'contemporary classics' – although there may be a few of these – but as the burning edge of the art form.

I have also excluded, arbitrarily, Australian nationals living permanently abroad, and this meant losing such writers as Glenda Adams. I narrowed the selection to people writing in Australia and in most cases interacting imaginatively with the 'Australian condition'. Even with the arbitrary rules of exclusion I was still left with about 1500 published stories and 1200 unpublished stories submitted by about 520 writers. I have, however, included as a narrative category 'Travelling About, Bumming Around, In Transit', which is about Australians travelling, and I have included one gothic tale.

The categories which I have used are classic. I did not seek stories that illustrated types of experience, such as 'life on the dole'; my concentration was on the *art* of story-telling.

'Stories from a journey' is the most successfully practised short story genre in Australia; about 20 per cent of the best stories were about travel. Travel is not only about encounters with foreign ways or the trying-on of foreign styles, it is an encounter with one's nationality. A traveller is stripped of nearly all identity through having long periods of being without back-home status, occupational identification and without a personal network. Often the only functioning parts of identity while travelling are wealth, sub-culture (if the people from other countries can read sub-cultural signs correctly) and nationality (if they can guess this). So before complete personality can cautiously emerge, it is nationality, 'being Australian', which sets the shape of discourse and interaction.

I was surprised to find that political life as a narrative site was hardly evident. No stories about being on action committees (or any committees), no stories about corporate or communal intrigue or of the governmental experience. The magazine *9-2-5* carries material mostly about work and grievance, but it is rarely in story form. The political stories I did receive had anger and sincerity, but in any story writing these equalities alone are insufficient. Politics was in some of the stories by implication, but the stories as a whole were unworldly, under-experienced in this sense. This may be a limitation of fashion. The current fashion in story writing is for the personal and the gameful. Overwhelmingly, the stories I read were domestic, in all its weird shapes.

The fashion of the personal is a clue to the flux of our times: the renegotiation of the terms of personal relationship, the redefinition of what a woman is supposed to be and what a man is supposed to be. Consequently this is written about – as a way of coping with it and as a way of recording it – and it produces its own aesthetic. The subject is political in the broad sense.

It is risky to make social extrapolations from fiction, but fiction is rich in clues and signs. About a third of these stories are from experiences that infringe upon conservative conventions, and the other two thirds I see as coming from main-stream experience. This seems to me to reflect accurately the way Australians live. The stories show Australia as a non-spiritual nation, an existentially casual community that does not brood about the meaning of life or the nature of death. We have become more interested in perceptions of the past and have developed the capacity to hold the past with one hand and let go with the other, instead of wiping the past with every generation. I think we are escaping from what I have called the 'genesis illusion': the belief that everv generation starts afresh and without trammels.

Australia appears to be still a robustly hedonistic society, but perhaps through art, and with heightened communication between men and women and within the sexes (about the meaning of gender), together with the cultural modification which comes subtly from travel, design, cuisine, we will add sensuality to the robust hedonism.

This book is full of delights, and putting it together was a task of serendipity. A good short story is like a good conversation, a sexual encounter with a stranger which turns out to be surprisingly good, or a beautiful handmade toy. 'Games, fantasies and lyricism' is one of the narrative categories of the book, and it is one of the most alive. This dialogue with form is one of the things I looked for. It can be the playing around with structure, language or arrangement to make pleasing shapes of meaning or patterns of sensation – beautiful toys – which is enough. But it can also be a way of prising or tricking fresh meaning from the form. It is a way of releasing verbal energy and can create a new exchange between the reader and the form.

But story writing is a social act of communication, and this dialogue with form (as in the dialogue with self) can become a closed network between writer and the writer's self. A little of this is acceptable as long as the writer comes back to the reader soon enough. A writer can never be sure everything that is tried also works. Sometimes, to fully enjoy the game, the reader has to be tuned to the form; all art is not equally accessible to all people. But the sales of short fiction in Australia in the last few years have shown that there exists a sufficiently bright and open-minded readership. Clever academics at conferences now sometimes present their papers as short stories, and academic criticism becomes increasingly playful. The readers are also players. William Hazlitt wrote that conversation is limited by the level of its reception, is made by its reception. Stories also exist within a context of reception.

Nearly all the other great dialogues found in short fiction are in this book. The dialogue with self, the dialogue with society, the dialogue with the past, the dialogue with the environment and the dialogue with gender.

And there is something I call the 'journey of the form': the results that come from working at a particular art form over a long period and finding where it leads (not all people who have written a good story take the journey; many move on to the novel or the film). But the pursuit of form produces a dialogue with the writer's own work as well as the inescapable dialogue with what has been written by other writers, past and contemporary.

My preferences are for stories that present an open-ended aesthetic experience which the sensibility can take for its own use. I have no taste for the story that leads me firmly to one destination. I like stories that let loose on the way. But everyone likes some stories that confirm their life perspective, assure them that they are not mad or damned, or at least not the only ones who are mad and damned.

The selection is not entirely a personal one. I have tried to present the landscape of the form to include good practitioners who might fall outside my taste. In making the wider selection I used the judgement of my editorial assistant, Bronwyn Bulgeries, the critical commentaries of Elizabeth Webby, the reactions of Jackie Yowell, senior editor at Penguin, and the advice of Don Anderson and Brian Kiernan.

Good writing not only liberates us from the limitations of our dominant cultural conventions but also from strident minor ideologies that try to capture us. Some writing is relievedly decadent, vagrant, errant and avoids contemporary social concerns.

C. K. Stead, the New Zealand critic, helped me to formulate what I like about stories. I like stories that are an arrangement of fragments within a personal field, which have a carefully judged incompletion.

This incompletion emphasises that it is the progression of the story which is important, not the 'ending'. And I like a density of reference to the public world – something I did not often find. The central performance of a good story is the fusion of the oblique, the unintended and the intended which together trigger reader reactions. Good fiction is 'not all there', and each reader brings 'the rest' to make a slightly different completion of any work (within boundaries and controls engineered by the writer).

The great need in Australian story writing is still that it should 'go too far' and resist blandness.

To repeat what I said in *Coast to Coast* (with some slight changes in my thinking), the short story is a natural form, a sophistication of the dream, the spoken anecdote (with all its great shapes) and the private fantasy. It has all the technological advantages of the printed word: comparatively unrestricted distribution, easily retrieved, portable and able to be consumed at a personal pace. It can simulate all the senses (convey the sensations of touch, smell, sight, hearing, which film cannot do). It has some special advantages because of its economics; it can be specialized in readership both in sensibility and in region, culturally and geographically. Unlike the novel, it can be published outside book form. The short story, like all imaginative work, can be an intense form which releases complex vibrations and oblique stimulations not readily reducible to simple political or sociological analysis.

I like to think that the art of the anthology is to make something similar to children's puzzles where numbers are linked to make a picture. If you join the lines of association, the outer and inner connections of all these stories, you have a picture of the Australian sensibility and an indication of the state of the art of living in Australia.

Marriage, Parenthood, Ancestors

Ranald Allan

YOUNG FATHER

1   The Pre-Wet: Top End, NT

You ask me how life is up here, as the tension builds while we
wait for the first rains to break the long dry. Sure we're wrestling
water buffaloes and crocs, screwing lots of velvet, drinking in
the gin, quaffing outrageous amounts of white/yellow/green/
blue: Carlton/Four X/VB/Fosters, catchin' a tunna' barra, paying alimony on something left down South. We've all pissed off
from *something*, to end up here on the Top.

I look around, I see the room in disarray. The insects are buzzing against the ceiling in the past midnight world of strange mag-
nified noises. Thinking back on the company of mixed voices all
shouting about 'bludging coons', as their monstrously bulging
beer-gut-egos become inflated with a Four X rating. Four X in
the yellow can – the favourite of these slurping Terrortornian
contractors working at the Aboriginal settlements. Four X's for
the seX they crave from the 'filthy gins', or the XXXXs on the
end of the occasional letter to Mum, back in Bundaberg. They
call the Territory Airline, Connair, 'Coonair' or the 'Canary-
coloured-Coon-Carrier', and still the flies buzz and drone.

I fix myself a whisky, wondering who gets the best deal. Is it
the wife of this midnight 'concerned' husband, or perhaps the
Aboriginal rock band still singing the blackened blues with electric guitars purchased from mining royalties? At the Uranium
Province town of Oenpelli, they got one of the traditional land
owners and stuck him out the back of the Border Store on a huge
pile of empty beer cans. They took his picture, which later

appeared in the papers down South, under the caption: THE RICHEST MAN IN THE WORLD. Some of the younger men of the tribe showed him the picture some days later and told him how he'd been conned. The old man died that same afternoon.

The young cow is stuck in the mud as the billabong retreats in the wake of the long dry. Wallowing in bull ants and covered with engorged tics, her cramped, bent hind legs are being crushed beneath her own WEIGHT. Death waits in the eagle-hawk laden gums. Eyes of terror roll back on a group of young Aboriginal children laughing at the cow's futile attempts to raise itself. They seem to have accepted the perverseness of the dying land's drying and eagerly show us the squashed guts in broken eggs of baby tortoises that didn't make it. Too much death at that corpse-littered billabong. Too much death for one morning. Too many bleached bones and time for lunch anyway.

EmbryO. Swirling in whirling warm liquid.

For lunch an egg nonchalantly cracked open to reveal blood red meat at the crack. The oval shape was bursting – its fertilized still-life, dead, overflowing through limp fingers. The child says,

'What is it? Is it dead? I want to look at it. Can I see? Is it a baby duck? It's dripping all yellow and red!'

The unnerving maturity of a child's insistence to witness (at night they lie awake trying to imagine who made God, or what's there at the end of space). He wants to gape full at the liquid bloodied shape but already flung towards the heat-hazed paddock, it describes an arc of yellow/red on blue sky – primary colours. Always the fluid, attending our 'raw' entries and 'well-done' departures (as if merely meat) in this spiralling of moments.

2   Honeymoon in India: Pre-NT

The Bodhi Tree is located at Bodhgaya in India. Under this tree the Buddha, Gautama, is said to have attained enlightenment.

I was reading near the Bodhi Temple when the shouts of children roused me. Looking up from the *Sutra on Compassion* to see two dogs stuck rear to rear, unable to disentangle themselves from their mangy embrace. The children laugh as they smash their contorted yelping forms with broken bricks, as if contemptuous of this instinct that compels us to reproduce our own kind, however pitiful or wretched.

The already stiff bodies of discarded puppies are heaped

together with piles of rotting fruit in the holy city of Varanasi – Benares to the British. No doubt the name was changed to protect the innocent – like the man at the bus station, lying in the fatal foetal grimace. His bare anus and genitals are pasted with shit and flies. He is wracked with the violent shaking of dysentery's dying dance. The children have built a mourning fire to immolate the corpse of a cat. Mourning ghats line the banks of the sacred Ganges. The pyres' fires blaze ceaselessly, giving off the acrid odour of sizzling human flesh. As the blood red sun dips on the Ganges, its reflection on the shimmering water forms an inverted exclamation mark. It flows, like the boys' kites drifting in the human thermal currents above the cremations. The corpses of the women are wrapped in shrouds of red, men in white – blood, sperm.

In the Bodhi dusk, hundreds of butter lamps sputter. Rows of mantra-chanting Tibetan lamas vibrate before the blessed tree. A new moon emerges from a cloud, a white owl gazes deeply into my eyes. As it perches on a branch of the Bodhi Tree, the spirit of our daughter pierces me.

A child points to my wife's swelling breasts.

'You've got milk coming!'

Thickening within her, a lightning, quickening flash of love.

3   'Pillow Talk': His and Hers
He says:

Placing a hand on your belly below the navel, feeling part of our life together kicking languidly in the fluid. That night I first saw you at a party, you had a moustache, long trousers and a waistcoat. (Now, in our bedroom, a picture of Marlene Dietrich wearing men's clothes, stares through the dressing-table creams and lotions.) You served mulled wine and were very electric but didn't 'see' me among the kitchen throng of hips and types. I was trying hard to be profoundly silent at the time (the effect of a recent Grotowski workshop), imagining I was smouldering – brim full of barely concealed depth.

Someone in your household (late sixties genre) had written a home brew/organically conceived/yin-yang extravaganza play, called *Paradise*. You played the principal female. WOMAN – the female principle. There was a DEVIL, a CHORUS and the man you lived with then (tall, musician – he'd been Grotowskied too) was playing MAN. He was only *playing* because as the fires blazed in the backyard of that old brownstone mansion and you both performed the 'cosmic dance', I WAS THAT MAN. It was *my* yang fusing yin you, not his. I loved you always and all ways and now feeling our baby signalling through the seven-layered veil of your swelling belly, I think of the first time I saw you and you were a man with a moustache.

She says:

Making love was a bit like that yin/yang, female/male parts in ourselves, that he goes on about. Anyway, he'd lie there and I would start fondling his penis, just to get him ready. He'd work his arms in some image of movie-female languorous sensuality, enjoying the expressiveness of the movement (he likes dancing). Then I'd sit astride him, put him inside and roughly (perhaps masculinely) force his legs apart, grinding my clitoris against his pubic bone. Making sure I held him inside, I'd move further up on him and really work until I'd feel the all-over melting rush. I guess I'm male screwing female, though it's good to keep my eyes closed so I don't see his beardy hairiness and obvious maleness. I know that's why his head is turned with eyes shut, sighing as he lifts his legs right up until his knees touch his shoulders and his heels dig into my buttocks. I know he's a woman and enjoying one form of the feeling of being 'fucked over'. Then I climb off him and kneel over with my vagina craving rear entry. He puts it bullishly (since I feel like a cow) and because in that position it's so tight and penetrating, both of us come. That's when he usually remains there, suspended in chrysalis, sinking back on his haunches and then forward until he is a little ball, back in the womb; dead perhaps, or just waiting to be born, while pleasant sweatness rolls from under the arms.

While I was pregnant we still carried out this 'yoga' as he called it. Always after it the pressure of my grinding left me in pain but I could never stop myself from going after it. The baby was just pressed between our role reversal fantasy – its own sex indeterminate to all three of us. Other times outside of these two definite states, our sex was just confused; well, it seemed to involve some kind of complexity, perhaps guilt, and certainly for him it involved a great deal of fantasy about other women. He said I was 'all women' to him. The baby *throbbed*.

4   *Love Dreaming*

This island – Arnhem Land, Arafura Sea. It's about people with sex drives and therefore babies who are played with like memories. There are fights, grog, gambling, sickness, death, hunting, smoking, teasing, ritual, spirit forces of land/sea/trees/birds/winds/currents/billabongs/animals – all the ordinary things but brought together closely and somehow lived as a whole.

Waiting for the birth, I needed a drink. The public bar where the Aborigines drank was as full as the occupants. An old lady pissed her pants, a young bloke wanted to fight me because I was white but maybe it was because I couldn't stop looking at the young Aboriginal woman moving to Tammy Wynette's '*Stand By Your Man*'. Her slacks were tight like the pool cushions, and she was looking right full at me at the bar and talked about us doing it together while we swam. As we left the pub there were no shadows or greyness – it was written clear in black and white, that this was a night for 'wasting' our beautiful brimming pumping bodies. When we reached that Low Level crossing, we lay down engorged with tingling as we breathlessly removed each barrier to lunge animal-like at our differences. Enveloped by darkness and feeling older than our blood, our juices blending in the flowing river.

'The sex hisses at me. I keep seeing soft black legs round yours, knowing your lust, when away from the family.'

The sperm lay on her belly like an impregnated cloud. The mythical snakes make rainclouds and lightning – their breath causes the clouds to form. These snakes are dangerous and sinister like the VD caught in the passionate river fuck, while she was in hospital, pregnant. It is important to get it down fresh before it becomes dreamlike or a fantasy, as so often happens with what is too 'real' to be coped with later. The fear of exposure to the light forces these stories to remain hidden in dark caves, like fish afraid that voracious predators seek to destroy them. (They use the same word for '*cave*' and '*vagina*' in her tribal dialect.) The tide retreats to reveal the myriad of sparkling shells and ochred rocks. Why should we expect coherence, just because the sky is clear above the perplexing black and white of rock and sand? At the core of these incidents is the certainty of our death.

The women are wailing loudly at the approaching death of the young boys who are soon to emerge reborn as men. The uncles of the initiates are lying down with the boys on top of them. They hold them firmly, forcing their legs apart by wrapping their own legs around their nephews. The sacred dilly bags are thrust in the boys' mouths – the stamping and chanting is packed with the memories of all the surrounding men who have experienced this moment of death as the old men cut away the foreskin. The initial cuts cause a white secretion like sperm to flow, just before the blood appears. When the foreskin is completely cut away, the newly made men are quickly carried to the bush. Here, their little bloodied spears are tended with special leaves, which experienced fingers keep constantly heated in the fire.

The sleek jabiru glides over the river which carries last night's sperm, as it drifts among the pandanus palms. The bird's black and white plumage is glistening in the early morning sunlight – like sweating bodies coupled in frenzy. I dream that I see thunder sticks standing upright in sand, with bird down stuck in rings of blood.

This mess seems even greater than the mystery of the Yirritja moiety wind, which copulates with Dhuwa moiety clouds – mixing together like sperm and vaginal juices, to bring new life to the long-thirsting land of the dry North. At last the Great Snake appears in its lightning form, forcing the clouds to give birth as they shed rain.

5   *The Day My Daughter Was Born and Other Labour Pains*
It was the day Gough was being challenged for the leadership. An hour after my daughter was born, the placenta having been checked, I cycled into the sunset. The smells that went with the contractions were as fresh as the tissue that had been stretched to the limit. Not far from the hospital was a cemetery next to a river. I leaned the pushbike against a coolibah tree and with the calculated spontaneity of a carefree napkin ad, I flung off my shoes and careened madly down the bank. I'd taken the big plunge of fatherhood and sleepless nights. Deftly avoiding the broken bottles, I flung my body towards the sand in a pagan embrace of Nature's profound fecundity, only to graze my knee on a concealed stubbie. Recovering bravely by meditating on the pain involved in the transition stage of cervix dilation, I bent forward in worship at the edge of the greeny river. The cosmic 'handshake and cigar' came in the form of the moon's reflection.

It was positioned directly above and appeared as the crown of a head pushing through from outside space. I flung myself backwards in paroxysms of universal wonder. As my cosmic chuckle leapt skywards, I saw the moon itself as a huge smiling mouth.

That night, while 'mother and daughter were both doing well', I smoked the whisky and drank full the delights of copious quantities of canabeers saliva. Since it was the town's folk club evening, I accompanied Pete's viola da gamba (of the Baroque period) with my didgeridoo in C. We improvised an Indian *raga* of welcome – to celebrate the fruit of an unlikely marriage.

BORN: A daughter
      5.27 pm
      May, 1977
      Katherine, NT

Nene Gare

ECLIPSED

Having a grown-up daughter means making a total reassessment of yourself and admitting that you've dropped too far behind ever to catch up again. You try, of course, but you keep failing: clearing away too quickly after dinner; using your scent to the last 'gone bad, mum' drop; totally unable to be nonchalant about her throw-outs (yesterday I found half a tin of Carnation corn pads and a tiny phial of Indian marigold ointment in the bin); tiring of sophisticated dinner parties after only two (Chris prefers roasts); being content with dull people to talk to or, rather, unable to summon the effort necessary to attract intellects; taking notice of one's husband's ideas of suitable frocking and hair-dos (why should you, mum?); and, last but not least, failing one's own idea of integrity by becoming garrulous on one's husband's faults.

What is it about a twenty-year-old daughter which loosens the tongue? Is it a desperate attempt to interest her in one's humdrum life at all costs or am I throwing the spotlight on Chris so my own imperfections can remain decently interred? Does that smooth young face with its faintly censorious gaze impel me to offer some other one for the slaughter?

I think I have become immune to Chris's frailties by now. I know I have. Left alone we are Darby and Joan, holding hands before the television, fitting snugly in our marital bed, complimenting each other on each's occasional effort to surface above the rest of suburbia, surely finding bearable the habits that formerly drove us mad. So long as Chris sits at the other end of the table I can endure the sound of mangled food and off my own bat I am teaching Chris to ignore my 'Beg your pardons' when I have heard perfectly what he has said. I am not deaf. I just take a while to process what I have heard.

I love my daughter. How I love her! But my days seem much fuller of work and of waiting when she is at home. Odd empty intervals vanish and the hard part is that not only is there more work to do but I must do it secretly or be accused of fussing to make things hard for Helen. If I work, she feels she must also. She does not but she feels she should – doubly irritating.

In three years my daughter has lived in two flats and a house and honestly to see these immaculate young people doing their amusing bits of shopping at the supermarkets one would never believe the filthy nests from which they stroll forth. My sister Margaret, widowed and working on old terrace houses, told me it takes her daughter Julie up to two hours to put on her make-up. Whilst Margaret is dashing hither and yon, washing up after breakfast, straightening the rooms, peeling things for dinner, starting the washing machine, Julie is sitting at her dressing-table selecting face pastels. In the time it takes Margaret to strip the bed and re-make it with fresh linen Julie will have perfected the curve of the top lip and be starting on the bottom one. Margaret says she does not have time to stop and complain.

I was at Helen's flat one day when a friend called to take her out to dinner. Helen introduced us. 'My mother has just come to clean,' she explained me. And I may say that I am becoming immune to grubby kitchens with over-flowing kitchen tidies strung with tea bags, where cockroaches rustle forth at night and little mice eat bits out of unwrapped bread and where refrigerators are defrosted once a year so that it is a wonder they function. The backs of refrigerators is where the cockroaches live. Judith, a friend of mine, once lent Helen a small refrigerator she was not using. Helen returned it with enough eggs in it to contaminate a couple of houses. Judith said she kept finding baby cockroaches all over the place. No wonder people are dropping like flies with hepatitis – around the flatting district near the university they are, anyway.

I have the greatest admiration for Helen despite all this. This is her honours year and as well she is a trainee journalist, working one morning and one afternoon a week. She earns enough to buy her clothes and a few chicken legs. We pay the rent of the flat. I wanted to be a writer once but there wasn't the time.

The dark sapphire colour which had spread halfway to the beach had been drawn back toward the horizon so that it formed the merest rim. I could see rain slanting down from the sky. Soon it would reach across the sea and over the beach and up the hill to the hut. I could smell it coming – washed clean air blowing over the wattles and banksias and greeting my nose with its sweet tang.

My daughter does not eat the same kind of food as us. Too fattening. Whilst we eat rotisseried chicken and four vegetables Helen cooks an omelet with tomato and parsley or she will eat natural yoghurt with wheatgerm and honey plus a plate of chicken jelly. I make this chicken jelly from the drippings of the rotisseried chicken plus vegetable water. I think to use it to strengthen the flavour of my soups and casseroles. Not if Helen is about, however. She has discovered it is nourishing, nice and contains no calories. Wherever I hide it she finds it. I don't really grudge it her but I too have to think of things to eat. On bad days my mind feels swept clean.

This morning a letter came from my sister for me but none from Ian for Helen. I'd have given a lot to have my letter change to one from Ian. Are one's daughters ever happy? We, Helen's parents, are never privileged to witness happiness. If it is not one thing it is another. At the moment, love. And so private the affair we are not allowed near its object. I don't know if we are to be broken to him bit by bit or vice versa. Before he went away he helped Helen babysit our grand-daughter. We were not available. Ian was not permitted to dine with us. Helen proposed to prepare his dinner after we were out of the way. 'What are we raising, a Queen bee?' Chris asked.

My son Christopher had his dinner with us and thereafter stayed in his room unless he wanted to go to the bathroom. Helen and Ian sat down to a four-course dinner with an avocado for starters. I bought that, hoping to please, and Chris said, 'How do I get to travel first class in this outfit?'

Having had my instructions that she herself would prepare the food I kept out of it except for the pear, thinking, erroneously as it happened, that any food I might buy would be the wrong

food. There had to be some hasty Saturday morning shopping
when I discovered my mistake.

Ian is good-looking, tall, nicely spoken, and after we got home
I managed a sentence or two before he was whisked away. We'd
rather like to have a yarn with Ian. He has offered to drive Helen
to Sydney at the end of the year and I feel we should know a little
more about him, other than that he did not finish university but
knows a good deal about Europe. One thing to be said in his
favour; he can't be afraid of work. He has gone to Newman to
make some money so he can stay in Sydney for a time looking
for film work. Directing, I think, or he may start a restaurant.
Helen says he is a good cook. Helen says his whole family cooks.

I wish often that my whole family cooked so I need not. Some
days, this is one of the days, I feel a big block between me and
ideas for dinner. I not only can't think, I don't want to think. The
ideal thing would be to choose an illustration from a cook book
and have it come to life. I wish that everyone would get whatever
he feels like and wash up after. I don't think I'd mind keeping
a refrigerator full of ideas so long as I didn't have to make the
final decision. I could stay here reading and writing and doing
a bit of water-colour and go in when I felt hungry to eat rye bread
and cottage cheese and lovely cold salad. Which Chris loathes.

*Almost out of the town a small boy with a dedicated face bounded
forward four or five slow paces, raised his right arm from behind
him in a wide arc and let fly. His hand was empty.*

Yesterday, Sunday, Chris took Helen and me for a long drive into
the blossom-covered hills where, as usual, I saw at least six places
I would rather live than here. Helen read in the back seat. I know
better than to call, 'Helen, do look at this.' She seemed content,
though, if not actually happy. We stopped twice, once for coffee
and buns for Chris and me – nothing for Helen – and once for
lunch. Helen had brought her own – two slices of chicken and
three lettuce leaves. It turned out she had seen everything a
couple of times before this but I had not. There was a perfectly
lovely old house at Toodyay overlooking the town and the Avon
– I'd have given a lot to have moved straight in.

One good thing about living miles from one's family; my children might start buying their own records instead of pinching

mine. Though they'd probably come to stay for longer and the records might go back with them just the same. Only more of them at a time. I wish I could remember about the records when I am at their places instead of always when I am at home and can do nothing about it.

Would a telephone call sound too peremptory?

Pale yellow grass sprang from the red summer roadside. Only the bunchy wattles cared nothing for the heat, and the scornful feckless sunflowers.

Helen has just been into town to shop. She was to have picked up my photographs. I ordered three of the one used at the top of her column. It is sweet. Every time I look at it I am reassured that the engaging Helen is there still behind that Helen-once-removed façade. But maybe this Helen is good for me. She keeps me alert. My son Christopher is too indulgent, minds nothing and laughs at some of my worst faults. But then he doesn't see so much of me, locked into his room with his philosophy books. Helen and I are together often and try as I might I continue to make mistakes which she zealously picks up. My biggest fault is my ingratiating manner. Expect to be found wanting and that's what you'll surely be.

I see Helen as a challenge. I WILL please her. Somehow! Not with food, though. That is a lesson thoroughly learned. Offering food means you are deliberately trying to make her fat. You know perfectly well that she's still on tomato and egg and can't eat another thing for four days more. I am always lying to her about thickening in the gravy and butter under the chop. Chris will eat watery gravy but he doesn't like it, preferring to eat less of the things he likes providing they are cooked the way he likes them – i.e., stodgy.

My point of view is lost in yours. I defend myself from the point of view of what you believe and only remember later what are my own beliefs. I betray myself.

Helen came home last week with two articles purchased from robbers at Cottesloe. A bolero of smudgy floral taffeta that was in fashion twenty years ago, for $18, and a scarf of pure silk, vin-

tage maybe 1918, for seven. The scarf is terribly grubby, the bolero cracking in places. I am learning to convert sharp indrawn
breaths into beginnings of sentences.

Like 'What!' to 'It is perfectly lovely.'

Today I have laundered them and I use the word in its most
precious sense. Lux flakes and rainwater and lukewarm at that.
Rolled into a towel to dry and ironed with a warm iron. The bolero came up beautifully, three shades lighter and proving to have
a warm cream background, not dirty fawn. Fondly I smooth it
with my fingers. This is the stuff of my youth.

The scarf, sadly, remains badly stained.

Helen is pleased.

*He forces us to recognize that good and evil spring from the same
source. He will not let us love his characters unless we do so know-
ingly, seeing them whole. If there is a single facet we do not embrace
then our love is no such thing.*

Helen rang at six this morning to tell us they have reached Mil-
dura. So thankful to know this after hearing that snow and floods
will hold up travellers for a couple of days. Helen says they are
ahead of this and will reach Sydney in two days' time. Charges
reversed – thank goodness Chris asked her to do this. Helen
sounded as if her cold were worse but she said no, just the same.
Thank goodness again that Ian is with her. She said it took 10
hours to drive over the rough patch just over the border. She also
asked me to telephone Ian's mother, which I was happy to do
until I came to do it. Who knew but what she might be thinking
Helen had enticed her son from his loving home to live a life of
sin in Sydney and my daughter not like that at all. But of course
she has met Helen and must have recognized a well-brought-up
girl. I hope I sounded respectable over the telephone. I tried to.

Ian's mother said she had been going to ring me later today
to see if I had heard anything of them because she knew they
wouldn't ring twice. Nor even once, I nearly told her, had it been
going to cost them.

Rang my friend Judith after. She disclosed casually that she
and Chris were at school with Mrs Bannister, Ian's mother. The
Rookes are an old south-west farming family. That was her
maiden name. I am delighted.

The first thing I noticed was the wind, though it was more like a profound disturbance of the air – a threat. The dry rustle of leaves accompanied the wind. Helen's room, which normally does not receive much sun, became a cavern. Then the whispers of the leaves stopped. The air was still, apprehensively calm. The light became dimmer inside. Outside it was like the reflection in a dark mirror. Shadows trembled and blurred at the edges. The loveliest were thrown by the leaves – light and feathery, dark only at their centres. The black moon glided over the rim of the sun.

Then it was bright again. The stillness left the air and life began again. The eclipse had passed.

Maurice Corlett

REUNION IN GUNYAH CREEK

The headlight shone on the road illuminating the occasional roadside tree. The bitumen road cut a path through the Riverina crop, and the motor bike headed west upon it. The rider was tired but not sleepy. Sitting astride the vibrating machine he travelled the strange road, chewing up the miles to reunion. He had left Sydney in the ebb-tide of week-end traffic, fleeing the metropolis for chosen country retreats. He had flowed with the stream until Wagga and was grateful now for this quiet backwater and the chance to recollect.

It must have been nearly two years since he'd seen Bob. Yeah two years next month when they were married. It didn't seem that long but it was. The weather had been perfect on their big day, warm and sunny, the beginning of summer. Although Karen came from the bush, her Dad had given her the wedding in Sydney as all her friends were there. Bob had stood at the front of the church, smart in his hired suit, his black hair and beard neatly trimmed. Karen, his now official wife, stood beside him, the full gown concealing the product of their earlier physical union. The reception, like the weather, had been a success, bountiful, boozy and bloodless. Bob had given his speech, occasionally stroking his collar-length hair, his blue eyes crinkling into a smile at his final witticism. Karen, her long blonde hair lying beneath the veil, her brown eyes sincere, thanked them all for the presents and for enjoying themselves. They had cheered and clapped and got back into the beer, they had danced and sung and talked earnestly of trivialities. By Monday, Sunday's suffering past, Bob and Karen were forgotten, left to get on with their lives as before and to see occasionally down the pub or in the street. The baby was born and Bob had been out of work a couple of months when Karen's folks came to visit. They saw the way things were in the big city and offered Bob work in the family store. They were gone in a week. He'd called round to see them off on that Saturday morning. The panel van had been chock-a-block with their worldly belongings, young Daniel in his bassinet tucked safely between the back of the seat and the pile of bedding and clothes. On the roof-rack, next to the ironing-board and brooms, was Bob's yellow surfboard gallantly holding its position against the rising tide of domestic flotsam. Bob had told him as they sat drinking beer on the floor of the empty flat that he was looking forward to a quiet country life.

Ahead, the rider could make out a gathering of lights. After a few minutes he eased back the throttle and rode down an avenue of gums into the township of Gunyah Creek. The gums gave way to peppercorns behind which houses sat in darkness. At intervals street-lights hung from telegraph poles, lighting the highway through the town. The lights were closer and brighter where the highway became the main street. The motor bike purred slowly down the deserted commercial and social centre of the town. It stopped near the end of the main street, just before the lights spread out again. The rider dismounted, walked beneath the verandah of a shop and peered in. In the darkness cooking pots reflected the faint light that reached them from the street and he could make out paint cans stacked near the glass. He assumed it was the hardware store where Bob worked, as Bob's Mum had told him it was the only one in the town. From here her directions were to take the next street on the left. This he did, slowly riding around the corner past the yard of the store and stopping outside the first house. Turning off the engine he leaned the bike on its stand, looked up and down the dark street, decided this must be the house and strode across the fenceless lawn. He stopped and stood before the verandah uncertain whether to disturb the silent darkness of the house. Would Bob and Karen appreciate being woken in the middle of the night? Maybe it wasn't even the right house. He decided to wait until morning and turned to go back to his bike when a dog began to bark – sharp, loud, warning barks. He hesitated for a few seconds then he heard mumbled voices through the fly-screened window. A voice boomed out of the blackness.

'Shut up you bloody mongrel.'

But the dog continued. Light stood on the verandah. Footsteps stomped on floorboards then a sleepy Bob Mahon flung open the fly-door and, cursing, headed along the verandah in the direction of the barking. He stopped dead after a couple of steps, sensing something strange on the lawn.

'Who's that?' asked Bob, naked and vulnerable in his jockettes.

'It's me Bob, Pete,' he replied from beneath his helmet.

'Who?' asked Bob unable to decipher the muffled language. Then realizing it was human and not immediately dangerous, said,

'What the bloody hell are you doing on a bloke's lawn in the middle of the night?'

Pete, realizing that he still had his helmet on took it off, and stepping into the light he said, 'Pull your head in you sour bastard. That's no way to welcome a mate.'

'What? No it can't be.'

'Of course it is. The one and only.'

'Peter Jennings you old bastard.'

Bob's tense body relaxed as he bounded off the verandah, grabbed Pete's shoulder and shook his hand vigorously.

'Long time no see Pete. How did you get down here?'

'On the bike,' replied Pete, indicating the silent machine with a nod.

'What, on your own?'

'Yeah, nobody else fancied the trip.'

'Christ it's good to see you mate. Come inside. Karen will be pleased to see you.'

They moved towards the house. Bob pulled open the fly-door and they stepped into the lighted hallway.

'Hello Pete.' Karen, who had lain listening, came out of the dark bedroom, lightly held Pete's shoulder and kissed his cheek.

'How are you?' she asked stepping back, squinting in the brightness.

'Good,' replied Pete. 'A little saddle sore but nothing a good woman couldn't fix.'

Pete winked at Bob who smiled back, they always put on this little act in front of Karen.

'I can see you haven't changed,' said Karen smiling. 'Still the gay bachelor I suppose?'

'Bachelor yes. Gay no.'

'No girl with any brains would have him,' stated Bob.

They laughed. Pete brushed his hand across his flattened brown hair and the tight wire-like curls sprang back to life.

'When did you leave Sydney?' asked Bob.

'Straight after work. The traffic was bad and I didn't get a clear road until well out of the city.'

'Have you had any tea?' asked Karen wrapping the towelling dressing-gown closer around herself.

'Well, eh, yeah I got a burger at Yass.'

'A burger at Yass, that must've been hours ago. Do you want something now? You must be hungry.'

'No, no. Don't bother, I'm all right.'

'All right!' stated Bob. 'When has Pete Jennings ever knocked back a free meal? Go and cook up something Karen, he'll eat it.'

'Well if you insist. I mean I don't want to break up the happy home.'

'Come on,' said Bob, walking after Karen into the kitchen. 'We'll sink a couple of coldies while we're waiting.'

Karen cooked Pete a steak. Then she made coffee and they sat reminiscing about friends and past happenings. As time passed Pete gradually became weary and his head slowly descended to the scrubbed pine table-top. Karen and Bob got the message and they all went to bed, Karen making up the spare bed while the boys wheeled the bike into the backyard. They peeped in to show Daniel to Pete before they retired. He lay coiled in sleep, sheets discarded, blond hair pressed by the pillow into crazy coiffure creations. Karen covered him as the early morning coolness penetrated the house. Pete climbed into the strange bed and listened to Bob and Karen talk, the words made indistinguishable by the bedroom wall. He thought of how Bob had got fatter and Karen older around the eyes, and how Bob had shown a strange despondency when talking of their situation. Then he was asleep, stirring occasionally as his nerves still travelled the road.

The morning came late to Pete. When he woke the room was light. Pete looked around the room remembering his whereabouts and recognizing the ache in his bladder. He threw back the sheets and sat on the edge of the bed. He massaged his face with his finger-tips then he rose and donning his jeans and tee-shirt walked into the kitchen.

'Good morning,' Karen greeted him dressed, fresh and smiling.

'Morning,' replied Pete, bleary-eyed in the doorway. 'What's the time?'

'Oh about ten.'

'Is it? Where's the toilet?' he asked, looking around the room.

'Up the back there,' replied Karen, pointing to the window.

'Where's Bob?' he asked when he re-entered the kitchen.

'At the shop. He works Saturday mornings much to his disgust.'

'Yeah I bet.'

'What would you like for breakfast. Cereal? Toast? Bacon and eggs?'

'Bacon and eggs, if it's not too much trouble.'

'It's no trouble.'

'Is it okay if I grab a shower first?'

'Yes of course,' replied Karen smiling.

Pete went back to the bedroom, took a clean set of clothes and his toiletries and found his way to the bathroom. The hot shower cleaned him and the cold shower freshened him. He brushed his teeth, combed his hair and deodorized his armpits. Feeling human he returned to the kitchen. His breakfast was ready so he sat down and ate, enjoying every bite of food and every mouthful of tea. He talked with Karen as he ate, commenting on the house and the big garden and Daniel who sat quietly in his highchair, vegemite face watching the stranger. When Pete had finished eating, on Karen's advice he slowly got down next to Danny, now playing on the floor. By the third time around the table legs they were the best of mates. Bob had left word for Pete to go over to the store. So he returned to the bedroom, took his wallet off the dressing-table, gave his hair another brush in the mirror and waving ta-ta to Daniel and Karen went out the front door.

Seven hours later Pete and Bob were drunk. Pete had met Bob at the store and after it had closed at midday they had gone across the main street to the Commercial Hotel. They had had a few beers, then a counter lunch, then a few more beers. On the suggestion of a couple of Bob's mates they had bought a dozen cans and gone fishing. Bob had called in at home to get some fishing gear and Pete had heard him say to Karen that they would be home at six for tea. It was now six and Bob had just bought two beers. The other blokes had gone.

'Shouldn't we be getting home for tea?' asked Pete as he took his beer.

'No, it'll keep for a while. Anyway I'm not hungry. Tucker only takes up good beer room.'

Pete shrugged. 'You're the boss.'

'Yeah you think so?' asked Bob as he sipped his beer. 'I wish I was then I wouldn't be in this bloody joint. I'd be back in Sydney with you and the rest of the boys.'

'It wouldn't be the same though Bob. Things have changed. You've got a missus and kid now.'

'Don't bloody remind me.'

The bar, although there were half-a-dozen other drinkers, seemed a noiseless unimportant background to their blurred perceptions. They gazed out the open doors across the main street at the teenagers standing at the front of the milk bar and at the occasional car passing. Bob finished his beer and banged the glass down on the bar.

'Your shout mate.'

'What about tea?'

'Stuff tea. Get the beers in.'

'Okay mate. Cool it. I didn't come down here for a blue.'

'Sorry mate.' Bob put his hand on Pete's shoulder. 'I'm just a bit pissed off at the moment.'

'That's all right Bob, but let's get home after this one, eh?'

'Yeah okay. We can always come down for a few at the RSL after tea.'

Entering the kitchen Bob slumped down at the table and spread his arms.

'Right where's this tea we've been breaking our necks to get home for?'

'It won't be a minute. I'll just put the steaks on,' replied Karen, seeing from the way Bob sat and the grin on Pete's face that the boys were well charged.

'What! You mean it's not bloody ready?' said Bob resting his big hairy hands on Karen's best linen table cloth.

'No it's ready. I just left the steaks until you got home. I didn't think you'd be home so soon.'

'What do you mean? I'm always home on time.'

'Well, if you say so,' replied Karen, smiling to herself.

'Don't smirk at me girl. I'm always on time.'

'Okay, okay,' replied Karen, realizing the futility of further talk on the subject.

'Might as well have a bloody beer while we're waiting,' said Bob rising and opening the fridge. He took out two cans and gave one to Pete. They drank while Karen cooked.

'How did the fishing go?' asked Karen breaking the silence.

'Good,' replied Pete, as Bob said, 'Bloody shithouse.'

'That bad,' commented Karen.

'Yeah. What else can you expect in a stinking swamp like Green Lake?'

'Dad has caught some good redfin out there.'

'Your Dad can catch anything Karen, especially if it's got dollars on it somewhere. He caught me two years ago and I've been working my arse off for peanuts ever since.'

'Christ Bob, Dad's not that bad.'

'That's a matter of opinion,' stated Bob placing the can to his lips.

Karen had finished preparing the meal. She carried two plates over and placed them before the boys. She returned to the bench and got her own plate.

'What's this shit?' asked Bob, pointing at his plate.

Pete looked at his mate confused by his attitude.

'Mushroom sauce,' replied Karen sitting at the table.

'Well I don't want any of it.'

'Thanks very much,' said Karen looking across the table at him, knife and fork poised beside her plate.

'Steady on Bob,' advised Pete shaking salt over his meal.

'Steady on, steady on you say when a man comes home to this shit.'

'It's not shit,' insisted Karen, face flushed. 'It's mushroom sauce.'

'Well here's what you can do with your mushroom sauce.'

Bob rose balancing the plate on his hand then threw it across

the room. The plate somersaulted into the sink, spraying mushroom sauce up the red check curtains. Pete rose, looked from the
sink to Bob. Bob returned the gaze, the anger in his eyes fading
through remorse to easy indifference, then he turned and strode
towards the door. Karen jumped to her feet, grabbed a coffee
mug and threw it after her husband. Pete swayed to one side as
the mug sailed past and smashed against the closing door. Karen
covered her face with her hands and slumped back into her chair.
Danny's screams suddenly registered with Pete and he stumbled
around Bob's empty seat and took the boy from his highchair.
He quietened after a few minutes and so did his mother. Pete put
the child down and laid his hand on Karen's shoulder.

'Look I'm sorry about this.'

Karen looked up through reddened eyes.

'Just leave us alone,' she said turning away, rising and gathering up the untouched dishes.

Pete moved after a few moments. He walked out of the kitchen,
gathered up his gear in the bedroom, stuffed it into his bag and
went out to the bike. He started it up, went down the drive and
past the store. He stopped outside the pub, dismounted and went
inside. Bob was sitting at the bar, hands cupped around a whisky.

'I'm off now Bob. I'll see you whenever you get up to Sydney.'

'Yeah, okay mate,' said Bob without looking up from his drink.
'But do me a favour will you.'

Pete stood silent looking at the side of Bob's face.

'Don't ever get married. I couldn't stand to see a good bloke
put down.'

'Okay mate.'

Bob, sipping his whisky, glanced at Pete. They looked at one
another. Then Bob said, 'Look mate just have a drink before you
go. I'm sorry about the blue and all . . .'

'No mate. I'll get going.' Pete put out his hand.

'See you pal,' said Bob turning back to the bar.

Pete headed for the door. He felt Bob's hand on his elbow.

'Have a drink mate.' Bob's eyes pleaded, watery and bloodshot,
for Pete to comply. For a few moments Pete looked at his friend.

'Okay Bob. But I'll get going directly.'

Philip Neilsen

A LOVERS' MUSEUM

He brought home a small bundle of knotty pine planks and two sheets of glass. She asked him what it was for.

'Something I'm making,' he said.

'What?' she asked, irritated by his persistent need to be secretive.

'A cabinet,' he answered, sanding down the golden pine planks, blowing the fine dust away after each frenzied bout of rasping.

'Must be a damn big cabinet.'

'Yes, it is.'

'All right, go on, what's it for?' She affected a tone of indulging him, but her curiosity was aroused.

He went on sanding for a second, then as he turned the sandpaper over he answered, 'A museum.'

'Oh yes? And where are you going to get the stuffed tigers and flint axe heads?'

'Not that kind of thing. This is a museum of our life together. This is a museum of our love.'

He paused to let the words sink in, then blew on the sandpaper and bent over his work.

The cabinet had five shelves enclosed by glass doors and it was consigned to the spare room under the house, with his collection of picture frames, a bottle containing a sad, thin, brown snake in yellow fluid, a cricket bat, a bicycle with flat tyres and an assortment of spattered paint tins. Two weeks after he finished building it, she went into the room to see if water had seeped through from the front yard after a heavy storm.

She noticed something on the top shelf. There was a neat pile of letters, a menu from the Tak Ho Wah take-away restaurant and a photo of the two of them taken at a party. She remembered his solemn pronouncement that he was making a lovers' museum and frowned at the glass doors for a minute before returning upstairs. She had half-expected more pathetic items like the snake, its eye shocked by the return to an amphibious universe. But this was a childish bit of nonsense and she wasn't going to indulge him by saying anything. She didn't care to have their letters – love letters he presumably called them – on display down there, but then who was going to see them? She wondered if it were possible to start the male menopause at twenty-eight. She wondered if he was trying to get at her. This could be another, more devious attempt to bring up the old subject of marriage again. They hadn't discussed it for over a year, and she had hoped he was resigned to her attitude. It wasn't surprising that men were so keen to formalize and conventionalize a relationship, to structure it in a way that suited them. He wanted something to make him feel secure in his possession of her. He would probably never grow up.

She sorted their dirty clothes into heaps. Lately she had been overlooking their agreement to do their own washing and had been doing his for the sake of efficiency. Not any more. She left his dirty pile in a pink basket on his side of the bed so that he couldn't miss it.

A month later the letters and menu and photo had been moved to the second shelf. In their place was a dog-eared and under-exposed photo of her and Nicholas at the beach. Nicholas was dressed trendily as always, wearing a cloth cap and baggy cream trousers and doing his very best male model smile for the camera. She had lived with Nicholas for a year while an undergraduate. Beside the photo was a crumpled pair of yellow shorts and a red comb. She remembered the shorts as Nicholas's.

That night they had an argument. He was matter of fact about having gone to see Nicholas and persuading him to contribute to the museum.

'We cannot escape the past,' he explained. 'It makes us. And a museum should serve two functions: it should show the past as well as having exhibits representing the present in order to better inform and educate future generations.'

She was sure he had been rehearsing his little speech for some time. She told him he was sick in the head and went out to visit some friends and get drunk.

At any rate, neither of them mentioned the museum for some weeks, and she was sure he was finished with the pathetic business; she had begun to forget about the cabinet. Then she looked in one day to see if he had left everything there. There were objects now on three shelves. She opened the doors with a sick feeling in her stomach. There was a pair of her underpants – black ones – a smeared tissue and a piece of birthday cake cocooned in Glad Wrap. She took the cake and tissue out gingerly and looked at them for a few seconds, then threw them back.

'There's no doubt now,' she said to him when she got upstairs.

'What about?' he said, putting the book down and looking at her expectantly.

'You're sick!' She tried to say it levelly, but her voice gave her anger away. She sat down opposite him and adopted a professional psychiatric tone that soon deteriorated into sarcasm.

'All right, I'm sure you've got another little speech prepared. Let's have it – let's hear about my underpants and the tissue and cake. Let's hear why they are significant, and not the work of a childish disturbed mind.'

He looked at her, hurt.

'No, look, you've got it all wrong. You were wearing those underpants the day we made love behind the dunes at Broken Head last week, and I found the tissue in the wastepaper basket yesterday. I've had the cake for some time, obviously. It was from your twenty-fourth birthday, when you said you were getting old. You see, I do only put in the museum things that are significant.'

She got up and walked quickly into the bedroom and closed the door. He heard her crying. When it was quiet he went in and undressed and got into bed beside her. When he touched her she moved away.

'What's the significance of my underpants?' She spoke with her back to him.

'They stand for passion.'

She groaned. 'Oh Jesus.'

She lay on her back, with one forearm across her eyes.

'You plan this in advance, don't you? You do things just to get exhibits. You just think of ways to add to your sick joke.'

'No,' he said. 'That's not the way it works. You can't cheat. The whole point is honesty; to make yourself vulnerable, to not have any secrets.'

She turned her back again and drew her knees up.

'Rob, I'm too tired now, but on the weekend we're going to talk this out. It's got to stop – because I think it's getting serious and I don't like the way you're behaving.'

'We can talk any time,' he said.

On Saturday he was in Sydney. She went downstairs to clean out the cabinet. It was the first step; and on Sunday she would persevere until he admitted it had been a stupid thing to do and agreed to stop playing this role of a weirdo.

Lying on the fourth shelf was a woman's hairbrush – not one of hers. There was also half a movie ticket.

On Sunday night she waited until they were in bed. He was reading a novel.

'You want me to think you're having an affair, don't you?'

He put the book down slowly, with his usual dramatic affectation.

'What makes you think that?'

She felt too depressed and angry to answer.

He resumed reading, then put the book down again.

'By the way, can I have that old red t-shirt you don't wear any more?'

She said, 'Why not,' very quietly. She knew there were some things that were best not looked at. He would find that out for himself eventually.

Tomorrow morning she would ring and say she wasn't coming in to work. It was a long time since she had devoted a day to herself. She thought about the cabinet in the dark room below them, its creamy, knotted pine and square glass doors inviting inspection.

She stood for a minute in front of the cabinet. Sunlight through the louvres in the rough besser brick wall gave it a benign, vaguely religious appearance. On her way upstairs she noticed a dead lizard, a big grey and black skink, lying beside the back steps, aswarm with ants. She picked it up on a piece of cardboard torn from a cornflakes packet and put it on the top shelf of the cabinet.

Let him think about that for trite symbolism. She smiled. She could still smell the pine.

Fay Zwicky

THE COURTS OF THE LORD

Growing older they have decided to separate. He thinks that he loves her but is tired of waiting for something to happen. He is not sure that happiness is what he should be wanting but this does not stop him from wanting it. She knows that anything would be better than the way they live together and has taken up yoga. They both fear that the children know them better than they know themselves.

Stumbling from what has been their bed in the early morning chill, he catches his foot in a pile of books on her side. Lillian Hellman's *An Unfinished Woman*, the diaries of Anaïs Nin, something about the crisis in sex hormones, and a couple of books about anxiety and depression. She reads a lot. Especially in bed. This morning she is already on the floor, helpless in the pose of the Locust, chin resting on the rug, hands by her sides in tight baby-like fists, left leg barely an inch off the ground. She is breathing heavily and fairly steadily. Breathing is important. He listens to the rhythm as he looks around for his underwear.

The spectacle of this self-help saddens and irritates him. His heart is wrung by the little roll of white flesh bulging over the elasticised waist of her green pyjamas. In what way is a humanist education relevant to this? He thinks he loves her and would like to touch her. He has wanted to touch her for years, but they have been too formal with each other.

Does she love him? She is not sure and keeps him at bay with the steady rhythm of her breathing. Her fists clench hard by her sides as he steps past her on his way to the bathroom.

'You will discover remarkable new strength and energy,' said her yoga instructor, elegant yesterday in a striped black and white leotard. 'Your mind and your body will experience the joy that is life at its best.' And, lying on the floor of the local Baptist church hall along with twenty or so other women, in that hour she looked for an answer. Lying down, stretching out, giving herself over to the slow rhythmical movements, she imagined herself briefly as graceful and sensuous and in pursuit of happiness.

Another colder voice was less sentimental about her chances. It reminded her that the body had a name. It also spoke of death.

Still helpless in the Locust position she turns her head in his direction and smiles apologetically for yesterday. She smiles at the way she must look today. He does not see the smile but watches the little white roll of flesh lap over the green of her pyjamas.

'This exercise will strengthen muscles in the lower abdomen, groin and buttocks,' said the instructor.

Groin. Buttocks. Buttocks. Groin. The parts that sound sexy in the books but which she has never related to herself. The buttocks are for sitting on and she has never been sure where the groin is.

She obediently tenses, remembering the instructor's commands to clench her fists under her thighs. He would like to touch her but, as so often has happened, he has to get ready to leave for work. Through the open doorway he hears the sawings of a baroque fiddle on the radio yield to a deep female voice. It is strong and steady and the enunciation is crisp and unaffected. Her old friend, Jenny Byrne, is reading psalms.

'My soul longeth for the courts of the Lord . . .' and she is back in the school hall listening to Jenny reading the morning lesson. Even as a child she had a deep voice. The sensuous images of the psalm wash over her soothingly. The courts of the Lord are full of green vines. Curling tendrils of the passion vine and the sweet starflowers of the stephanotis. And there is water in the courts of the Lord. In the trees are singing birds.

She wonders what happens to those who were once happy. 'Did you know I went to school with her?'

'What did you say?' His voice sounds impatient in the bathroom. 'I went to school with the woman who is reading.' 'Oh?

Have you seen my other sock?' 'She always knew what she was going to do.'

'Yea, the sparrow hath found a house, and the swallow a nest for herself.' The voice was balanced and purposeful.

'She knew exactly what she wanted, and did it. She sounds very happy. She never married.' 'Sensible of her.'

It is all talk and gesture now. Both know that sensible isn't the word. Both know that words are running out. He finds the pathos of the sparrow and the swallow unendurable. She, who once had a home, can handle the idea of having none. He has had to build one from scratch and does not want to put words to the loss. Her old friend finishes the psalm and starts on a passage from Isaiah.

'Have a look in the top left-hand drawer.' Her voice is tense. Her body is now contorted in another position. Still on her stomach, she bends her knees, reaches behind her and attempts to grasp her feet. They are broad and white. There is a bunion on the right foot. The effort is too much and she is forced to let her feet go. Stretching her legs behind her, she rests helplessly on her chin. He has found his sock and stands looking down at her. Her defeated posture moves him strangely and he defends himself against her. 'Hello! What's it like down there?' She winces and, as if challenged to fight, bends her knees and again tries to grasp her feet. Her breathing comes fast and awkwardly. She looks resolutely ahead, grasping her feet in both hands. He walks across to the window and flings it open wider. 'You'd be better off if you didn't smoke so much,' he says. 'Thanks. Thanks a million.' She is trembling, but still holding on to her feet, looking straight ahead.

'The wilderness and the solitary place shall be glad for them . . .' Her friend's voice gives her courage of a sort. '. . . and the tongue of the dumb shall sing.' She loses her balance and slowly hunches back into a sitting position. She is fighting silently with herself. To get up as she has done many times, or to stay on the floor. She finds it difficult to go near him and yet she has once promised to grow old alongside this man. They scarcely hear each other now. She is still listening to the radio.

'Jenny never left her parents' house. I think she still lives with them.' Was that the secret of that confident, purposeful voice? 'You know you can't go back,' he says, putting on his shoes on his side of the bed. She laughs and says, 'Perhaps not.' 'There's

no perhaps about it.' He knows. He has never wanted to go back.
There is nothing for him to go back to. There is nothing for her
either but she doesn't know it. Yet. They are both in need of
instruction. They are both growing older.

'I'm sorry I said anything but her voice brings so much with
it. She had the most comforting mother when we were nine.'

He shifts on the bed away from her bowed body. She suddenly
looks years older and yet seems younger and more helpless than
their youngest daughter. She shrugs, pushes back her hair from
her forehead, and begins to cry. His heart contracts but he moves
further away. 'No lion shall be there nor any ravenous beast . . .'

'I wish I weren't so childish. I want to die every morning but
I don't because of the children.'

'What about you? Don't you care about yourself?'

'. . . and sorrow and sighing shall flee away . . .'

He doesn't have any more conviction about this new utopia
than she. But he is trying to stop the avalanche.

To live for yourself? What does this mean to either of them
who years ago promised to live for each other? Who have given
each other the rich unhappy hoard of their patience? How can
one such say to the other 'You don't know what it means.' Never-
theless, she says, 'You don't know what it means.' And, because
he believes in agreeing to anything that will put a merciful end
to this guttering life they share, he agrees that he doesn't know
what it means. What he does know, however, is that when he
looks at her bowed head and the little lines round her eyes and
mouth, he, too, wants to die. But right now he has to go.

'I'm late already. Please don't be too depressed today. I don't
know what it all means any more than you do. We'll have to talk
about it later.'

He looks at his watch and gets up, hoping she hasn't seen him
looking. It always makes her furious. No, she hasn't seen the gesture. She is looking straight ahead, the tears streaking the front
of her green pyjamas. He bends down and puts an arm around
her bent shoulders as she shrinks into herself. 'Perhaps you
should go and see the doctor.' One of their well-worn formulas.
He uses it when his head aches and he hasn't had any breakfast.
The children are making noises out in the kitchen and there
probably won't be any bread left because it's Monday.

'It's just that –' she stops short.

'What? What is it? What can I do?'
'I just want you to feel what it's like.'
'That wouldn't help either of us.'
'It might if you tried.'
'If I had ever known what you felt like, we wouldn't be talking about leaving each other right now.' She is obliged to agree, always proud of her capacities to summon control at critical moments. She gets up and goes to the kitchen.

He is surprised to discover how well he feels as he gets into his car to drive off to work. He will buy her a present this afternoon. Something beautiful. A statue for the garden maybe. A stone angel or a bird-bath. Something that no younger man would ever have thought of and certainly couldn't afford.

Ken Leask

GAMES MY PARENTS PLAYED

I can still remember how people outside my family circle would look at me at first with astonishment and then with obvious distaste or even repugnance when, at the age of five or six, I used what they considered were 'adult' words. They assumed I was showing off, parading my knowledge, but really it wasn't this at all. It was simply that my parents always, or almost always, spoke to me as if I were an adult of their age and understanding. One result of this was that I used adult words from my early infancy, and even when I tried to avoid offending strangers by eschewing the use of polysyllabic words I still used words which belonged rather to the adult world than to the world of the child. I suffered a good deal on account of this during the first few weeks of my first year at school. I was laughed at by teachers and bullied and beaten by other boys, and to save myself from further torture I was forced to learn two languages: the language of the classroom and the language of the playground. I was multilingual from the age of six.

My parents were intelligent people and enjoyed playing games of skill. Chess was their favourite. My mother used quite frequently to win, and this may have been why my father began teaching me the game soon after my fifth birthday. I had already learned to play draughts. Every night they played one game of Scrabble, and I listened to sometimes logical and sometimes specious arguments from both my parents when one or the other questioned the use of a word. Sometimes my father did the morning crossword, but not often. When he did he set his stop watch and frowned if he hadn't completed it in three minutes.

Occasionally when I was with my parents it was clear that they wanted to converse but to exclude me from their thoughts. For some months in my seventh year they managed this by speaking in French, but I began to pick up some words, apparently including obscene and merely vulgar words, for they discontinued this practice when I began to enliven my own speech with French expressions. They were more successful when they resorted to a kind of code, using English words but in such a way that the surface meaning was quite different from the real meaning. They continued this practice from time to time even though I told them I considered it despicable.

I was seven when my parents began a new game. At first I was puzzled by it, then, as I learned that I also had a role to play, I took a keen interest in it. Later still I became bored by the whole thing and told them I considered it childish, but they still played it out until they themselves at last tired of it. I was glad when it was over. There was not a great deal of intellectual challenge in it, and I never could understand why, for a full week, it became such an obsession in their lives.

I say I had a role to play in the game, and I use that word 'role' deliberately for the game was in fact a play for a cast of three. It consisted of what I might call two acts and an epilogue.

The first act began one evening when my parents had a short conversation in code. (I always knew they were using a code when their gestures and facial expressions did not accord with their spoken words.)

'I'm glad to see, Len,' my mother said, 'that you're getting along so well with Marge's young friend.'

'Any friend of my sister's is a friend of mine,' my father said. 'I thought you liked Elsie too.'

'I did like Elsie once.'

'She likes you, Celia.'

'Not, I think, as much as she likes some people. I think some people make it very obvious that they like Elsie and then Elsie makes it obvious that she likes them.'

'Other people of course may be merely jealous.'

'Only when such people have good cause, when, for example, they have seen some people disgracing themselves at parties.'

'In what particular way do some people disgrace themselves?'

'By devoting a great deal of attention to certain people who would be suitable for the role of the other woman in cheap melo-dramas.'

My father raised his voice very slightly.

'Are you aware,' he asked, 'of any other so-called disgraceful conduct of some people which less prejudiced people might well call simple fun?'

My mother also raised her voice very slightly.

'Yes,' she said. 'On one particular occasion some people have been known to tell their next-of-kin that they have been working late when their next-of-kin knows from reliable sources that some people have in fact been out with people who would be suit-able for the role of the other woman.'

My father threw down the newspaper he had been holding and left the room.

The next day my father came home later than usual, and he was drunk. He was quite polite with my mother, but he was unsteady on his feet and he slurred his words even though he was attempting to speak very carefully.

When I was in bed that night I heard them talking rather loudly, and still later I heard bumping noises followed by my father's footsteps.

In the morning when I went in to say good-morning to them I saw that my mother was alone. I thought at first that my father must have risen early, as he sometimes does, but my mother told me that my father had decided to sleep in the guest's room from now on. I asked why.

My mother was silent for an unusually long time. Then she said, 'It's a kind of game we're playing, Bertie.'

I said, 'What kind of game? Can I join in?'

'It's an adult's game,' my mother said. 'A kind of communi-cations game. I doubt whether it would amuse you.'

I said, 'It doesn't seem to amuse you, either.'

'Bertrand,' my mother said, 'go and say good-morning to your father.'

My father looked very strange huddled up in his new small bed and he gave a strange laugh when I told him that my mother had told me they were playing a new game.

'It's a game I don't like much,' my father said.

'So why do you play it?' I asked.

'Your mother wants to play it,' he said.

At this stage I wasn't much impressed by this communications game so I asked if I might spend the morning – it was a Saturday – with my cousin Phillip. He was fond of drawing and painting and we sometimes sat for hours in his room while I read and he painted. We didn't talk much and I think this is one reason why we liked each other's company.

'You'd better ask your mother,' my father said.

'She doesn't seem to be in a very good temper,' I said. 'Will you ask her?'

'No,' my father said. 'You'll have to ask her yourself, Bertie. Your mother and I have agreed not to talk to each other.'

'Why on earth not?' I asked. 'What's wrong with you two?'

'Nothing's wrong,' he said. 'It's a part of the game, and don't you bloody well speak to me in that tone.'

'All right,' I said. 'Keep your shirt on. You don't like it when I use expletives.'

I went back to my mother and asked her and she agreed I could go. She even said she'd drive me over after breakfast.

It was during breakfast that the game developed some interest for me. I quickly understood that there were two basic rules: I was to address my parents individually and never collectively, and they could not converse directly with each other but only through me as an intermediary. On this first morning, the conversation went something like this:

MOTHER: Bertrand, ask your father if he's going out today.

MYSELF: Dad, Mum wants to know if you're going out today.

FATHER: Tell your mother I shall remain at home during the morning but that after lunch, thank goodness, I shall be going out for my usual round of golf.

MYSELF: Dad says he's staying home this morning but after lunch he'll be going out for his usual round of golf, thank goodness.

MOTHER: Tell your father I agree with his sentiments as far as the thank goodness is concerned.

MYSELF: Dad, Mum says she agrees with your sentiments as far as the thank goodness is concerned.

FATHER: I see. Ask your mother to pass me the butter knife.

MYSELF: Dad says he sees and will you pass him the butter knife.

MOTHER: Tell your father he will find the butter and a butter knife at his end of the table.

MYSELF: Mum says there's butter and a butter knife at your end of the table.

FATHER: Tell your mother I want the butter knife I always use. The silver one.

MYSELF: Mum, Dad says he wants the silver one he always uses.

MOTHER: Tell your father it's not silver.

MYSELF: Mum says it's not silver, Dad.

FATHER: Tell your mother I don't give a damn what it is. I want that one.

MYSELF: Mum, Dad says he doesn't give a damn what it is. He wants that one.

It took some time for my father to get the butter knife he wanted but it was pleasing to see that we had all learned the rules quickly and were following them closely.

After breakfast my mother took me over to Aunt Marge's place and Phillip and I had a very companionable morning. Usually my father called for me and spent some time talking to Aunt Marge and her friend Elsie, but this time it was my mother who came. She had very little to say to Aunt Marge and it happened that Elsie was at that time in another room. On the way back my mother asked me how I'd enjoyed the morning and if I'd seen Aunt Marge's friend. I told her that Phillip and I had enjoyed ourselves in our own quiet way and that Aunt Marge's friend had talked to me for some time.

'Did she have anything interesting to say?' my mother asked.

'No,' I said, 'mostly trivialities, although she amused me once by saying I was a genius.'

My mother smiled at this.

'Do you like her?' she asked me then.

'She's a very pretty young woman,' I said, 'but she talks a good deal and giggles a good deal. I really haven't considered whether I like her or not.'

My mother said no more about Aunt Marge's friend but looked seriously at the road ahead and concentrated on her driving.

The communications game was played again at lunch time and I enjoyed it again, still finding it something of a challenge to remember and repeat phrases and sentences. However, when it was continued after lunch before my father went out for his round of golf and again at dinner time when he came home I began to find it a little tedious and sometimes gave merely the gist of messages as I passed them on.

I was surprised at the seriousness with which my parents continued to play this game over the next few days. I was required to relay messages from master bedroom to guest room, from living-room to kitchen, and even from one part of the garden to another. And of course at meal times they continued to follow the convention that what one said the other could not hear until I repeated the words.

The game still had occasional amusing moments, but by and large it had begun to pall on me, and after a full week of it I had had enough. In fact I began positively to dislike the game and I decided to ask my parents (individually of course) to discontinue it. I confronted my father first, in the guest room, while he was changing for dinner, and it was only later that I realized we were now beginning the second act.

'Compared with chess,' I said, 'this communication game's monotonous. All the moves are alike. Couldn't we think up some more interesting game?'

My father looked at me rather seriously and sadly. At last he said, 'I'm willing, Bertie. Ask your mother.'

'Can I tell her you're tired of the game and don't want to play it any longer?'

My father considered carefully, then nodded, but as I was leaving he stopped me. 'Tell her something else, too.'

I could see he was having some trouble making up his mind and choosing his words, but I was impatient now.

'I'm waiting,' I said.

'Tell her – tell her some people never did anything more than talk to certain people.'

'But that's in code.'

'No matter. Your mother will be able to break it.'

'Well,' I said, 'I think it's unfair. Will you explain the code to me?'

'No.'

'Do you think I could work it out for myself if I thought hard about it?'

'No. There are some codes you can't break till you grow up, no matter how clever you are.'

'All right,' I said. 'I'll tell her what you said. But I still think it's despicable.'

I went to my mother and relayed the messages.

'What's it mean?' I asked, because I could see she was interested, first smiling then frowning then sighing a little.

'It may mean a good deal, Bertrand,' she said. 'Did your father say anything else?'

I was annoyed. 'I know the rules,' I said. 'I've told you everything.'

My mother smiled slightly, not seeming to mind my show of annoyance.

'Tell me,' she said, 'did your father seem glad or sad or what?'

'Are we changing the rules?' I asked.

'It's all a part of communication.'

'He looked serious and a little sad,' I said, 'but I'm not going to talk any more about that. I think you are changing the rules.'

'Sometimes,' my mother said, 'it may be wise to change the rules.'

'Well,' I said, 'what do you want me to tell him?'

'Tell him,' my mother said, and then stopped. She thought hard then began again. 'Tell him everything I said.'

The game was becoming complicated now, and I went from room to room relaying all kinds of messages, most of them still in that objectionable code.

Later, when we were seated at the dinner table, I felt sure we were indeed very close to some kind of climax. Everyone was silent through the main course, but my father and mother glanced at each other from time to time and looked away again quickly. We were beginning on our dessert when my mother said, 'Bertie, tell your father I had a ring from Aunt Marge this afternoon. Her friend Elsie has gone home to Auckland.'

I passed this on. My father looked down at the ice-cream in front of him. He had eaten only a spoonful but he passed the remainder over to me. He knows I'm very fond of ice-cream. He fiddled with his spoon for a few seconds, then said, 'Tell your mother Elsie told me she was going home. She rang me at the office yesterday and talked for a considerable time. She is a great talker.'

I repeated the gist of this but didn't bother much how I put it because it was quite clear that my mother had been listening carefully.

They sat over their black coffee in silence for some time. At last my mother looked directly at my father, although she was still ostensibly addressing me.

'Tell your father, Bertie,' she said, 'that some prejudiced people make fools of themselves because they so easily become jealous.'

I repeated this, although my father took no notice of me. But he said, looking directly at my mother, 'Bertie, tell your mother I love her.'

'Mum,' I said, feeling that the drama was now reaching its climax and also the ultimate in absurdity, 'Dad says he loves you.'

Of course I knew quite well what was coming.

'Bertie,' my mother said, 'tell your father I love him, too.'

'Dad,' I said, 'Mum says she loves you, too.'

While I was finishing my ice-cream my father got up and went over to my mother and bent over and kissed her. I couldn't help thinking it was like the ending of one of those mawkish children's stories I had once read. I said, addressing them both, 'Does this mean we've finished with the communications game now?'

But they hardly heard me. They were very selfish, I thought, ignoring me now that the game was over. That is, if it really was over. I couldn't be absolutely sure, because they still didn't say much to each other after dinner, just a word now and then which I found hard to hear. And there was no way of being certain at this stage because when I settled down with the book I'd been reading, *Tactics and Strategies in Chess*, my father told me I could read it in bed if I liked. I was comfortable where I was, but I went readily enough because I could see they wanted to get rid of me, and in those circumstances I found it almost impossible to concentrate on my book.

In bed I read for about half an hour and then put out the light. I was sleepy but found it difficult to get off for some time because my parents began whispering and creeping about.

In the morning I went as usual to the master bedroom and was only a little surprised to see that my father had returned from the guest room and that he and my mother were in the big bed they had always shared until a week ago. If the kissing last night had been the end of the second act and the play proper, I thought this was probably what was known as an epilogue. I said good-morning to them (collectively) and my mother kissed me and held me to her for some time, and even my father hugged me. It was rather an emotional scene, and embarrassing to me, but I was able to respond with an adequate show of affection because it was abundantly clear now that the communications game was over – the play had reached its, I suppose, satisfying end. And it was pleasing that my parents were now showing, even though somewhat belatedly, some recognition of the key role I had played.

Kenneth Gaunt

SUNDAY SESSION

I'm whispering on the back seat to nobody, though it seems everyone can hear. Crammed into Knobby's green Simca, we can see the board rollers through a hole in the roof. I can tell Knobby is chewing by the way his hair moves. Dave beside him is rocking out to Neil Young. And beside me Marty looks at Di who is gazing out, tapping her ring against the glass. Knobby and Dave put Clapton into the dashboard two streets away from the Sunday session.

My grandmother died today.

It's a jazz session at the Ocean Beach and we sit on the white tabled lawn, looking out past Rotto. It's been a hot day, the sun is red as it dives into the sea. Only Di watches until that final moment of disappearance. Dave is buying a jug and Knob is trying not to be seen pointing out two damp bikinis coming up from the beach. The beer. The beer is good. Soon I'm whistling obscenities at the group over Marty's shoulder as he tells me about the show I missed last night for being at the hospital.

She loaned me her golf clubs when I first started playing, and kept up with my scores. And during the footy season she'd ring me up when our teams were playing and we'd have a little wager on the result. I must have been ten and broke when that started. My team was always on top, but it was exciting anyway.

Behind Marty she sips on an orange drink. She's laughing with her tanned friends and I'm finding it hard to keep going. There's too much lust in me to keep the flirt façade going. Too much desolation. I want her beside me now, tonight, forever. I don't

50

want to whistle, my moistening eyes can't play. And if I look around I want her too, and her, her.

Di asks what's wrong with me today. I'm just tired. The beach really drained me today. I'm really into this West Coast Jazz Band. Really good for a Sunday arvo. Yeah. It's really incredible how many people are here. Knob says he'll probably make it back next week. Might roll along myself.

For a long time Granny ran a boarding house with two giant pines out the front. When I was home from school she'd look after me and at lunchtime make banana sandwiches. We'd watch the war movies together. Once a programme with Diana Ross and the Supremes came on and she hummed along. Ooooh oooh babylove, my babylove, pleeeeese don't forsake me love . . .

Knobby's Simca is buzzing along the coast highway and they laugh when he manages to pass someone. They break up when Marty says he's really worried about the little green wonder's brakes. I begin making soft noises again, trying to imitate the distant breaking of waves. We pull into a pizza place and there's that chick with the red t-shirt again. I'm pissed.

Eating a slice out of the Ham'n'Pineapple I look at myself in a laminex panel. There's me, the day Granny died. Normal. But what else, where else? She'll never know what I remember. She'll never know her warmth, how she is connected to all these people, every girl I've ever wanted, all my lust.

Dave says we should see what's going on down the Scarborough beachfront. And we're all in the mood so we put on the Beach Boys. We're all singing along and swaying and banging our hands on the paintwork outside.

I'm curled up years ago, in darkness under my blankets. I can hear my sister practising the piano. My mother is there, watching her feeble fingers. I pretend I'm a foal, kicking in the womb. So warm I can hear the world and I'm so warm.

We swerve into the carpark singing so loud if I close my eyes I can hardly make out the tape but it doesn't matter. Knobby's Simca closes us in and we're gently kicking and I'm thinking I can hear a few generations humming keenly behind us . . .

Morris Lurie

UNCLE GAMES

Once more at the uncle's. (Saturday afternoon, two o'clock.) Who, before Moses is even properly in the door, before he has even said hello, how are you, how's things, has scooped up, from an uncooked stack of at least three dozen, two fat cheese blintzes, dropped them into a frying pan, is prodding, is turning, is manoeuvring, is sliding them – with the liberal use of his fingers, a cigarette in his other hand – on to a plate. 'Eat,' he says. 'What do you want, a fork? Here's a fork. You want sugar? Soda water?'

Moses sits down at the kitchen table. His uncle stands, watching him, hands on hips.

'Good?' he asks.

'Terrific,' Moses says.

'You want another one? Another couple?'

'No, no,' Moses says, eating quickly. 'This is plenty. Terrific. Honestly. Look, I've just had lunch. Twenty minutes ago. A big lunch. Sit down.'

His uncle doesn't move. 'A cup of tea?' he asks. 'A cake?'

'Please,' Moses says. 'Relax. Sit down.'

His uncle sits. He puts out his cigarette and immediately lights another. His uncle has a curious way of sitting. He sits on his knees. Moses asked him once why he sat like that. 'Doesn't it hurt?' he asked him. 'You get used to it,' his uncle said. 'What's the difference?' Moses' uncle has a fruit shop. He is sixty-eight years old.

Moses finishes his cheese blintzes. 'Fantastic,' he says. 'I don't know how you do it.' He looks around. 'Where's Auntie?'

His uncle points with his cigarette.

Ah, there she is. Of course. Moses sees his aunt on the sofa in the front room, this is where she always sits, her place, by the television set, which is positioned so you can also see it from here, through the kitchen doorway. The television, as always, booms.

'Hello, Auntie,' Moses says, waving from the kitchen table. There is no reply. His aunt is a static shape, a lump in the flickering dark.

'Asleep?' Moses asks.

His uncle shrugs his shoulders. 'Tired,' he says. Moses sees mockery in his eyes, mockery mixed with resignation. Women. Wives. What can you expect? Moses' uncle is never tired.

'Maybe you should turn the television down a bit,' Moses says.

'What for?' his uncle says. 'She's asleep. She can't hear it.'

Moses gazes for a moment at the television. A children's programme. Nonsense. Two fat men dressed like birds. One is poking the other with a stick. Moses turns back to his uncle. 'It's rubbish,' he says. His uncle shrugs. 'So don't watch it,' his uncle says. 'Are you watching?' Moses asks. His uncle shrugs again. 'So turn it off,' his uncle says. Moses smiles, but doesn't move.

Moses has never been here when the television has not been on. His uncle switches it on the minute he gets home from the shop. It is the last thing he turns off at night. 'How can you watch that much television?' Moses asked him once. 'Who watches?' his uncle said. 'It's company. A voice, a human voice.' But he watches too, Moses knows, watches a lot, watches while the dinner is cooking – he does all the cooking – and when the washing-up is done – he does that too – and when he's alone, when no one has dropped in, when Auntie is asleep, either upstairs in bed, or sitting on the sofa, he sits here at the kitchen table, propped up on his knees, late into the night, lids drooping, smoking cigarette after endless cigarette, brooding impassively through the smoke at the booming screen. 'How can I go to bed?' he said to Moses once, when Moses asked him why he stayed up so late. 'I haven't smoked enough cigarettes yet.' Moses' uncle smokes 140 cigarettes a day.

'So,' his uncle says. 'How's things?'

'Terrible,' Moses says.

'Terrible?' his uncle says. 'What's terrible? You're working?'

Moses writes television plays. 'Well, yes,' he says.

'So it's not terrible.'

Glancing up, Moses catches on his uncle's face the hint of a smile. Uh-oh, Moses thinks. Here we go. The games.

And he feels himself tempted to take the bait, to step into the ring, to leap aboard for the ride. He smiles at his uncle, and is about to speak, to amplify, to give details, but instead he pauses. Be careful here. Tread warily. Some circumspection is needed. He looks down at the large red glass ashtray crammed and crowded with butts – his uncle stubbing out yet another cigarette, with his other hand reaching out automatically for the pack – and he remembers the time, a month ago, six weeks, when he came here, sat here, at the kitchen table, just like this, and when his uncle asked him how things were, he couldn't contain himself. 'Terrible,' he said. 'Terrible?' his uncle said. 'What's terrible?' 'The house,' Moses had said. 'It's cracking. It's falling down. You should see the walls. There's water getting in underneath. I had an architect in. I need drains, reblocking, I don't know. New plaster, new everything. The architect said if it was his house, he'd do it straight away. It's really bad. It can only get worse.'

'How much?' his uncle had asked. 'Eight thousand dollars,' Moses had said. He looked at his uncle. 'I haven't got eight thousand dollars,' Moses had said. 'I'm a writer. Writers don't earn money like that.' His uncle had looked at him. A long silence. 'Eight thousand?' his uncle had said. 'Yes,' Moses had said. 'Maybe even nine.' A further long silence. 'Hmm,' his uncle had said. 'You're a writer?' 'Well, yes,' Moses had said. 'So,' his uncle had said. 'Write faster.' And Moses had looked up to a smile that was like a door slammed in his face.

'Actually,' Moses says, moving the ashtray a fraction, and his thoughts and words just as carefully, 'things are not so bad. I've been asked to write a film script.'

'Oh?' his uncle says.

'Thirty thousand dollars,' Moses says.

'Hmm,' his uncle says. 'That's nice.'

'I said no,' Moses says.

'What?' his uncle says. 'Thirty thousand dollars?'

'Maybe forty,' Moses says. 'I don't know.'

Moses stretches his arms, flexes his back. 'God, I'm tired,' he says. 'Exhausted.'

'This film,' his uncle says. 'How long would it take you, a thing like that?'

'Oh, I don't know,' Moses says. 'A month, six weeks. You don't really know till you get into it. Not long.'

'Thirty thousand dollars for six weeks' work,' his uncle says. 'What's the matter with you?'

'Naah,' Moses says, stretching some more. 'Who needs it? I'd lose it all in tax, for a start. Listen, where's that cup of tea you were talking about an hour ago?'

And he stands up, giving yet another stretch.

His uncle sits, shaking his head. Moses, standing beside him now, pats him on the shoulder.

'Relax, relax,' he says. 'Don't worry about it. It's only money. I know what I'm doing.' He prowls around the kitchen. 'Listen,' he says, 'what's with all these blintzes? You going into business or something?'

'People drop in,' his uncle says. 'You have to have.'

Moses looks at his uncle – he is standing behind him now – and feels suddenly sad. He sees, as though for the first time, the grey hair, the slumped shoulders, the rounded back. He is so *small*, he thinks. And he remembers the old days, when the house was always so bustley. People coming and going. The doorbell. The phone ringing non-stop. His uncle's three sons. Friends. Family. If you were hungry, this is where you came. There was always something. Latkes. Chickens. The kitchen full of steam. Soup. Fresh rolls. His uncle cooking, smiling, smoking, serving, filling up the table. Cups of coffee. Cups of tea. Now one son is in Canada and another is in England and the third is always busy. Grown up. Grown away. And the family, Moses' uncle's brothers and sisters, old, tired, diminished. Or, like Moses' mother and father, gone, dead.

Moses sits down again.

'Listen, don't bother with the tea,' Moses says. 'I couldn't have it. I'm really full.'

'Who's bothering?' his uncle says. 'For people who say no to thirty thousand dollars, I don't make tea.'

And again that smile, that hint, that door slammed in the face.

Does he like me? Moses thinks. My mother's brother. He was closer to her than to anyone else. He remembers how his uncle cried at the funeral. Would he help me, Moses thinks, *really*, if things got bad?

He looks at his uncle's tough hands on the kitchen table, the stubby fingers, the black-rimmed nails.

'Well,' Moses said, 'and how are things with you? What's doing? Anything new?'

'Painting,' his uncle says. 'We're going to paint.' And he waves with his cigarette around the kitchen.

'What?' Moses says. 'You're painting the kitchen? What for?'

'Not just the kitchen,' his uncle says. 'The whole place.' He shrugs. 'Don't look at me,' he says. 'Talk to her. She gets these ideas. We've got to paint.'

Moses shakes his head. 'Crazy,' he says, looking around the kitchen, at the gleaming walls, the shining cupboards, nothing looking older than seven minutes, and the rest of the house the same.

'This doesn't need painting,' he says. 'If you want to see needs painting, come to our place. Unbelievable.'

His uncle looks at him. 'So take the thirty thousand dollars,' he says.

Moses smiles. He laughs. 'Come on,' he says. 'Leave me alone with that thirty thousand dollars. I'm sorry I even mentioned it. What a mistake.'

He should have been a lawyer, Moses thinks. That brain. That way he never lets go. What a shame. What a wasted talent. What a life.

They sit for a moment in silence, save for the booming television. Moses' uncle lights another cigarette.

'You shouldn't smoke so much,' Moses says, as he says every time. 'Really.'

'Ha,' his uncle says. 'What are you talking? Am I ever sick? Not even a cold. My body hasn't got time for a cold. It's too busy smoking.'

'Still,' Moses says.

'Listen,' his uncle says. 'Does she smoke?' His chin points to the front room. 'She goes to doctors. I'll tell you doctors. They gave her last week a pill, straight away she was dizzy, she couldn't see, she couldn't even sleep with it. And what for? Because she was stupid. Because she went to them.'

He gestures with his hands. 'I never go to them,' he says. 'And that's why I'm never sick.'

'Well, OK,' Moses says. 'But if I hadn't gone, I'd be blind.' Moses two months ago had had an operation for a detached retina.

'Well,' his uncle says, shrugging. 'An eye. That's a different thing.'

'What's different?' Moses says. 'I had headaches, flashes, I didn't feel right, I went . . . he said if I'd left it another week, I could have lost the eye.'

'Naah,' his uncle says. 'That's what they tell you. They have to tell you something. How can you give them all that money and they don't tell you something?'

Moses looks at his uncle, the thwarted lawyer, the courtroom ace. The logic, he thinks. Have you ever heard such logic?

'Actually,' Moses says, 'it's still flashing. I went to see him again last week. He said it's a cyst, on the back of the eye. Don't worry, he said. They used to operate on cysts, he said, but they don't do it any more. Not worth the trouble. So it flashes a bit. Forget about it. Live with it. Ha. Well, it's not his eye.'

Moses touches the ashtray. 'He's supposed to be the top man,' he says, his eyes down, 'but I don't know. I'm still worried.'

'Hmm,' his uncle says. 'You know Mrs Zuckerman? You remember her?' Moses nods. 'She was here last week.' His uncle shakes his head. 'One eye she's got completely blind, the other one . . .' He looks down at the table, at his cigarette, at his hands. 'She was sitting here,' he says, 'at the table, exactly where you're sitting, and she says to me, "How's Peshke?"' Peshke is Moses' aunt. 'Peshke was sitting next to her,' Moses' uncle says. 'Right here. Ten inches. I had to turn her around, she reached out her hands, she put them on Peshke's face. "Ah!" she said. "There you are!"' Moses' uncle looks suddenly up, straight at Moses. On his face there is not even that hint of smile. 'So don't tell me blind.'

Is it because of my brother? Moses thinks. Is it still that, after all these years?

For Moses went away, when he was twenty-five, went to England, went to Europe, leaving behind his brother Ben. 'So how long you'll be gone?' his uncle had asked him. 'Three months?' 'Well, I'm not sure,' Moses had said, bending over suitcases, not looking his uncle in the eye. For a year he and Ben had had a flat together, took it when their parents had died, Ben just a boy, fourteen, fifteen, Moses suddenly cast in the role of mother and father. And that started fine but became increasingly claustrophobic, cooking meals, always being home, until finally Moses could stand it no longer. He booked passage on a ship. Ben understood. Moses went to see his uncle. 'You'll go to Israel,' his uncle had said. 'A look, a visit, why not?' 'Thanks,' Moses had said. Only it wasn't three months, it was seven years. And not once a letter from his uncle, not a word, about how much it all cost.

Yes, Moses says to himself, but what could I do? If I had stayed and looked after Ben, if I hadn't gone, what would that have done? Would that have pleased him? Is that what he wanted from me? Impossible. I had to go. I was going crazy. Anyhow, you can't do things just to please other people. Not with your whole life.

Moses sneaks a look at his uncle, who is lighting yet another cigarette, and he feels – what? Guilty? No, not just guilty. Worse than guilty. Something else. He feels himself hemmed in, trapped, impossible to explain, the way he used to feel when he was in the flat with Ben, all those years ago. 'There's no life here!' he remembers how he used to shout. 'You can't *do* anything! It's all so *dead*!' And Ben not saying anything, averting his eyes, or worse, looking at him, those big, clear eyes.

'Listen,' Moses says, pushing away from the table, starting to stand up. 'I think I might go.'

'What?' his uncle says. 'What's the rush? Sit down, I'll make a cup of tea.'

'No, no,' Moses says. 'Really. We've got people coming for dinner, I'd better . . .' He makes a quick business of looking at his watch, opening his eyes wide. 'God!' he says.

His uncle starts to stand up too. 'Rush, rush,' he says. 'In on one leg, out on the other, what's the matter with you?'

But Moses is going, smiling, waving, backwards down the hall to the front door.

'No, no, don't come,' he says to his uncle. 'I can do the door. Oh, and listen, say hello to Auntie for me, OK? Tell her I was here.'

His uncle is up, walking to the door with him. 'All right,

Moishe,' he says, 'all right. Thanks for dropping in. Come again. Any time.'

On the doorstep, Moses turns. 'Gotta run,' he says, but doesn't move, stands there with his uncle, as though there were some unfinished business, something yet to do.

'Oh, and thanks for the blintzes,' Moses says. 'You're still the undefeated champion.'

'Drive carefully,' his uncle says. 'The car's going good?'

'You're joking,' Moses says. 'Fourteen years old? The steering, the suspension . . . I had it in at the garage last week. You know what they said? It's not worth fixing. Throw it away.' He looks at his uncle. 'How can I?' he says. 'You know what a new car costs these days?'

'So take taxis,' his uncle says. 'Who needs a car? It's a liability.'

And there is that smile again, but this time Moses is ready, and he matches it, smile for smile. 'Thanks, uncle,' he says, and pats him on the shoulder, warmly, but quickly too, let's not get too involved here, and then takes off, running.

Angelo Loukakis

I TOLD MAMA NOT TO COME

Whether he was born with it, or whether it started when he was a kid, I'm not sure. If it started when he was a kid I'd like to know exactly when, how, who was to blame.

This morning I've been trying to remember the last time I ever saw him. In fact, I've been trying to recall all the people who have gone out of my life. I thought I'd start with the ones who had something wrong with them, and so Dionysios, Denny, has come back to life in my head this morning. Why the sick ones? Because I've got a few questions. You can't help it when you've been sick yourself.

My mother reminded me of Denny when she was in here visiting me yesterday. She saw Denny's mother. She hadn't seen her for years, hadn't spoken to her since they had an argument when we were kids. She's the one who really got me going, thinking about Denny. She always makes things worse by holding things back, not telling me the whole story when I want to know more. I can't help thinking about it then.

1961, if I was about ten, which seems right. I must have been about ten the last time we visited the family Zagaris: Costas, Theocline, and son Dionysios. That last visit itself I can't remember. But there's not much to do here, and I've been putting it back together pretty good. I know the story, I know what it must have been like, if it was like any of the others.

They ran a food shop, just as we did. Theirs was in Sans Souci, and ours was in Newtown. My parents came from the island of Mytilene, like his, that's how they knew each other. The

Zagaris's had their home away from the shop – in Ramsgate or Kogarah? – so they must have been doing better than my parents. Denny was an only child, like myself. But if I was ten in 1961 he must have been pushing twenty, for sure.

We used to catch the tram out along Rocky Point Road, Mama and I, on the Sundays we went visiting. My father never came with us because he had to keep the shop open. He always had to keep the shop open. His excuse was that we needed the money that came in on Sundays when the 'big shops' were closed. But Denny's father was always home on Sundays. He even went to church, which my old man never did.

Of the tram trip out I can't recall too much. One thing. There were trees, palm trees I think, along a kind of narrow island between the tracks.

They lived in a brick place, really something to me who lived in the weatherboard rooms behind our shop. A red brick house, a palace with a lawn out the front and a garage at the side. We must have been the poor folks. That's probably the main reason my father didn't want to come. He hated anybody who was making money.

I had nothing like the amount of junk Denny had been given. He had everything, but I see now that this was part of his problem. Dionysios had an electric train set, a Meccano set, an incredible number of *National Geographics* among other things. He spent his life with toys, but, as I say, he would have been nearly twenty. He was mentally retarded. The ten years between us made no difference.

What we did together that afternoon wouldn't have been very exciting, or so different from what we usually did, which was to play. We would have cleared a space in the middle of his room, and got one of the toys out. If it was the train set (he had a Hornby, the best), he would have pulled it out from under his bed and silently pieced the track together, and just as silently made the thing run. He hardly ever let me work the switches. The magazines were another thing. Those, which he kept in cardboard boxes I think, he would let me flick through myself, unless there was a new one. A new one he would have to show me himself. He would stop at a picture that amused him and he would smile very quietly and point it out. I can't remember how I acted, probably just nodded so he wouldn't get upset. Sometimes for

some reason or other he would get tears in his eyes and I would
have to go and get his mother.

We had to be kept an eye on anyway. Every so often one or
other of the mothers would open the door to see if everything
was all right. If the sweets had been produced in the living room,
sometimes a few would be brought in to us. Mrs Zagaris, like my
mother, always went in for serving coffee and sweets to visitors.
A little cup of black syrupy stuff would be brought in to the living
room, along with a glass of water, and a plate of *kourabies* or
preserved fruits with a little spoon. All on a showy, chrome tray.
Whatever was left, we had to finish.

What was the argument about? What could they, who had so
much in common have argued about? When she was here yesterday (this morning?) she didn't want to talk about it when I asked
her. But after a while she had to tell me or I would've gotten
upset, wouldn't I? She thinks she has to humour me because I
am in here. What it was about, she said, after I kept at her, was
that over the years she had become more and more annoyed at
the way Mrs Zagaris was bringing up her son. Instead of encouraging him to grow up, she kept treating him like a little boy. He
had a problem, yes, but she was making things worse, spoiling
him, always buying him toys, always sheltering him. No wonder
he turned out the way he did.

I don't know if what she told me was the truth or not. Thinking
about it, Mrs Zagaris would have kept quiet about her son's
handicap for sure. She would have also kept him away from
people as much as possible. The kids have to be perfect, or you
shut them up in their rooms.

The number of people my parents have told about my own
thing you could count on your fingers. And I'm redeemable! Just
a bit of a nervous collapse, nothing serious, but enough to put
me in here for a while, and enough to put her on her best behav-
iour. The old man's just as bad though. When he comes at all,
he gets all jolly, like I've got a broken leg or something, or like
nothing's happened and I'm here just for something to do.

I don't believe this story of my mother falling out with Denny's
mother about bringing up children. What could they have
argued about? What was so different about the way she brought
me up? I was kept indoors. I was bought books to keep me distracted or occupied so that I wouldn't bother anybody. I wasn't

allowed to join anything, like the cubs, or sports. Couldn't go to the beach because I would drown. Couldn't go to the school dances because the girls there were no good. Little Golden Books and a World Encyclopaedia from Woolworths. She even used to bring my lunch to school and feed me in a corner of the play-ground! With all the other kids watching and laughing!

When I get out I'm going to try and find him, see how he is now, what he is up to. You never know, he might be okay. I reckon that where we all went wrong was in losing contact with each other. We should have stuck together. People like Denny, funnily enough, could help me a lot today. Even if I am thirty, it's not too late.

Or what about Peter? Peter from up the road whose old man worked in the drum factory. They shunned him because he did no good at school and he nearly went crazy. He kept running away and the police had to keep bringing him back. But he turned out all right in the end. He joined an airline and flew away forever. Into the skies, the beautiful, huge skies. I'd like to see him again, too, if I could find him.

He finally got away. He left his mother and father and started his own life. He had to stop being the good, obedient, respectful son. I tried to stop being those things too, but tried staying at home at the same time. It didn't work, and all I got was fights. So many, many fights. It's a wonder I never killed one of them. For a while I thought I *had* killed someone. For about a year I thought I had killed someone. I wasn't sure who, but I had this tremendous feeling of guilt. It's gone now, thank Christ.

They should be bringing lunch around soon. I asked for fish fillets. What a laugh, they give you one bit and it always has bones. One thing I could never attack Mama about was the food she cooked, which was always fantastic.

She usually brings me something extra when she comes around, which I hope she doesn't today. I'm having a good day, and I've got quite a lot to think about and work out . . .

No, I can't remember any harsh words or red faces that after-noon. There must be some other reason why we stopped going to Denny's which she hasn't told me about. Maybe she really had the argument with *Mr* Zagaris. But about what? Maybe some sex thing. Maybe they were doing it together and somebody found out.

Ha! My mother would never do that sort of thing, even if she wasn't religious. She just wouldn't do it to me.

I told Mama not to come, but I hope she does come today. I'm starting to miss her again. And I've still got some questions to ask her. With her help I'll be able to get out of here soon, no worries. I'm feeling better. I hope she does come.

Low
Life

Helen Garner

DID HE PAY?

He played guitar. You could see him if you went to dance after midnight at Hides or Bananas, horrible mandrax dives where no one could steer a straight course, where a line of supplicants for the no-cost miracle, accorded to some, waited outside the door, gazing through the slats of the trellis at his shining head. Closer in, they saw him veiled in an ethereal mist of silvery blue light and cigarette smoke, dressed in a cast-off woman's shirt and walked-on jeans, his glasses flashing round panes of blankness as they caught the light, his blond hair matted into curls: an angel stretched tight, grimacing with white teeth and anguished smiles. In the magic lights, that's how he looked.

He was a low-lifer who read political papers, and who sometimes went home, or to what had once been home, to his fierce wife who ran their child with the dull cries of her rage and who played bass herself, bluntly thumping the heart rhythm, learning her own music to set herself free of his. They said she was rocking steady.

'To papa from child' wrote the little girl on his birthday card. She was a nuggety kid with cowlicks of blonde hair, a stubborn lower lip and a foghorn voice. Her parents, engaged in their respective and mutual struggles, never touched her enough, and imperiously she demanded the bodies and arms of other grown-ups, some of whom recoiled in fear before the urgency of her need. A performers' child, she knew she existed. She knew the words of every song that both her parents' bands played. You'd hear her crooning them in the huge rough backyard where the dope plants grew, chuckling in her husky voice at the variations she invented:

'Don't you know what love is? Don't you love your nose?'

'Call me papa!' he shouted in the kitchen.

'Papa! Papa!' she cried, thumping joyfully round him on her stumpy legs. Having aroused this delight he turned away, forgot her, picked up his guitar and went to work. The child wept loudly with her nose snotting down her face; like her mother, she was accustomed to the rage of rejection and knew no restraint in its expression. In her room she made a dressing-table out of an up-turned cardboard carton covered with a cloth. She lined up a brush, a comb and an old tube of lipstick on it.

The parents had met in a car-park in a satellite town, where kids used to hang out. Everyone wondered how they'd managed to stay together so long, given his lackadaisical ways and her by now chronic anger. The women knew her rage was just, but she frightened even the feminists with her handsome, sad monkey's face and furious straight brows. It was said that once she harangued him from the audience when he was on stage at one of the bigger hotels. Somehow it was clear that they were tied to each other. Both had come from another country, as children. 'When he's not around I just . . . miss him,' she said to her friends. It cost her plenty to say this.

'Old horse-face,' he called himself once, when they ran an unflattering photo of him in the daily paper, bent like liquorice to the microphone, weighed down by the heavy white Gibson, spectacles hiding from the viewer all but his watchful corner-smile. He was sickeningly thin; his legs and hips were thin past the point of permission. In spite of guitar muscles, his finger and thumb could meet round his upper arm. One of the women asked him why he was doing this, in bed one morning. 'Finger-lengthening exercises,' he said, and she didn't even laugh.

He was irresistible. His hair was silvery blond, short, not silky but thick, and he had a habit of rubbing the back of his head and grinning like a hick farmer, as if at his own fecklessness. He would hold your gaze a second longer than was socially necessary, as if promising an alliance, an unusual intimacy. When he smiled, he turned his mouth down at the corners, and when he sang, his mouth stretched as if in agony; or was it a smile? It did for women, whatever it was. Some people, if they had got around to talking about it, might have said that there was something in his voice that would explain everything, if you could only listen hard enough. Maybe he had a cold; or maybe he did what everyone wants a musician to do – cry for you, because you have lost the knack.

Winter was a bad time in that town. Streets got longer and greyer, and it was simply not possible to manage without some sort of warmth. He was pathetic with money, and unable to organize a house for himself when his wife wouldn't have him any longer. Yes, she broke it. Not only did she give him the push, she installed another man, and told her husband that if he wasn't prepared to be there when he said he would, he could leave the child alone. He ground his teeth that day. He hadn't known he would run out of track, but he knew enough to realize he had no right to be angry. He walked around all afternoon, in and out of kitchens, unable to say what the matter was. He couldn't sit still.

After that he drifted from house to house between gigs, living on his charm; probably out of shame rather than deviousness, he never actually asked for anything. Cynics may say his technique was more refined: pride sometimes begets tenderness, against people's will. He just hung around, anyway, till someone offered, or until it eventuated with the passing of time: a meal, a place to sleep, a person to sleep with. If someone he was not interested in asked him to spend the night with her, he was too embarrassed to say no. Thus, many a woman spent a puzzled night beside him, untouched, unable to touch.

In the households he was never in the way. In fact, he was a treat to have around, with his idle wit and ironic smile, and his bony limbs and sockless ankles, and his way of laughing incredulously, as if surprised that anything could still amuse him. He was dead lazy. He did nothing but accept with grace, a quality rare enough to pave his way for a while at least. If any of the men resented his undisputed sway, his exemption from the domestic criticism to which they themselves were subjected, their carpings were heard impatiently by the women, or dismissed with contempt as if they were motivated only by envy. Certain women, feeling their generosity wearing thin, or reluctantly suspecting that they were being used, suppressed this heresy for fear

of losing the odd gift of his company, the illusion of his friendship. Also, it was considered a privilege to have other people see
him in your kitchen. He had a big reputation. He was probably
the best in town.

After his late gigs he was perfect company for people who
watched television all night, warmed by the blue glow and the
hours of acquiescence. The machine removed from him the
necessity of finding a bed. The other person would keep the fire
alight all through the night, going out every few hours to the
cold shed where the briquettes were kept, lugging the carton in
and piling the dusty black blocks on to the flames. He would flick
the channel over.

'That'll do,' she'd say, whoever she was.

'No. That's *War and Peace*. No. Let's watch *Cop Shop*. That's
all right, actually. That's funny.'

It wasn't really his fault that people fell in love with him. He
was so passive that anyone could project a fantasy on to him,
and so constitutionally pleasant that she could well imagine it
reciprocated. His passivity engulfed women. They floundered in
it helplessly. Surely that downward smile meant something? It
wasn't that he didn't *like* them, he merely floated, apparently
without will in the matter.

It was around this time that he began to notice an unpleasant
phenomenon. When he brought his face close to a woman's, to
kiss, he experienced a slow run of giddiness, and her face would
dwindle inexorably to the size of a head viewed down the wrong
end of a telescope, or from the bottom of a well. It was disagree-
able to the point of nausea.

All the while he kept turning out the songs. His bands, which
always burnt out quickly on the eve of success, played music that
was both violent and reasonable. His guitar flew sometimes,
worked by those bony fingers. He did work, then? It could be said
that he worked to give something in exchange for what he took,
were this not such a hackneyed rationalization of the vanity and
selfishness of musicians. Let us divest him of such honorable
intent and say rather that what he played could be accepted in
payment by those who felt that something was due. He could play
so that the blood moved in your veins. You could accept and
move; or jack up on him. It was all the same to him, in the end.

He worked at clearing the knotty channels, at re-aligning his hands and his imagination so harmoniously that no petty surge of wilfulness could obstruct the strong, logical stream. It was hard, and most often he failed, but once in a while he touched something in himself that was pure. He believed that most people neither noticed nor cared, that the music was noise that shook them up and covered them while they did what they had come for. Afterwards he would feel emptied, dizzy with unconsumed excitement, and very lonely.

Sometimes guitar playing became just a job with long blank spaces which he plugged with dope and what he called romance, a combination which blurred his clarity and turned him soggy. In Adelaide he met a girl who came to hear the band and took him home, not before he had kept her waiting an hour and a half in the band room while he exchanged professional wise-cracks with the other musicians. In the light that came in stripes through her venetian blinds she revealed that she loved to kiss. He didn't want to, he couldn't. 'Don't maul me,' he said. She was too young and too nice to be offended. She even thought he liked her. Any woman was better than three-to-a-room motel nights with the band. He was always longing for something.

A woman came to the motel with some sticks for the band. She had henna'd hair, a silver tooth earring, a leopard skin sash, black vinyl pants. She only stayed a minute, to deliver. When she left, he was filled with loss. He smoked and read all night.

When the winter tour was over, he came south again. He called the girl he thought had been in love with him before he went away.

'I don't want to see you,' she said. 'Have a nice band, or something.'

She hung up. At his next gig he saw this girl in the company of his wife. They stood well back, just in front of the silent, motionless row of men with glasses in their hands. They did not dance, or talk to each other, or make a move to approach him between sets, but it was obvious that they were at ease in each other's company. He couldn't help seeking out their two heads as he played. Late in the night, he turned aside for a second to flick his lead clear of an obstruction, and when he looked back, the women were gone.

When he got to the house the front was dark, but he could see light coming from the kitchen at the back. He knocked. Someone

walked quickly up the corridor to the door and opened it. It was
not his wife, but the girl. He made as if to enter, but she fronted
her body into the doorway and said in a friendly voice,

'Look – why don't you just piss off? You only make people mis-
erable. It's easier if you stay away.'

The kitchen door at the other end of the hall became a yellow
oblong standing on end with a cut-out of his wife's head, sideways, pasted on to it halfway down.

'Who is it?' she called out. He heard the faint clip of the old
accent.

'No one,' shouted the girl over her shoulder, and shut the door
quietly in his face. He heard her run back down the corridor on
her spiky heels. He thought she was laughing. Moll.

That night he dreamed: as the train moved off from the siding,
he seized the handrail and swung himself up on to the step.
Maliciously it gathered speed; the metal thing hated him and was
working to shake him off. He hung on to the greasy rail and tried
to force the van door open, but the train had plunged into a mine,
and was turning on sickening angles so that he could not get his
balance. There was roaring and screeching all around, and a
dank smell. Desperately he clung, half off the step, his passport
pressed betwen his palm and the handrail.

The train heeled recklessly on to the opposite track and as he
fought for balance the passport whisked away and was gone,
somewhere out in the darkness. Beneath the step he saw the
metal slats of a bridge flash by, and oily water a long way down.
He threw back his head and stretched open his mouth, but his
very lungs cracked before he could utter a sound.

The band folded. He might get used to it, but he would never
learn to like the loosened chest and stomach muscles, the vague
desolation, the absence where there ought to have been the
nightly chance to match himself against his own disorder and
the apathy of white faces. He got a job, on the strength of his
name and what he knew about music, doing a breakfast show
on FM radio. You could hear him every morning, supposed to
start at 7.30 on the knocker, but often you'd roll over at 20-to,
flick on the transistor and hear nothing but the low buzz of no
one there. Lie back long enough and you'd hear the click, the
hum and at last his voice, breathless but not flustered.

'Morning, listeners. Bit late starting. Sorry. Here's the Flaming Groovies.'

He had nowhere much to sleep now, so different women knew the stories behind these late starts. Shooting smack, which he had once enjoyed, only made him spew. One night when nothing turned up he slept on the orange vinyl couch at the studio. The traffic woke him, and at 7.30 he put on a record and chewed up a dried-out chocolate eclair and some Throaties. He thought he was going to vomit on air.

With the radio money, dearly earned by someone with his ingrained habit of daylight sleeping, he took a room in a house beside a suburban railway station. There was nothing in the room. He bought a mattress at the Brotherhood and borrowed a blanket. He shed his few clothes and lay there with his face over the edge of the mattress, almost touching the lino. In the corner stood his Gibson in its rigid case. He dozed, and dreamed that the drummer from his old band took him aside and played him a record of something he called 'revolutionary music', music the likes of which he had never heard in his life, before the sweetness and ferocity of which his own voice died, his instrument went dumb, his fingers turned stiff and gummy. He woke up weeping, and could not remember why.

The girl who kissed arrived from Adelaide one Saturday morning, unheralded. She invaded the room with her niceness and her cleanliness and the expectation that they would share things. That night he stayed away, lounged in kitchens, drifted till dawn, and finally lent himself to a woman with dyed blonde hair and a turn of phrase that made him laugh. When he went back the next night, the kisser had gone.

There were no curtains in the room, and the window was huge. He watched the street and the station platform for hours at a time, leaning lightly against the glass. People never looked up, which was just as well, for he was only perving. At 5.30 every morning a thunderous diesel express went by and woke him. It was already light: summer was coming. He supposed that there were questions which might be considered, and answered. He didn't try to find out. He just hung on.

Michael Wilding

READING THE SIGNS

It grew under the apple tree. It got a start because nothing much else ever grew there. We did try potatoes occasionally, but you caught your fork in the tree roots trying to dig them up. So that from the apple tree to the fence at the right was my garden, and from the apple tree to the path at the left was my sister's. She put in rocks and moss and things for the fairies.

It grew there with its stubby wooden stem and its bushy branches of leaves and then this amazing pinkish-purplish bugle of a flower. We let it grow because we had never seen anything like it; even before the flower, it had this presence, this numinousness. But the flower was a clarion of mystery. Then the seedpod formed, green and spiky at first, and then it darkened and became rounded and leathery.

We asked everybody what it was, and no one knew. Even Dad must have accepted some of its mystery, because he never pulled it up. Even though under the apple tree was not productive and even though he didn't believe in stripping off all unplanted vegetation like some of the people in the avenue, the bigger weeds got pulled up and put on the compost heap.

So nobody knew, and we picked the seedpod and kept it in a little fish-paste jar in the kitchen window, sitting in the fish-paste jar like an egg in an eggcup on the windowsill above the sink, among the rubber rings that sealed the fruit we bottled in jars, and the hairpins, and the used razor blades, and countless other things. Sometimes the robin would hop in through the open window and peck around. Year after year the windowsill was in the robin's territory.

The seedpod cracked open, and we kept the dark-brown seeds in the bottom of the fish-paste jar through the winter, and they stayed on the windowsill with all the other accreted things and got forgotten. The plant died beneath the apple tree, and the dried stem was tossed onto a bonfire.

The next year, it came again. But the next year it had come all over the rest of England, too. Neighbours had them. The newspapers reported its mysterious appearance throughout the country. The California thorn apple, they called it. Jimsonweed. *Datura stramonium*. Said to be deadly poisonous.

'Wonder you didn't poison the lot of us,' Dad said. Poisonous, they all said. No one said it was a hallucinogen. But they stamped them out and burned them just the same.

Once the plant was everywhere and had been named, we didn't know what else to do. We knew there was a mystery, but the naming and the reported spread of it were made to do service for the revelation. We never did take any of it, boiled or brewed or powdered or smoked or rubbed into the skin. The newspapers never suggested you could do that. That sort of knowledge hadn't survived. It was about this time Mum had her fortune read at a village fête and was told that in a few years she'd be doing the same herself: reading fortunes. She was always able to read the signs. If she dropped a big knife it would be a tall visitor coming, and a little knife a short visitor. The magpies would fly over the fields, one for sorrow, two for joy. But the uses of the thorn apple had been stamped out in the witch burnings. Everything comes in threes was another of Mum's sayings. But the third year the thorn apple didn't come back. And the seeds had got thrown on the fire because of everyone's saying how poisonous it was. I think that was a mistake, not keeping the seeds.

'That flying saucer you saw,' I asked Mum.

'Oh, Michael, did we?' she says. 'I can't remember now.'

It was like this when I needed my precise time of birth for the astrological chart. 'Here we are. Five. One. Or was that the date? Wait until I find my specs.'

'When we were living up the avenue. You remember.'

The avenue was a row of twenty-seven houses, with fields in front of us – because they hadn't built on the other side of the road – and fields behind. They stopped building when the war started. The prisoners of war used to hoe in the fields at the back.

'We were in the back garden talking one evening and it just came across,' Mum said. 'I can't remember if it was our back garden, even.'

'And it just came over the garden?'

'I think so,' Mum said. 'It wasn't very high. It was just like a bright light. It had a sort of tail, I think.'

'And where did it go?'

'It just vanished. It just went. It wasn't there anymore.'

'No,' said Dad. 'No, no, no, it was in the front of the houses. We were standing in the road. It was going up the river. It was a meteorite. It was going up the river.'

'What, following it along?'

'That's what it looked like.'

Dad wrote to the paper. 'As an iron molder, it seemed to me like a glowing red ball of molten iron.'

Sometimes he would be at home with burns on his hands or feet from molten iron that had spilled. Now he is at home dying of emphysema from the foundry dust.

'It was just like the molten iron when it comes out of the furnace.'

Mum was furious, embarrassed. She went red.

'I never expected them to print it,' Dad said. 'I just wrote it as information for them.'

Other people in town had sighted it. There were other letters.

'You might have known they'd print it.'

'No, I didn't, so that's that,' said Dad.

Mum was mortified. On the forms at school we wrote 'Engineer', not 'Iron molder'. Filling in the forms for university, I went off to a private place and my stomach wrenched for a long time, and for 'Father's Profession or Occupation' I crossed out 'Profession' and wrote 'Iron molder'.

The man at the appointments board, just before I left, congratulated me.

'Well, well,' he said, 'you're tipped for a first, you edited the university paper, you've done very well for an iron molder's son.'

Dad said, 'It went along up the river glowing like molten iron and then it exploded. It was a meteorite.'

'There wasn't any noise,' Mum said.

'I didn't say there was any noise,' Dad said. 'It exploded in a big flash.'

'But explosions usually make a noise,' Mum said.

I don't know whether Dad clipped the letter or not. I've had letters in print that were not intended for print. I think I kept them but kept them beneath dark stacks of things.

'People who've seen them don't seem to talk about them much,' I said.

'That's right,' Mum said. 'We didn't talk about it much, did we?' she said to Dad.

What they talked about was the letter. The shame of being a manual worker and the ridicule for having seen a flying saucer and the breaking of the taboo in revealing these things in print.

C.C.Catt

GRAFFITO SPY

You might have seen it if you've ever walked through the tunnel under Railway Square. I know there are a million there but its right between 'PUNK SUCKS' and 'SOMEBODY, WHERE ARE YOU?'. And anyway, it stands out so that people can hardly go by without being forced to look at it. I've seen people reading the blurb on the other wall or talking, and then as they get to it their heads seem to jerk around to it as if they know they are missing something.

It's funny how it started as just something to write. I walked out of the party at our flat with a mug of rosé and sat on the front wall. We're right between street lights and there was no moon, no stars, no cars, no lights from open windows. I could have been a bit drunk too so I sat there in pitch black for a while, sipping by feel and spilling a bit, before I started to see the shapes of things. Like the footpath. I wondered how old the cement was. It was cracked and crumbled enough to be hundreds of years old, except for a new strip across the path where someone had dug to fix some pipes. I remember moving the beer mug around in front of my face to try to catch the light gleam in the rosé but there was no light or my eyes weren't working. So I looked at the new cement because it was the lightest grey around, and tried to absorb the light into my eyeballs.

I just happened to find the lipstick in my overalls pocket and the thought of lipstick and mouths made me think of him and the next thing I knew I was kneeling on the cement with an empty mug and writing with the soft lipstick on the rough cement. I don't know how I thought of it. The cement seemed to eat the lipstick, crunch it, and as I finished, the metal case was scraping with each downstroke. The funny part was I couldn't remember what I'd written.

I had to rush back inside and scream out for a torch. Of course no one had one and they kept asking me why I wanted it. I grabbed some guy's lighter and I could see that he was going to grab it back but then he decided that it would be sort of cool to lend his cigarette lighter to a drunken chick. I heard them saying that someone should go with me because I was worse than they thought but I ducked out the door and behind the wall before they had argued over who should go. The guy must have decided to worry about his lighter because he came out for a look. But he went back when I wasn't around.

I know it's taking me a long time to explain it but I wanted you to see how unpremeditated the whole thing was when it started out. Here I was, a bit under the weather, stumbling around with a cigarette lighter in the blacked out street and trying to find a bit of new cement in the footpath. Then as soon as I flicked the lighter and saw the first line it came back without the need to read it.

    I MET HIM
    I LIKED HIM
    I LOVED HIM
    I LOVED HIM
    I LET HIM
    I LET HIM

    I LOST HIM

I think you can see it, even if it's only on the page instead of the cement. It's sort of banal I think but still it's incredibly poignant; has a certain sorrow, pathos. Piquant. A little raunchy too. My own little revelation. Epiphanies, Brenda calls them.

Graffiti is highly contagious apparently. The next day when I went outside someone had written 'ANARCHY SUCKS' with white chalk right beside mine. Everything seems to suck around here.

There were at least a dozen blurbs on the footpath by the weekend but I wasn't concerned with the graffiti generating process. I was only concerned with what I had written. Crumpled paper lay all over my room where I'd written it at least fifty times, fifty different ways, trying to make it better, I tried:

    I SAW HIM
    I MET HIM
    I LIKED HIM
    I LOVED HIM
    I LOVED HIM
    I LOVED HIM
    I LOVED HIM, LOVED HIM, LOVED HIM
    I LET HIM

    I LOST HIM

I thought that might accentuate how I loved him but it looked a bit overdone. I tried:

    I MET HIM
    I LIKED HIM
    I LOVED HIM
    I LET HIM
    I LET HIM
    I LET HIM
    I LET HIM
    I LET HIM
    I LOVED HIM

    I LOST HIM

I thought that one might show a bit of the feeling of throwing myself into him, completely letting go, discarding everything, diminishing everything except the physical need.

But the original probably expresses the spontaneity that I'd felt and I decided that's how it should stay. The trouble was, the lines sort of filled me. It was as if I'd written them on a long sheet of paper and then folded it in a circle and kept revolving it in front of my eyes. The lines just kept rolling and I began to lose the beginning and the end. I'm like a teletext, I thought. World headlines flashed on a skyscraper. I knew it couldn't just end on the footpath.

Railway Square tunnel was the place. Empty. Hollow. Shuffling feet and transience. The graffiti – contemporary epigrams. The place echoed the forlornness of my lines.

The size of the letters worried me. Too big or too small could have ruined it. I also agonized a bit about whether to take one of the girls with me. Brenda would have come and I almost asked her. I fought against it even though I needed the moral support. It had to be done alone, I decided.

Strangely, I felt little as I scrawled on the pale yellow tiles with the black pen, hands slightly shaking. There were footsteps echoing but I didn't know if they were right beside me or way down the tunnel. I shut them out as a presence and made them into just noises.

I forgot the full stop. I just left.

I think it's better without the full stop anyway.

'PUNK SUCKS' was already there when I wrote mine in but 'SOMEBODY, WHERE ARE YOU?' came later. It had to be a response to mine.

Don't you think?

Even on that first night I had to go back and walk past it.

Echoes are endemic in the tunnel. A fug of echoes.

I just walked up and down the tunnel slowly to read all the graffiti. There's too much there to read all at once and a bunch of guys started annoying me so I left.

Nearly every night I go there now. If there's a busker near it I can stand there without attracting attention. Some people stop to listen and they invariably start reading between songs.

Or I just walk slowly till the faster walkers go past and then I turn as if I've forgotten something and go back. People don't notice.

Facial expression is what I look for. In the tunnel I feel sort of dead. Like some of my senses are anaesthetized. Then I watch as someone reads it and I get an incredible buzz. I can almost feel them physically. It's a real jolt. I even saw a group of musos with a couple of guitars sitting underneath it and trying to write a song. It didn't have a chance because they tried to fit my words into their music. They reckoned that they had something but I could have told them it was hopeless.

Well I haven't heard it on the radio yet, have you?

I suppose you're wondering who I'm writing this to. At first it was for him but after the first page or so I realized that I'd been thinking so long now of a 'him' that I don't think of him any more now as a 'you'.

There's just the lines now, not him.

He even came back to the flat one night. The other girls called me to the door and he obviously wanted to get back together.

'Can I see you?' he said.

'What for?' I asked him, trying not to sound hurt and realizing just then that he didn't hurt any more.

'I thought we could talk.'

'There's no need to talk.'

'I'd like to explain.'

'No point.'

'Look, I came to see if you could understand . . .'

'If you want to know what I understand, go to Central Railway tunnel.'

'What?'

'Go take a walk along the tunnel.'

'Don't talk ambiguities.'

'And when you get to the end keep going up on to the platforms and jump under the first train that comes along.'

He patted the air with both hands. 'Okay,' he said, 'I'm not going to push it.'

I didn't even bother to watch him walk down the steps.

Even at that stage watching was becoming important. Seeing the effect of my lines. Some people have a printout on their foreheads. Their brains are so vulnerable. I can see the stifled whimpers and I know that they are fuller people from reading it. I know they understand.

Even the shrieks from the other end of the tunnel don't jar my nerves. They could be laughter or a rape. From this distance it's all the same. Like I said, I get kind of in a trance and I'm only responsive to people's reactions.

Leaving it is the biggest problem. I don't like to leave it with the possibility that some bureaucrat may stab his pen in a sheet of paper and send people down with paint brushes or cleaners.

So I wrote it on my bedroom wall.

It seems more fragile on its own.

It needs others around it. What I had to do was transfer that living tapestry off the tunnel wall to my bedroom. I've studied each one minutely to get the detail just right. I've adopted the same method they use to rebuild historical structures. They number every brick and stone to make sure that it fits together just as it did originally. But its just not the same with graffiti. I don't know why.

I've just thought of a camera, too. If I shoot all of them and blow them up I can fit the photos together.

Then I'll have it there at any time, along with the others.

But I'll always go back to the tunnel. It's the faces I need. The endless traffic of strangers to read the lines and give off their little facial epiphanies.

Suzie Malouf

SPEEDIE LADY

I lost my identity in my sleep, in a dream. I can't remember at all what happened except that when I woke up I felt an overwhelming sense of loss and none of the things in the room seemed to belong to me. Which of course they don't anymore.

I have a job now, under a false name. I work in Grace Brothers. I have to dress up to go there. I wear the clothes that the girl wore, when she was younger, before she found feminism. Apparently she kept the dresses and the skirts in case she ever needed them for a straight job. I found them hanging in the wardrobe that is opposite the bed I woke up in the day I didn't know who I was. So I wear dresses and skirts to Grace Brothers.

I catch a bus there and see vaguely familiar streets on the way. When I get to Grace Brothers I become this person I have never seen before. I ask people if they would like to know about the heaters. (Those people who are looking at the heaters.) When they say, 'Yes. How does this one work?' I tell them. I tell them about the fan heaters, how you have to hang them on the wall at least six inches off the ground. And I tell them about the oil-filled heaters, how you can put clothes on them and how they are cheaper if you leave them on all the time. I don't know how I know so much about heaters, but I do.

I told one woman all about the heaters and she seemed to like it. She asked me what my name was and I couldn't tell her that. But she read it off a little badge that I wear and she repeated it a couple of times. I forget what it was now, but she said she'd try and remember it. I don't know if she did or not. She ended up buying a Breville steam iron. Later on the demonstration Breville steam iron went missing off the stand. The woman told me she had just come back from holidays in Coolangatta. She was very brown.

I don't know who I am except that I am the SPEEDIE lady. As well as the customers I have for my other companions women who work with me. There is a SUNBEAM lady and a BREVILLE lady and a SANYO lady and a GENERAL ELECTRIC lady. Some of them cook cakes and sausages in the crock pots and electric fry-pans. They let me eat some of it, what they cook. They make coffee too, in gadgets that always have coffee in them and it is always nice and hot.

The girl's friends tell me that it is good that I can handle this job. I don't see why I shouldn't be able to as I can't remember what I used to do before. And if I was not in the store I would have to sit in the room where I sleep, all day. I do not like the room because I am frightened the girl will come back and want to know why I am wearing her clothes. But I don't think the girl is coming back. She may even be dead, who knows? A lot of people think I am her but there is a lot of confusion about that. Apparently all the people who knew the girl really well have gone away somewhere too. People ask me, 'Have you heard from so and so' and 'Did you know thingummy was living in such and such.' But I don't know who they are talking about, except that they are someone to do with the girl.

When the Breville iron went missing, they asked me about it. I didn't know what happened to it. It could have dematerialized I suppose and gone off into the cosmos like the girl. But I think it much more likely that someone pinched it.

When people ask me where Haberdashery is I say, 'I wish I knew.' I would like to buy some shoulder pads to sew into the girl's clothes.

Gary Dunne

THE PRINCE PHILIP BLUES

Nick moved in following an evening that by all standards of romance should have been memorable. The film on TV, flagon of wine and the routine. Actually, *The Bed-sitting Room*, following a Monty Python replay on Seven.

And a new cure for premature ejaculation. Racy oral sex during commercials and as the two minute point of no return arrives, the film begins again. Glasses back on and return to mild petting. Very Pavlovian. Probably explains the ABC's low ratings.

Anyway, following him mentioning being cut off the dole and currently minus an abode, I said, 'You want to stay here?' And he said, 'Thanks. Maybe just till the cheque comes.' Such is probably the nature of modern romance.

Before he moved in I would have said that we were more good friends who screw than lovers, the difference being greater than just class and semantics. On the second day he returned home with a wreath, original card removed.

'Gee honey, I brung you deese here flowers, aww shucks.' With corny grin and appropriate gestures. Living together changes things.

It was summer so the leaking roof was no problem, but with two of us, the attic was smaller than ever. Nick didn't own much. Beyond a determined skinny body with freckled features, it all fitted into one carpet bag. I borrowed a double bed mattress to put on the floor and we threw out the squeaky single bed. He shop-lifted some satin sheets and a quilt. The nights became more comfortable. Using a found bankcard, he bought some curtains and the bits and pieces necessary to fix the roof. I asked him if he was basically a criminal type and he ran a hand through his spiky hair saying that he only did things like that when he was on the dole. He had never talked about his employment record so I gave up. It really didn't matter.

We were poor. There was just my fortnightly cheque to see us through. After experience with Wayne's patronizing handouts, I was careful. Once the rent and food were paid for, the rest went into the tobacco tin.

'There's the money. It's got to last till the next cheque.' The first definition. Understood.

Once or twice I had to crack it. Tight clothes and a trip up to the park. A couple of hours with a bored husband and back home, $30 richer. Nick didn't ask any questions but then I had said no more about the bankcard.

If all else failed, we'd go out busking. Nick could sing and played mandolin fairly well. I'd accompany on guitar and gravel my way through the chorus. Practising a more bland expression is quite an art. We made enough most times for tobacco, papers and a drink on the way home. The largest amounts dropped into the mandolin case when it was directly in front of Nick. My clothes being one size too big for him, plus the waif-like blue eyes, created a ragamuffin effect. It didn't suit his personality but it seemed to attract cash.

At home, despite the lack of space, the room had a comfortable, busy feel to it. I went on writing and reading in much the same manner as before. He had his own activities: music, reading or sketching. Neither expecting to be entertained by the other. The only time we really talked a lot was in bed, TV on, under the bankcard quilt, ashtray in the valley between.

And we screwed from time to time, but by unstated consent, it didn't intrude on our friendship. Minimal athletics followed by cuddle, kiss, cigarette and hazy conversation. I didn't make the first moves; they were up to him. Because of the economic situation. A desire to keep the balance. It must have worked; he was certain enough to joke about the times he had had to fuck to put a roof over his head.

But there were still his 'Prince Philip Blues' days. Times when he liked to be left alone, a curled up, blanketed ball in the corner. I'd offer to talk, then go visiting if he didn't want to.

'It's what comes from living off a relatively rich queen,' he said, 'It'll pass.'

In part, it was the seemingly endless wait for his dole cheques to start coming through again. We lived as if they never would. Nick didn't consider the dole to be very respectable. I didn't see it that way. Two years of sharing a house with Sarah and watching her battles with the SS over her wages had left their mark on me.

The first cheque finally arrived. We found it sitting on the table downstairs one Friday evening and went straight out to buy a bottle of scotch to celebrate. Upstairs, we had drunk about half of it when one of the three pigs downstairs banged on her ceiling. Too much noise. We headed back out, planning to catch a bus anywhere.

On the jetty at Watson's Bay. Just the two of us. Looking under the railing at city lights and other distant things. Legs dangling over the edge. Conversing, as people do on cold still nights, in mouth mist and cigarette smoke. Very drunk. Flicking cigarette butts out to sea. Red tips turning over and over.

'Wanna build a sandcastle?'

I chased him down the jetty.

The sand was too cold and damp so we drank the rest of the scotch instead. Nick dumped the empty bottle in the bin then threw the bankcard in after it.

'That's that. Sooner or later someone would check the list or have a computer handy. Mustn't be greedy.'

'No more dinners in restaurants.'

'You could consider paying for them.'

'True.'

On the other side, the Gap. Waves pounding in far below. A mist coming in from the sea. Despite a well-tuned sense of the dramatic (forties movie addict), I didn't want to ask him then and there. I waited until we were on the bus going home (sixties movie style).

'What are you planning to do now that the cheque is here?'

'It hadn't occurred to me. What do you mean?' Blank face.

'You said once that you would stay until it arrived.'

'Yeah, well . . .'

The cynical butch mode as an Australian conversation style can be limiting when it comes to expressing feelings. We agreed that we both wanted to go on living together but it took a long time to battle through the complexities of an unstated relationship. We probably missed the point. The effect of double the income.

But that was the only way it could be done. Discussing economics in emotional terms. And emotions, like ready cash, a distant luxury.

Penelope White

PARTING

This house I live in, it always smells rancid. Lingerings of other people's sweat and tinea and toenail cuttings. In summer no fan cools it, in winter nothing warms it. Now it's winter, the water dribbles down windows and bedroom mirrors in the mornings and rooms are icy. I hear the children coughing at night and wonder if it's water that's in their lungs. If it's water they're bringing up.

Old houses. Always old houses. Never anything with clean new walls and immaculate bathrooms. Because of the children who leave handprints and footprints over everything. Because of the dog who moults over everything and sleeps on the table. And mostly because we're poor.

I have few possessions – some paperbacks, mostly novels by women writers and some poetry. A few potted plants. God knows how we'll move them next time. Last time, the time we moved here, my plants got tucked in between the record player or chair legs sticking up naked or bags of blankets. Chairs and blankets left over from my dead marriage. The record player my ex-husband bought in Singapore duty free.

He'd paid the cost of moving us into this house. And the bond. For the kids' sake, he said.

I pick carefully at my toast this wet winter morning. Pick slowly, pick neatly at each tiny piece. Put each tiny piece in my sorrowing mouth.

My friend Coral rushes through the house, up the long hallway, back to the sunroom, arms loaded with crepe gowns and coat-hangers. 'I left some cosmetics for you,' she says as her back disappears into her bedroom. What was once her bedroom. Now it's a nothing room. Just a room with a bed. And a wardrobe. And a yellow dressing-table. The one with the deceptive handles that make you think there are two drawers when there's only one.

I am a person who's always bitten my nails so has to deliberately try not to bite them. Instead I pick and bite at the quicks. Long nails and torn quicks. I have short hair and grey eyes and a little nose and little feet.

My friend Coral is going to England. It was my idea. Two years ago I'd told her, 'You're young. You've got a job. You should be saving. Don't sit around wishing you could go. Do it.'

Coral has hair that's growing. Over the past two years since I met her, she's had long hair every shade of red and brown and hair that's frizzed and hair that's tipped silver. The last cut was short but now it's growing. Getting ready for England. She is part Irish, part English but mostly Chinese. She laughs at her Chineseness, her miserliness with money. She has a talent for finding bargains and rich men.

For weeks I have watched her packing. Piles of clothing, bags of it, boxes of it have been sealed and sent to Coral's married sister. The stuff Coral will never wear again. The stuff she won't take to England.

Her sister's my age, twenty-nine. The small dainty one (not like me, Coral laughs) whose photo was always on the yellow dressing-table. My rival, though I never let Coral know it.

Coral's twenty-one. She had a party, but that was in Melbourne where she comes from. After we started living with my children in this rotting old house we all had the first Christmas together. With my lover whose mother wasn't too happy about it. Well she wasn't too happy about the whole thing, their being Catholic and my being divorced. After two years Coral said, 'You're too good for him, Sandra.'

I have a new lover who's moved in with us.

That Christmas was the only celebration we shared. Coral has always gone to Melbourne. Always sending cartons of once-used clothing ahead of her. For her sister. To take up or put a tuck in or even alter for their mother.

Coral's bought things for my children. Outfits and cheap toys from Woollies and sweets and bits and pieces. And she's given them her old junk jewellery and painted their fingernails and curled their hair and sometimes allowed them into her room. She's given me tea-sets and coffee mugs and little pots from the gift store where she works. And brought home uncollected dry cleaning – curtains and table cloths – because there's a dry cleaning business in the gift shop.

She's rushed round for weeks collecting her own bits and pieces bought for her glory box. She has a fiancé who is in despair because of this trip. I think he'll fly over to join Coral.

None of Coral's lovers has been very satisfactory. Except this one. He has the tiniest tightest bottom. 'Ooh yummy,' Coral said. She'd taken him to a psychologist.

The fiancé had told him, 'One of us is very sexy and the other one is having trouble keeping up with them.'

The psychologist had said, 'I understand. Women can be a bit reluctant sometimes.'

The fiancé said, 'No no, you don't understand. It's the other way round.'

Coral had always thought there was something wrong with her. Perhaps she was a lesbian or bisexual. She was always getting unsatisfactory lovers. She always thought she was frigid. Until this one. They quarrel a great deal but she said, 'You have to have someone in your life. There's nothing worse than loneliness.'

While he was visiting she would keep coming from her room to get creams for rubbing into her sore fanny or she'd sit soaking for ages in a hot bath to ease the rawness.

Today I sit eating my toast and sipping my tea (I like it hot).

Coral has changed over the past two years. Now she is striding self-assured back and forth with her washing, her ironing, a bit here, a bit there. When I met her she used to walk with a scrunched, hunched up walk. A Chinese walk Coral would say with a giggle.

My face over the teacup is trying to give nothing away. My eyes watch the beautiful crepes, the skirts, the shirts (bought at sales or bargain prices, some pinched).

'Are they going to your sister?', so casually. And I'm thinking, that blasted sister. What did SHE ever do for you? Always telling me how clever and intelligent she is. New house, new baby, up and coming husband. Big deal. Why should she get everything if she's so well off? And what did she ever do for you, Coral? Did she encourage you, did she invite you to live with her and her 'poshe' husband and your precious darling nephew . . .?

'No, these are last minute packing for the ship.' For the dances, the dinners, the Captain.

The fiancé has bought Coral a pigskin pouch for her papers. He's bought her, over the past months, red carnations, silver jewellery, a kangaroo fur coat. Her mother has sent gifts, some to me, and thanked me for being so good to her daughter.

I have never bought Coral anything. I took her to all the parties, introduced her to all my friends, arranged dates, listened to complaints about her constipation, menstruation, men, Coral's mother, everything that worried her. Until the fiancé came. Then Coral's bedroom door closed for good. She started a busy new life, and now . . .

Now you don't need me anymore eh?

I watch the comings and goings and try to hide my jealousies, my selfishness, my self-pity. And the other things.

At first there'd been my rousing and telling off. 'You're dirty, you don't even bathe.'

Now it is hard to get into the bathroom. Coral has developed a passion for cleanliness. The sad, unhappy, unclean and miscarried Coral has developed into an assertive, spotless, tailored woman who has her own specially made contraceptive pill. No more sweaty armpits, no more rolled up jeans and cheap Indian bracelets, no more body bras. Now she spends ages in fitting rooms selecting the right bras for her heavy breasts. Gone are the vivid knee socks and garish make-up.

She still pinches things. She walks out of boutiques with blazers over her arm and trousers in her bag. 'The stupid sales girls ask for it.' She takes the children to the discount stores and fills them with chocolates and chips while she saunters round the aisles. The empty bags are secretly disposed of before they come to the check out. She switches price tags on underwear and laughs at her daring. 'I'll get caught one day, I know it.'

Probably in London.

Men have said that Coral's not quite right in the head or she's not all there and they'll tap their heads.

She has a high whiny voice except when she gets angry, then she slams through the house yelling 'Fuck! Fuck!' as she bangs every door she can find and clomps threateningly up and down the old echoing hall.

She loves black singers and eating. We have been dieting for two years. I simply starve myself. Coral has a lot more trouble giving up the cream cakes and chocolates. The kids and I never know what we'll find when we open the fridge door. Half-eaten yoghurt and one measly chop might be side by side with a cream bun and a custard tart. With every new man friend there were half empty bottles of wine vying for place of importance with jugs of bluish, watery skim milk. To convince herself she's dieting Coral occasionally cooks herself a boiled egg, which she peels with finicky precision and dedication. Then her lover rings, she moans at her own weakness, and off they go to some lavish meal at a Chinese restaurant.

She always dresses with the utmost care. Next to eating and black singers she loves clothes. She has no intellectual conversation, no academic qualifications, no working skills. The feelings I have had for her have ranged from pity to exasperation to rage that she can't even use a can opener and has to ask me to do it, that she boils kettles dry, leaves the gas on and fridge doors open and clogs pipes with her multi-coloured hair. She knows her shortcomings better than anyone else and laughs behind her hand at herself when she thinks she's done anything silly. And there's been my jealousy. Jealousy that Coral's figure is shapely and unblemished even when she's overweight. Of her height which allows her to wear anything and look attractive. Of her desirability. For although men comment on what they think is her lack of intelligence, they still want her. And of her freedom. Her freedom to save and go to England.

'You're all right Sandra. You are going to be wonderful. Everything is starting for you.'

I am trying to be an actress. I have a small face which I've been told I tighten to give a look of maturity and self-reliance. I suppose I'm the sort of woman people see as competent, efficient, decisive. There've been moments I've allowed this tight hard look to soften. Not many. Today, a wet winter day, I'm watching my friend preparing to leave me and I wonder how long it will be before I can think of her in the past tense, of used to do instead of doing, of used to be instead of being.

The boyfriend is here, the fiancé, bustling about with cases and make-up bags. He is like a mouse scampering back and forth saying a hasty, head down, 'Hallo Sandra'. All of us are like mice, except the children. All the grown-ups lately poking heads out of bedroom doorways before venturing into bathroom or kitchen. Ensuring no one is around, ensuring there is privacy in order to move freely not furtively. Coral would giggle, 'Look at us, all running back to our mouse holes if someone sees us.' But only lately, only in the last few months.

The children break all the rules I have laid down: 'No noise while the adults are sleeping'.

They still run into each other's rooms and yell and wrestle and bang doors and fight and squeal in the hall. At first I was constantly apologizing for them. After a while I realized Coral liked them and thought they were funny. She is always coming to me, laughing so much the tears are in her eyes, to tell me about their latest mischief. And I feel my mouth twitching but I try to stay in control for I feel I must maintain discipline . . .

Oh Coral who will I share woman secrets with now? Who will make me laugh now? No man has made me laugh. Not one.

'My cabin is so low down it'll take me an hour to find my way to the dining-room. Knowing me, I'll probably get lost,' she grins.

I leave the protection of the table.

'Are they gone yet?' My lover is still in bed, needing reassurance.

I have to tell him when it's safe to trot off to the toilet. When they're packing up the car. He's not quick enough and he and the fiancé bump into each other, 'Morning', then scuttle into their women's rooms, into their sanctuaries.

'We're going now, Sandra,' Coral's voice outside the door.

'Oh? Oh yes. All right,' so casually, so matter-of-factly.

I peek out the front door and see my friend's face in the car. Serious, puzzled.

I'd told the fiancé, 'You come and visit. You're very welcome.' But I know I'll never see him again.

'They're gone.' (No waves, no smiles, no tears, no promises to write, no goodbyes.)

All that's left are half-empty shampoo bottles, perfume bottles, a few bobby pins.

Nothing else of her.

Inez Baranay

THE SEX PART

How could she do it? What if she didn't like him?

The unknown man. He puts his papers in a neat pile. He puts them in his briefcase. He has a shower and puts on a bathrobe. He has a shower and gets dressed again. He waits to have a shower with her. He doesn't think about a shower until she arrives. He thinks about a shower but does he want her to know he just came out of the shower? He has a shower and smears on the deodorant. He hopes she's a girl who appreciates personal freshness. He hopes she's as good as the last one. He hopes she's better than the last one. He doesn't think about it. He catches up on some phone calls while there's time. He has a drink. He orders champagne. He doesn't order yet, not until he has a look at her. He remembers why he called. He hopes it'll be worth it. He doesn't care.

She knocks at the door. She's immediately at home, sitting at ease, kicking her shoes off, hoping he hasn't waited too long, it was hard to get a cab. She lets him notice her relief and pleasure that it's someone more attractive, young, distinguished or something more than she had dared to hope. She'd love a drink. Better get you-know-what out of the way, enjoy ourselves. Is it cash? He wants to know how much, how long, how good. He doesn't ask a thing. It's ready. It's in an envelope. He has to find his wallet. Is there any hurry?

He can see he has her attention. He has her interest. Interesting. Where does he live? Oh yes, so he said. Never been there, is it nice, interesting. He's looking at her. She's got nice tits. She's

96

got tits. She's got nice legs. Those awful pantyhose or real stockings? Suspenders, lace, black, red, flesh, silk, nylon? He wonders. He hopes. He doesn't care about these things. She's wearing pants. Casual, kinky. She's got personality. He likes the smile, a mind of her own. Smart. Professional. But not too blasé. Oops. He likes her passive, feminine, dumb, admiring. That's better. Has she been doing this long? Of course, it's relative. But he can tell it wouldn't be long – she's not hard. Don't get hard. That's right, he laughs – nervously, heartily, not at all – ladies shouldn't be hard. Men should be hard. A hard man is good to find.

Another drink? Maybe later. After. Get comfortable now. Take off the tie for a start. How do you feel? It'll be good. He watches her undress. She loves it. Show-off. Nympho. Sex maniac. Bullshitter.

Her hands on her own breasts, her own thighs, the hips moving against the cold sheets, the cold sheets making her giggle. Come here, make me warm. Put your hands here. She replaces her hands with his own over the cunningly hardened nipples. He lowers his face to hers. The big moment: does she kiss? She moves her head swiftly at the last second, bites his shoulder, leaving him thrusting his tongue at the air stupidly like a fish. She's got a boyfriend, you can tell that if she doesn't kiss him. He doesn't think of kissing her. Kissing has no part in this. He doesn't want to kiss. He begs for a kiss. He won't ask again. He'd better not. She pushes his head to her breast. There, nice, like that, don't bite, careful, gently please, no teeth. He kisses the nipples. He sucks gently. He sucks hard. He's not into tits at all.

He hasn't got this far. He's sitting on the end of the bed. He has to tell her. He sometimes has a bit of trouble. It's all right, and she looks him in the eye, steady, confident, you won't have any trouble with me. She undoes the top button of his shirt. She pulls the shirt apart and presses her mouth to the bare triangle of flesh. Next button, her wet mouth sliding down. Next button. Down to the belt. Her tongue flicking over his nipples. One side. The other side. Down to the belt. He takes it off, she can't. Good. Pushes him back, says don't do a thing. Her wet sliding mouth on his bare stomach. Lifts the underpants, eases them over, aside. He's growing. He's hard and eager. He isn't yet. He soon is. Her hands underneath him, cupping, holding, stroking. Her hair on his bare stomach. Her tongue flicking, slurping, sliding. No trouble with me. He's ready. A bit more. That'll do. She tugs at the pants. He takes them off. She rolls over on the bed. He's busy pulling his pants off his ankles. She quickly spits the gathered saliva onto her fingers and applies it. She is posed, classical, her hands pushing on her thighs. She's wide open. She glistens, she beckons, she flows. Come on, come on.

Oh god he's the nouvelle cuisine type. He had minted eggplant puree for dinner topped with pickled prawns in a marmalade glaze. He knows these days it's ladies first. Gentlemen come later. It's his turn for her turn. All right then. Good, don't bite, gently please, no teeth, no, there, like that. She's tensely ready to jerk his head off by the ears. She's never been so relaxed, sinking, flowing. She can't stand it any more. It's time for the killing to start. They should never have been told about the clitoris. Her most hated question, did you come? Oh god he's a talker. Tell me you want it. What do you want? Where will I put it? What am I doing? Tell me. Say it. Do you like it? Where is it? What is, what's in your cunt? Baby. Baby.

It wasn't like that. He had a plain steak for dinner. He grabbed her arse, got on top, said nothing, grunted once, it was over.

It wasn't like that. He's a stayer, an athlete. He turns her over, he's read magazines, he wants her on top, he turns her over and over again. He knows tricks, he can make her move, he can make her moan. Don't stop, she moans to him, don't stop. He has stopped. He's finished, she said the wrong thing. She listens. He moans, she sighs. He yells, she cries out. He doesn't make a sound, she's dead, coming slowly alive. She places her hands to check his heart. He's already quietly finished. He's just starting, building up speed, ready to pound furiously, announce his arrival, a fanfare. He takes her with him. He fills her. She's throbbing, streaming, clutching.

Are you wet? Are you hard? Can you feel it? Do you like it? What am I doing? Do you believe me? Do you want more?

Suppose there's more. He's well read, he knows things. He goes for the works. The endless falling into darkness, falling into his iron manly flesh, the hot kisses gulped like wine adding heat to her body drinking deeply, the sucking mouth melting into mouth seeking the leaping tongues, the eyes alight, the febrile waves trembling there, the pools of madness, the exquisite torment, her hair damp as seaweed, her taste like a seashell like a camellia like a rose, the velvet the silky salty flesh. Tigerlike he's tearing open the fur, the frenzy, the steaming tides, the hot springs, the wound of ecstasy which rents her body like lightning, the beatitudes, the tightness like a sheath closed over him softly caressing, gripping, the sweet insistent stabbing, her back arching to meet his thrusting, the flicking darts of fire, the molten langour spreading through her body.

It wasn't like that. He rolls over silently and turns his back to her. He rolls over and lights a cigarette. He holds her as if it should never end. He asks about her boyfriend, children, interests. He pays for another hour. He says she can go. He wonders why he does this. He feels gratified. He doesn't think. She has a shower, careful not to get her hair wet, drying herself hurriedly (or slowly) she looks at his after-shave, his pills, his toothbrush. It's a night to remember. They never think of each other again.

There's something about it that's rather like the real thing.

Ania Walwicz

HOSPITAL

I go to hospital. I go to the hospital again. I went there very early
in the morning. I go there today again. In the hospital there are
very clean and shiny. Linoleum floors. And everybody saying
kind things to me. And I get lost and they find me. And everything makes sense. And what is the name and address. And
please. And talking slowly. And I really exist. Here. And everything you do has a point to it. They tell me to follow the line.
A red one. I know what to do. And I had to have a tooth taken
out. And they did. I didn't sleep all night. The dentist asks me.
How old I am. I'm only twelve everywhere. In here. I'm always
twelve. Or even less. And they had these kind girls. Nurses. From
the country. With rosy red cheeks. And a nice smell. And they
tell me. Don't worry. Don't worry. Don't you worry baby. Gave
me a cup of coffee. Tell me. To wait. Try to make me comfortable. Are you easy now. Gave me my card. And is somebody looking after you. Nobody is. So I can always go to hospital. I go to
hospital. They have these big buildings. Meant to save my life.
They let me go on. This hospital. Had pink curtains. Around the
beds. And green ones. And yellow ones. Pastel and the colour.
Glows. So sharp. This hospital. Has blue cards to fill in. And red
ones. And white ones. But I don't like the white ones. At all. No
I don't. And I sat on the red rubber couch. On grey linoleum. And
the disinfectant smell that was like the school. First grade. And
the shiny walls they painted. So you can wash them. And I was
waiting. And there were these trolleys. And elegant thin alu-
minium. And instruments. And they sat me on a kidney bowl.

And I wasn't embarrassed. At all. And they told me to press my bare chest against the machine. And it was cold. And I didn't mind. And the nurse was very nice to me. And the lady doctor had a starched white coat. I'm always going to the hospital. And they put me on a special chair. And turned these lights on. And the dentist was very young. And it was his first time. And he pulled my tooth out. And I heard him drop it in a little dish. And he was so scared. That I was so scared. And a drop of sweat fell like a tear on my cheek. And they told me to lie down. And there were such nice clean sheets. And the air was warm. And I was slower here. And peaceful. And they put a needle in my arm. And I didn't have to pay anything for this. And there were these very kind ward attendants. That would do anything to make you smile. And they saw everybody the same. And they liked me. And when she came to the hospital. I could tell how she was. Just about to jump out of herself. Through the top of her head. And I go to hospital. And when everything was very bad. I'd take a taxi. I took taxi. When I can hardly walk. And I would call him on the phone. And he'd say do come down. And they would go where. And in my father's clinic there was this operating table for horses with big rings where to tie down. And I used to think that I was a gelding. And born horse. And my father did it to me. And I don't want to go to hospital. And I do go to hospital. And I was nearly crying and so weak. And I stood in Royal Parade with a wad of cotton in my mouth. They take care of me here. And the trolleys glisten. And the pincers took the cotton in my mouth so sure of every movement. And everything anybody did. Made such sense to me. And nothing to spare. Or laugh at. And everyone so serious. And kind. And I fell on the street. And my knee ran through my stocking. And they clean me here. And comfort me. Yesterday. The liqueur bottles shone at me all evil red. And I was feverish. And hot in the head. And today I'm well. And at ease with me. And these red skaters moved in my television set much too quickly. And now I'm just so peaceful. I get love here. I get loved.

Travelling About, Bumming Around, In Transit

Kate Grenville

HAVING A WONDERFUL TIME

There's something about travel that brings on generalizations about the meaning of life. Maybe that's why we do it. Every departure's like a brushing acquaintance with death: getting in practice.

Even at the bus station in Earl's Court my bed-sitter seems like an abstraction on another planet. Desk here chair there bed here. All the flimsy brown paper makeshifts fall away and leave us shivering. Standing by our bags waiting for the bus we eye each other. At the end of the next three days some of these strangers will have become people, and who knows what might happen? Anything can happen. Three days on a bus is not an attractive prospect, but think of it this way and it will be an adventure. Think of it like that.

Yes John it will be like that. An adventure. Being your second-best woman has not been an adventure. Being your Wednesday woman has only been fun on Wednesdays.

You know what your trouble is, you're too introspective you know that? Snap out of yourself a bit. Travel. Do you the world of good.

There are a lot of Australians going to Athens, like migratory birds. That girl over there with the flat face looks Australian. That low shining forehead, that sharp chin, that lipless slit of mouth. Her huge breasts are contained in a well-upholstered bra like a comfortable armchair. The point of each nipple is grubby where they've brushed against things.

Is it because I'm one of them that I have to sneer?

The colossus in the check shirt looks American. His enormous hiking boots have curved up at the toes and look like cobblestones on the ends of his legs. Great arms like hams, this man's a real meat-eater. Beside him, a dark, dapper little man sits neatly on a neat pack with not a loose strap anywhere, as tidy as a block of butter. He sits and methodically eats a sandwich and makes something in me shrivel.

Is that what you mean, getting out of myself? Seeing how the other half lives?

I've got to get a window seat. Three days and two nights of falling into the aisle will not be an adventure. Or if it is, in my generosity I'll let some other poor bugger have the pleasure. Get the elbows in there. Pretend you don't see them thinking she jumped the queue the bitch. A foot on the bottom step and the bag casually held at the side blocking any bright ideas from the crowd behind me. Okay now. In we go quick. Not too far back, it bounces. Not over the axle where the floor runs in a ridge. This one will do nicely thanks. Now sit back and look innocent.

The man who sits beside me is like a blond Greek god. I imagine his pectorals erect launching a javelin. An adventure! We exchange hellos. We establish that we are both going to Athens. We establish that he is Greek, but studies in England.

'I study to be a pilot.'

'That must be interesting.'

'It is all right.'

We're still in dreary Penge or somewhere but the driver is giving us a taste of Greece. The beginning of our journey coils around and swallows its tail, and suburban London stands amazed, blank windows exclaiming an empty O as the shimmering thump of bouzouki music fills the bus.

'What is your name,' I ask.

'Costas. Means King,' he explains with a modest smirk.

I think of my collection of conversation stoppers. I know someone once who lived in that street. I bought this suit five years ago for ten pounds.

'I have a friend who learnt to fly,' I say.

That's not much good. I knew a man once who lived in that street.

'He had to learn morse code, do you learn that too?'

Costas leans in impatiently.

'What?'

'Morse code.'

I enunciate so clearly that in a moment of sudden silence the whole bus hears.

'Moose . . .?'

'No, morse, you know, dot dot dash dash. With a little machine . . .'

I mime the flickering wrist of a morse operator. Costas watches stonily. Dot dot dot dash dash dash dot dot dot. Help I am sinking. Mayday. Costas calls out in Greek and the driver turns up the volume of the bouzouki.

Is it really such a good thing to have quite that number of St Marys and St Christophers and St Whoever-Else and rosary beads and bunches of good-luck garlic dancing against the front window of the bus? And that large efficient-looking clock trying to tell us it's one o'clock at half-past nine? Never mind, it's got to be right twice a day. And we can eat the garlic if we get marooned. We going anywhere near Transylvania?

Here I am. Travelling. Broadens the mind. Maybe I should be taking notes. Look at these houses. Like boxes. Not very original. The hedges. What would I say about the hedges? Very neighbourly the way that one is clipped like a poodle to exactly the point where it becomes the next-door hedge and then sprouts wildly. Not an inch more. A man is trimming with an electric hedge-clipper, standing back to admire before he hovers in to take off one last errant leaf. Well another day gone, anyway. Yairs, spent the weekend in the garden.

On the boat across the Channel there's a sudden sense of being in the team. 'You're on the bus too aren't you,' whispers the girl with the grubby nipples. 'Do you know what we're supposed to do?' A gangling man in front has reached the tea counter and clutches the top of his head with his arm as he says, 'Aaaaaah, cn Oi ev two cips a coffee? Na tye?'

When we get off the boat there's a long unexplained Greek wait. I decide with profundity that waiting bears the same relation to travelling as matter does to anti-matter and fight the suspicion that the bus has left without us. Another Australian girl with a face like Head Nurse, wearing a singlet and tight shorts, follows me around the wharf.

'Then I got the boat to Cairo, only twenty-seven pounds. Then, there was this train down to Khartoum and from there I got the plane to Algiers. Really dirty. The toilets, well you wouldn't credit it.'

On the wharf where we stand hopelessly waiting, a group of Americans is also waiting to be saved from the empty glare of this hazy non-place. They stand in a circle talking to each other with their bright backpacks ringing them around, like colourful humped birds. Everyone's on the move.

Keep looking, keep looking. What are you after anyway says John. You want to learn to relax.

France is a blue smog haze. Great tangles of pipes and tanks twisting solidly up into the sky, huge blank buildings the colour of nothing as we speed past. Tall dumb chimneys forever point the way: up there it's up there. Neat triangular heaps of slag rise out of the mist, monumental, lingering. As one is left behind, fading into distance, another takes its place. Or is it the same one fooling us?

Before John there was Jim. My wife doesn't understand me. Before Jim there was Jerry. Baby you're dynamite, see you round. Before Jerry there was Jack. You're a million dollars baby, don't call me at home.

'Then I got the plane to Madrid and from there I got the morning train to Lisbon. That would have been the twenty-eighth of July, no I beg your pardon the twenty-ninth. Then I got a bus to this little place called Ortago, quite nice but the toilets were that smelly. Then must have been the second of August I took the plane from Lisbon to Barcelona.'

Electricity pylons walk solidly off into the haze, striding with long praying-mantis legs, unswerving. Some march along with a bundle held aloft in each hand, others like amputees hold only one set of wires. The power must get through.

It's starting to get warm in here. Around me a great rustling of paper bags has begun and in a moment the air is full of orange peel and cheese sandwich. I root in my own bag and bring out an apple. On second thoughts I snap out of myself and get a bit involved and offer another one to Costas. He takes it with hardly a glance. Gotta learn to give a little, give and take, that's what it's all about.

In front of me two more Australian girls with tight shirts and closed smug faces are really getting organized. Long loaves of pre-buttered bread. Salami. Tomatoes and the right kind of knife, no squelchy mess here oh no, these girls didn't come down in the last shower. Even salt, in a shaker with a special lid so it doesn't spill. Paper napkins, I don't believe it. They sit munching while around me others spill biscuits out of burst paper bags, dribble oranges on their legs, and spray exploding drink cans into the back of my neck.

'Gee sorry.'

The two young men behind are looking apprehensive and also trying not to snicker.

'That's okay.'

They are polite and watch each others' mouths as they speak, watch mine as I speak, although they are not lip-reading deaf mutes. They are a pair of nice boys, off to Athos, they tell me, to check out the monasteries. No women are allowed anywhere on the peninsula of Athos, they inform me, not even female animals. They cannot stop themselves snickering at this. Boats containing women are forbidden to come closer than half a mile to the shore. It's almost enough to give you the feeling women might have something after all. Wonder if they strip you off at the entrance to make sure. And what is it they really get up to in there? Little leather lap-laps like the Masons maybe, standing displaying their paraphernalia at cock-crow.

Afternoon wears on. Are we still in France? Belgium? Luxembourg?

The drama of a frontier: this is Germany. Everyone's important with their passports. Head Nurse with her trembling thighs in shorts shows me her visas. Look I've been here and here and here and the toilets were that smelly. Travel broadens the bum.

Night falls and the Australians in front produce air-cushions and blow them up. No doubt about these Aussies they've got themselves organized. How come I didn't turn out like that? A blanket over the knees, snug as a bug in a rug.

Hey what kind of bitch are you? Where's your sense of adventure? Your joy in the rich pageant of multi-faceted humanity? The glowing tapestry woven with a thousand gleaming strands which is Life? Where were you when the smiles were handed out? Huh?

Costas twitches and slumps beside me, trying to sleep. Bugger him if I'm going to offer my seat.

At some dead time of the night we stop for petrol and pisses. Grubby tits is clutching herself between the legs; ooooh a I've gotta go. We line up in the toilet staring at our reflections in a leprous mirror, listening to each other. Unbuckle unbutton unzip. Aaaaah.

Everybody has tried the coffee machine beside the bus. English money doesn't work and nor does French. No one has any German money. When everyone has tried and gone away, the bug twins come over and produce a little bag marked *Foreign Money*. They stand sipping coffee while around them we all blink blearily. Sorry, that was all we had, they say. But here have a sip.

In the morning when we wake we're twisting laboriously through mountains. The Andes? The Alps? The Himalayas? It's raining. Drops streak sadly down my window and on the windscreen huge wipers bend gracefully into each other like dancers. De de de de DAH, de DAH, de DAH.

Around a bend in the road a deep valley spears off into mist, a twisting V weaving between interlocked spurs. Above us the ridges claw the dull sky with serrated edges like a child's scribble. The bus is very silent.

As the valleys flatten out and the rain stops, the bus comes to life. The bug twins squash the air out of their cushions with a rude noise. They tuck the blanket beneath housewive's double chins and fold it carefully. Then they produce little bottles and clean – cleanse – their faces, and settle back without any expectation of surprise for another day. Oh yairs, we did Europe.

The last night with John, before goodbye forever, he said as we got into bed, 'I've decided I like the outside of the bed best.' Then he told me the one about the condemned man being led to the gallows. Someone offers him brandy. Oh yes he says eagerly. Never tried it before, maybe I'll like it.

Horses and mountains and chickens and cows pass. I discover that by rubbing a finger on my teeth I can make an internal squeaking noise. Locked in solitary confinement, a person could become a virtuoso on teeth.

Boredom's like that. Someone should start a brain bank for when you get tired of your own. Better than shuffling through the tired old pack of Europe.

When we stop again we hover near the bus like nervous children afraid of being left behind. We've lost track now, no one knows for sure what country we're in.

'So anyway then I got the plane to Rome and I went to Florence on the train. Nearly missed it, they've got another name for it. Really dirty train with all these peasants stinking of that garlic. Rude and ignorant. Not a word of English between the lot of them. Don't talk to me about Italy.'

Head Nurse has a voice of such authority it threatens to burst her singlet, but boy she's been everywhere. You name it, she's been there. And the toilets were smelly and the peasants were rude and ignorant. She says to Grubby Tits, who's staring open-mouthed and impressed, 'Why'ncha sit next to me, we'll have a real good chin-wag.'

Her chin is muscular, the fittest chin in the world, the Mr Universe of chins, from so much wagging. A leathery peasant shuffles past staring at her. His toothless face is like a squashed shoe.

'Wotcha staring at, dumb-bell,' she says loudly.

These mountains are rather nice. Silhouetted pine trees walking up their spines, like black paper cut with pinking shears and pasted on a white sky. Orange autumn trees among the dark pines give a stippled effect like trout. The hills hold blue shadows in their laps, their peaks crisp in the sun. Pines as straight as pencils spear up the slopes. We speed through a village while a cracked bell tolls clang clang clang. There's a church of soft ochrous plaster painted all over with small pink crosses. The ambitious sign on the Hotel Moderna is almost too faded to read.

We stop and the man with the neat pack gets out, waves tidily and walks off. There's a man who knows where he's going. Quick as a flash Costas takes the window seat he's left empty.

The border into Yugoslavia seems all guns and stubbly big-jowelled faces and those peaked caps that South American dictators wear. The border guards swagger through the bus, rudely going through everyone's plastic bags full of orange peel and embarrassing crusts. Costas gives them a couple of packets of cigarettes and they leave him alone. No flies on this boy. They thumb laboriously through our passports while we sit waiting and sweating. I promise I'm not a terrorist. Honest, I've never seen a drug in my life.

We trundle off into dusk. Slavic faces stare sternly at us from doorways where kerosene lamps hang, and in the fields wooden carts creak along behind horses. A late worker in a field trudges behind the horse, ploughing, bored, dreaming of soup.

In the early morning we pass Mount Olympus and I remember that this is my adventure. We're nearly there. The mountains sprawl over the plain like vast sleeping hounds lying with their paws towards a fire. The gods are up there on that lumpy mountain, and somewhere not far away is the navel of the world. How feeble and faulty those gods are: Zeus with giant godly prick raised at some poor wee thing in the woods. Maybe I should turn into a tree, this is my chance.

Athens. Hieroglyphics instead of street signs. Not a word of English between the lot of them. My feet are huge as I hobble off the bus. Grubby Tits is moaning, 'Ooooooh, me feet are that swelled up.'

Head Nurse strides away, map in hand, to the youth hostel. 'Then I got the bus down to Greece, nice bunch of people, gave them a few tips about where to go and that.'

I'm alone. I think I'll like Athens. The pavements are made of marble but everything smells of shit.

Now drop a card to John. Make it nice.

Dear John, had a great trip down on the bus. A nice bunch of people. Got chatting to a few Australians and a handsome Greek too. Saw lots of Europe. You were right, I needed an adventure. See you round, Louise.

S.F. Melrose

MOVEMENTS BEFORE FALLING

The hospital ward is typical: Turkish. (What does that mean? It announces itself clearly but I find it hard to isolate the significant parts of the message. European reflections over deep chaos?)

A cold bare bulb over the bed. We have been here for hours. Sami bey's expression of resigned humour is unchanged. (I have never seen it otherwise: is my reading of the signs defective? No ... the message is clear, only falsified by its constancy.) Anje's hand is damp. I give it a squeeze and try once again to remove my gaze from the red bubbling smiles: tiny reddish globules, thousands, in neat rows. Instead of teeth. Such a smooth, honey-brown rotund – is that the word? A word for fat that lacks the insult? – peach, until she was split open to expose millions of fig seeds, pink-red and glistening. Barbed wire bites deep. They – who was it? One of the affable stained-white-coated medicos seemed just to amble over and penetrate the peach skin with a hypodermic; butterfly pinned to the board. Fat glossy butterfly ... they've given her a tetanus shot. (Should I ask about VD? How broad is Sami's English? What register to use? And then the insult implicit – to Turkish manhood. 'Every Turkish male is a potential rapist,' my mother had quoted in her letter, to pass on the message while refusing the responsibility of insulting the country I love. What about drunken Australians in Balmain, Ma? What about 'every man' in the manic Glebe graffiti? What about every woman tantalizing with the external signs of that deeply etched slit, Ma? Now that the veil has been stripped away. No, I won't ask Sami bey. It hardly goes with the story of the fall . . .)

A medico ambles over with a tray of needles and threads. The needle sinks into skinny lips – aren't they going to anaesthetize it? – and I grin fixedly into Anje's face and squeeze her hand and make a bad joke about her ex-president, expletives retained, and she rewards me with a grin. Her face is very calm. It's less the reflection of the three mogadons I made her swallow in Sami bey's bathroom where she squatted in the tin bath while I swabbed and lathered and scrubbed and douched; the college gateman brought her in and we knew already that something was wrong even before the kid was sent to hammer on our door. You can smell the buzz in the air when something's up, and we were already feeling and accepting *our* guilt reflected in every Turkish face – our guilt! And what about *his*? Uncommented, even amongst ourselves . . . It's less the reflection of the sleepies than her apple-smooth self smiling. But her hand holds on hard. If we let go we'd both be alone. Last time I was here, the only time I was here before, I was alone – not *alone*: the wards overflowed and the good doctor my language student was 'showing me around' and into his resident's room. 'Are you married to your hospital, Doctor Halit?', and his startled defensive eyes reflected married until his brain caught up with hospital and he made the correct substitution, and he fed me raw peanuts and worked his way into me.

'Although she submitted we do not consider that she consented.' There's the stint in the local gendarmerie at two in the morning where we sit on our hands and stiltedly translate for Anje the message of our own foolishness and consequent guilt and the need not to bother the embassy, and we swallow it all with endless glasses of *çay* and Anje's face glows with a certain stunned glee as she looks at her black stitches – stuffing back in. The gendarme doing sentry on the door doesn't move and his eyes don't even flicker. Nothing's real, and especially not the pantie hunt in the ditch below the barbed-wire fence, in the dark, on the way home.

I must find some excuse to stop Şöhret's private lessons: it's not English she wants but friendship and counsel, and I can't charge for one and can't supply the other. No longer. It's dangerous. After each session when she's gone, recomposed, I sit and turn inside out the phrases I've used, which she only understands through the accompanying facial expression and tone, which she won't recall, never use. *I can't help her.* It's not like Lee in Sydney where the rebellion could be fed and channelled and could flow into an expression already established and accepted. There's *nowhere to go* here: no mature-age studentships, no dole, no alimony for deserting wives, no social status for a newly freed psychologically bashed wife. Second wife. No refuge.

We sit on the beach out past Güzelyali. Until he comes she won't go near the water. No women come here unattended – unless they are *kötu kadin* – and the status conferred by the accompanying foreigner is less substantial when it comes to the test. I have not met him before. The Mercedes we arrived in is flanked by his own. His thick hands flash with his trademark and he takes a handful of Şöhret's belly through the thick black stuff of her swimsuit and he gestures with it towards me: 'I no like. Very fat.' Şöhret has told me that his first wife is sixty-five and that he spends every second night with her. Her eyes are downcast as he releases the snatch of belly and my gut is gripped around a grey impotent rage. I say nothing and look away over the water. He leads us to another, empty beach and we have lunch in a little restaurant which was closed until he ambled in and took over and the table nearest the water was swept clean and the cook woken from his post-prandial slumber to spear chunks of *trança* on sharp prongs. I cannot eat but must. I have learnt that at least. There is *beyaz peynir* for me, and yogurt – they won't touch it with fish and marvel politely at my tastes, united against me. I feel myself withdrawing. In mid-session when she asks me again 'Susan what must I do what must I to do?' my response is examined, appraised, stifled, silenced. I disengage her soft white hand from my wrist and the sixteen solid-gold bangles – one for each birthday of her marriage since she gazed into his window, sixteen and lush and nubile – slide together into her lap. I dream of detachment.

I am growing thinner. I am pleased. But the secretary at the Institute suddenly asks if I will continue teaching. The question takes me by surprise. I nod, wondering if her English is correct. Perhaps I am ill? There are no mirrors in our flat but I stare at myself in the teachers' cloakroom. I can't see past the surface of my eyes, which are wide and staring in the harsh light. Perhaps it is the sleeplessness as I lie and re-examine the phrases of the day, troubled that it is my self that I am teaching with. Sometimes at 3 am I think about Enderby making up a famous author and laying the facts on his Lit. class and getting it back again in the rehash. Poor stupid fools – just words on a page. If you look far enough in and pull and poke and turn everything inside out you end up not needing to sleep and afraid to sleep because of that great empty space inside, where words echo and echo and the softest whisper comes back as a shout and a scream, billowing and flooding. At 3 am the baker across the road is at work and the dull slap of the raw loaves sliding down the shute and the thud of the long-handled board sliding them into the open oven imposes itself over the silence of my stifled breath and I stop spinning and come to crouch on the floor by the window so that I can see the smooth white loaves through the slit in the curtain and the glow of the mouth of the oven. My breath comes and goes in the rhythm of the bakery. When they finish their first shift after the *muezzin*'s five o'clock call to the faithful, and the window opens for early business, I fall back into the depths of a sleep which lasts till noon. I get up and wash quickly to go to my first class.

Celalettin grins, the perfect replica of the toy-town admiral in his sergeant's uniform. He tells us that he wanted to be an *imam*, in his village near Bandirma, until the travelling nurse told him that it was one of the *imam*'s duties to lay out the bodies of the dead. He is neat and immaculate and it has little to do with his uniform, although at first I assume that it results from that. But his child is the same, slicked and shiny. Celal always grins, even when he is telling us something serious. He has learnt not to take himself seriously, working at Land South with wise-cracking US Nato forces. He tells the best Hodja stories; he's told them before. It has become a ritual; the point is the telling, and the sharing. This is a special class. We all have our roles. If I try a limited Enderby I give it away by signs that they have learnt to read faster than they read the American-English – 'it's gotten so I can hardly' – of the prescribed texts. After class Celal walks me to the bus stop. The 10.15 bus is still all right for lone females: it is full of girls going home from university or the Institute. Celal encircles my wrist with his forefinger and thumb: 'You know what I want.' And he's still grinning so I grin back. It's part of the game, or we let it be part. I'm safe within the rules. He invites us to tea with his family each week, and when we accept I meet his wife, who is nameless and without any English. We talk with my limited Turkish but she is mainly silent because Celal chatters away in his US slang (unconsciously?) excluding her. She doesn't seem to suffer from the confusing babble of voices. The child sits with her, grinning with delight at his father. She doesn't grin, but she looks very calm and contained. I find little to say – Celal talks for us all – and I watch her silence, startled when Celal stops and asks me, 'Why do you not talk? You say so much in class and here you say nothing.' I don't need to answer; Celal is off on a complicated commentary on the regional differences in the Turkish language.

Then summer comes and the classes end, and I don't need to talk any more. There are long walks through the labyrinthian passages of Kemeralti where I am the eternal tourist – in their eyes – despite the well-thumbed *Ikamet* stamped and approved and kept inside my passport in my pocket. Although the shopkeepers must see me every day that I follow the same trail through the maze, their eyes never acknowledge me as *déjà vue*. I am alien territory. I am alone, walled in by my foreign tongue. When we make our summer trip to Istanbul to take the boat along the Kara Deniz to Rize and Trabzon the cocoon of permanent residency is dissolved, and I return to the ranks of the tourist, only to surprise – it comes and goes in a flash – now and again with the slight Turkish I possess. And only in the market. Nobody tries to talk since it is written beforehand that I am alien. *Déjà damnée* . . . I am turning into a shadow.

On the way to the boat, loaded down with food for the trip, I stop stunned in the middle of the Galata Bridge. The city is just stirring and the bridge rocks gently as its roots are shaken by the awakened *muezzins* who set up their wail from minaret to minaret, ringing the skyline, piercing the sky, invading the senses with wash after wash of plaintively rhythmic ululation, on and on until it forces the faithful out and down on their knees. The rocking of the bridge forces my legs apart as I try to hold my balance.

The sky is stiff and grey, masking a strident ochre sun. There is no wind all day. And then it starts, blowing across from the mountains and shifting the thick air which lifts the dust to lash against exposed skin and to penetrate eyes and mouths. I go out only to buy yogurt and melons in the market which spills through the alleys of the village. The *karpuz* are small and round like cannonballs, with thin blackish-green skins heavy and warm. It is past the clean heat of full summer and the season of decay begins. The lanes are full of rotting corpses of melons too ripe to be sold. The smell is thick and slow, rising from the warm surface of the earth. Rats scuttle from pile to pile. Each morning uniformed council employees with apparatus like aqualungs strapped to their backs go from heap to heap spraying them with a substance more offensive than their own odour. Still there is nothing I can eat other than *karpuz* and yogurt. The smell of the turgid *yağ* in which red beans and eggplant and meats are drenched turns my stomach.

The yogurt at least is cool and pure, if I eat it at once in the shadowy corner of the shopfront where it is made. I can no longer sleep. It is too hot, too heavy, too thick. I go out for yogurt after the first *ezan*: the yogurt-maker is devout. He opens his shopfront after going to pray at 5 am. Melons are not sold, legally, until 8 am when the the market police restore to the sellers their scales and weights. But there are one or two who do business at all hours, sleeping on a mat surrounded by melons, their homes miles away in the hills. They won't go back to their families until the season is over. They weigh the black balls in one hand and we go through the quiet ritual. They know I will buy, and hardly care. Most have given up the practice which marks legal selling: when the buyer has picked over the enigmatic globes and found one which is firm and densely heavy in the hand and approached the seller with the scales dangling from one hand, he must watch and move quickly and with care if he wishes to carry home his choice intact. The seller moves imperceptibly and fast to penetrate the skin with the tip of his knife. He carves a neat triangle with three deeply etched slits; the *karpuz* opens up and spills its red juice onto the dust. And we must gather around to acknowledge the perfection of the red glistening flesh, the shiny black seeds, before the wedge is re-inserted. You carry home your prize, taking care not to let its fluids run down your arm. It is warm in its centre from the endless heat of the earth.

It is earthquake season. Three times already the heavy grey air has turned livid and a low roar accompanies the aching stirring of the earth. Instinctively I become motionless, my feet clinging to the ground, riding it out and expecting the walls to part or the windows to crack open. The latest comes just before dawn: it is the fasting month. The baker continues his own ritual. Women and children are sometimes exempt from the fast, and everyone eats after nightfall. The baker makes special unleavened *pide* which is sprinkled with sesame seed and propped in the window of the shop for the hordes who come all night now. I have no need to sleep. There are no classes to go to. My sole expenditure of energy is minimal: three times I go out for food, the rest of the cycle consists of the watch, crouching near the window. Just before dawn, before the morning *ezan*, the drummer passes through the streets, signalling the last moments of the permitted eating hours. Time is inside-out: there is endless activity as the eaters' daily abstinence turns into nocturnal gluttony. Their hours meeting mine. When the tremor comes everything is transfixed but moving, spinning motionless like the dervishes when the music, mounting to the plateau, flattens into the rhythmic cycle of the trance. The earth stirs and kicks, and then stirs again. It is troubled and lethargic and stirring to break free from its enclosing skin. I cannot breathe. The light turns cruel with menace and the electric bulb in the bakery goes out, followed by the rasping gag of the water pipes. Is this the end? I cannot close my eyes, cannot see, am not seeing. It cannot be that the image transfixed before my eyes is real, breathing – it is mirage-like, transparent, the after-image of life. I am not aware of the tremor ceasing, of life starting up again. Until I am pierced by the sun, by the sharp bray of the milk-donkey in the lane in front of the bakery, by the daily, day-time life in the cliché of my gaze. Where have I been? There is no water to wash my face, which is stiff with salt. I spit on the cloth and wipe my eyes, and go out to lap at a bowl of yogurt.

I can sleep again. But I must not sleep. In the dark space behind my eyelids I am visited by spectres. In each dimly lit space there is slow agonized movement and faces that move toward me, mouths working and black. And I push out my arms to shield my face and my body from the plucking of their fingers. And when I push them away they are as thick as the blanket of air, and my hands pass through their entrails and they are upon me, butting at my body, penetrating me, clothing me, suffocating me, entreating me. What must I do what must I do. But when fighting an enormous invading weight, I push open my eyes in the dark, they are still around me, hiding in the shadows, waiting. In Rennes last year a letter came from my mother to announce that my little dog had died after a series of fits that shook his old body and left him stunned and pale-eyed. I did not cry. It was only words on a page. And now in the night he is there and I am holding his soft age-thinned brittle body as it shakes and kicks with the death tremor; and his eyes hold mine and ask some question that I cannot decipher and will not answer. And the bed rocks to the tremor.

I must not sleep. I must sit and watch. I drag myself through the heat to the yogurt shop and bring back the bowl of soft white slime, and lay it down beside me and crouching there with arms wrapped tight around my body I bend my face to the bowl and lap at the warm, thick milky white. My gaze turns inward, and I must sleep because, waking, I feel the tremor of the small brown body that lies soft and heavy in my arms, cradled there against the world and against the penetration of death. I bend my head down to the velvety brown brow and softly engage the flicker of the black still eyes. If I can make a perfect circle around his body, of our two bodies, then we can be safe from the tremor that shakes the earth. I roll over gently onto the floor, enclosing the small soft brown body in the circle of my knees and arms. We are safe. He will not be taken.

John Bryson

DREAMING OF GLORY

The restaurant was once a golf-house. Trophy cases in the hallway still displayed the chromium shapes of putting irons and golf
balls and a wood that was once the instrument of a hole-in-one
by a member of the Imperial Family. The names of winners of
Japanese tournaments were celebrated on rosewood panels high
on the wall. The titles were all in English. Old photographs of
uncomfortable golfers in plus-fours and cloth caps were mounted
on both sides of the doorway. Humphrey had not seen them when
he came in. He was surprised to find a date as early as 1919.

He found Butcher and the four Japanese delegates already on
the terrace. They were not waiting for him. Butcher struggled
into the flaccid burden of his overcoat and his gasps fumed into
the cold afternoon as if he were puffing at a cigar. He turned his
back for Humphrey to lift the coat by its collar and held out his
arms in the half-mast gesture of a heavy knight readied for the
fray. Higher, he grunted, higher.

Their limousines had waited through lunch under trees at the
edge of a driveway that touched the building only for a moment
before curling back to the road. The guard box had a despondent
air as if it were empty. The chauffeurs opened the car doors wide.
Butcher wrapped the flaps of his overcoat about his thighs and
took the last space in the rear of the first car. He took time to
settle himself. Humphrey stooped to climb into the front. No,
Butcher called to him, you ride with the others. He waved to the
driver to close the doors and Humphrey turned away.

Humphrey rode in the front of the second car. Though conversation at lunch had been brisk, and often jolly, the two Japanese sitting behind him fell silent and only occasionally pointed out places that might be of interest to a foreigner. The traffic into Tokyo was heavy and slow in the wet. They crossed the river Sumida by a stone bridge Humphrey was told was famous for its age, and swung into the river-side boulevard. The kerb was lined with riot police.

For nearly two kilometres they picketed the sidewalk at intervals Humphrey judged to be ten paces. Every plane and articulation of their bodies was cased in black cladding and the carapaces gleamed with the intensity of wet paint although the light was dull. Their scaled fists held staves upright in unwavering enfilades for as far as Humphrey could see. There must be hundreds. Narrow shields hung from their forearms with no emblazonment of heraldry so that they seemed to be responsible to no identifiable authority. Each visor reflected an unyielding and malevolent glaze behind which Humphrey could find no flicker of life and sloped at an angle that recalled nothing so much as an iron mandible.

The cars turned off the boulevard at a roadblock that had not been there before lunch and Humphrey felt a relief he thought was very foolish. He turned to Hogara. Why, he asked, were there so many police?

Hogara shrugged. Today, I don't know, he said. Maybe the safe movement of some important people, he smiled, big shots.

The air of the conference room was still stale from the morning session. Its warmth was welcome. Humphrey sat on the same side of the long table as Butcher but left an empty chair between them. He expected to take no part in this final and summary session. He had taken no part in the earlier three. On the morning of the first meeting Butcher had tapped with his thick finger the brief and its twenty-eight appendices; he asked Humphrey if he was familiar with the figures. I am the author, Humphrey told him with a smile, of their every digit; if you have any trouble, just ask. I see, Butcher had said, your reward for diligence, I wondered why you were here. I will do the talking, he said, I'm going to pitch it to them.

Butcher began. His voice had the stock-in-trade confidence of a door-to-door salesman. He had, Humphrey knew something of it, joined Mincorp as a publicist for petroleum extracts after a year with Lancia in Turin, he had spent two years as advertising manager for one of the toolmakers of the Ruhr and had directed promotion for a breakfast cereal, a brand of low-tar cigarettes and an expanding line of executive games from California. He had less German and Italian than he claimed. I am a marketing man, he said, as if there were no higher credential.

Humphrey thought of Butcher as having the mannered bon-homie of an anglican prelate. It seemed unmanly and unvirtuous to disagree with anything he said. His weight must have been over a hundred kilos but at parties he danced intricately and with a sureness in his own centre of gravity that unnerved his part-ners and they clung petulantly to him. His headstrong driving had killed his first wife and Humphrey had met only his second, a singer he had married in Munich. He spoke as though misfor-tune had deprived her of leading roles in Marschner and Wagner, but sometimes late at those parties her voice made the vulnerable and searching notes of the blues and her thighs worked the slits of her skirt. She was not often with him. If asked about it, Butcher told of their asthmatic daughter whose sickness stifled her frantic breath at unpredictable, he said, and inconvenient hours.

None of the four Japanese took notes while Butcher spoke. Their blue folders lay on the table. All were executives of the same company, a corporation of immense size and diversifi-cation, through the baking of plastics, the harvesting of food-stuffs and the invention of pesticides. And all were from the plas-tics division; the plastic arm of your corporate body, Humphrey had said as they first met, but everyone seemed to be smiling already, and one after the other exchanged business cards with him, accepting Humphrey's always with the left hand then hold-ing the card toward him at arm's length in the expectation of a motionless instant, beginning with the minute narrowing of an eye's aperture and ending in the sudden flash of a smile, so that card and face were together printed in a single frame of perma-nent cognition. They bowed him on with a grateful excitement which Humphrey found impossible not to parody a little in return.

Strangely, Butcher had become uncomfortable and sat behind his placecard at the table before he realized the introductions were incomplete. Perhaps he was nervous. I want you to show complete attention, he had whispered to Humphrey. Do you realize how important this deal is to us? Yes, Humphrey said, I do indeed.

Humphrey opened his folder, slowly so as not to distract them, and turned the pages of 'What's On In Tokyo'. He passed quickly over advertisements for orchestral concerts, Japanese traditional theatre and movies. Massage parlours, skin flicks, escort agencies and night clubs took up the last four pages. He marked 'Charon, intimate, drinks from 600 yen small beer, English speaking hostesses, piano music with song'. And on the last line: 'stress'. Oh, songstress.

He drew out another pamphlet. It had the rectangular shape of a travel guide but its pages were firm and glossy with a bulky presence. It was a public relations brochure he had plucked from a display box in the foyer for the Japanese corporation.

Although the text stood in inaccessible lines of characters with the teetering columnar quality of alphabet blocks, the pictures were captioned also in English. A frontispiece laid together a montage of ships at dock against paddy fields and office blocks and textile looms, all to promote the variety of the corporation's enterprise. Although Humphrey had researched these painstakingly for his masters, he had found and dealt out merely figures, quantifications and categories. Here the incidence of effort were displayed as if through an opening of windows in the page: these looms hummed with countless threads unravelling the warp and weft of the spectrum; mimicking rows of rice plants wore a fresh and humid green from the flush of morning rains; painters in bosuns' chairs swung against the iron side of a ship and painted over spreading ink stains that had wept from her blundering deck on bitter southern nights as deck-bins overflowed the slime of squid dying in their thousands under a cold halogen glare visible for as many miles as the far corona of a small city.

A chart gave the corporation's income over a decade. Its yearly turnover ranked twelfth of the companies of the world and was exceeded by the revenue of only fourteen national governments. A photograph showed three chartkeepers marking a map of countries bordering the Pacific Ocean with points of their company's conquest. Their mouths were bunched from sucking rows of sharp pins like ageing seamstresses. Humphrey looked up. That chart hung on the wall opposite him. The seaboards glittered with coloured pin-heads but its surface was surprisingly faded and the clusters did not match those in the photograph.

On another page the executives of Plastics Division sat, as they did at this meeting, behind nameplates in the manner of a press conference. Okura, Inter-Group Liaison, speaks English with a Cambridge accent; the tiny Production Co-ordinator Hogara acts also as an interpreter for Kogo of Finance, who will try no English at all and scratches marks into his agenda margin but does not take them with him overnight; Shimizu, Marketing, brown from much golf at his club where green fees of each game cost more, he will tell you, than a labourer's monthly wage, and chatters only about sport over lunch in his high tone of an excited spectator; and other faces from other divisions and other places, all photographed in the foreground of factories so their capacity for industry is incontrovertible, or before attentive groups of scribbling trainees, or behind busy desks and holding a calculator or a pen warily still only for the interruption of the snapshot. None of them had the appearance of being, even momentarily, at rest.

Butcher paused at Hogara's politely diffident port de bras and coffee was served at a buffet table at the end of the room. The lacquered cups were of paper lightness and painted with a small and modular emblem reminding Humphrey of a pagoda: the mark of the company president, Hogara told him as he faced Humphrey toward a portrait on the wall, holding him by the elbow with a flattering courtesy as if introducing him to an ancestor. The portrait was of an old man, perhaps in his seventies, and of a sepia quality that may have been either of emulsion or of pigment. The figure sat in an elaborately carved and high-backed chair. Yes, Humphrey said, I noticed it earlier.

Butcher began to close his summary, the run home, he put it. He used the shiny phrases of car yards and appliance show-rooms directed across the polished table to Shimizu. Shimizu is the opinion-maker of this group, Butcher had said after the first session, every grouping has one. Shimizu is the power-broker.

Their case finished. Butcher asked for questions, for clarification, he put it, of our proposition. But it was the tiny Hogara who asked them while the others were silent, and who recorded

with the quick strokes of a court reporter and with an interest
only in the fulsomeness of the answers, as if their worth was a
matter for some absent tribunal.

Humphrey found Hogara's president on the last page of the
brochure. There were two pictures of him. In the first, he sat in
a miniature of the sepia portrait on the wall. Underneath him
were nine pillars of Japanese text and a photograph with the
harsh shadows of a newspaper reproduction: a prayer offering,
Humphrey thought at first, on the deck of a ship; a red-necked
and awkward solemnity at a blessing of the fleet. But the faces
have none of the compressed anticipation of waiting fishermen.
Their posture is strict and their eyes are not on the sea but on
the sky. They are airmen.

The president, Shikoru, is small for the chair carved with four
hundred and seventy years of tumbling chrysanthemum petals
but sits precisely in the centre of them with a frail dignity, on
the light bones of the carefully aged, his spectacled eyes the
fading grey of incense drifting in the wake of solemn pro-
cessions, his white shirt-collar stiffly hiding folds in his throat
with the mute decorum of a Shinto cassock. He sits easily still.
The grey pin-striped suit is exactly pressed. Slim hands lie gently
folded in his lap. His fingers wear no ring.

Every morning he rises a half hour before dawn and, wrapped
in the plain kimono of the bereaved, walks from his bare
sleeping-room across a marbled courtyard. His wooden sandals
make always four slow beats over the narrow timbers of the
bridge, above the ancient carp whose silken tails lazed, as his son
had said in childhood, to hold their sleeping in mid-stream;
through a low doorway and into the consecrated cell to wait
before its stone shrine, his wisping head bowed during the perceptible bleaching of walls, until first light darkens the frame of
a photograph fastened above the altar and he can again begin
to make out the raised eyes of the boy-pilot and his ghosted reflection in the curved cowling of a fighter plane already trembling
with the deafening heat of the last long thunder. Twenty-eight
tilted wings in a herringbone pattern across the flight deck in
hard crosses behind one and a half rows of tomorrow's faces,
fourteen, again he counts them, rigidly to attention; and standing
alone facing the boy is the braided figure of a Flag Officer of

the Imperial Forces, his rimless spectacles misting in the salt air, the silver imprimatur of the Emperor's own command heavy on his shoulders. His steady fingers hold a white scarf to the boy's neck, the banner of sacrifice fluttering in the photograph's instant. The Commander's thin throat is already too old for his prime, his hair is wisping and his eyes fade in the grey wake of five years' war.

When he can no longer see the detail of that day beyond his misting spectacles he leans forward and again kisses the chill over his son's glazed face and again draws back only far enough to whisper to him the soft syllables: Heiwa.

Peace.

Re-crossing the narrow bridge he feeds the carp.

Some illusions can assume the status of truth. Humphrey knew it no longer mattered that the details of his day-dreaming were invented and hallucinatory. He knew, in a way now indelible and complete, that this Japanese corporation is guided not with the careful powers of delegation drawn from the teachings of London or Harvard, but in the manner of a kingdom, of old and familic loyalties and enmities, for which the tabular logic of immediate opportunity and risk are of incidental interest. Decisions will be taken only by this ageing ruler or those related to him through a linealogy of belief in the nobility of ultimate conquest and the knowledge that time is not measured merely in terms of the accountant's year, or the historian's war.

Humphrey was suddenly aware he was the centre of an expectant silence. He closed the folder. I'm sorry, he said, I didn't catch that. He looked along the table. They looked at him with the counterfeit enthusiasm of their subordinate authorities. None of them ranked as – he thought of Hogara's use of the words – big shots. I said, Butcher repeated while the others waited, that about wraps it up. Yes, Humphrey said, I'm sure it does.

On the stairs Butcher slowed him by the sleeve so they lagged behind. We are going great, Butcher said, Shimizu asked us for drinks and dinner. I said you fly out early in the morning, I want him alone, okay? He did not wait for a reply. On the ground floor his stride was long and his arms swung. Humphrey trailed to the position of an adjutant. Sure, Humphrey said, pitch it to him.

Geoffrey Bewley

CHICKEN STREET

Ah, she's gone now, man. She left here a week ago, I think. She was staying a while in Sigi's, with the big chessboard pieces, you know? Then I went again and she wasn't there, so I don't know where she is now. I think maybe she went on to India, she said she was. Maybe she went back to Europe again. I don't know now.

Ja, right, it's a pity. But it's the way it goes, man you know. It was because we were so, so, I can't think of the word in English. Incompatible, is that it? Ja, not fitting. That was us all right.

We could say ja, ja to each other, that was a word we had, but otherwise we both talked English. What it was, she was Dutch, and she was so Dutch, you know? You know what's Dutch? You know what they're like? They are so clean, man, that it's unbelievable. And they are so arrogant, they really push you around, you know? You don't do like they want, man, you get pushed.

In the beginning, you know, it was all right. It was good. Ja, right, when you were here before. We really got it on together. Because she had plenty of money, plenty of Afs, plenty of guilders, plenty of marks, and she wanted to be into the dope, and I knew where, so that way it was good. And she was a good screw, man, you saw how she was. When we were stoned it was unbelievable, man, it was so good.

Then when we weren't stoned it wasn't so good. After a while she was arguing all the time. She was saying I coughed all the time. Okay, man, I cough, I do cough all the time. So what? It's the smoke, man, sometimes it's the bad shit you get, all the impurities. It's this bad air here, it's high up, it does different things to your lungs inside. But she was saying, you're sick, you get pneumonia, you must do this, do that, all the time, you understand?

Ja, I should have, man, I should have kept her stoned all the time. But we were both stoned and it still went like this. She was saying I didn't eat enough. That's the Dutch, man, they all eat like pigs, all the time. It's like their whole life for them to eat. So I said, ja, ja, and we were eating all the time. We were eating vegetarian, and the rice and soup and all the strudels, the cakes. You really eat good here for cheap, for nothing. But she was saying, not enough. I said, if I wanted to be a fat-arse like you, then I would eat more, too. And she was saying all the time it was her money for the food, and I said, I don't care if it's your money or whose it is, if you want eating then you eat for me too, okay? But it was never any good with her.

And also, she was talking about going to India still. I said I was going to Pondicherry, to the ashram, only I had no money, and she said, all right, we both go. And I thought, yeah, but all the way with this Dutch chick, it's a drag, you know? All the time being hassled, eat, drink, wear the warm clothes. I thought, I can do better without this. So I said, no, we go in a little while. Always a little while, you understand?

So anyway, in the end it was too much. She was always do this, do that, like a mother, you know? And I didn't want a mother. I just wanted a good screw with a good body, which she was. But then she changed about that; then she wasn't so good any more. She just lay there like a sack of flour or something. And this was because of me, because she wanted me to do these things she said, so it would be like a reward.

I said, maybe you want me to stop the hashish also? And she said, ja, maybe that's the best thing. But I told her, no, no way, if I stop then so do you. But I don't stop it. Why should I? This is the best place in the world for hashish. This is the big reason for being here. So there was no more about that, because she liked the hashish too much herself. And man, for a hundred Afs here you can get stoned for a week.

I said, you should think you're lucky it's only the hashish, it's not the needles, the bad stuff. But she said, the hashish is just as bad when it's too much. Because she wasn't really into the drugs, you know. She liked the hashish but it was only a trip for her, it wasn't the real thing where she was at. She was a little bit scared about it.

But she was still all the time hassling me, you know, like a housewife. All the Dutch chicks, they're all like that. I was like a kitchen or a piece of the furniture that she had to make clean all the time. And it was always India, go to see India, and, man, I didn't want to see India with her. I still don't care if I see there. I mean, India, so what? It's people dying all the time, man, and disease, and getting sick, the diarrhoea, the shits, you know? I think it's better up here.

So I was telling her this, but it was no good. Shit, she was stubborn. She was real Dutch. So then she was doing these little things all the time, she was with my clothes, these patches and buttons, this here, see? And at the beginning I thought, ja, why not, it's good for me and she likes to do it. But then I learned why she was doing it, and it was all this housewife thing again. All this eat and wash and clean, do this, wear this. And in the end it was too much.

In the end what happened was, she started to wash things. She was wanting to wash my clothes all the time. And I woke up one morning and my clothes were gone, and I could hear the washing outside in the room for the shower. She was washing the things so there was nothing for me to wear. But I was so angry that she was doing this without my permission, and I got out of bed naked and took the clothes off her, out of her hands. And she tried to keep them and I hit her, man, I was so angry, and took the wet clothes out of the bucket and started getting them on, and I said, you fat-arse Dutch, you wash your own clothes if you want to wash anything.

Then the other guys, the Afghans, they all came to see, you know, what's the big noise, what's the hassle? So I pushed her out and I locked the door to put the clothes on, and I could hear noise outside, all these people, she was arguing with these guys, and then when I came out she had her pack and all her bags and she was giving them money. And she said, I'm leaving you now, goodbye and thank-you.

I was amazed, man, and I said, it was when you took the clothes, I didn't know what I was doing, I was acting on my impulses, you know? But she was so hostile about it, man, she was totally unable to relate to me any more.

I said, I'm sorry I hit you, but why did you do that with my clothes? But she said, there are your things, there's the dope, there's some money for you, now goodbye. So then she went. And I saw her once at Sigi's but she went away as soon as she saw me, and that was the last time I saw her.

That's how women are, man. They start off and then they start to think that they own you. Then it's always you that's wrong, and then in the end they leave you. I don't know, man, you can't trust them.

Michele Nayman

THE HOUSE ON LAFAYETTE STREET

I had bought a cowboy hat – a real Stetson – in Cheyenne, Wyoming, and on the bus to Denver I was able to cover my face with it and sleep.

After arriving at the Greyhound Depot on Nineteenth Street, and after collecting my suitcase, I straightened my hat and grinned. Denver! Denver, Colorado. Tracing the footsteps of Jack Kerouac and Neal Cassidy, larrikin angels of the Fifties, automobile fanatics in an automobile city (parking lots where landmarks should be), symbols of irresponsibility and irrepressibility. Denver! I emerged from the depot, bus-trip tired, bus-trip happy.

The guidebook suggested the YMCA (women accepted in addition to men), so the YMCA it was. I found a taxi, the driver of which told me it would be quicker on foot. He gave me directions and I walked along the flat, wide streets, passing anonymous office blocks in various stages of construction, aware of a preponderance of cowboy hats and boots and belts. Later I discovered that I had stumbled into town just in time for the annual National Western Stock Show. I was delighted, and thought that perhaps I might be able to pass off my Australian accent as some regional variation from an obscure part of Texas. No one believed it for a minute.

The YMCA did not look promising. It was already dark, and several men of undefined age and various racial backgrounds were standing or sitting on the steps at the front. I walked up the steps, trying to achieve the optimum combination of aloofness and friendliness: I wanted no trouble. One of the men whistled at me; the others seemed bored.

The price of a room – payable in advance – was one dollar fifty more than the price listed in the guidebook. 'Take it or leave it,' said the middle-aged man with the thick glasses who sat behind the desk. His hands were stained with nicotine, and I noticed that he had trouble writing my name even though I had slowly spelt it out for him. He gave me the key to a room on the sixth floor ('you should be safe there') and said that check-out time was 11 am.

There was a drunk in the corner of the lift, asleep. I pressed the button marked 6. A man got in at the second floor and ignored both me and the drunk. When I got out of the lift, I found myself facing a large expanse of window through which could be seen an uninterrupted panorama of buildings and streets. An elderly woman in a pink cardigan sat at a card-table in front of the window by the left wall. She was painstakingly piecing together a jigsaw puzzle, and the light provided by the window created an almost halo-like effect around her white hair. 'But no,' I said to myself, 'that is how Kerouac would have seen it. You are not Kerouac, and it is not the mid-Fifties. It is 1979, and you are Eileen Scott, and you are here to see Denver with your own eyes.'

There was a long corridor to the left which smelled of urine, vomit, and disinfectant. (Vomit? I thought. Are there junkies here?) In the doorway of the room next to the one allotted me stood a tall man – a Puerto Rican I think – who stared at me but without interest. I wondered if maybe I should try to find a hotel. But my room was furnished and more or less clean, and I turned the lampshade around so that its faint bloodstain faced the wall.

After having a shower, I put on a delicate patterned shirt, hid the pieces of camera equipment in different places around the room (in a pillowslip, under the bed, in the bottom drawer), locked up, noticed uneasily that the Puerto Rican was still standing in his doorway, retraced my steps down the corridor, found that the drunk was no longer in the lift, and entered the evening.

Josephina's is a restaurant in Larimer Square, a rehabilitated nineteenth-century collection of shops. The restaurant was full, and the man at the front told me that a table would involve a ten-minute wait. I took a seat at the bar and ordered a glass of milk.

Ten minutes later my name was called ('Miss Eileen,' the man said; I hadn't given my surname), and I gathered hat and handbag and was about to follow the waiter when I heard a deep voice behind me ask for a table. Partly out of kindness (I knew there would be a wait for a table), and partly out of curiosity, I turned around and said; 'Are you dining alone?' The man with the denim shirt, denim jeans, and thick greying hair nodded. To which I replied 'I am too. You are welcome to share my table.'

We followed the waiter and sat down.

'Graeme Tyler,' announced my dinner companion. 'Actor extraordinaire – theatre, television, film, radio. Drama, comedy, documentary, farce. I'm thirty-nine and I've lived here for ten years.'

'Eileen Scott,' I reciprocated. 'My friends call me "The Eel". They say I'm slippery.'

Graeme looked at me as if he expected me to say more. 'Well?' he demanded when I didn't continue.

'Well what?'

'Is that all?'

'I've just completed a degree in Literature,' I said. What was I meant to say? I'm not too clear on who I am? I've come to Denver to follow Kerouac's ghost?

'What are you doing in Denver?'

'Trying to order a meal.'

Graeme smiled and we ordered *paella* for two, which turned out to be an excellent choice.

There was a band playing: a four-woman band called Sunday Ladies. They alternated between gutsy rock and gentle folk, and the lead singer, a full-bodied woman with thick black curls, sang with a strong, round voice. Graeme immersed himself in it.

'I've been to see her every night this week,' he said. 'Her name's Marie. I think I'm in love with her.' He got up from his chair. 'Excuse me,' he said, and walked over to the bar. A minute or so later he returned to his seat, and the barman placed a bloody mary on the loudspeaker next to Marie. Graeme got up from his seat again. 'If we move the table,' he said, 'we'll be able to see better.' And move the table we did.

At eleven-thirty the band announced its last song, and Graeme, from the middle of the restaurant, sang along in a deep baritone, applauding vigorously when the Sunday Ladies had finished. The band started packing up. Graeme walked over to the platform and said to the lead singer, 'I think you're terrific, can I see you sometime?'

'No,' said Marie, and that was that.

Somewhat crestfallen, Graeme asked if I was interested in accompanying him back to his house to read some children's books. I said that I was.

After seating me on some cushions in his living-room, Graeme took three children's books from an old mahogany bookshelf and began to read one to me. It was a fable about a caterpillar. Graeme chuckled as he read aloud and made me examine the illustrations – 'No, look more *closely*' – so as not to miss all the funny little objects and visual surprises that ordinarily I would have missed. 'A child's world is so magical,' Graeme said. 'Actually, I'm still a child myself.'

I was offered the couch for the night. 'Don't worry,' he said, 'there are no strings attached. A few loose threads, but no strings.' But I was concerned about my camera equipment at the Y and so I asked Graeme to take me back. He did, and I didn't move into the wide-verandahed house on Lafayette Street until three days later, by which time I had become so ill I could hardly breathe.

Graeme insisted I move in so that he could 'look after me'. When his doctor said over the telephone that he was not prepared to take on new patients, Graeme became furious and announced that henceforth he was looking for a new doctor. He hung up and paced around the kitchen, his forehead furrowed and his eyes bulging slightly. 'I've been going to that bastard for six years,' he said. 'I first went to see him when he was just starting up and had no patients at all. And now he won't see my *friend*.' It took Graeme quite a while to wind down when he was angry. I was to discover this several times over the following few days.

But we did find a doctor, who gave me penicillin for a strep throat and various other prescriptions for an ear infection and swollen glands. Having a temperature of 101° made me feel as though there was an invisible wall surrounding my head. Everyone and everything appeared not quite real. I started laughing a lot. Graeme gave me a pair of his pyjamas that had shrunk ('I'm not too good on laundry,' he explained), and plumped me up with pillows, a hot water bottle, a portable colour TV, a radio, and a selection of children's books.

The bedroom was an attic with a sloping ceiling and a large window facing the street. The window was part of a small alcove with ceiling levels different from the rest of the room. In the alcove was an antique drawing board ('I bought that from a sale of government furniture in El Paso twenty years ago') and a chair with a broken leg ('I don't like objects which aren't defective in some way.' 'People too?' I had asked). It was a fairytale room.

I stayed in bed for two days. Graeme woke me every four hours to remind me to take my assortment of pills. If he wasn't home, he would telephone from wherever he was. At night he got into bed and watched that night's ice-hockey game on TV. He wore headphones, so I was spared the sound. I could, however, hear Graeme's odd whoops of encouragement or disapprobation at unevenly spaced intervals. After the game, Graeme read for a while then turned off the light and wrapped his arms around me after placing a chaste kiss on my forehead.

When I got over the worst of the virus, I came to realize that there were two other people living in the house. One morning I heard Graeme espousing his views on the tyranny of government interference, a topic I had heard him broach several times. There was a low murmur in reply, though I couldn't make out the words. Graeme left to tape the voice-over for a documentary film. A couple of hours later, I went downstairs to make a cup of tea and found a cuddly bear-like man wearing a cream sweater and heavy black-rimmed glasses. He was drinking coffee and reading a newspaper.

'Hello,' I said.

'Hello.'

'I'm Eileen.'

'Yes,' said the cream sweater.

'Who are you?' I asked hesitantly.

'Tate Tyler,' he replied, and resumed reading.

When Graeme got home that evening I asked him about Tate. 'Is he related to you?'

'No,' said Graeme. 'Tyler wasn't his original name. It is now, though. He changed it by deed poll.'

'Why?'

Graeme didn't answer my question directly. 'Tate has been living with me for seven years. After I had been in Denver a while I wrote Tate and said that if he wanted to leave Texas he would always have a home here.'

'What does Tate do?' I asked.

'He reads a lot,' Graeme said, 'he introduces people to one another.'

'Yes, but what does he do for money?'

'He doesn't really need much money. He lives frugally. I don't charge him any rent.'

The other person in the house was Caroline Tyler, who called Graeme 'daddy'.

'Her original name wasn't Tyler either,' Graeme explained, 'and actually she wasn't really my daughter. But she is now.'

'Did you adopt her?' I asked, wondering by this time why the questions I asked – which seemed perfectly reasonable to me before I asked them – always came out sounding silly.

'Actually, no,' Graeme said, then started talking about something else.

I started feeling well enough to go out. Donning cowboy hat, I went a second time to the exhibition of livestock and agricultural machinery at the Coliseum, which probably was where I had picked up the virus. Thin teenage boys sauntered self-consciously, munching hamburgers, and wearing T-shirts printed with slogans like 'If you ain't a cowboy, you ain't shit'.

The rodeo was checked shirts, frenzied broncos, hats thrown on sawdust, and muscled cowgirls on stockhorses, manoeuvring obstacles and cracking whips. I clapped and whooped with everyone else and managed to push aside that tight chest-lump of anxiety that had been following me around ever since I had left Australia.

After the rodeo I started feeling healthier and more positive.

I still didn't know what I'd be doing when I got home, but not knowing began to worry me less.

It was time to leave. I had stayed in Denver far longer than I had intended. But each time I said I was thinking of heading off, Graeme would say that I wasn't ready yet. And so each day I would venture out and discover a little more – the parks, the mountains, Bill Cody's grave, the Red Rocks Amphitheatre, the town of Boulder – and come back again to the house on Lafayette Street.

One day I returned to find a large blonde woman sitting with Graeme in the kitchen.

'Hello,' she said pleasantly, 'you must be Eileen. I'm Janice Tyler. Thought I'd drop in to say hello.'

'Are you Graeme's wife?' I asked.

'No,' she said, surprised.

'His sister?' I asked, determined to get to the bottom of this.

'No.'

'A cousin?' I asked faintly.

'Why no,' said Janice, her face expanding into a grin.

And then something clicked. I grinned back.

The next day I packed my things and took a taxi to the bus depot. I bought a ticket to Albuquerque and looked forward to another two months on the road, after which there would be the trip home. Graeme and I hugged when the taxi came, and I promised one day to return.

I felt light-hearted, and this feeling must have been obvious on my face because a man of about twenty-seven came up to me and said, 'You look happy. Our bus won't be here for nearly an hour, so I thought I'd come up and introduce myself. I'm Jim Davis.'

'Pleased to meet you, Jim,' I replied. 'My name's Eileen Tyler.'

Damien White

YOUNG MAN WITH PADDY PALLIN WALKING BOOTS

Walking in Rome, walking in Rome on my first morning in my Paddy Pallin walking boots, I crossed the Tiber and stood in the piazza before St Peter's. I stood and stared and walked and stared before stopping near the obelisk and the two fountains there. Between the obelisk and each fountain is a round porphyry slab, and if you stand on these slabs you get the illusion that the colonnade around the piazza has only a single row of columns instead of its actual four. I stood on both of them. I climbed the steps to the main door of the basilica, reached out to push it open, but then turned back. I had time, time to go into everything more thoroughly. I took a different route back to my pensione. It was a Sunday. The Poste Restante office wouldn't have been open.

Walking in Rome, walking in Rome every morning after a couple of hours' work, I criss-crossed the city, ambling down side-streets, stopping to read every inscription on every monument, waiting to be surprised by the paintings and statuary and architecture in the churches, big and small, I found on every block. On these excursions I always bought a copy of *Il Messagero*, to practise my Italian and for its listings of apartments to rent. But apartments in the centre were always too expensive, and the cheap ones were too far away.

Well, why Rome, he said.

My first conversation in English in over a week, and it had to be with a middle-aged American trying to pick me up in the trattoria. I shrugged.

Come on, he said. You must've had some reason.

I grew up Catholic, I said, so I guess I've always been curious about Rome.

Yeah. All roads and all that.

Walking in Rome, I always returned to my pensione via the Poste Restante office. I had been in the city for almost a fortnight and still hadn't heard from Katie, even though I'd written twice to her. Often, though, I could picture what she'd be doing. During the days, her art history courses. In the evenings, concerts, plays, opera, movies. And each Monday evening her Mind Games group.

Walking in Rome, walking in Rome that morning, my Paddy Pallin boots gripping the lava cobblestones, I found myself in the Piazza del Popolo, near the Flaminian Gate. The church of Santa Maria del Popolo was just inside the old city wall. I went in. The tombs and statues, the altars and paintings, the Virgin above the main altar, all held me for several minutes, but then I turned to go. I had time, time to go into everything more thoroughly.

Just as I turned another tourist dropped a coin into the light machine near the side chapel next to me. And there, illuminated, were the two most magnificent paintings I had ever seen. *A Crucifixion of St Peter. A Conversion of St Paul.*

St Peter being crucified upside-down because, so the story goes, he didn't consider himself worthy to die the same death as Christ. Three men tilt the cross while St Peter half lifts his torso to stare at the nail through his left hand, to stare in pain, yes, but in astonishment too that now it's actually happening to him. In the foreground the expansive bum and dirty bare feet of one of the executioners as he strains under the cross. The cross itself slashing the composition in two. And the details, the details lit and picked out from the darkened background – the arms of the three executioners and St Peter's own arms, the nails through his feet, the crumpled blue cloak, the perfect grain of the timber in the crossbeam.

St Paul, in military uniform, his sword glistening darkly where it has fallen, lies foreshortened on his red cloak, his eyes blinded, his arms stretched to heaven, just at that point in the story where he has been thrown from his horse by a flash of light and has heard the voice accompanying it say, 'Saul, Saul, why do you persecute me.' The horse's rump leads into the upper foreground, and over its crupper St Paul's peasant companion stares at him.

A compositional fault that makes it hard to see just how this companion's legs can connect to his head and shoulders somehow adds by its clumsiness to the power of that frozen, stark, perfect moment.

When the light went out the other tourist left. I dropped my own 100 lire coin into the slot.

Just after my third coin I became aware that more people were beside me; a stylishly dressed middle-aged Italian couple. Next time their coin activated the light. I glanced at them again, and just in time to hear the woman murmur, ah, Caravaggio, with such a blend of pride and humility, of wonder and familiarity, that my Paddy Pallin boots seemed instantly heavier on my feet.

They left. I sat down in one of the pews there to read my guidebook. The church was described as 'one of the artistic treasure-houses of Rome', but my eyes skimmed over everything else until they came to rest on the name Caravaggio.

I fed in two more coins, my last. There was no one else in the church. As I left, not even glancing at the treasures to left and right, I murmured to myself, ah, Caravaggio.

Michelangelo Amerisi, known as Caravaggio from the name of his native village, came to Rome in 1592. For several years he lived hand-to-mouth, supported by various patrons, trying to establish himself as a painter. A *Young Boy Peeling Fruit* is perhaps the earliest work that can definitely be attributed to him. Some of his patrons objected to his naturalism, to his peasants, to their ragged clothes and dirty bare feet, claiming he wasn't treating religious subjects with enough reverence.

The post office lay on the direct route back to my pensione. I handed my passport over the counter, and recognized Katie's script even before the English stamps as the attendant handed the passport back to me with a letter. I didn't open it until I'd found a table and had ordered coffee in the bar at the Piazza Colonna.

The resumption of her course. A night at the Royal Shakespeare. A walk in Regent's Park. And at the bottom of the second page the news that after her Mind Games session the night before she had stayed with Joel, the convenor of the group. The letter was dated the first Tuesday after I had left London. By now she would have spent at least one more night with him. This was a

Friday now, so that even if they hadn't met since the previous Monday they would be seeing each other again in three more days.

The story goes that when the persecutions under Nero began St Peter decided to leave Rome. But on the Appian Way he met Christ, walking towards the city.

Where are you going, Lord, St Peter asked.

To Rome, Christ told him, to be crucified again.

And so St Peter turned back, went back to his upside-down martyrdom in the Circus of Nero, the site where the basilica of St Peter's now stands.

Back in the pensione I checked in my guidebooks for everything I could find on Caravaggio. And that afternoon I tracked down four more paintings, in churches not far away.

After dinner I wrote again to Katie, telling her of my discovery of Caravaggio. I knew that she would have studied him at some point in her course. I told her too that apart from an occasional twinge I felt fine about her and Joel, told her I was glad we felt free enough with each other to expand.

Between 25 September 1600 and 10 November 1601, Caravaggio completed those two pictures for Santa Maria del Popolo. In 1600 too he is first mentioned in police records for having been involved in a street brawl.

On the Monday I saw his *Madonna of the Serpent,* that and five others in the Galleria Borghese.

It was just after 8.30 as I walked back to the pensione after dinner in my local trattoria. That meant it was 7.30 in London. That meant that Katie would be leaving for the Mind Games group. That meant that within half an hour she would be seeing Joel again. Taking my guidebooks I made a list of all the Caravaggios in Rome that I hadn't yet seen. I finished at 9.10. That meant it was 8.10 in London. That meant the group would be starting.

St Paul was martyred under Nero. As a Roman citizen he was privileged with beheading instead of crucifixion. The story goes that his severed head bounced three times on the ground, and that at each spot where it struck a miraculous fountain sprang up.

I was trying to read, but couldn't concentrate. I walked out again, to the Campo dei Fiori, a busy market during the day but mostly deserted now. I'd read that Caravaggio used to play football there. It was 9.55. That meant it was 8.55 in London. That meant the group would be well under way.

Caravaggio had been involved in many more brawls by 29 May 1606, when he killed a man in a fight after a game of football. Under threat of capital punishment he fled Rome.

Black coffee and grappa at the bar in the next block. A circuitous route back to the pensione. Through the little door set in the giant portone. Up three flights of stairs, my Paddy Pallin boots squeaked at every step. Through the door of the pensione. My key from the rack. Through the door of my room. It was 11.05 as I undressed. That meant it was 10.05 in London. That meant the group would soon be finishing.

With patrons working for his pardon Caravaggio came in 1610 to Porto Ercole, just outside the Papal States. There he was arrested by mistake, and by the time he had been released his boat had gone on without him. The story goes that he ran along the shore, half-demented under the blazing sun, trying to catch the boat that was taking away his pictures. The resulting fever proved fatal.

Reading. Turning off the light. Trying to sleep. On my left side. On my right. On my back. Turning the light back on. Reading. Turning off the light. Trying to sleep. On my left side. On my right. On my back. It was 12.35, 11.35 in London. That meant the others would all have left Joel's place. All of them but Katie. It was 1.45. It was 2.30. It was 3.25.

And then it was 7.40. My list was on the bedside table. I reviewed which of the Caravaggios I would visit that day.

Games,
Fantasies,
Lyricism

David Brooks

THE LINE

Late, on the hottest night of the year, he sits by the window. For a long time he searches for a line and at last he finds it, beginning at the tip of his pen and continuing across the page beneath the words 'continuing across the page beneath' until it reaches the edge and, independent of ink and human motion, pausing only briefly as if about to dive, moving thence on to the desk and past the candle and the glass toward the sill.

From there, against the first faint stirrings of a cool breeze from the river, it slips through the wire screen and out across the fuchsias and the lawn. Traversing the pavement, rising above the trees, and following no streets or feasible cross-country route, it passes westward over Roe Street and the Beggar's Lane to the playing-fields and the old stone buildings of the university. Not stopping at these, or in the cafés, and following roughly the course of the river, it passes through the wide updraught of denser oxygen above the park, directly above the last bedless lovers in an EJ Holden and the pointing arm of the statue of Sir John F, the founding father of the city, and thence across the long, perfect reflection of the Great Port Bridge and into the sleeping suburbs. After almost one mile of these, just grazing the upper branches of an avenue of flowering gums, it slows and descends, approaching cautiously the third front window of a darkened house four miles or three pages of the city directory from where first it left the orderly confines of the introductory paragraph of a tale for which it may, in truth, have never been intended.

To follow it by car (public transport, needless to say, is unthinkable), one would have to begin on page 48 – to employ again the city directory – in the square designated by the fine blue lines that descend from either side of the letter B, and those which stretch toward the left from the number 53 at the far right-hand margin. Bearing in mind that one's general direction must always be westward, one would then move at first in a southerly direction along Alison Road until Balcott and, turning right at the church with the great rose window, move diagonally across two map squares to where the page joins 47 and, crossing at first Charles Road, Balcott leads into Dean Parade. Now moving directly westward, one traces Dean through four squares of the light blue grid – past the city pool, the council offices, and the Ladies' College – and passes beneath the freeway into Estuary Road, where the Floral Beach Parade and map 46 begin. Following the Floral Beach Parade diagonally across the upper right, beside Dog Swamp and the Herdsman Cemetery, one finds oneself, having strayed north-westerly, referred to map 36, where the Floral intersects Green Street and turns toward the sea. At Herbert Street one takes a left-hand turn. Moving again southward, one drives beneath flowering gums to a lane beginning, of course, with the letter 'I', and halts at the darkened frontage of number 38, at a considerable disadvantage and at least half an hour behind the line which, unshackled by a pedestrian imagination, has already entered the third window from the left – left open to catch the cool sea breeze – and passed between billowing curtains toward a bed upon which sleeps a woman with alabaster skin and auburn hair, her face partly hidden by her furled right arm and a fold of the single sheet. Uninhibited by this last barrier, the line has long since found her, and, not without an initial parabolic digression, proceeded along her left calf and thigh and come to rest, peacefully and without thought of return.

She, of course, knows nothing of this. She has, in fact, been borrowed from Alain Dufort* and was last seen on a balcony above a courtyard lined with palms. All she could tell is that when she awoke, she had been dreaming of an old man on an esplanade, feeding seagulls that, for their own mysterious reasons, suddenly rose and, banking westward, traced with their soft grey wings an ambiguous message, free of grid or narrative, on a dark sky promising rain.

Font du Nuit, Alain Dufort, Hibbert et Fils, Paris, 1914, p. 27

Wendy Jenkins

THREE INTO FOUR

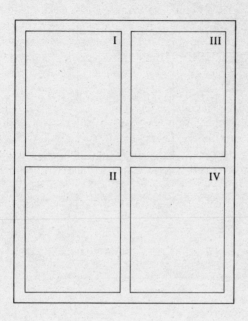

I have tried many times to get it right, to get four perfect yet different shots from the machine. What you see above is the closest I have got. The first time I tried was in a London railway station – I needed some passport photos. Not knowing the habits of the machines and being self-consciously uncertain whether to smile or play it straight, I blew it, obtaining only one good shot. As I held the card in the air, watching it dry, three bleached and vacant faces looked back at me as from a mirror.

The terms were set. My dialogue with the machines had begun.

This is how I usually appear in photographs. It is how I look when I know that my photograph is going to be taken. I don't have to think about it. My body naturally assumes this shape. It has the right feeling from the inside. And when I see it reproduced like this, so that I am looking at it from the outside, it also feels right . . . If I kept a photograph album, and if I wrote captions in this photograph album, beneath this picture I would write: *Me as myself*. If someone who knew me well saw the photograph there, they would say: Yes, that's a good one of you. What they would mean is, that looks right, that is typical, that's how you usually are. This is, as you would expect, the first face that the machine and I agreed on. The natural first shot. I do not have to describe it here – it is not a problem. It is not even really a choice. I carry this potential with me like the colour of my eyes.

This is the shot that I try for second. You will notice that it is a smile. There is a degree of choice in this, and also something of a problem. When a person with a camera says, 'Do something different, can't you smile or something', they are asking for an intervening process, a performance, a lie against the machine. What they get back from the chemist (stiff grins, defensive teeth) is not your problem. But what is revealed to you privately by the machine after a process of intimate co-operation – this is differ-ent. I feel it may even be crucial. I can understand tribal people believing that a camera can reveal their souls . . . This shot has slowly become easier, more routine. I have to think about it less. Over time, the machine has revealed to me certain truths that have helped a great deal. Notable among these is the fact that I am not consistently capable of refinement in the expression of pleasure. Wry and subtle grins require a degree of control and a sophistication of gesture that I do not have. I am not and never will be a sophisticate. Once this was accepted and the shot mapped out (half to full laugh), the nature of the problem changed. It became a question of execution rather than of conception. It freed my energy for the problem of the third shot.

She talks of the second shot being arrived at through the exercise of a degree of choice. Having used up only one possibility in the framing of the first shot, it naturally appears to her that a sea of alternatives remains into which she can dip at will like a bird fishing from a rock. This is a nice image, but a false one. You do not have to look very closely at the first shot to notice that she isn't smiling. In fact, there is little show of emotion at all. Given the terms of the dialogue (four perfect yet different shots), does it not follow that the second shot will be poles apart from the first – that it will be determined not freely, but in opposition to what has gone before? Does it not follow that, given a certain demonstrable penchant for opposites (black jacket on white background, this sentence and this context), and given the culturally determined set that she brings to the exercise (you smile at a camera), that the second shot will, in fact, be a smile and a full one at that? Does it not also follow that the third shot is likely to be some kind of blending, a synthesis of both possibilities?

The third shot, or I should say, one attempt at it. This is the window that interests me the most. The one my eyes scan first when the card drops into the tray. It is constantly evolving, shifting, being defined. Each session with the machines reveals a little more of what is achievable and what is not, within the limits set by the first two shots. The possibilities are constantly in my mind. I can't relax with this shot. It is too important. There is always the chance of the unexpected, the possibility of news, good or bad. My part in the dialogue is not very easy. There is nothing quite like being presented with a black-and-white portrait of your own failure.

This shot is still a long way from 'perfect'. For one thing, it is not really natural. (Note the 'poetic' cast about the eyes, the 'sensitive' fingering of the symbol at the throat.) There is some degree of will at play here. An attempt to impose an image on the machine. She is only partly aware of this, putting the failure of the shot down to a certain tenseness and a need for more information. It is more than that. The shot is forced. She is not, despite what has been said above, truly listening to the machine. She is flirting with the image for its own sake. This is the constant danger – the kiss of death. To love the image or process for its own sake, losing touch with the basic facts that keep it real.

Three is a fascinating number. By definition it is poised equally between two and four, yet in my mind, it is not fixed. I see it sometimes closer to two, sometimes to four. It's in a constant state of tension. A step forward or back could change its nature completely ... *She has become fascinated with threeness, seeing it everywhere. There were three kids at the corner of the street this morning, a threeness pattern in a friend's new poem, three trees suddenly moved together when a turn in the road changed the perspective. She has started to see threeness in people: He's a three-shot man she tells herself, that woman's a definite two and a bit. Beyond these signs, she senses the larger forms: past-present-future time/my mother-myself-the child I do not have.*

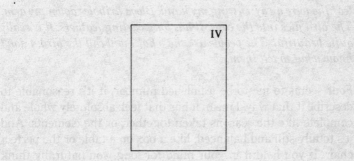

The fourth square. Last frame. There is little I can say about this. Nothing is clear. It's like I'm looking for my image on open water. Sometimes I think I see a hint of something, a direction. Then it is gone completely, as if the wind or the sea itself had cancelled it. I believe it will come, in its own time, all being well. I believe in the possibility of the fourth. There have been signs, and the image – the metaphor – stays.

She has written down this dream: I am holding three pigeons. They are my birds, acquired one by one, and each accustomed to my touch. Suddenly a strange new bird appears. There are people there and they tell me how to catch it. I am fairly certain that it doesn't need to be caught. The cage is clogged with wire – perhaps the bird has been prevented from entering rather than having resisted. I tear the wire away, cutting my hand. Blood dribbles down my arm. The bird flies into the cage. It has long curling feathers. It is really quite beautiful. The people ask me what I will call the bird. I don't know what to tell them.

Four seems to me to be a finished number, if it's reasonable to describe it that way. I mean it has that feel: absolutely whole and complete like the seasons taken together, or the elements. And it's totally still and balanced, like a box on a table or the perfect chair. If you hold it in your mind for long, you naturally think of a square or rectangle. You are completely familiar with this image – it has framed you over and over since infancy. It can hold you like the walls of your house, while being every door, every window.

As she came down into the Main Gallery he was kneeling on the floor, the paintings for the new exhibition all around him. He was positioning the panels of a triptych onto the fourth element – a grey-backing board. She stopped, watching the pieces come together: three panels, each separate and contained yet moving into the others with strong narrative and conceptual links; four parts, each squared and boundaried, yet totally textured into the larger work. She said nothing, held by the image, the simple, perfect parallel.

Brian Cole

THE BAY OF ISLANDS

'Always wanted to see a whale on the Islands.'

Mallee is thinking, there have to be whales.

'You was born there Mallee, you know there aren't any.'

Jess drove the old Peugeot fast. Mallee lies across the seat, one leg hooked under his arse, his head on his elbow, watching branches; spinnakers in wind, passed. There were dead whales. One had washed up on the Islands a week ago and Mallee was going to see Noel; he'd know about the whales.

Jess turned the Peugeot into a bend, looked a vagrant grin across the dash at Mallee.

'You're weird Mallee . . .'

Jess thinks, 'Cause you drank too much sea-water . . . swam too much, out to the Island, that was looney.'

Forest rain, clouds tree-top close and autumn. Jess reckoned looney was the wrong word. He guarded that swim, storm swelled ocean to the furthest Island, Jess had always wanted someone to swim too. He knew only Mallee could swim it. Mallee tilted a bottle of beer to his mouth; brown colour, sun's codes of light. He remembered Jess' rites of dare and double dare, naked testicle swim to the furthest Island. Something like fear, slower than fear, lonelier than fear; Island felt, cape-like without land, forlorn in its secretive kelp wet tides.

Jess said, 'But no one's swum it since, Mallee.'

'Maybe a whale.'

'Na, no one's swum it.'

Slow falling turns, ragged brushed mist. A shrill bell cry in grey
ash trees. Cigarette ash fell on Mallee's shirt, and he brushed it
off or in with a flick of his bottled hand. Pastures with rye grass
spiked yellow.

The Peugeot sounds, gallop, gallop on a plank bridge. An egret
flew away from the car, it swirled and landed further along a narrow creek. Mallee had his head out of the Peugeot's window. He
watched the egret's strange gulp of neck, hesitant foot forward
landing. A weird crab-eating bird. Weird as whales; as Jess
thought Mallee. Mallee thinks a whale must swim to the Islands
to die on the Islands.

'Storm coming.'

A storm moved across the heath coast, discolouring the ocean;
dents of blue, darker blue.

Mallee gulped beer.

'Mallee don't drink sea-water no more, drinks beer.'

Light rain.

Jess grinned.

A fallen black kernel of storm, heavy rain moths the Peugeot's
fenders, through Mallee's open window. He wound it up as they
turned off the road into Noel's house track.

Noel heard them drive up and he came out in the storm. Robin
on the verandah. She hadn't met Mallee before, only heard of his
weirdness and she glanced at him warily. Mallee brought some
wood inside for Noel's fire. Noel always had a fire. It was damp
wood and the fire shuddered.

Noel put a kettle on. Mallee asked him about the orchard work.

'It's all right, it doesn't pay much and there isn't much around
until July.'

Mallee had quit his city storeman job. He told them.

'I've quit.'

'What are you going to do,' Robin said dryly.

'Dunno,' Mallee shrugged.

'Wanted to come back to the Islands.'

'Mallee wants to see a whale.'

Noel, who'd know about the whales, sat in an old cushioned
chair across from Robin and the fire. Mallee wanted Noel to tell
them about the whales. Noel shoved wood into the fire and looked
at Mallee puzzled.

'Ain't ever seen a sea-whale.'

'Must of seen the dead one.'

'Yeah, saw it.'

Noel's thumb angled his fingers along his mouth's break as he eyed Mallee.

'Dead one . . . maybe it floated in dead from the Antarctic.'

Jess grinned his agile grin. Mallee submerged in Island sea.

'Sharks would of got it before it floated in dead from the Antarctic.'

Noel nodded agreement to sharks or nodded and said, looking at Robin who had her legs up on his chair, her buckled paper face on her knee, 'They die, when they land on the Islands.'

And Jess joked, 'Maybe we oughta take Mallee's boat to the Antarctic to find a whale . . . sank more places than anyone fished.'

Mallee would row it out, swim it in. Noel always said that was why Mallee could swim so good. And they talked over other tales of the Islands into evening.

Jess had to drive back to the city. Mallee opened the house gate. A different wind whine in Noel's English trees. Mallee walked down the field's muddy slipping slope leaving Noel to redraw stories of Mallee, less weird than before. A Mallee that arrived.

'He's not that weird.'

'Weird enough.'

'Brought in the wood.'

Robin said cautiously, 'Guess so.'

'Where's he gone?'

'Gone off.'

Mallee went off, over road fences to the Bay of Islands. There were three Islands, two smaller Islands and a massive Island he'd swum to. A slow breathing sea, thrusting waves to the bay cliff edge. Mallee's jeans were wet to the knees; the water had a slight summer warmth.

There were small storm-chop ridges across deeper sea swells and white breaks like diving whales.

Mallee's whale thoughts – they die here.

Mallee swimming an empty sea triangle of Islands, a feeling

so close to fear. Waves; spray stung Islands holed hulls of rock.
Every wave inventing a word, wave words, wailing words.

'A whale song.'

'There aren't any whales . . . a mellow-choly song.'

Mallee's mellow-choly song. The Island calls something like
a whale song in an Island's forlorn whaleless bay.

Peter Carey

LIFE AND DEATH IN THE SOUTH SIDE PAVILION

1

I was employed, originally, as a Shepherd 3rd Class. That was in the days of the sheep, and even now that the sheep have been replaced by horses I believe that my position is still Shepherd 3rd Class although I have had no confirmation of this from The Company. My work place is, to the best of my knowledge, known officially as THE SOUTH SIDE PAVILION, but it is many years since I saw this written on a delivery docket and I have never seen it anywhere since.

Yesterday I wrote to The Company asking to be relieved of my post and I used the following description: 'I am employed as a Shepherd 3rd Class in the South Side Pavilion.' I hope it makes sense to them. I had considered a more detailed description, something that would locate the place more exactly.

For instance: 'The pavilion is bathed in a pale yellow light which enters from the long dusty windows in its sawtooth roof. In the centre, its corners pinned by four of the twenty-four pillars which support the roof, is a large sunken tank which resembles a swimming pool. The horses require the greater part of this area. I, the Shepherd in charge, have a small corner to myself. In this corner I have, thanks to the generosity of The Company, a bed, a gas cooker, a refrigerator, and a television set. The animals give me no trouble. However, they are, as you must be aware, in danger from the pool . . .'

I didn't send that part of the letter, for fear of appearing foolish to them. The people at The Company must know my pavilion only too well. Probably they have photographs of it, even the original architect's plans. The pool in the centre must be known to them, also the dangers associated with the pool. I have already made many written requests for a supply of barbed wire to fence off the pool but the experts have obviously considered it unnecessary. Or perhaps they have worked out the economics of it and, taking the laws of chance into account, must have decided that it is cheaper to lose the odd horse than to buy barbed wire which, for all I know, might be expensive these days.

I have placed empty beer cartons around the perimeter of the pool, in the foolish hope that they will prove to be some kind of deterrent. Unfortunately they seem to have had quite the opposite effect. The horses stand in groups perilously close to the edge of the pool and stare stupidly at the cardboard boxes.

2

The television is showing nothing but snow. The pavilion is bathed in its blue electric blanket. Another horse has fallen into the pool. Its pale bloated body floats in the melancholy likeness of a whale.

3

Marie arrived early and discovered me weeping amongst the horses.

'Why are you weeping?'

'Because of the horses.'

'Even horses must die, sooner or later.'

'I am weeping because of the swimming pool.'

'The swimming pool is there to help them die.'

When Marie tells me that the swimming pool is there to help the horses die, I believe her. She has an answer for everything. But when she leaves, her answers leave with her and the only comfort in the pavilion is distilled into a couple of small sad marks on the sheets of my bed.

4

I AM HERE TO STOP THE HORSES FALLING INTO THE SWIMMING POOL.

5

Marie, who helped me get into the pavilion, now wants to help me out. Personally, I would like to leave. I have sent my resignation to The Company and am, at present, awaiting the replacement. Marie said, 'Fuck The Company.' She arrived today with colour brochures and an ultimatum: either I leave the horses or she will leave me.

'Do you love the horses?'
'No, I love you.'
'Then come with me.'
'I can't leave them alone.'
'They fall into the pool anyway. You can't stop them.'
'I know.'
'Then you might as well come.'
'I can't come until they've all fallen into the pool.'
'But you are trying to stop them falling into the pool.'
'Yes.'
'You can't love the horses if you're just waiting for them to fall in and drown.'
'No, I love you.'
'Ah, but I know you love the horses.'
And so it continues.

6

Marie sleeps beside me, enveloped in the sweet heavy smell of sleep and sperm.

There is some movement in the pavilion. I lick my fingers and wipe my eyes with spittle. For the moment the tiny shock of the wetness is enough to keep me awake. I stare into the dark, among the grey garden of gloomy horses, trying to distinguish movement from stillness.

There is a large splash. A high whinnying. I block my ears. Once they are in the pool there is nothing they can grip to get them out.

7

The men came with a truck fitted with winches. They dragged the horse from the pool and put it on a trailer. They had to break its back legs to fit it in properly.

I imagined that they looked at me reproachfully. Probably it is simply that this is a part of their job that they dislike, and, having paid me five visits to remove dead horses, they are not kindly disposed towards me.

I asked them if any of the dead horses would be replaced. They seemed too busy to answer me, but I have always assumed the answer is no.

Today I explained that I wished to be relieved of the job. When they could offer no helpful suggestions I asked about the barbed wire. They looked shocked and expressed the opinion that barbed wire was cruel.

8

Marie didn't come tonight. She is giving me a free sample of her absence, letting me know in advance what it will taste like. She needn't have bothered. It's just as bad as I thought it would be.

I leaf through the brochures she has left for me, staring at beaches I can never imagine visiting. I have never seen so many beaches. On the beaches there are beautiful girls, girls more beautiful than Marie. Perhaps she thinks that the beautiful girls in the brochures will provide the extra incentive. What she will never understand is that I want to go with her to these beaches more desperately than anything else in the world. She accuses me of having a misplaced loyalty to The Company, but I care nothing for The Company which has never deigned to answer my letters. If I could leave the pavilion I would go to The Company's offices and settle everything once and for all. If need be I would kidnap a member of The Company's staff and bring him back here as a replacement.

The strange thing is that once I have left the pavilion I know I will detest the horses. I can feel this new attitude waiting in the wings of my mind, waiting to take over. I have tried to explain this to Marie but she thinks I am being dishonest with myself, that I simply wish an excuse not to go with her.

But now I am responsible for the horses. Each death is my responsibility and I have no wish to be responsible for so many deaths.

And now that I am unable to make love she thinks it is because I have an unnatural attraction to the horses and that I find her unattractive in comparison. But I am unable to make love because every time I make love a horse falls into the pool.

EVERY TIME I FUCK MARIE I KILL A HORSE.

Perhaps the noise of fucking upsets them and they panic and lose their bearings. I told Marie about my feelings, that the love-making was unsatisfactory because of the danger to the horses.

She said, 'You attribute great power to your cock.'

'While it is limp it will do no harm.'

'No harm,' said Marie, 'and no good either.'

9

Another night without Marie.

Her absence has cured my limp cock more quickly and effectively than either of us could have guessed. I toss and turn in my tangled bed dreaming of involved and passionate love on the distant beaches of her brochures.

At this moment I am prepared to fuck until the pool is full of horses.

10

The horses are standing in a circle around the pool, their tails swishing through the grey air. It is not difficult to imagine that they have gathered around the pool to look into the black water and dream about death. The blackness of death must seem attractive to them after the grey nights and yellow days of the pavilion. Or perhaps they are simply aware of my decision and are now standing in readiness.

The whip has always been there, thoughtfully provided by the same company that refused to supply me with barbed wire.

I have no wish to remember the manner in which I drove the horses into the pool. It was sickeningly easy. They fell into the water like over-ripe fruit from a tree, often before the whip had touched them. In five minutes the pavilion was empty and the pool was boiling with horses. I retired to my bed and pulled the pillow over my head.

In less than an hour there were twelve horses floating in the pool. They bumped softly into one another like bad dreams in a basin.

11

They have brought replacements. They unload the twelve new horses from the truck with the flashing yellow light on its roof.

Then they proceed to winch the drowned horses from the pool.

I plead with the men not to leave the live horses in my care, to transfer them to another pavilion. I offer them everything I have: my television set, my refrigerator, my bed, the brochures Marie left with me.

The driver flicks through the brochures sullenly: 'The TV is company property.' He adds that he intends to confiscate the brochures.

Dorothy Johnston

PIECES ON PROSTITUTION

The Codpiece and the Diary Entry
(In which a window is opened into the romantic adventures of H. Cod,
regular client at number ten, with Maria as lady-in-waiting.)

Harry came to Maria with his velvet hose crinkled around grass-hopper knees, so thin and sharp they made ladders within minutes of donning. One heel caught on the front steps as he scraped the mud off and prepared to stride in a bullish manner. Dressed for the conquest, he had some difficulty extricating himself from his close-fitting head-piece of calfskin and ivory, his velvet breeches and anklets of new spring jasmine. The stench of an authentic Shakespearean codpiece, preserved for centuries in a mixture of camphor and methylated spirits, overpowered the jasmine which promptly withered and died on his bony ankles.

'Would you give me a hand to get out of this?' asked Harry, one hand on the massage table, another feeling its way over his crumbling button-holes.

'I can't take my shoes off,' he told her, 'because when I get excited my feet swell up and then I can't get them back on again.'

Maria was startled, but only for a moment. The shoes themselves looked as if they would fall apart at a touch.

'Would you like oil or powder at the finish?' she asked him.

Harry said that perhaps powder would suit him better.

'If you would wear white,' he whispered before he left, 'or a blonde wig, or the mask of a young virgin, I could submerge myself in the part with greater vigour.'

'I can make a great lover out of you,' he began again next time.

Maria put her hand over his eyes with the swift gesture of a mother protecting her child. She slipped an enquiring, dark hand beneath the quilted, embroidered *fleur de-lys* of his breasts.

Night fell outside the parlour. Harry's eyes gleamed yellow through the dusk. She knew that when the dawn light got behind their faded make-up, showed up the worn patches on the prized codpiece resting in its bath of camphor and metho, and they talked about the principle of disorder in the universe, floating under them like the curse of an angry god, that someone, somewhere out there, had prepared for them a shabbier end than was theirs by birthright.

Sometimes Harry came to the house disguised as any other client, in a grey suit and pale blue shirt, but more often he was a combination of historical characters, bearing on his thin body the knick-knacks of centuries. Striding the boards like any period actor, taking his cue from some internal clock, his short legs tripped over the spongy floor-boards, down the corridor that led nowhere but to the bathroom and the ancient shower. He came and went as regularly as the towels and the money folded neatly in the oven every night. 'For the fairies,' Maria answered, when Harry asked her why she left the day's takings there.

Maria, whose daily experience was that of being inhabited by another, saw landlords and tenants everywhere. She saw coffee laced with brandy and hot orange tea disappearing into the bodies of her clients. Outside, she was like a person who wore stage make-up on the street. She did not consider it her place to ask why Harry had chosen her, or why he chose such a variety of obstacles to put between them, which he spent many minutes disentangling, or why he returned, taking the name John like every second stranger who found himself on the door-step in a blue suit or bricklayers' overalls. She thought she could have nothing to say to a man whose preparations of love were so elaborate that he came back once a week for five years – or was it longer? – with his hand raised in a warning that she would recognize him only as a stranger, through an extended confusion of courtesies.

'Oh little sail-boat floating in the bay,' sang Harry at three o'clock on a Thursday afternoon. 'Carry me away to my own country.'

'Since we're so close to the sea,' he would murmur, and appear next time in an admiral's cast-off underwear.

He could side-step innocently, on nimble feet, saying playfully, 'Why don't you hop up on the table this time?', as slippery, though she had not yet oiled his white, liver-patchy skin, as porous as a child's.

Sometimes he brought paintings to show her, and to decorate the room for his visit. He held them up for her to see, under his lined chin of an actor so old that he could not help muddling his parts together.

Maria thought it was almost as if there were a military band in the background, so automatically in time were her fingers, then the movements of her body, on the rug laid ceremoniously under the massage table, with the little flat cushions shining white in the shadow of the table legs, his castle, Harry called it, arching over her, his tent, his cottage, his semi-detached.

They floated together in a bath-tub sea. Maria swam through the juices, though this time they were hers and saw, where the horizon was broken by dirty buildings, how the waves would lift over her and seep away.

Harry lay with his eyes closed. Maria ran her fingers lightly down the inside of his arm.

'Don't fall asleep here,' she whispered. 'I'd never get rid of you.'

They listened to the rain, standing by the window waiting for it to clear so that he could leave – Had umbrellas been invented then? – Harry frowning at the thought of spots on his padded frock-coat, Maria standing by his left elbow, her mind stretching out through the rain towards some backyard of a future house of love.

The old house would not have held its cracks together for half an hour if the storm that they watched from the window had gone on long enough to bring the sea up over the wall, with a noise in which the heart-beats of fear were still audible, and the low sounds of timber giving way. Harry lifted his hand and Maria watched it, with its dark patches of age, on their side of the teeming window. The bitten silverfish holes in his jacket and the thin patches, where the lighter material of his shirt showed through, matched the holes in the plaster and woodwork, almost piece-for-piece. They were stopped up with odds and ends against the rain.

'Weather like this,' said Maria, 'is a constant reminder of some-thing, but you can never remember what.'

When Harry left, Maria knew that it had been a mistake to act as if it was always three o'clock on a Thursday afternoon. It was simply that time had been on his side. Why didn't he come back for me? she asked herself. With his frog's posture and thousand-year-old smile, he should have know that no one else would have him.

When Harry said good-bye for the last time, standing on the door-step in the rain, it took Maria a week to realize he was gone, so perfectly had she fallen into the pattern of repeated movements. For some time Harry had been unable to do much, had exhausted himself simply with getting there. She would shake her head at him standing at the front door, as helpless as an albatross caught in a fishing net, and undress him piece by piece, admiring the latest bit of flotsam hung about his body. It wasn't surprising that she went about in a daze long enough for fungus to grow around the rim of the bath, and that she'd lost count of the weeks since she'd seen him, when it finally dawned on her that he was her last and only client and that he was never coming back.

On the day when she noticed the smell of decay in the kitchen hanging around the bottle of methylated spirits and realised that this was all Harry had left behind him, and opening the oven, saw the ashes of the money she had left to be picked up, on that day, after she had thoroughly cleaned out and aired the kitchen, Maria began a diary.

The first thing, she wrote, was that we fitted. In the beginning, that was all I knew and it was enough. Most pricks fit most cunts – that is the heterosexual experience. You could write it like an equation. Even ageing, battle-scarred cunts will lick their lips and smile as if for the camera, since, though they know in their deepest folds that every long, feeling shaft of love most likely turns into a frog prince, still, still . . . the mind may know but the cunt, in spite of its struggle with rubber rings, wads of cotton and every kind of imposter, the cunt is naively generous.

We do not put aside our knowledge that love disintegrates and the ash is dry in the mouth and the warm places are empty holes. We kind of wrap it tenderly around. It is a kind of Christmas present, for we have only half abandoned our belief in Santa Claus.

The Man Who Liked to Come With the News

In spite of everything, it gave her a secret pride to know that she did her job well.

Her practice was to start with a client's legs, moving in soft figures-of-eight from ankle to thigh. She did ten, maybe twelve strokes like this, both legs at once, her hands moving in time with each other. She liked particularly to feel her fingers press lightly on the small of the back, curve down the slope where the buttocks swelled and brush the balls with the tips of her fingers, or the soft skin just below them.

One hand helping to push the other, she worked on each leg separately, using the same figure-of-eight, taking care with the inner thigh, tucking her fingers under the part of the leg that rested against the table. Then with her thumbs in circular movements she worked up, following, as far as her ignorance of anatomy allowed, the lie of the muscles and tendons. The backs of the knees were often stiff. Feeling resistance tighten under her fingers, she would take the knee between her hands and rub it, jostling and nudging the client into relaxation.

The buttocks were straightforward. If she sensed that the client enjoyed it, she gently worked at opening the anus, testing along the ridge of skin towards the penis, but only after she'd completed her customary number of strokes, both buttocks at once, then each separately, following the pattern of the legs with her thumbs and the flats of her fingers, stretching the palm of her hand into one curved line.

She ran her knuckles up the spine and back with light strokes, barely touching the skin, then worked the vertebrae apart with her thumbs, starting at the base of the spine where Kundalini the curled snake lay resting before his journey. The large muscles of the back claimed her attention for a full five minutes, with many up-and-down knuckle and butterfly strokes. She moved the head gently into position, kneading, with one hand after another, the muscles at the top of the spine. Only then would she say to the client, 'You can turn over now.'

The man who liked to come with the news said, 'I only want a six inch massage. From here to here.'

His left hand spanned an octave, from the top of his thigh to where his hip bone made a ridge under brown skin.

He asked her to turn on the radio and then, if she wouldn't mind, to tune in to the twelve o'clock news.

'How can I give you a massage,' she said laughing, 'when they're talking about government scandals and the gala premiere of *Jaws*?'

She had to work quickly while he lay on his back, neck arched, straining to finish before the weather report. He came with his eyes open and she watched them clear.

'Would you like a cup of coffee? No, tea, we're out of coffee.'

He didn't answer, and after a moment she asked, 'Are you all right?'

'Well,' he said, 'that was worth every penny.'

She smiled, wiping her hands on a towel. 'Would you like a drink now?'

He allowed his head to flop back on the pillow. 'Do you think we could go again?'

'You want another massage?'

'I think we could go again, don't you? I'm not in any hurry.'

'I thought you were in your lunch hour.'

'They can wait.'

'You'd have to pay the same again.'

'Of course.'

'No, she said, 'I don't want to massage you again. Save your money for another day.'

'After all, I think I will have some coffee.'

'Tea.'

'Tea then. Black with two sugars. That is, if you'll join me.'

She washed the strong sweet stuff around in her mouth and her eyes clouded over with steam. Every movement made in that room she remembered having made before, in a sequence with only the slightest of variations. Each had a price attached and added to the next, refused to be an occasion.

'What were you doing before this?' he asked her.

'I was on the dole.'

'I see. What made you decide to work here?'

'It's a long story.'

He smiled. 'Are you always this talkative?'

She smiled back, though she was irritated.

'I'm thinking of leaving and going back on the dole.'

'You'd better do it soon. Anyway, it doesn't matter about the massage I enjoyed the one you gave me.'

He dressed quickly, without speaking. He was already away, his mind on the next thing, steps in an orderly sequence.

The following week he turned up again. This time he paid for extras while in the background, overshadowed momentarily by a passing train, they heard that a minister in the Labor government had been dismissed.

'I thought you were Labor from the way you poked and prodded me,' he said. 'I could tell you were angry. I'm Labor myself.'

'He doesn't seem to have done anything so terrible. Apart from talk to the wrong people.'

'Absolutely the wrong people, especially at midnight, alone in his office.'

'I suppose he tried to cover it up, and that's what they got him for.'

'He put the wind up the mining companies. If he'd had his way, the government would've gone into competition with them.'

After he left she sat at the window and day-dreamed.

She didn't see him again for several months. She kept the radio on all day, imagining for some reason that she'd recognize his voice and find out his name. She learnt the voices of the different newsreaders with their trained stops and starts.

One week she took all the furniture out of the room, except for the table covered with a white sheet and two white towels. She gave away the few prints, ornaments and pot plants with which she had tried to make the place her own.

Each half hour was separate, distinct, measured by the alarm clock and the news, regular accusations against the Labor Party. The changes to the room, plus her attachment to the radio, gave her a sense of security and at times a kind of cleansing relief.

When the newsman appeared again, the first thing he asked her was. 'Didn't I see you at the Melbourne Cup?'

'You might have,' she told him. 'I went with one of the other girls. I saw Kerr on TV – did you see him? It was a bit of a victory for us, to get the day off. We never get clients on public holidays. They're all home mowing their lawns. Why didn't you come and say hello?'

'You were a long way off.'

She massaged him in silence. At the end of the news there was the weather report. They were perfectly timed. She noticed that she could concentrate on the movements of her hands in such a way that the announcer's voice receded almost to a whisper. Then she felt something else, a slow betrayal of pleasure creeping up from the balls of her feet.

'We're all overworked here,' she told him. And then, because he nodded, 'Why do you come here, then?'

He couldn't tell her or didn't want to. She guessed that his reasons were as mundane and predictable as anyone's.

'Will you vote Labor if there's another election?' he asked as they drank their tea.

'Sure,' she said. 'I don't think they'll win though.'

'Don't say that,' he interrupted with a quick laugh.

He turned to the mirror. She was about to offer to fix his tie. Sometimes the small services – tying their ties, washing the oil off their backs – pleased them more than the massage. She stayed where she was, half sitting on the table, swinging one leg, because he was already wearing his work face.

'I guess there's bound to be another election,' she said, 'and there'll be a big drama, but in a few months' time everything will be back to normal.'

The client gave his hair a last stroke behind the ears and put the comb back in his pocket.

'What's normal?' he asked as he folded the money neatly under the ashtray. She didn't look at it.

'I suppose this place is normal.'

'You think this is normal?'

'As normal as shitting once a day,' she said.

She never saw him again. She became skilled enough to concentrate on giving a massage and at the same time to absorb each bulletin without missing a thing. That was how she followed the political crisis to its climax, in sharp, speedy bursts of news that paused over a single phrase only long enough to be scandalized. When the announcement came that the government had been sacked she felt a bond of confusion with other listeners who were preparing tea meanwhile, or driving home through the suburbs. If any drivers swerved, coming back to themselves with that shudder from the groin which said, 'another inch and I would have hit something', if any housewife cut a finger instead of the beans, watched a thin horizon of blood cover the barely porous green vegetable and was brought back to herself with a start, if any of these things happened because the newsreader's voice broke long enough to allow ordinary concentration to shift, then it was quickly over and everything began again as if perfectly normal.

Mary Fallon

WORKING HOT

you toss me about toss me around between your hands 'not your common garden variety fuck' said Freda Peach I roll my palm back and forth across your pubic hair pudenda rolling soft dough flat on a board I have you dancing on the end of this pin doll I can wind the music box to a torture of a fever pitch I can make you toss and twitch a white boat on a sea of spit a white corpse eyes wide open that old rock and roll washed over and into brought to life with these here electrified wires – ten fingers – in the right place plug into sockets I feel the jolt right up to the eyeballs you have been condemned to the electric chair I am the one with the responsibility to pull the switch but I must admit I am the one whose back arches it is then we are in the thicket together the thickest and tightest part of the night's exercise and I know on this Godforsaken planet in this world of scarcity and lack you lack nothing there is nothing stinting nor niggardly that you are gorged and sated and that I have provided that there is no give and take no economy worth speaking about does the ocean count the number of waves it gives and tick and tote it up against the number returned there is no checkout chick in this bed no invoice or inventory.

that body that Vienna loaf that Camembert that avocado that glaced fruit that marzipan iced fruit cake

you come over and over
so quick
so many times

I'm thunderstruck
I'm flabbergasted
I'm in awe of my fingers
(the tips tingle if we haven't fucked for a few days)
'come and give me a kiss' said Toto
'here and here and here and one here'

'I can't get enough of your mouth' said Freda Peach
and she couldn't

I was a mouse running along a live wire between two terminals
– your hands
you ran me back and forth
back and forth I ran

going to sleep with you holding me saying I love you because
. . .
over and over – and you even had reasons reasons like a contract

'the girl with the magic mouth' said Freda
and I was

'. . . you could cry like that every day' said Freda Peach cold
'. . . do you mean me do your mean I could or one could' asked
Toto
'. . . anyone could we could all cry like that every day if we
wanted to if we didn't stop ourselves'
'. . . come to me' she said
how many people can say that without it sounding ridiculous but
she can Freda can Freda Peach

the essence of what is in my hands running through to you in
my mouth batting like a moth tongue around a bulb but breaking
the bulb breaking through to the live wire between my teeth satisfied (a knack for loving a skill something I do well – well well
well good for me)

such pleasure this morning – pleasure – the word warms my
groin runs circles around my clitoris rings it a noose a festoon
that is strung from the tree in my guts and they strain and bend
with a weight as ponderous as pleasure – pleasure pleasure
pleasure singing down through my mouth open onto yours and

into yours and your jerked head and your shut eyes your left arm outstretched going down on you is all joy all exploration the eroticism of trust (even respect) saying you you you . . . with my tongue

(where do you hide your knives and the red eyes even going down and coming up I am vigilant for the touch of steel blade of pain you must hide something somewhere we women have all baited booby trapped our bodies I am not naive enough to believe there is no concealed weapon come on now honey let me frisk you)

'Ah I madly love . . .' Genet 'but fate had ways of opening my eyes or of opening the darkness in two so I could see into it.'
– the orgasm the point of intersection the point where all erotica erotic language etc attain that apex of vibrating life (a snapshot – this is me on my wild goose chase)

'Then I was filled with the gloom that suddenly comes forth at the approach of death. Our hearts cloud over. We are in darkness.'

waking up arms around your neck and breasts thinking oh shit the washing pay the rent buy the wood for the bench and you wake up and we're kissing and it's so warm and drowsy and I say no no today we won't spend all day in bed today I must do the washing pay the rent get the wood for the table ring about the paint . . .

'what about the washing?'
'it won't get washed'
'what about the rent?'
'it won't get paid'
what about the table it won't get made
what about the paint it won't get bought

– passion and excess (yum yum)

bereft stranded beached

image
a woman with her legs apart masturbating furiously under flood-lights in an empty stadium

image
a swamp being drained

image
you deliberately sopping up gravy with chunks of bread

image
you treadling determinedly and mechanically on an old Singer
sewing machine the needle stabbing in and out of material under
your keen eye

image
the image as tight as a pearl milked from me
realizing you're just lazy
'You're just Freda, just a fucking lazy lover'
'Yes I know. It's true. I am.'
Toto masturbates
a voyeur rubs her breasts and belly
saying to herself
'It means too much
   divest it
It means too much
   divest it
It means too much
   divest it'

Oh I am bereft stranded beached
your body is then sometimes
such a honeycomb
then
such a rock
I am suddenly
   breaking
      my
teeth
   and
fall back
off you
humiliated

'We desire to be desired,' says that bitch Freda Peach, 'chew me,'
she whispered hoarsely, 'chew me.'

    and
in my mouth full
my imagination and
imagining full of
a flesh flower

– a fat marzipan rose
– an intricate radish rose

a sex salad
a lucky muff diver
what a lucky licker
muff diver dyke
sportswoman chewer
glutton to some

you say
'You'll never have enough'
    or
'You'd come at anything'
to be full of you
is to be full of myself
like a fat shadow
(here is a secret for you
I have discovered the shadow orgasm)

you fall asleep like a kid with a belly full
apple cores and passionfruit skins
composting at the bottom of the bed

at the bottom of the bed
is where your head was

I found a tongue twister
engorged in the tuft of your muff
I stuffed

OK now you try it

Joanna Murray-Smith

AND SHE GAVE ONE TWIRL

The shadow has reached the wreck. The rusty old *Saint Nicholas* is clothed in warmth for a last few seconds, and then swallowed in darkness. That means it's eight o'clock. Henri should be back by now.

I run out along the track at the top of the cliff above our beach and search the bay. I long for the brightness of day. It's so hard to see anything, now the sea's skin is darkening purple. The williwaws are starting, the wind coming up. On the sked* this morning I heard the lighthouse keepers talking to each other, jovially sympathizing with the nameless yachts caught between anchorages.

The wind is coming! The wind is coming! Goodbye to those quiet days, the lazy evenings sitting on the Dragon's Teeth listening to the cool music of the lapping water. The wind is coming! How long, I wonder, before the hut is pounded by the breath of Bass Strait. Henri and I must pull everything up off the beach. The tides will drink deep tonight. The nets must be carried up to the shed, and the life jackets and the dinghy must be tied down. It's too late to swim the raft in – I should have done that earlier, in the lunch-time sun.

Well, perhaps it won't be so bad. If the rain comes, the rest will quieten. The sun is now well past the wreck and has almost caught up with me. Another five minutes and the whole beach

*Short wave radio schedule

and bay will be consumed. The big light will go out and our lights will go on. They're getting stronger! And where is Henri?

Henri is always playing games with me. He thinks I am too serious. He thinks these islands are a playground, and that he can train me to enjoy life more by scaring me – that a few frights will make me react less. It doesn't work and I don't like it. I love Henri but I don't like his games. He hasn't grown up on this island. He hasn't weathered its blows.

I suppose that Henri is watching me look for him. Huddled in one of the far coves in our little dinghy with the motor stilled. He is probably laughing because I'm standing on the cliff-top beginning to get frantic. He can see me worry, pulling my scarf around me, clutching it, waiting to hear the growl of the outboard over the water. I will scream at Henri when he comes back. I have had enough. If he could see my eyes he would come home.

In front of me where I stand two curving arms stretch out either side, embracing the bay, gathering in the water. The hills rise from the cliffs, nursing the clusters of spitting sand-blows. Then the land flattens and dips to the other side. It is strong, and I can feel its mass supporting me. Perhaps I could pinch out the wind?

Just as I decide that Henri is drowned, he comes in. The boat turns the corner and I run down to the water to hug him. He grabs me in his vast woolly arms and kisses me passionately, as he likes to do when I am angry. We pull the boat up on the rollers and turn it upside down so the wind cannot flip it. Henri ties it down and we carry the odds and ends up to the shed. He washes from the tank and puts on his red jumper and corduroy pants, his evening wear.

I light the wood stove in the kitchen and fill the box with billets to last the night. He lights the gas mantle. He looks so tall in this little hut. The white-washed, sailcloth ceiling and wall-linings billow in the breeze that creeps in through the crannies. Henri takes out his diary and ink and pen and sits at the kitchen table in thought while I prepare the pie. He looks up and smiles at me.

I don't feel so happy. For one thing, he has no right to be so content when I have been so upset. For another, the din outside is growing. I am still annoyed about the raft, and the unease I felt earlier is still with me. Henri is safe, but I never feel quite safe when the winds get loose to savage us.

'Henri, please don't stay out so late. I was getting worried. Especially in this weather. Don't go to Nautilus Bay again. Don't turn the corner of the bay. The nets can wait for daylight, Henri, or for another time.' I look at him pleadingly. My mind is beating fast, don't laugh at me, Henri, don't laugh.

Henri puts his pen down slowly and looks up at me with his sly eyes. His mouth opens. He looks serious, but I know that mouth too well. The line breaks and he laughs, throwing his head back.

He sees me glum. I put the pastry leaves in the centre of the pie and put it carefully in the oven. I throw some more wood into the stove and fill the kettle. I look sad. Henri reaches out and puts his arms around the tops of my legs, pulling me over to him. I sit on his knees. He speaks gently, and my anger flows away.

I wake in the dark and wonder if the hut will survive. I try to calculate the age of the drift wood it's built from, battered by the sea even before it was hammered into place on these walls. The wind could have come millions of miles to taunt us. Starting as a little breeze in South America, or Morocco, or amongst the ruins of Delphi. And we have just three rooms here. The gale butts the corners ferociously, and the curtains billow out like sails. I am too scared to move. Can the sea consume us? I wish I knew. Can tidal waves come from anywhere? Are we safe? Where is the yellow brick road?

Henri sleeps beside me, his brow unfurrowed. Why doesn't the wind eat away at his ears, as it does at mine?

I lie next to him and beat out the puzzles in my mind. I am part of this island. And Henri is not. It is simple. How can I expect anyone to live here who cannot feel with it? Henri is not of this island. For him it is only a scene. Henri's life is carefully con-toured to his body.

When I look out the window in the morning I see vast splinters on the sand, lumps of shredded wood. The waves pound over and over. Where the raft used to be is swirling grey. Henri brings me a cup of tea. He has already spoken on sked to the light-keepers over the way. He has ordered some supplies to come out on the next boat. It was force ten during the night, and the wind is not subsiding. Perhaps it never will.

I sit in the kitchen and try to concentrate on my book while Henri writes his articles. His typewriter grates at my brain. I wonder what is happening on the other side of the island. It's possible that some boats are caught there. You can never know. A year ago a yacht from Devonport was trapped there for two weeks, without a radio, running out of supplies, and we didn't know. There could be a boat there now.

'Henri, do you think there could be some boats over the other side?' What do I mean, 'could'. Of course there could. Why do I have to be so tentative with Henri. It's ridiculous.

'Shall we go and check, Henri?'

Henri looks up at me and grins, as if I had just said something naughty. Go suck eggs, Henri.

I grab my coat from the back of the door and rush out. I can hear him push back his chair and come to the door. I am already half-way down the track. My cheeks are stinging. He calls out, 'Don't be so silly, Joanna!'

The island is strained today. There is the heaviness of battle everywhere. I find the cattle sheltering in the casuarina grove in the centre of the island. They look tired. I am tired too. The weather tears at me. But over the saddle the island is sheltered from the easterlies – I can hear the wind, but the air is still over here. No boats. I think I'll sit and watch for a while.

Henri cannot fit into the grooves of this island. He uses it, or challenges it. He plays games with me, and he plays them with the island. He teases it. It's his way of demonstrating his strength. But he doesn't understand his adversary. The island is playing games with Henri.

I have always thought that Henri knows everything, but now I see that he does not. I rush back to save him. The wind lifts me up and across the island.

It is chaos back on our bay. I have never seen the weather this tough before. The *Saint Nicholas* will be a junk-heap by morning. The rocks each end of the bay are quite submerged, the waves bashing half-way up the cliffs. The beach has been swept bare in graceful patterns – completely deserted, not a bird in sight or sound. In a minute my head will be pushed off my shoulders: is it hinged solidly enough?

I can barely see the other island across the Pass. Has it sunk? No, I can see the light. Flash, flash, flash, long pause. It's only two o'clock and they've lit up already. How many sailors will go down tonight? She gave one whirl and she gave one twirl and she sank to the bottom of the sea, the sea, the sea, and she sank to the bottom of the sea.

Henri will laugh when I tell him he must leave. I walk into the hut to face him. But he is not there. His pen and ink lie on the table, and the fire is still burning in the stove. The hut vibrates and shudders. I check the shed, and he's not there either.

'Henri!'

'Henri! Henri!'

My voice is hopeless – a tiny whisper caught up and carried away by mighty currents. I'd have to rip my guts out to get my words a yard away. Jesus, such desolation! Where is he?

The boat is gone. Nothing can survive out there.

I turn and walk to the hut. Waves leap and loom across the Pass. I lie down on the bed to sleep. Henri would be pleased – I am calm. I can even manage a smile. I'm alone.

J.M.S.Foster

OH I DO LOVE TO BE BESIDE THE SEASIDE

She's dead as earth . . . No, no, no life!
Why should a dog, a horse, a rat have life,
And thou no breath at all? Thou'lt come no more,
Never, never, never, never, never!

Shakespeare, *King Lear*

Memorandum

I recall the day was bright and sunny. Ladies in white muslin
with parasols of many shades walked easily up and down the
prom. The air was alive with the screech of gulls; children laughing excitedly as they rolled their hoops up and down the street.
The hawkers cry, 'Boiled mussels, get your boiled mussels. Sweet
floss my prettys, pink and sweet.'

It was mid-afternoon; in front of the hotel the red and white
marquee rolled lazily in the light breeze. Iced lemonade was
served. A small girl with violets on a worn brown tray wandered
through the crowd.

It was the summer holidays. We stayed there every summer;
my mother enjoyed its easy formality. She had many friends, politely inclining her head at every greeting. She looked beautiful
that day, a pale lilac dress, with delicate lacing covering her
slender arms. She wore a large hat surmounted by a white egret's
plume.

'Would you like an ice-cream, John?'

She ran her fingers through his hair. He was small and dressed
in a blue and white sailor suit.

'Yes please, Mama.'

He jumped up and down beside her.

'Now John don't get too excited, you'll only tire yourself out
... Simon would you like one?'

'No thank you, Mama.'

She didn't even look at me.

Madeleine

A pretty girl with a snub nose; a riot of blonde curls. She was
said to be pretty with her deep blue eyes and rosy cheeks. She
was staying at the same hotel; her father was away on business,
something to do with tin mining. John liked her, and they played
together in the small rose garden, played tag. She would run and
John would chase her, emitting little cries. My mother smiled
indulgently, saying often to Madeleine's mother, 'Don't they
make a pretty pair.'

We met her that day at the ice-cream stand. She smiled coyly
at John who stood there, legs astride, like a conquering hero.

The beach was covered with deck chairs, each one bearing the
insignia of the hotel, a crown and scallop.

I grabbed my mother's arm; her skin was soft and smelt of powder.

'Mama, do you know what the crown and scallop represent?
Mama?'

She turned. For a brief moment she looked annoyed, her brow
was furrowed.

'What is it Simon? No I don't know what they represent.'

I let go of her arm, blushing deeply.

'The scallop is the symbol of pilgrimage to the shrine of James
of Compostella; the crown represents martyrdom. It is said that
James calmed the uneasy conscience. Why do you suppose they
have them on the deck chairs?'

'I really don't know Simon, perhaps you should ask someone.'

She turned away from me.

'Now John, why don't you and Madeleine go and play on the
beach, but don't go too far.'

My mother smiled wistfully, her fingers toying with the lace
collar of her blouse.

'Come along Simon,' she said. 'We shall sit here and watch

them play. Or better still, why don't you go and build me some castles. I'll sit and watch you.'

'Mama, I would sooner sit with you. I can read to you.'

'No Simon, it is such a lovely day, you should be out playing. Now off you go.'

She waved me away, did not even look at me. She was watching John and Madeleine wander off down the beach.

I dug a hole, the sand was wet and the sides continually fell in. I found some shells . . . (The family went swimming, but the cliff collapsed and one of them was drowned. The funeral was lovely, the small coffin covered in white lilies. My mother cried, but I took her hand and consoled her.)

'Simon, can you see John and Madeleine?'

'No Mama, I can't.'

I quickly climbed the steps and joined her.

'They've been gone for a long time. Where are they? I told them not to go far.'

She was very pale, her eyes roved distractedly over the beach.

'Come along Simon, we have to find them.'

She took my hand and squeezed it tightly, pulling me along after her.

We soon left the promenade and walked into the main street which ran along the beach front. With each step my mother was becoming more and more distressed. I kept tripping over her skirts.

The accident

My mother stepped off the kerb. I dropped my book and stooped to pick it up. Suddenly someone was screaming, 'Watch out lady.'

My mother stood frozen in the centre of the road, her mouth open in a soundless cry, her hands shielding her face.

The cart smashed into her.

She crumpled like a doll.

'Maaaaaaammmmmmmaaaaaaa!'

The weapon

A rag and bone cart with heavy iron wheels. The driver was terrified.

'I just turned my back; it must have broken loose from its holding. God it was an accident.'

The murder

She lay on her back, her eyes nearly closed. A thin trickle of blood ran down one side of her mouth. Her breathing was heavy; it rattled. She looked surprisingly calm. I knelt beside her, covering her face with kisses.

'Mama, Mama, please don't die.'

The wheels had rolled across her chest.

She merely closed her eyes.

The murderers

Judas and Babylon.

I am the mighty hand of Judgement said the Lord.

Simon

Listen, the old train is on its last legs, mid-morning run mid-week to Sutton-on-Sea. The carriages are all but empty – an old woman with a snub-nosed Pekinese; in mourning, no doubt for all the dear departed. A gentleman and his white chalk pipe, the front of his suit covered in a fine grey powder – billows of smoke hang about the trunk rack. A smart young man, neatly pressed suit, stares langorously out of the window at the passing landscape.

It hasn't changed much; still the same black and white cows wandering lazily between bright yellow gorse. The sky is a pale grey, dotted with seagulls, the spire of Saint Stephen Martyr a stark silhouette.

A light rain; out of season.

The young man pulls a watch from his waistcoat pocket, taps the glass and then places it to his ear; 11.30. At least the train is on time. He will not have been waiting too long. Why on earth does he want me to meet him here of all places. I suggested the city, but no it was important. (I don't ask many favours of you . . . try to put yourself out just for me.) His telegramme had been abrupt yet commanding. 'Meet me Sutton-on-Sea, 11.25 Monday. You will not refuse, love . . .' I feel a strange responsibility for him. I can't explain it, probably something to do with his weakness, his inability to pull things together. I rang him.

'Hello.'

'Hello.'

'It's a bit awkward. It means taking time off work.'

'Well, you can do that can't you?'

'Yes, of course I could manage it, but that isn't really the point.'

'The point is that you will come.'

'Yes, of course, but . . .'

'No buts, be there. I will meet you at the station.'

'Yes, all right. Goodbye.'

'Goodbye.'

He slammed the phone down. I stood for quite a while with the receiver buzzing in my hand.

Why on earth Sutton-on-Sea, and at this time of year.

I pleaded death in the family.

The last time I was in Sutton, besides the honeymoon with Madeleine, was the day of the accident. We had gone down for the summer holidays. We were to go boating, or at least I was; he built castles in the sand. It was a warm day. The red and white marquee in front of the hotel tossed and turned in the wind. A small girl – Madeleine was her name – wore a white dress. We ran along the beach and hid behind some rocks. I bet her half a bag of sweet rock she wouldn't dare show me her knickers. She slowly lifted her skirt . . . white cotton with small blue ribbons about the legging.

The train pulled to a halt. He was standing on the platform, clouds of smoke from the engine obscuring his face, his left hand, palm outwards, level with his shoulder. I busied myself with my bags. On the wall of the restroom the Sutton sea girl perched on her rock, long brown limbs in a pale yellow bathing suit. She smiled invitingly: Welcome to Sutton-on-Sea, playground of the North.

Suddenly there was a knock at the window. He had pressed his hand to the glass, the splay fingers drumming slowly. I smiled and waved.

He is shorter than I am, in fact much smaller. His shoulders a little stooped, they always were. Still wearing the same rimless glasses. His eyes, though small, have a strange intensity; due to short-sightedness of course, but nonetheless . . .

He tapped again.

'Will you hurry up.' His voice was faint. I smiled, manoeuvring my baggage out of the door.

'How nice to see you,' I said extending my hand. He took it limply.

'Things have been good to you,' he said.

'Yes,' I said laughing, 'I suppose they have.'

'You suppose?' He was suddenly very serious, the corners of his mouth drawn down.

'I won't help you with your baggage,' he said. 'My back isn't terribly good.'

'Yes of course, that's quite all right.'

'My car is just outside. Come along.' He took my arm. 'Do you remember this place?' he said.

'Yes, it really hasn't changed much. Still the same Victorian functional.'

The station is of the ugly red-brick type, standard design, mock gables, small medieval windows.

'Of course you're an architect aren't you. I saw your picture in the newspaper. Something to do with concrete and glass; a big affair.'

'Oh that; nothing much, merely a swimming pool,' I said.

'Anything else about this place?' he said.

'Yes, the Sutton girl; they can't have changed that billboard for years.'

He glanced at the poster.

'She is either incredibly well preserved, or else they haven't had the courage to change the photograph; ugly thing really, always was,' he said vehemently.

'Oh no, not ugly, she's quite attractive.'

'How's your wife?' he said.

I stopped. 'She died last year.'

'Oh yes,' he said, dragging me forward. 'I forgot. There are so many deaths, one can hardly keep tabs on them all.'

The car bumped along the road, deeply pitted with holes. Dirty brown water splashed across the windscreen as the car lurched from side to side.

'I see they also haven't fixed the roads,' I said.

He was silent; the windscreen wiper scraped back and forth, forcing the water down and through little cracks in the mounting. Droplets of water ran across the dashboard and crashed onto my knees. I shifted my legs attempting to avoid them.

'We are staying at the Crown Hotel,' he said, 'in exactly the same rooms we always used to have.'

'That should be nice, although I don't suppose you had any trouble getting them at this time of year.'

'That isn't the point,' he said.

'For old times sake then,' I said, curling my legs hard against the door.

The hotel had been built during the boom of the late 1890s; heroic, preposterous. Flag poles atop the building flying the special insignia of the owner. A crown and scallop shell. They even went so far as to use it as a letterhead. Now it was somewhat jaded, the whole place duller than I imagined.

'Can you remember what I once said about the crown and scallop?' he said, as the car pulled to a halt in front of the hotel.

'No I can't,' I said.

'They are the symbols of pilgrimage and martyrdom. They were worn during the Middle Ages to signify one's intention to worship at the shrine of James of Compostella, the balm of conscience.'

'Oh yes, now I remember,' I said. 'You told us about it that day on the beach. You were fond of carrying those large books about with you. But why use those things here?'

'I was fond of reading,' he said dryly. As for the symbols, you can surely see the point.'

'Yes; let's go in, I'm getting drenched sitting here. Your car leaks.'

I opened the door and got out, staring up at the façade of the old hotel.

'How long have you been here?'

He slammed the door shut and moved to open the boot.

'The trip down is quite enjoyable,' he said. 'The train still has the same compartment we used to travel in. The one with the picture of the Sunday band, the promenade of ladies in flowing muslin, a bright sun, boiled mussels for sale. It's reassuring. Here's your baggage.'

'Thank-you,' I said, puzzled by his avoidance of my question. Are there many others staying at the hotel?'

'A few ladies,' he said as we mounted the broad sweep of steps facing the building.

'If you don't mind, I will leave you to your own devices until dinner. I'm sure you would like to refresh yourself. The staff will take care of anything you need.' He took my hand, stroking it rather than shaking it. 'Until this evening.' He turned and walked out of the front door. I watched him disappear down the promenade. His heavy overcoat billowing in the wind.

The room was exactly the same as I remembered it; an ugly conflation of bits and pieces, the old armchairs still wore the same sweat-stained anti-macassars with appliqued peacocks. The room faced the seafront; it was cold and damp. A dull grey sea tossed itself against the seawall, scattering a fine spray back across the prom into the sand bowl, falling against small trees, coating the windows with a soft mist. Away to the right, the old wooden pier jutted into the sea. It visibly shifted as the water rose and fell. I could see him pacing the deck, every now and then raising his arms like some large bird attempting to take off.

'I've taken the liberty of ordering dinner,' he said, unfolding his napkin and placing it on his lap. 'I hope you don't mind.'

'Not, not at all.'

He sat very erect in his seat, dressed in a black suit and tie, his face still flushed from his afternoon walk.

'Anyway, if I recall correctly the food never was terribly good here, was it?'

He slowly removed his glasses, cleaning them on the edge of his napkin.

'The food is plain but well prepared; it is sufficient,' he said. 'You have a very curious way of dressing.'

He placed his glasses on his nose and peered at me over the top of them.

'Oh come now, a sports jacket and a polo neck jumper are quite acceptable, surely.'

'It depends on where one is I suppose,' he said.

'This type of dressing is quite run of the mill these days,' I said.

'Yes of course. Eat your soup or it will get cold.'

The dining-room was empty except for two ladies primly seated by the bay windows, the silence complete but for the sound of soup spoons intermittently hitting the sides of the bowls.

'How long have you been here,' I said, attempting to subdue a mounting sense of discomfort.

'A few weeks,' he said. 'Why?'

'Oh, I just wondered. Why did you come?'

'Surprising as it may seem, I've always liked this place. I find it very peaceful.'

'I would have thought it would be too painful.'

'Painful? Why painful?' he said.

'Because of what happened here.'

'What did happen here?' he said, laying down his spoon and leaning back in his seat.

'The accident of course. You must remember.'

He sat there with his chin propped on his clenched hands. His eyes fixed on me.

'Yes I remember,' he said. 'Perhaps you could tell me what you remember.'

His voice was strained, the knuckles on his hands white.

'I really don't think there is any point in going over that.'

'No please, I am genuinely interested. Memory is such a deceptive thing, our very nature makes us prone to distortion. You should be familiar with that, remembering some things, forgetting others, a dash of colour here, a paling there. This instance should prove all the more interesting, the two of us, related, remembering something that has presumably affected both our lives. Call it a swapping of information. Pretend we are cameras, the more information, the more true. To make it easier I will get us both a drink. Yours is scotch, isn't it?'

'Yes, but . . .'

'Please, if nothing else, it could prove amusing.'

He rose quickly from the table and walked off towards the bar. I was decidedly uncomfortable, the whole atmosphere of the place conspiring to add to it. The fog horn blared out its melancholy note. Small bracket lights had been turned on and their pink shades threw a sickly light over the room. Shadows loomed in the corners; the windows appeared boarded up; the air close, heavy with the smell of ox-tail soup and old foxgloves.

'Here we are,' he said, placing my drink down in front of me and sitting down.

'Thank-you. Tell me, how often have you been back to this place since then.'

'Many times. I told you, I find this place peaceful. Now, please go on.'

'I've been here only once, on my honeymoon with Madeleine; she said it reminded her of our first meeting.'

'Yes, the little girl with the blonde curls. You met her that very same day didn't you.'

'Yes, on the promenade, we stopped to buy an ice-cream.'

'How did she die again,' he said turning the glass in his hand.

'You know she was run over,' I said.

'A hit and run. A milk truck wasn't it? Out on Shipham's Road, just to do the shopping, she stepped off the kerb and the truck literally rolled over her. She didn't die instantly; crushed ribs, punctured lung. You were off drinking with a friend and by the time you got to her it was too late. A tragedy they called it.'

'Yes, damn you, it was a tragedy,' I said, placing my glass heavily down on the table.

'Please, there is no need to get upset. I am merely trying to arrive at the truth.'

He reached across the table and squeezed my hand.

'Going back to the other accident, where were you when it happened?'

'I was with Madeleine. We went for a walk. How was I to know Mama would come looking for us.'

'But she did . . . and the cart broke loose.'

He closed his eyes, his lips tightening.

'Where were you?' I said.

'I was following her, trying to tell her not to worry. She was so distraught. You did say you were only going for a small walk. She stood for ages gazing down the sands.

'But she knew I could take care of myself,' I said, hurriedly drinking what was left in my glass.

'You were only eleven. Heroes are very rare at that age.'

'You speak as if it were my fault. How could I have known?'

'If you had been more attentive you would have known that it was in Mama's nature to worry. She did after all adore you . . . her strong little man.'

'You sound almost bitter,' I said.

'Bitter? What on earth for, you obviously had all the talent. One small cry from you and Mama was the replica of God's ministering angel. Your mission, if one may call it that, was to be her strong, happy little man. You did it beautifully.'

'I don't think there is any point going on with this conversation, it merely causes us both pain. Goodnight,' I said rising
from the table. 'I will see you in the morning. Perhaps tomorrow
you can tell me why you brought me down here.'

'Isn't it perfectly obvious?' he said.

'No it is not,' I said angrily. 'Goodnight.'

I could not sleep so I sat by the window watching the rain fall
about the street lights, forming multi-coloured haloes. A strong
wind blew off the sea, the window rattled incessantly. I placed
my hand against it, the heat causing a shifting film to trace its
outline. Slowly I became aware of a figure pacing the seafront;
he wore his long black coat, his arms rising and falling in the
same gesture that I had seen that afternoon.

I was suddenly seized by a desire to see his room. I opened my
door and peered down the hallway. Only row upon row of those
pink lampshades.

His room was exactly the same as mine except that it looked
more lived in, as if he had been there for years; indeed, as if he
had never left the place. On the wall above the bed was a drawing
of the crown and scallop shell surrounded by thousands of
minutely drawn heads, all eyes fixed on a point above the crown.
There, sketched in exacting detail, was a picture of my mother,
her eyes blank.

To one side of the bed stood a small table, heavily laden with
what looked like picture frames. I turned on the bedside lamp
to discover literally hundreds of pictures of my mother, myself
and him. I remembered how, upon my engagement to Madeleine,
he had demanded all the pictures of my mother in my possession.
I had given them to him largely because Madeleine had insisted.
She felt sorry for him; he was so pathetic. He had called for them
one evening. Standing in the open doorway, his large coat
wrapped tightly about him; more like a spectre than a human
being. When I handed him the shoebox full of the photographs
he smiled in a way that I had never seen him smile. He looked
almost relieved, as if some part of a great burden had been lifted
from him. And now, here they all were. I looked at them closely.
In each of the photographs he had scratched out my face, placed
a small black circle about his own, and actually painted in, with
gold paint, a halo about my mother's head. In the photographs

taken the year of my mother's death he had cut me out of the picture and draped my mother in long robes, with himself in the attitude of an adoring putti. My mother wore a crown, he wore the scallop shell.

The question he had asked upon arrival at the hotel suddenly became frighteningly clear. I felt sick, realizing that my exclusion from this obsessive reverie could mean only one thing. I was the damned, hers the martyrdom, his the pilgrimage. I turned off the light and left the room.

When I came down to breakfast the next morning I found that he had already eaten but was sitting there waiting for me. He merely stared as I sat down, gesturing to the waiter who stood poised by the scullery door.

'Good morning, did you sleep well?' he said.

'As a matter of fact, no I didn't. The storm kept me awake for most of the night. Did you?'

'No, I was out walking.'

'Walking, in that weather?'

The waiter handed me the menu and stood to one side waiting to take my order.

'I'll have the kippers, thank-you.'

'What do you mean you were out walking?'

'As I said, I happen to like that sort of weather.'

'Simon, tell me,' I said, adjusting my chair, 'how long have you lived here?'

'I told you yesterday. Not long, a matter of weeks.'

'That is not true, I checked with the desk staff. You have lived here for a number of years.'

'Why did you do that?' he said, drumming his fingers on the arm of the chair.

'I don't know, just curious. You seemed far too settled.'

He gripped the arms of the chair and leant across the table, his eyes startlingly bright.

'Since when have you been interested in what I do?'

'This place isn't good for you Simon. How long have you been here?'

'Fourteen years.'

We were disturbed by the entry of the two old ladies who

assumed the same places, modestly nodding their heads as they walked past us.

'Fourteen? That's how old you were when mother accidentally died.'

'Exactly, fourteen years this week. This little reunion is a sort of celebration.'

He leant back in his chair, smiling triumphantly.

'Simon,' I said, rising from the table, 'I am afraid your little celebration has come to an end. I am going back. I refuse to be a party to your malevolent little jokes.'

'Jokes? Oh no, you take it all too seriously. But if you must go,' he said, moving around the table and taking my arm, 'let us at least say our goodbyes in private. Your train doesn't leave for at least another hour. We will go for a walk.'

I was unable to refuse. He pulled me towards the door. We stood for a moment at the top of the steps, the sky was clear but overcast.

'Come, we'll go to the garden,' he said.

A pale sun slipped from behind some clouds, briefly illuminating the small puddles of water on the steps. The sea, flat and motionless, resembled, for a moment, a large bowl of quicksilver.

'When did you say your wife died?' he said suddenly.

'Last year Simon, you know that.'

'Yes, unfortunate hit and run.'

He stopped and took hold of me by both shoulders.

'Do you feel deprived? What punishment do you think would be fitting for the murderer?'

I shook myself free, and stepped back.

'As far as I know Simon, it was not murder. Anyway it would be out of my hands, a matter for the law.'

'The law, oh yes.'

He rushed ahead of me, flapping his arms, laughing loudly. Suddenly he stopped and screamed at the top of his voice.

'Retribution is mine said the Lord. An eye for an eye, tooth for a tooth. Much better isn't it.'

I followed him into the garden. A series of formal rose beds surrounded a leafless tree, small gravel paths of loose red stone snaked their way between the beds.

'Simon, for God's sake pull yourself together. It was an accident, any number of things could have caused the driver to keep going; fear, anything.'

'Or pre-meditation,' he said. 'You can't discount the possibilities.'

'Simon that's preposterous. Who would want to deliberately hurt Madeleine, she was . . .' The way he looked at me made me stop in mid-sentence. He stood with his head bent low, his arms raised in the air.

'Go on,' he screamed, 'she was?'

'Nothing Simon, I must be going.' I turned back and walked towards the gate.

'Before you go, I have a present for you.'

He handed me a large yellow envelope.

'Go on, look at it. A little gift to remember our reunion.'

I opened the envelope. Inside were two photographs and a letter with the word memorandum scribbled across it. One of the photographs was of my mother and the two of us taken in that sorry year. I had been cut out and tacked on to the bottom of the photograph upside down. My mother was encased in a golden light. Simon smiled triumphantly out of the picture. Somehow, he had exaggerated his usually nervous smile into a grimace, at once triumphant and vicious, the fingers on his left hand pointing downwards.

'What does it say, read it.'

His voice was shrill; he was balancing from one foot to another slowly raising and lowering his arms.

Around my neck hung a small sign, and on it in a tiny script I read the word 'Judas'.

'Simon, this is not funny. What does it mean?'

'It is not meant to be funny,' he screamed. And now the next one.'

The other photograph was a picture of Madeleine and myself on our wedding day. Simon stood in the background staring glumly at the camera. He had filled in the eyes of my wife and traced what looked like tyre marks across her chest. His left arm was extended over my head, and rested above Madeleine's, in imitation of the hand of judgement.

Simon broke into an appalling laugh as I stared at him blankly. He turned away and walked off towards the pier. Suddenly he called.

'Goodbye Judas, think about it.'

He ran off, his arms flying wildly about his head. A gust of wind scattered sand in my face. I raised my hands to shield my eyes and walked slowly back towards the hotel, out of the garden.

Growing, Ageing

Murray Bail

HEALING

The quality of miracles has declined over the years. In Adelaide, a flat city, 'the city of churches', we all went around on bikes. I am speaking here of the mid-1950s. My father, for example, rode an Elliott. It was a heavy machine, bottle green, with leather cleaning bands rolling around the hubs, silver-frosted handlebars, and a seat sprung with two thick coils like hair curlers. My father with his grey face and his pitted bike clips; arriving home after the Magill Road climb, he'd lean the bike under the grapevine and rest in the darkened kitchen with a sarsaparilla. It was a three-mile ride from where he worked. Yet – and I still believe this – our bikes and the pedalling past dry hedges somehow signify the period, the white light and optimism of the fifties. They fit in very well. The man across the street subscribed to the *Saturday Evening Post*. Things just seem more complicated now.

I said Adelaide is a flat city. Well, it is and it isn't. It looks flat on the map or from the air, but the wide intersecting streets contain an inbuilt slope of private dimensions, barely perceptible, often invisible to the naked eye. The city centre is located halfway between the sea and the perpetual purple backdrop, the Adelaide Hills. Our days consisted of coasting into the hot empty air, then pushing slowly back toward the hills. Magill Road here was a classic. It ran from the foothills to town, about four or five miles, straight and smooth, wide and harmless-looking. But try cycling up one day.

It was on Magill Road, about a third of the way down, that I saw the accident. I was one of the few.

Denis Hedley was considered a smart-alec. His bike was an Elliott, like my father's, but he had stripped it of the mudguards and painted the frame canary yellow and black. Around the wheel rims he'd painted a checkered flag pattern, which at low speed made old people dizzy. But its most conspicuous feature, and the thing that attracted ridicule, was a plastic aeroscreen he'd fitted, as on a racing motorbike, over the handlebars. The handlebars were black and horizontal, also like a motorbike's. Hedley had made them from a piece of pipe. Closer inspection – though we tried not to give Hedley the satisfaction – revealed other significant modifications. Every possible strut and clamp, even the bell, the wing nuts, and parts of the pipe frame, had been drilled with holes to save weight. Hedley was too smart to talk much, but he confided casually one day it gave him extra speed. And it was a blurred yellow-and-black fact that he dominated the upper reaches of Magill Road. Crouched behind the aeroscreen, legs pumping like wheels, Hedley would streak past trams and the small British sedans at thirty-five or even forty-five miles an hour and, reaching the Burnside Road intersection, which is near our street, would suddenly sit up and coast no-hands, sometimes combing his hair or scratching the small of his back. Then he'd brake, turn around, and laboriously climb back for another run. That was how afternoons were spent in Adelaide. He was thick-necked and of course had pimples and oily hair. He wore tight khaki shorts. Hedley was also well known for his fourteen-year-old sister, Glenys. She had damp hands and a cowlike smile. She was the first girl in our district to suddenly begin wearing a brassiere. On this particular morning, my chain had come off and I was squatting down by the footpath. It was a quiet Sunday, hot; not many cars. As I say, I was one of the few to see everything. I happened to look up as Hedley went past. He had Glenys sitting sideways on the top bar – something I had not seen before. I could see they were going too fast. Hedley seemed to be struggling with the handlebars; Glenys was rigid, holding too hard. As they passed No. 1839 Magill Road – and, oddly enough, I realize now, that was the year the bicycle was invented – Hedley's specially lightened frame appeared to buckle slightly, or fold, and because of his indiscriminate drilling this placed sudden strain on the brake strut. It snapped. It had been drilled too much. The back wheel then slid forward, throwing the chain and all hope of braking. What followed could only be called a chain reaction. The atrophied pipes of Hedley's bike, the drilled and countersunk sprockets and levers all began cracking and splitting, the little aeroscreen flew into the air, bits of broken metal and spokes fell off and jumped all over empty Magill Road like black sparks. The machine, no longer a bicycle, began weaving and contracting, approaching the intersection.

And then from behind came Boardman (that rings a bell for me!) on his mauve Healing. It was the latest model, with alloy guards, three-speed gears; Boardman was the local Healing dealer. As usual, he was riding with a lighted cigarette. With superb balance and strength for a thin man in his forties, with tremendous cool, he rode in close and, pedalling in top, lifted Glenys off and onto his serene handlebars. By then Hedley's tangle was almost at ground level, still sparking at high speed, and Hedley had one leg trailing. Again Boardman leaned over and down, this time more like a polo player, and grabbed Hedley by the collar, supporting the careering machine and halting further disintegration, while with the other hand he applied the chrome-plated brake calipers on the Healing, weaving to a halt across the intersection. At the last second Hedley lost his grip. His bike somersaulted in the clarity of that Sunday morning, snapped around the veranda post of Townsend's corner shop, and lay in two or three pieces. Glenys's blouse was badly torn; I could see her ochre brassiere. She immediately began swearing at her brother, and I realized she had grown up. She was no longer a girl.

Hedley stood there, one shoe missing, surveying the wreck. Boardman lit up another cigarette, waved, and rode off. I have not seen anything like it since. Boardman is dead now, and I don't know if they make Elliotts anymore. Hedley and his sister must still be alive, grown up. My father is dead. A Shell service station has replaced Townsend's corner shop, and the intersection has been fitted with lights.

Rob Duffy

UNTITLED

Today i am meeting with a school friend in the mid city centre. he is greeting me. 'long time.' we are adjusting to unfamiliar appearances and to a belief that this happens. he is ignoring my smoking and introducing his fiancée. she is looking young and carrying kitchen utensils. i am pretending to be excited and wanting to know how long has this been going on and when is the date. it's soon. i am already inhaling with greater frequency finding less to say and wishing i'd walked along market street.

i am unaware it is ridiculous to feel embarrassed because i do not have a fiancée.

Today i don't have a fiancée and am cast as interested: i am listening like school and the whole story is coming out neat in period time. he is being adult about a project home at mount warrigal and modest about the deposit. she is looking at her reflection because she is involved. he is pretending not to notice that the passing of time makes conversation difficult. he is dealing with our problem by summarizing his recent life like a novel plot outline. i am encouraging him to reach the climax by asking about his job which justifies mount warrigal and the kitchen utensils. he is grateful and talking confidently about a traineeship at the steelworks but then has to ask about me and learn i am still studying.

i am unaware it is ridiculous to feel embarrassed because i don't have a traineeship at the steelworks.

Today i am not a member of the Steelworks Family and have to emulate his Confidence and Ambition. it is sounding as hollow as the plastic rolling pin protruding from her package. she is telling me what school she went to and hoping i know one of her friends. i do and light another cigarette. (he looks away.) they used to play netball together. she is telling me about this person who is apparently just the same as when i knew her and this confirms for all of us that nothing ever changes. i am pretending for a moment that i still do not smoke. after my politeness i am asking if he still plays tennis and for this he is even more grateful than the traineeship. but i am trying to avoid saying i haven't played for years.

i am dimly aware it is ridiculous to feel embarrassed because i haven't played tennis for years.

Today i am not a Tennis Player and i am asking about his family. we are each newly embarrassed at the large number of topics in our short conversation. his mother is being pedantic about wedding arrangements. his father is resigned and unenthusiastic. the Generation Gap has never been so welcome. sister is flying in from the states with two year old kid. (no mention of husband.) none of this has happened yet. we are already talking about school, as if education had something to do with the future. i am being invited to the wedding. i am writing my phone number on a foolscap sheet. it is looking isolated and ridiculous as i am fumbling, folding, handing it over. 'take care.' i am smiling like a loon.

Walking away i am unaware that tomorrow i will decide with relief that she must be pregnant and that she has not found True Love.

Helen Lewis

SKINNING PEACHES

Tears of sweat are trickling down the girl's face. She's lying in the sand now, thinking. The hot sand is stinging her skin. Leon is stinging her mind. She wonders what she wants of him and is uncertain. She fears though, there's no disguising that. She fears the surrender in her mind.

Lately, this gorge hasn't been the refuge that it used to be. The heat is leaden. It squeezes the water out of her. The river moves slowly, as if it, too, struggles under the weight. Only the cicadas have energy. Incessant, unthinking energy.

The gorge is full of symbols. Instincts. That's why she comes. At this moment she is poised between langour and desire for the cool murkiness of the water quietly turning close by.

She stands and walks slowly into the water, one step at a time; feeling the chill creep higher, watching her feet disappear into the algae suspended depths, leaning forward, parting the water and slipping underneath. All becomes washed and light. Sounds rise and die as the water laps against her ears.

The gorge wants to contain her. She wants to comply; to lie supported by the strength of this body of water and loose the animal.

She leaves the water, accepting the full weight of her body again, sinking back into the langour, reflecting that Leon would like this place. Her skin tightens as he strokes her neck, sliding his hand down to her breasts. She moves her hand as if to push his away but stops involuntarily. The pressure of his hand is

smooth and gliding. Opening her eyes she sees the black head
of a snake resting between her breasts.

The snake remains motionless. She likewise, afraid to breathe,
remains motionless. The snake moves again, slipping forward to
her belly, pausing, then moving again. She can feel the un-
dulations of its body pushing against her. She can just see its
head moving through the curl of hair, disappearing between her
thighs, under the arch of knee and across the sand. The rest of
its body follows slowly. Shuddering, she sits up to watch the
snake drop into the water and curve its way across the gorge.

'Why does the snake cross the gorge?' she says, laughing, then
stops. Somehow the question isn't so funny. She lies back in the
sand disquieted, wondering why she wonders so much, wondering if the snake knew the erotic path it had traced down the
length of her body. Did it pause strategically?

A shadow moves across her. Looking up she sees three boys,
young teens. She notes the interest and embarrassment in their
eyes. They are lean and brown, wearing surfie shorts, towels
round their necks.

'Hello,' she says.

There is a pause as they exchange conferring glances.

'Are you a skinny dipper?' says the tallest one.

'I suppose so,' she replies. 'A closet skinny dipper.'

The other two shuffle their feet. 'C'mon Nol,' says one.

'Closet,' she answers to Nol's challenging gaze. 'A place where
you do things you don't want anyone else to know about.'

'Oh,' he grins. 'Like playing with yourself.'

She smiles. 'Something like that.'

Nol looks at his two uncomfortable companions. 'Sam and Poss
here, think you don't want us about. Do you mind?'

'No, I don't mind. Stay if you want.'

'C'mon Nol,' says Poss. 'Let's get at the water.'

Nol lingers a moment staring at the girl. 'Okay, let's go.'

Dropping their towels they run; throwing themselves into the
water, sending spumes of foam cartwheeling through the air,
bouncing their voices across the gorge. The girl watches, leth-
argically in awe of their energy. At last, panting and dripping,
they relinquish the water. Nol flings himself on his towel beside
the girl. After some hesitation, Sam and Poss do likewise.

'Did you see a snake?' she says.

'No,' says Nol. 'Why, you 'fraid of them? I bet you are.' She shakes her head. 'Huh, I bet you are too.'

'Would you like a drink?' she says reaching for a basket that is in the shade of a casuarina tree.

'Yeah, what you got?' Nol still the spokesman.

'Rosé, soda water or orange juice. A mix is good.'

'I'll try it,' says Nol.

'How about you two?' she says.

'Okay by me,' says Sam nonchalantly. Poss is trying to avoid looking at her. When he does, his eyes seek and hold hers a little desperately. She feels that he of the three of them has not lost the caressable look of youth.

'Would you like some?' she says holding the eye contact and smiling specially for him.

'Yes please.' He stares at his feet.

She pours the drinks saying, 'We'll have to share, there are only two cups.'

They drink and refill, drink and refill, until sated. They take the peaches she offers them. Poss and Sam start to laugh at the peach juice running down their chins. Nol is carefully pulling the peach skin back and flinging the red cloying strips in the sand.

'I can't stand all that fluff,' he mumbles to himself.

The girl laughs at this. Sam and Poss laugh with her for laughter's sake. Nol just smiles the smile of someone who knows he has not quite grasped the joke.

'What do you do?' he says quickly.

'Do?' she says, stifling her laughter. 'I'm a student.'

'Does your boyfriend mind you skinny dipping?'

'You're assuming I've got one.'

'Does he?' Nol demands.

She hesitates. 'It's . . . it's not his problem.' She searches Nol's face for the look of triumph at having been proved right. But it was not there; not a smug assumption, just a childish tenet.

'What's the problem then?' says Nol. The question draws blood, but Nol is not aware of it. It is the alcohol making him parrot her words.

Feeling hunted, she looks at Poss. He is curled at her feet, no longer inhibited. He smiles at her, stroking the soles of her feet. Sam is playing God with an ants' nest. Relaxing she turns back to Nol. 'What's Nol short for?'

He scowls limply in reply.

'Well?'

Sam has been waiting for an opening. 'It's Noel. He doesn't like it 'cause we always used to sing that carol to him. Y'know, thee firrrst Nooel . . .'

'Shut up.' Nol looks belligerent. Sam and Poss break into giggles.

'Who's the Noel Coward fan in your family?'

'Who's he?' says Sam.

'Just a writer,' she says, trying to catch Nol's eye.

Sam and Poss are clutching at each other with repressed laughter. 'Not much like Nol then,' Sam manages to say. 'He can't write anything – he hates English and . . .'

'Yes I could.'

'You said you . . .'

'Schools different, isn't it?' he says, appealing to her. 'I mean things at school are never like real things, are they?'

'No, there is a lot they teach you that's never like the real thing,' she says, closing her eyes and leaning back on one elbow. She is aware that Nol is watching her and that he realizes he is still on the outside of her thoughts.

A piercing cicada silence opens between them.

'I'm going to skinny dip.' Nol is on his feet and pulling off his shorts. 'C'mon,' he says to the bemused Sam and Poss, 'get y'gear off.'

They mumble their reluctance. Poss looks from the girl to Nol. Sam is dragging his shorts off. Kicking free of them he reaches across and tugs at Poss's shorts. Poss looks at the girl again but she is fumbling in her basket. He slides his shorts off slowly.

'You'd better put some of this on.' She surveys the translucent whiteness of their exposed parts. Nol takes the block-out lotion and begins to slap it on carelessly. He passes the bottle to Sam and Poss.

'All over,' says the girl to Nol. 'That would be the worst part to burn.'

Nol flushes slightly, hesitating to touch himself. He complies quickly. Finished, he turns his face to the sky and yells. The sound starts far back in his throat, rolling up in pitch and volume. Sam and Poss pick up the cry. Siren like, their cries gather in intensity as they echo through the gorge in a strange primal round. Giving a final cry, Nol sprints away towards an outcrop of rocks. Sam and Poss pursue him.

For ten minutes they run, leaping, hiding, shouting and crashing through the scrub, then, without word or signal, stop and return to her. They kneel in the sand, sucking in the air, sweat dripping from them.

'Let me do that,' Nol gasps as she starts to apply oil to her arms and legs.

She hands him the bottle. 'Could you do my back please?' She turns her back towards him.

Nol pours the oil into the palm of his hand and gives the bottle back to her. With both hands he starts to rub the oil in, moving from her shoulders to lower back. The oil makes the movements smooth and gliding and she begins to be aware of the rhythm of his hands as they move further round the sides of her body.

'Thanks, I can do the rest.' She turns to look at him, but he moves quickly.

'It's time to swim,' he says as he splashes into the water. He turns and mouths a jet of water at Poss and Sam who are lagging. 'Let's explore those rocks.' He points to the other side of the gorge. They strike out fast and splashily; their voices become indistinct as they near the other side.

The girl watches them until they reach the rocks and haul themselves out of the water, then she lies back in the sand. The heaviness of the heat and the wine is upon her again. She remembers the snake; the ease with which it glided over her and through the sand, its suppleness, its place in the gorge. Soon she is arguing with Leon.

He remonstrates with her over keeping the snake. She replies softly, trying to reassure him. He is no longer listening, he is speaking at her. His voice becomes shriller and louder. She wakes suddenly, clenching handfuls of sand.

The boys are screaming their strange primal round. It is harsh now, sharp-edged. The gorge shudders with the reverberations. She feels fear crawling across her skin. Standing up she can see the boys on the other side of the gorge. They are crouched with sticks in their hands. She knows they are hunting.

Nol motions the other two to wait while he climbs up to a narrow overhang of rock. The ledge is in shadow and she cannot make out what he is stalking. They fall silent as Nol edges forward to the overhanging rock. He stops, swaying slightly as he settles his feet for a better grip. The cicadas claim the silence briefly. Then Nol, taking the stick in both hands, lunges forward shouting. He makes a wide scooping movement under the ledge and a black snake comes spinning out with the force of the thrust. It lands on the rocks just in front of Poss and Sam. They hesitate momentarily, but Nol leaps from above, yelling and beating frantically with his stick, and they follow his lead.

The girl watches. Her lips move to form the word 'NO' but it is too late and too soft. The snake twists a few times, after which it dances only to the beating of the sticks. The yelling dies from the gorge and the boys fall back from the body of the snake. It doesn't move but Nol pokes it with a stick cautiously. With both hands he lifts the stick above his head and cheers. Then all three of them turn towards the girl, waving their sticks and cheering.

Nol picks up the body of the snake, dives into the water and starts to swim back. Poss and Sam dive after him. The girl stands motionless in the sand. Nol stops swimming and stands. He walks forward until the water is down to his thighs. Poss and Sam are besides him. Smiling he holds up the limp body of the snake.

He assesses the girl's expressionless face. 'It's okay, it's dead. It's really dead. You're safe now.'

She stares at the dangling body, forming her hands into fists. Tension sets in her face, the veins of her throat standing out. Poss is watching her closely. He moves towards her.

'Well?' says Nol impatiently.

The girl looks away from Nol to Poss. She opens her mouth to speak but is stopped by Poss moving towards her. Falling to his knees he clings to her waist, pushing his face into her belly and sobbing.

Nicholas Jose

THE INCOMPARABLE

When we were young we thought of her as the incomparable. Our yearning for art and romance was naive, but no less intense for that. To our budding selves she was the embodiment of all that was beautiful. By magic or privilege she had the grace and knowledge we all awkwardly strove for. It was an article of our faith, as well as a fact, that she was exquisite. Her tallness helped to set her apart. We argued about whether she was slender or just thin, which was a question of whether she was more Renaissance or more avant-garde. When she danced she was stiff, which we took to be a high mode of expression. Sometimes she was uppity despite herself. I've often wondered how conscious she was of her rare gifts. Whether she wanted it or not, she had us all ravished. It does seem rather ridiculous now. The girls used to go round whispering of their special intimacies with her. The wildest, sexiest girl in the group went mad with mocking jealousy whenever she was near. Each of us boys at one time raged or ached for her. One bloke, in drunken frustration, kicked in a plate-glass window to show what he would dare. For my part I had a fine and subtle perception of her, and I flattered myself that she valued my just esteem above all else. I had a print of Botticelli's *Primavera* on my wall, the loveliest thing mankind had ever created. In my eyes the middle lady, the garlanded one in a swathe of damask, not quite touching the ground, was the image of her. Only in this case life surpassed art. When I looked into the particular violet of Willa's eyes, it struck me as quite incredible that such perfection should be there and alive. But I never said anything about it, of course.

You mustn't think our relationship was superficial. Willa and I spoke of everything under the sun, except ourselves. As we grew into sharp logical people, for whom honest communication was vital, we recognized in each other the staunchest of friends. As others in our group drifted into ephemerality, Willa and I became more important, and constant, to one another. We were both a little surprised by our maturity. You suspect it won't happen, until one day you discover that you've become sensible, can cope, and have taken control over your life. Willa had an impressive grasp of the world and showed me the way. In long evenings she toughened up my feeble notions of politics and power. She was remarkable, and no future seemed beyond her reach. Yet an effortless enchantment clung to everything she did. Even when she was unhappy, and pressed her fingertips against her temples in sheer impotence, it was lovely beyond words.

My twenty-first birthday came on the eve of my long foreshadowed departure for Europe. I was off travelling. When people asked how long for, I replied, 'Forever.' If they scoffed, I added in defence, 'Even if I do come back one day, I won't be the same person. You'll never see this me again.' That always got a laugh, perhaps out of affection for the old self who was making his last appearance. The party was an aimless affair with a throng of guests who knew how to have a good time, even when there was little sense of occasion. It spilled from the cramped backyard of the townhouse to the scrub-covered reserve beyond, which marked the end of the suburb and sloped up to a great black hill. Willa was there, looking spectacular. She wore a heavy blue velvet robe she'd got from God knows where, and from her ears hung glittering drops of outlandish crystal jewellery. Her long wispy hair was piled up on top. Towards midnight began the ritualistic playing of classic rock songs. The speakers were outside under the trees and everyone was drunk. Willa led me by the hand to a clear space where we could dance. Her movements as she started were angular, even fierce, as she stepped and turned on the strewn bone-white bark. The weight of her dress was lifted outwards and the moon was in her face. It was as if the song were hers. I don't know if anyone else even noticed.

But her solitary circling dance has stayed in my memory absolutely.

At the end she fell against me and burst out breathlessly, 'What will I do without you? It's going to be *awful*! You're very precious . . .'

It took me some time to settle after that. I roamed about for more than a year, alone or with casual companions, leading a spare existence that was large in self-indulgence, uncaring except for the petty inconveniences of travel and the odd glimpse of the sublime. I was in Italy, where things were cheap, and finally in Venice, a consummation devoutly wished, except that the youth hostel was putrid and I couldn't afford a gondola ride. I was sick to death of my backpack, and also, I suppose, homesick. One dank evening, when my ears were pained by the relentless clang of my own feet against the green flagstones, I saw a concert poster. *L'Incomparabile!* It announced a song recital by a lady currently reckoned the *prima donna assoluta*, so through a maze of alleys I sought the illustrious theatre, got a seat and waited. The other tourists in the gods looked as crumpled, as hungry and blank as I felt.

The singer was a statuesque, silver-haired Italian with a gypsy sway from the hips up. Her accompanist was an unobtrusive, mottled Anglo-Saxon whose quiet attunement allowed the soprano to give herself to us with such passionate singleness. I listened carefully, through Mozart and Mahler. Then, at a certain point, I was physically transported. I don't mean that I left my seat. It was a sensation I hadn't had before, nor since. No doubt my loneliness was a factor. Suddenly, as in a vision, the large-spirited lady on stage became a Renaissance grace, resonant in flesh, who told me forcibly to wake up to myself.

L'Incomparabile. I knew what that was in my terms. That night I wrote to Willa. I've blocked out what I actually said. It embarrasses me to think of it. It was long and roundabout and full of talk of 'the thing I value most in life', the highest pitch of my romantic worship. In an oblique form, which I was sure she would understand, I proposed that we should come together in a life-long bond. Simply putting it on paper seemed enough to make it happen.

As usual it was some time before I heard from her. When it

caught up with me, her postcard addressed me warmly. She made no reference to my letter – either way. She gushed briefly about Venice and said it was ghastly at home without me. She said she had no one. I really didn't know how to take it. The problem was I couldn't be sure my letter had reached her. But I took it as a defeat and admired her superb tact.

Half a decade slipped by. We both prospered, I in my studies and career, Willa in her commitment to social reform. We met, under changed circumstances, when I moved back to the same city. She was married to a whizz-kid from the Treasury who was a nice bloke, though I never got far with him. They had set themselves up well and had a busy, good-humoured, engaged life together. They were very kind to me when I hadn't quite found my feet. They entertained frequently, and it was always a pleasure to be with such intelligent, civilized people. When at the end of a long afternoon's lunch Willa offered me a second cup of coffee, and another chocolate, I was truly content. She would beam with serenity and gladness, or stifle a tiny yawn, and perhaps in her eyes I could catch a shadow of her old surprise at how things turned out.

   Once, as a gesture, she invited me to a party after a rally in which one of her community groups had been active. Her friends were interesting, but on this occasion I couldn't involve myself with talking to them. I preferred to stay in the kitchen, helping Willa prepare savouries or running about as waiter. I worked hard, clearing away debris and replenishing glasses, and cherished the sense of a connexion with Willa that was older than anyone else's at the party. We began to talk in snatches about what had happened in the intervening years. But she sniffed disdainfully at any hint of reminiscence. She was strictly concerned with what the past could show of directions for the future. 'It's incredible how long it took us to learn not to waste our energy on childish things,' she said. 'Don't you think?' She was tired, and her strained expression seemed to underline the lessons that had made her pragmatic.

   But I couldn't resist easing back into our old intimacy. There was nothing she would not fully understand. I was about to speak when she was called away to see someone off at the door. I had to ask her about my letter from Venice. I was curious to know, and the time had come when it was possible to speak. It was necessary to discover if she'd had my tribute, now when she was exhausted from the rally, and sociability, and spreading a hundred biscuits. But she was stuck at the door in a demanding discussion of political strategy. I could hear how clear and tough-minded were her views.

Her husband found me waiting in the kitchen and joked that I was the last one left. He offered me another drink and abandoned me to it. 'I've had it – tell Willa I've gone to bed, will you?'

When the front door slammed I knew my chance had come. I caught up with Willa in the hall and we stood there anxiously in the dim light. She smiled and leaned against the wall, pressing her palms flat to its surface. She knew I had something on my mind, and was uncomfortable.

'Do you remember,' I began, 'when I was in Venice? Did you ever –,' I stopped.

'Don't,' she said, as if she'd had enough of all conversation. But for a second she was lit up with joy.

'Did you ever –,' I repeated solemnly.

At that her face became very stern, and she laid a finger on my lips to hush me. Then she opened the door for me to go, and I complied. We said our goodbyes and thank-yous and I hurried across the lawn, waving back when I reached my car. She closed the door, and in the last of the hall light I think I saw a further quick incomparable flash of joy, because that is what I felt, too. She had known what I was going to ask and that was proof. Although she didn't want it brought up to the light, she hadn't forgotten. The house went dark as I drove away. I had offered my utmost, and she had taken it.

Frank Moorhouse

FROM A BUSH LOG BOOK: GOING INTO THE HEARTLANDS WITH THE WRONG PERSON AT CHRISTMAS

That Christmas he went into the Sassafras bush with Belle, his decadent friend.

They had debauched in motel rooms and restaurants along the coast while he turned forty, spilling champagne on the bed sheets, games at midnight with live lobsters, and sadistic conversational games over restaurant meals because they had exhausted amiable conversation and because she was so young and did not have true empathy with his 'becoming forty'. He wanted now to be in the bush away from the clatter of breakfast trays, away from the somnolence of lying on beaches, and away from cars and roads and towns.

He also had some home-yearnings which came on at Christmas. His family was not in town for this Christmas, but anyhow his home-yearnings had been displaced over the years away from his family in the town to the bush about a hundred kilometres away from, but behind, the coastal town where he had grown up – the Sassafras bush in the Budawang Range.

It was where the Clyde River started as a trickle and then quickly cut a steep, deep gorge and flowed down along the coast in wild country hidden from the highway until it appeared fully grown and slow, moving into the sea at Bateman's Bay.

On Christmas day Belle and he left the motel at Bateman's Bay at the mouth of the Clyde and went up to the other end of the river. He had put the camping gear into the car when he left the city, half intending to go into the bush somewhere. They drove as deep into the bush as the road permitted and then left the car and backpacked their way, meeting up with the trail originally marked in 1939.

As they walked in the bush he kept glancing at Belle to see if she was being affected by the dull day and the bush. He knew about the creeping hysteria and dread which the Australian bush could bring about.

She saw him looking back at her and said, 'I'm coping. Stop looking back at me all the time.'

They walked into the bush for an hour or so and came to what is called Mitchell Lookout.

'This is called Mitchell Lookout,' he said, 'but as you see it is not a lookout in the Rotary sense.'

It was just a shelf of rock.

'The growth is too thick,' he said to Belle. 'You can't see down to the river in the gorge.'

'I can see that the growth is too thick.'

'Laughably the only thing you can see clearly from Mitchell Lookout is directly across the gorge – they could have another lookout there which looked across at Mitchell Lookout.'

She looked across at the other side of the gorge and back again. She made a small movement of her mouth to show that she didn't think it was all that laughable.

'I don't go into the bush for views,' he said.

'You tell me, Frank – what do you go into the bush for?'

'I go into the bush to be swallowed whole. I don't go in to look at curious natural formations; I don't marvel at god's handiwork.'

'I don't mind looking at god's handiwork if it is theatrical enough.'

For reasons he could not explain and did not record in his log, he decided to put the tent there on the rock ledge overlooking the gorge.

'You'll find sleeping on rock okay,' he said. 'It is really much better than you imagine.'

'If you say so,' she said, dumping her backpack.

'I go for the unanalysed sensory experience,' he said. 'I don't go in for naming things geologically or birds and so on.'

'You don't have to apologize for not knowing the names of the birds and stones.'

He cut some bracken fern to lie on, more as a gesture towards the idea of what made for comfort.

He put up the tent, pinning each corner from the inside with rocks and tying the guy ropes to rocks.

'It's really okay,' he said. 'I have at times used a rock for a pillow.'

'I believe you,' she said, sitting, one leg crossed over the other, cleaning dirt from her painted fingernails with a nail file.

He instantly doubted whether he had ever used a rock for a pillow and whether sleeping on rock was okay.

'There,' he said, 'the tent is up.'

She looked across at it, got up and peered inside the tent but did not go in.

'How about a drink?' she said.

'Sure, it's the happy hour.'

She laughed at this to herself.

'I'll cook the Christmas dinner. That'll be my contribution,' she said.

'No,' he said, 'that's okay – I'm used to cooking on camp-fires.'

'Look Frank, you're not the only one who can cook on camp-fires. I can cope. I grew up in Australia too, for godsake.'

As they had their bloody marys, pre-mixed by the Company of Two, Fresno, California, he doubted whether she could cook on camp-fires.

'I came through the Australian experience,' she said, making a gesture at the bush.

Belle was a sexual friend. They saw each other now and then out of good simple lust – which was never quite enough to support their doing anything much else together. Nothing very extended. They had already over-extended this jaunt. He had never seen her cook a meal. It was always restaurants and Hilton hotels.

'I've been out in the bush quite a bit,' he said. 'It was my idea to come out here – so let me do it.'

'I'll cook the Christmas dinner,' she said. 'Don't you worry yourself about it.'

'Well okay, if you feel happy about it.'

'I feel quite happy about it, Hemingway.'

She made a low slow fire just right and rested the pannikins

and camp cooking dishes on the coals. It wasn't quite the way
he would have done it. He would have had stones in the fire on
which to sit the pots. She sat them on the wood coals. But he didn't
say anything – it was her fire.

Wood coals looked stable until things tilted and spilled as the
wood burned away. Unless you kept pushing the pots down into
the coals to stabilize them.

She squatted there at the fire. She put on the rabbit pieces –
which they had not themselves hunted – after smearing them with
mustard and muttering to herself 'lapin moutarde' and laughing
to herself. She wrapped them in tin foil and then wormed them
down into the coals with a flat stick. Then she crossed herself.
She put the corn cobs on to boil, candied the carrots with sugar
sachets from the motel, put on the beans, wrapped the potatoes
in foil and placed them in the coals. She then heated some lobster
bisque, throwing in a dash of bloody mary.

She put the plum pudding on to be warmed and mixed a careful
custard.

She did all this with the dishes right down on the coals of a
slow fire, squatted there on her haunches.

She squatted there at the smoking fire, stirring and moving
pots as needed, throwing on a piece of wood at the right time,
all with what, he thought, was a primitive control. He swigged
bourbon from a World War I officer's flask and passed it to her
from time to time. She squatted there in a silent trance, full of
attention for what she was doing.

He swigged the bourbon and, on and off, became a World War
I officer. She had slipped into postures which belonged to the
primitive way of doing things back – when? – a thousand years
to when the race cooked over camp-fires.

He sat off on a rock and took some back bearings using his
Swiss Silva compass and Mapping Authority 1:25,000
topographic maps, trying to identify some of the distant peaks.
He was in a different technology from her.

'We are at Mitchell Lookout,' he said, after some calculation,
'definitely.' He was not really so positive.

'Good,' she said.

He kept glancing at her, marvelling at her sure control of the
fire and at the postures she had assumed from another time.

He opened a bottle of 1968 Coonawarra Cabernet Shiraz; it was in superb condition.

'It's ready,' she said, muttering something that he could not catch.

She presented the meal with perfect timing, everything right, at the right time, no overcooking, no cold food, no ash or sand in the food. It was served on the disposable plates they'd bought for the meal.

As they ate the Christmas dinner and drank the wine in the Guzzini goblets he'd bought for camping, a white mist filled up the gorge and stopped short of where they were so that they were atop it, as if looking out the window of an aircraft above the clouds.

It came almost level with the slab where they were camped and where they were eating.

'Jesus, that's nice,' he said, staring down at the mist.

'I thought you didn't go in for god's handiwork.'

'Well I don't go searching for it. When he does it before my very eyes, I'm interested.'

She looked down at the mist while chewing the meat off a rabbit bone, as if assessing the mist aesthetically – eating mainly with her fingers, with their painted nails.

'It's all right,' she said.

It was warm and there were bush flies which worried her and she kept brushing them away with her hand.

'Piss off you bastards,' she said.

'I've made peace with the flies,' he said. 'Sooner or later in the Australian bush you have to stop shooing the flies and let them be.'

'I'm not going to make peace with the flies,' she said.

'Please yourself,' he said.

'I will.'

'You did the meal perfectly.'

'You aren't the only person in Australia who can cook a meal on a camp-fire.' She laughed to herself again, 'Actually it was the first time I had cooked a meal on a camp-fire.'

'It was perfect.'

'Thank-you.'

'You looked very primitive – you went back to primitive postures.'

'I felt very primitive,' she said, 'if the truth be known.'

'I meant it in the best sense.'

'I assumed you did.'

They sat there with food-stained hands, smokey hair, food and
wine on their breath and lips. She hoisted her skirt to expose her
legs to the misty sun.

She stared expressionless at him, her hand methodically
waving away the flies, and she began to remove her clothing.
They had sex there on the rock slab surrounded by the mist.
They knew each other sexually and played with the idea of her
naked body on the rock slab, the bruising of it and the abrasion.
He held her head by the hair and pinned her arms, allowing the
flies to crawl over her face. She struggled but could not make
enough movement to get them off her face. She came and he
came.

They drank and became drowsy around the fire.

During the night he got up because he liked to leave the tent
in the dead of night and prowl about naked. He said to himself
that although he did not always feel easy in the bush – in fact
he sometimes felt discordant in it – he'd rather be out in it feeling
discordant than not to be there.

'What are you doing out there for godsake!?' Belle called from
the tent.

'Having a piss.'

He crawled back into the tent.

'I thought for a moment you were communing,' she said.

In the morning he said, 'Well, it wasn't unsleepable on the
rock?'

'No, not unsleepable,' she said, 'nor unfuckable either.'

It was still misty and the air heavy with moisture but it was
not cold.

Neither of them wanted to stay longer in the bush. He thought
that he might have stayed on if he'd been alone.

Gritty with the night and damp, and having nothing much to
say to each other, they had coffee and packed up.

'I liked having it off on the rock,' she said, 'I seem to be
bruised.'

'But were you bruised enough?' he asked.

'Hah hah.'

It was a grey sky. The bush was close to Marcus Clarke's weird melancholy. The dampness quietened everything down just a little more than usual and the dull sky dulled everything just a little more.

'Just because I enjoy all that sort of stuff doesn't mean that I don't understand what's going on,' Belle said as they walked.

'On the rock?'

'Yes. I know all about punishment and esteem. But with me it's a game now.'

He shrugged, indicating that he wasn't making any judgements about it.

"It's no longer the whole damned basis of my personality,' she said.

'You have to be a bit like that to go into the bush the way I do.'

'I was thinking that.'

They walked a few metres apart. They passed a stand of kangaroos some way off that speculatively watched them walk by. Belle and he indicated to each other by a glance that they had seen the kangaroos.

'More of god's handiwork,' she called.

He realized as they walked out that he had a disquiet about being there with Belle. When he looked at the Christmas they'd just had together – on paper – it was an untroubled and memorable and enriched event: the mist in the gorge, the perfect campfire cooked meal, the good wine, Belle naked on the rock, his standing on the ledge in the middle of the night, the melancholy bush, the speculative kangaroos.

The disquiet came from having shared all this memorable experience, in a very personal district, with Belle. Belle didn't belong there. Belle and he didn't have the sort of relationship where you shared such potent emotional things. This Sassafras bush was a place of his childhood fantasies, it was overlayed with family, it was the place where he'd been tested as a child, it was the place where he'd learned his masculinity. He had taken Belle to the very centre of his emotional life and his male self.

Now she had become a photograph snapshot which did not belong in album.

He looked at her up the trail plodding through the swampy part in her Keds, dripping wet.

Nor did he think that he was the sort of person she would have ideally chosen to share Christmas with. They were making do with each other.

By bringing Belle into his heartland and giving it to her as a gift he had left an irradicable and inappropriate memory trace across the countryside. It was a category mistake.

These sad thoughts did not alter his fondness for her, and he caught up with her and touched her fondly.

'Sorry about the mud,' he said.

'Don't think that I can't take it,' she said. 'I can take it all.'

'I'll get you a new pair of Keds.'

'They come from the States.'

'I'll get a pair sent across.'

'You probably won't.'

He thought that, curiously, her tenacity in the bush was not so much to win his approval as to demonstrate her Australian spirit.

He found that curious.

In a motel on the coast they showered off the mud, dried off the dampness, turned up the air conditioner to warm, and got slowly drunk on the floor.

He spread out a map of southern New South Wales.

This is my territory, he showed her, from up here at Camden near the city, down the southern tableland through Bowral, down to the lakes and the snow of Jindabyne, to the old whaling town of Eden, up the coast along the beaches, through Bateman's Bay to Kiama where I took my girlfriend from school for an irritable, make-believe honeymoon after we had married in the hometown Church of England.

'How sweet,' Belle said.

'That's my territory,' he said, 'my heartlands.'

She looked at the map. He marked it out possessively with a felt pen.

'There, that is the boundary of my heartlands,' he said, more to himself.

He realized as he stared at the map with that alcoholic concentration which was both focused and then discursive, that it coincided with the territory his father had controlled as a farm machinery dealer and which he'd travelled with his father, and which his father had commanded as commander of coastal defence.

'It was my father's territory exactly,' he realized with wonder.

He told her how he had been a student at schools there, had been a rebellious but proficient scout, had played hard football up and down the coast, had been a soldier on manoeuvres there, had swum the rivers, surfed the whole coast, camped out in all the bush and hunted there.

'You're a very sentimental person,' she said.

'No, I don't think I am.'

'I think you are.'

'I think not.'

'Well, a sentimental drunk then.'

As he stared at the territory he'd marked out on the map he felt as if there were someone leaning over his shoulder looking at the map, like a high-spirited late arrival at a fading party. It was mortality.

'Let's go,' he said, 'let's check out now and go back to the city. I think it's over. I'm forty now. That's over. Christmas is over. Let's drive back to the city.'

'Sure,' she said, 'that's okay with me.'

Two weeks later he went to the Sassafras bush along the trail and camped in the same place – alone. It was a trip to erase the mistake of having gone there with Belle.

After a couple of days of being in the bush he realized that it was a misguided effort. He was making too much of having gone there with 'the wrong person', and coming back to erase it had only more deeply inscribed it – and the inscription had been added to.

Now whenever he passed the place he would think of having gone there with the wrong person and of having attempted to erase it. He would laugh about Belle squatting there cooking, about the flies on her face, and her saying, 'I feel quite happy about it, Hemingway.'

Ian Kennedy Williams

THE SWALLOWS RETURNING

'Miss Cameron?'

'Yes, Mickey?'

'What'll I do with this?'

He was a small, lean adolescent, part Aborigine, and with his long dark fingers, he caressed almost lovingly, her father's old stockwhip.

'Put it in the shed with the other stuff. I really don't know what it's doing in here.'

Coiling the whip carefully, he carried it off. She listened to his clumsy footsteps on the bare floorboards, and then the sound of the screen door clanking shut as he let himself out into the yard. A few seconds hung on the air, releasing only the slow tick of the grandfather clock in the study, and far off the indignant screech of a magpie. When it came, though she was expecting it, the cold crack of the whip set her nerves on edge. She pulled herself up from the floor where she'd been kneeling over the bottom drawer of the dressing-table, and sat moodily on the edge of the bed.

The boy returned after a short interval.

'Where've you been?' she asked petulantly, 'I thought you'd gone home.'

He chose not to answer, but dug his fingers into the pile of damp smelling agricultural magazines filling the bottom of the wardrobe, and dreamed of unearthing even greater treasures.

Ruth clicked her teeth irritably and returned to sorting the bottom drawer.

It was four weeks now since the car leaving the highway some metres short of the intersection had taken in an instant the distant lives of her parents. The accident had occurred late at night, when the couple were returning from the RSL club in town. A post-mortem determined her father had drunk more than was good for him. Informed the morning after, when the wrecked car was found by a neighbouring farmer, the daughter wept briefly for her parents but refused to be too emotionally moved. After the funeral she notified a local stock and station agent that she wished her father's house, sheds and four hundred acres of grazing paddocks to be put up for auction, and then made enquiries about the purchase of a small cottage with a five-acre paddock she had seen closer to town.

John Cameron had not actively farmed his property, which the agent estimated to be worth about $150,000, for a number of years, owing to poor health. Instead, he let his paddocks out for agistment, and kept a few horses of his own for the pleasure it gave him. His wife Jean bred exotic birds in an aviary constructed at the side of the shed, and for company (for her husband had grown moody and insular with the years, and the only daughter had never been close) kept an old blue cattle dog she called Rufus to which she was devoted in a way that neither husband nor daughter approved. In deciding how best to dispose of the property, Ruth determined the horses an asset and let them stay. The birds, however, she sold privately, and the dog was put down. It had pined terribly for its mistress, and quite frankly stank, though her mother had never owned to smelling it.

'You wanna burn this lot?'

The boy had pulled the yellowed magazines from the wardrobe, and found nothing of further interest.

'Yes, and then you can clear these drawers out too. I've been through them, and there's nothing of any use.'

The boy looked at her accusingly, as though she'd said something offensive.

'That's all your folk's private things, ain't it, Miss Cameron?'

'It's just old clothes, Mickey, they're no use now. Unless you want to take them to St Vincent de Paul.'

The sour look remained on his face, and she wondered how much he resented the casual way in which she was disposing of her parents' effects. She had thought of asking him whether his family could use any of the old clothes, but was afraid he'd think her patronizing. Really, she didn't care what happened to the small stuff, as long as it was out of the house before the auction. Only the furniture was to remain: that too was to be auctioned. Most of her own belongings had already been moved to the cottage which (luckily being untenanted) she was presently renting until contracts had been exchanged. The daughter preferred not to sleep in the family home, fearing neither ghosts nor solitude, but rather finding the ten-mile drive into town to sort out her parents' affairs tiresome.

Had Ruth Cameron been accustomed to making the trip daily, she would have found it less of an effort now. But for nearly twenty years she had remained at home, a spinster, unemployed, though to all intents and purposes she helped run the farm, and then, when her father found the work detrimental to his health, she stayed on as company and help to her parents in their early retirement. Yet surprisingly she'd never been seen in town on business, or even a shopping excursion with her mother, though occasionally at night she could be found entertaining herself in the clubs and restaurants, indulging a succession of lovers, none of whom was ever invited home.

The boy had returned from the yard where he'd been stuffing the incinerator with paper. His father worked at the mill where Frank Sym, her present lover, was employed as a foreman. It had been Frank's idea that she hire the boy for a few hours this and last weekend to help clear out the rubbish before the auction. Frank had offered his own services, but she had refused them, saying priggishly that she didn't like the thought of his nosing around her family possessions. The boy seemed a much safer proposition. Frank, grown used to her ways, was neither offended nor piqued. He'd called at the home once while she was still ostensibly in mourning, and wanted for a change to make love to her in her own bed. The prospect horrified her, but aroused, she took him to the shed where they indulged each other on a blanket covering a discarded and much abused mattress. She was, she said afterwards, too old for such games, and warned him away. Once in the cottage, however, she received him more freely and without caprice, though the narrow bed was uncomfortable and poorly sprung.

'Perhaps,' she said, 'it would be better to put all the stuff from the drawers into a clean rubbish bag for now, and I'll decide what to do with it later. It would be rather a waste to burn it, wouldn't it.'

Whether or not it would, he was not saying. She told him to finish the job, and then come into the kitchen for coffee. He lumbered off, his easy unworried gait annoying her with its indolence. She tried to recall her own adolescence, but it was buried beneath two decades of unvaried, tedious existence. Only one painful post-adolescent event stood out, and that she hastily pushed from mind.

'Sit down, Mickey, there's some cake there, but the biscuits have gone soft. I forgot to put the lid on the tin when we finished las week.'

The boy might have reproved her, having previously enjoyed the biscuits particularly, but merely grunted his thanks, and stuffed himself self-consciously with cake. She guessed she overawed him somewhat, possibly because she was potentially a wealthy woman. Mickey Gunn's large family lived in a spare-looking cottage and shed that was prone to flooding in wet conditions. The council, with its policy of buying up properties on the flood plain, had offered them $5,000 for it. The father, so far, had decided against selling.

'Well, we've done well today,' she told him. 'We should be finished inside this afternoon. Tomorrow we'll clear up the yard. You're all right for tomorrow, aren't you?'

He nodded, and took a mouthful of coffee which evidently was not to his taste.

'I suppose you're glad of the bit of extra pocket money,' she said. 'What will you buy? Or will you save it, you know, put it in the bank?'

The idea seemed alien to him.

'Might buy that stockwhip,' he said at last, 'if you're gonna sell it.'

'The stockwhip?'

'Yeah, she's a beauty.'

His eyes danced a little, and she noted in them a life hitherto kept from her sight.

'How much do you reckon it'll be?' he wanted to know.

'Well . . . actually, I don't know. It'll probably just go as part of the shed stock.'

The boy's eyes clouded once more, and his jaw dropped slightly with contempt. She sensed then he harboured some grudge against her for the strength she possessed. The knowledge caught her breath short.

'Do you really want it?' she asked stupidly.

'Wouldn't mind,' he admitted with evident reluctance.

'What will you give me, then?'

'Eh?'

'Make me an offer. If it's to be auctioned, tell me what you think it's worth.'

The boy chewed on some hidden gristle, and eyed her suspiciously.

'Dunno,' he said slowly. 'What do you want?'

'Think about it,' she insisted, 'and tell me tomorrow. You must make me an offer.'

It would be, she reflected, the second offer she'd had in a week. The previous Wednesday evening Frank had called on her at the cottage, and though she would have rather gone to the club, persuaded her to stay in. She guessed he was short of cash, or more likely, as he had not arranged to call, in the mood for sex. While he nursed a warm beer (she'd turned the fridge off by mistake earlier in the day) she slouched around in a much-loved dressing-gown, and looked, with her hair down and lack of cosmetic rejuvenation, about ten years his senior. She delighted in his discomfort.

'What's the matter Frank? You've hardly said a word since you came in.'

'Nothing's the matter,' he said sourly, 'except this bloody beer. Jesus, Ruth, how can you turn a fridge off by mistake?'

'I plugged the iron into the double socket,' she explained vaguely.

'It's a bad show when a bloke's got to drink warm beer,' he complained.

'You don't have to drink it,' she snapped back at him, 'you can clear off to the pub, and drink with your mates. Do you want some money?'

He pulled himself up, and looked appropriately hurt. 'Give over. I've never bitten you for money, have I? Can't I pay a sociable visit on you without being treated like a poor cousin?'

She passed him a small sympathetic smile and poured herself

a large sherry. Shortly she left him, and went into the bedroom.
When he followed, she had discarded the gown and was sat on
the bed, her knees pulled up to her chin. Her stomach, flabbier
than in former years, pressed into her thighs.

'Come on lover, get out of your strides.'

He undressed hurriedly, but seemed preoccupied with matters
other than those of the flesh. He was lazy with his fingers,
entered her roughly, and climaxed in seconds rather than minutes. She wondered if he was punishing her for serving him
warm beer.

As he withdrew, she complained with some irony that he was
giving her poor service.

'What do you take me for,' he cried indignantly, 'a prize bull?'

She could smile at that, but refrained from answering.

Frank left the bed immediately, and started to dress. Without
turning to face her, he remarked that it was time she bought a
new bed.

'Why?' she asked. 'I like this one. And you don't spend enough
time in it to warrant buying a new one.'

He turned to her then, and said flatly, 'I will when we get married.'

'Married!' She might have laughed. 'Who said anything about
getting married?'

He fastened his belt, and then sat on the bed next to her. 'Come
on Ruthie, don't give me a hard time.'

'Hard time nothing!' she cried angrily. 'What in Christ's name
makes you think we're going to get married? Who the hell gave
you that idea?'

'Well . . .' he faltered, taken aback. 'I just thought . . .'

'Thought what, Frank?'

'Jesus, Ruth, use your loaf! Do you want to grow into an old
bag on your own? Do you think I'm gunna be coming round here
twice a week to give you a screw when you're sixty?'

'You're finding it hard now,' she sneered. 'By the time I'm
sixty, you'll be past it, married or not.'

His face crumpled, and she laughed almost joyfully. 'Oh
Frank! I'm sorry. You know I don't mean that. But really, mar-
riage, for Christ's sake. What on earth made you think of that?
We're not kids!'

He looked at her peculiarly, and didn't understand. 'Don't you want to get married?' he asked in a small, uncomprehending voice.

'No, I don't. And after knowing each other for two years, I'd have thought that was obvious.'

'Nothing's obvious,' he maintained, 'with you. As I recall, the one time we discussed marriage, you said you were perfectly happy living with your parents. I understood that to mean you felt you had an obligation to look after them, and that that obligation came before your own interests. Though I felt you were wrong, I respected your view. You were obviously very close to your parents. However, now . . .'

'Now they're comfortably dead and out of the way, little Ruthie, with half her life wasted, can now get married and waste the rest of it. Which presumably is what every woman deserves.'

'Don't mock me, Ruth, it's you I'm thinking of.'

'It's yourself, damn you,' she spat at him, 'you presumptuous bastard. Why on earth should I want to put up with you in your decrepit old age? Mend your clothes, feed you, wash your stinking underwear, all for what? What I'm getting now, and probably less. I don't have to put up with that. Frank, you seem to forget, I'm a woman of private means.'

'Private means! God, what an empty woman you are when it comes down to it! Your friggin' money won't buy you what you need most when you're an old bag before your time.'

'And what's that, Frank, tell me?'

'Love.' The word, released from his lips, was like a ripe plum, round, smooth to the touch; and vulnerable.

'Love!' From Ruth's mouth it was ejaculated like a gob of spit. 'What the hell would you know about love? Your first wife left you because you were a pain to live with. Your kids avoid you like the plague. You love no one but yourself!'

'That's not true!' he said hoarsely. 'I love you.'

'My arse, you do! You've never damn well said it.'

'Yes I have!'

'Only when you're sticking your thing inside me, and chewing me bloody ear off like a beaver. That's not loving me, Frank, that's loving your cock!'

Shortly afterwards, he left. In the meantime they managed to cool off somewhat, indeed indulged once more each other's bodies, though Frank was careful to say nothing, and kept his teeth clear of his beloved's ears. The result of this second embrace, not surprisingly, was even less satisfying than the first.

When he was dressed once more, and ready to leave, she drew him to her, and murmured, 'Just because I don't *need* you, Frank, it doesn't mean I don't *want* you.'

He nodded, apparently understanding, but left her without a word.

Driving out to the property that Sunday morning, she passed the boy cycling furiously along the highway. She tooted the car horn, but he saw fit to neither wave nor indeed look up. The act of cycling had absorbed him.

That morning they swept the yard and verandahs of fallen leaves, brushed down the network of spiders' webs, and burned off the remains of the rubbish from the house. While Mickey mowed the lawns, and weeded the flower beds (though most of the flowers, unwatered, had long since died), Ruth checked through the cartons and crates in the shed to ensure there was nothing remaining of a private nature. She found finally a small leather suitcase of her mother's, strapped but not locked, which she took into the kitchen to sort while she prepared morning coffee.

For the boy's sake, she'd brought fresh biscuits.

The suitcase contained little of interest; some old books of her mother's, a few of Ruth's textbooks, her school report cards (she'd been a poor scholar), and numerous photographs evidently considered unworthy of mounting or collecting in the family albums. Her mother had been an enthusiastic, though undisputedly amateur, photographer.

When she went out to call the boy, she nearly collected two zooming birds that might have been using the verandah as a speedway. The sudden whoosh as they shot either side of her head sent down her spine not just the chill of surprise, but a peculiar sense of *déjà vu*, as though she'd stepped out on to the verandah of years past. The phenomenon left her strangely elated.

The boy, called, threw down his trowel and approached, wiping his grubby hands in his shorts. The birds, she noticed, were darting in and out of the mango trees, like lovers chasing each other's tails, their sharp blue-black backs flashing alternately with throats of reddy brown.

The boy caught her looking.

'Swallows,' he said matter-of-factly. 'They're nesting behind the shed.'

'Yes.' She laughed hesitantly. 'They nearly dive-bombed me as I came through the door. I suppose they've got used to the place being empty. It gave me quite a fright.'

He remained poker-faced, indifferent to her experience.

In the kitchen he noted the suitcase with its scattered contents. 'You burning that lot too?'

'Yes, most of it.' She poured coffee and thrust the plate of biscuits under his nose. 'I brought some fresh biscuits for you.'

He nodded, and looked at her slightly askance, as though suspicious of her thoughtfulness. Helping himself, he turned his interest to the photographs spread across the table. 'Gee! Some of these are old, ain't they!'

'Yes, they're not very clear though. That's why they were packed away.'

He singled one out for inspection. 'Who's that?'

'That's me with my father. That must be, oh, thirty years old. The house, you can see, looks just the same.'

He looked up at her, his eyebrows knitted in deep thought. He was calculating her age.

She sat opposite him, and asked if he still wanted to make an offer for her father's stockwhip.

'Dunno . . .'

'You don't know if you want it, or you don't know what to offer?'

He nodded slowly, and she assumed the latter.

'Well then, let me make a suggestion. You know where I'm living now?'

'Old Mr Brody's place.'

'Yes, and no doubt you've seen the garden. It's a mess. How do you feel about cleaning it up, and then keeping it tidy on a regular basis, say a few hours each Saturday morning?'

'For the stockwhip?'

'No, silly, I'll pay you each week. The stockwhip's a sort of bonus and agreement between you and me that you'll keep it up. At least until you leave school. How old are you now?'

'Fourteen.'

'Well, we'll be set for a while then, won't we. What do you think? Do you want to ask your folks first?'

He swaggered a little to demonstrate his independence. 'Nah! Don't have to ask them! I'll do it.'

'Good. You come over next Saturday morning, and we'll make a start.'

'Okay.' He was shuffling through the photographs again, and plucked out one that had been folded in half. Opening it out, he viewed it for a few seconds, and then looked straight into her face, and grinned. 'That's you too, ain't it.'

She took the photograph from him, and looked at herself as she'd been at nineteen, hair lank about the shoulders, skirt above the knee, her blotchy face thankfully lost in the poor quality of the print.

'You looked real pretty, then.'

'Thank you,' she said, the unintended implication not lost on her.

'Who's the feller? Was he some bloke you was courting?'

The young man in question was stood self-consciously by her side, his new suit marginally too big for him, his hair greased and hurriedly combed back for the photograph. The lovers were holding hands.

'Was he?' the wretched boy was insisting.

'Yes. He was my first –' she looked quickly into the juvenile's face, '– boyfriend.'

'You didn't want to marry him then? He looks a bit of a dag.'

She smiled thinly. 'We were engaged for awhile, but nothing came of it.'

'Why not?'

'My parents didn't approve.'

Mickey screwed up his face in contemplation. 'Didn't approve of what? Wasn't he no good?'

'They didn't believe he was suitable. He had no money or profession. He worked as a labourer on the railways and had rather strong political opinions which my father thought unhealthy. My father was very conservative.'

'What's wrong with that?'

'Nothing's wrong with that,' she said irritably. 'Now stop asking stupid questions. I'm not paying you to sit on your backside and stuff yourself with biscuits. Come on, move! Coffee break's over!'

He moved as though struck, and took off through the kitchen door. The screen clanked shut behind him, and the magpies that had been foraging in the yard scattered squawking into the trees. She was left with her rage and despair.

Holding the suitcase at the edge of the table, she swept into it the books and photographs, bar the one creased, and then carrying it into the yard, flung it at the foot of the incinerator where it spilled its ragged contents into a heap. Striding round to the front of the house, she called the boy from where he'd resumed his weeding.

'Go over to the incinerator, and burn that damn lot.'

'Now?'

'Yes, now!'

Leaving him to his task, she returned to the shed, but was in no mood to continue sorting. She set up, and flopped into, a deck chair that had had part of its canvas chewed by rats. They'd had a cat once, a good mouser, but it had gone with the advent of the aviary. The cat had preferred birds to rodents.

She took from her skirt pocket the creased photograph and looked again at the lovers. The shock of seeing him was all the greater because the affair was long past, and she'd thought no photograph of him existed. Certainly she'd never expected her mother to keep one. In the yard the incinerator crackled, its belly consuming but never obliterating memories long soured.

When she was sure the boy had finished, and returned to the front garden, she left the shed and explored the other buildings behind it. They'd been built to house various pieces of farm machinery but had fallen into disrepair. Only the potting shed remained in good condition, because her mother had been using it up to the day of her death.

Pushing open the door, she was surprised how quicky the spiders had taken control. She had no fear of them, and was content to let them stay. Along the shelves odd-shaped pots awaited their new handler. Looking at the floor, she recalled, with something akin to fright, how she'd lain there once, bleeding slightly from a torn hymen, while her young lover wiped himself down. The pain she remembered was her father's voice sounding from the yard, getting nastier as his temper flared. He'd known they were out there somewhere, hiding in the dark, because he'd heard the car pull up half an hour earlier. She remembered pulling on her pants, the movement of blood nothing compared with the bruises she received later when her father took the butt of his stockwhip to her.

Outside, she stood in the sunlight rubbing her groin that ached slightly; psychosomatically she might have thought, if it hadn't been for Frank's antics last night, demonstrating how much the prize bull he could be when he put his mind to it. She could see him in a more approving light now that he'd stopped talking of marriage. She liked things the way they were, though she was not so foolish to think they'd stay that way forever. Frank was a little older than she, about forty-two. She entertained the thought of younger lovers.

Underneath the eaves of the shed she could see a small cup-shaped nest made of mud, and hardened in the sun. The swallows were still away from home, enjoying the freedom of her garden and verandahs. In twenty years she'd not once paused at this side of the shed to observe the swallows' nests, though she guessed they'd always been there. She liked being made aware of their presence: it was as if, after being absent for so many wasted years, they'd returned.

Folding the photograph back into her pocket, she made her way to the front garden where Mickey was digging furiously with a spade, turning the crusted earth. He ignored her as she approached, and went on digging even when she stood close to him. He'd stripped off his tee-shirt, and though it was late autumn, beads of sweat rolled down his back.

'I'm sorry I snapped at you in there,' she said. 'That photograph brought back sad memories for me.'

He paused at his digging, but refused to look her in the face.

'Is that why you never married,' he asked at length, still avoiding her eyes, 'because you couldn't marry who you wanted?'

'I suppose it is.'

'You just stayed at home, and looked after your mum and dad.'

It was one way of putting it.

'Not exactly. They looked after me.'

He looked at her vacantly, his mouth open slightly, drawing long deep breaths.

'It was the penalty they paid.'

He nodded slowly, but she could see he still didn't understand. He had no reason to. Presently he resumed his digging, pausing only when she lightly took his arm and reminded him to pick up his stockwhip before leaving.

Andrew Lansdown

ARRIVAL

September 17 Ray said that Mr Gallagher will exchange the old 1924 Overland for a cow and our hay cart. I am reserved. The car is dilapidated; it has been sitting out in the paddock for six months. But Ray is convinced. He's been bartering with Gallagher for weeks. I didn't try to dissuade him. It would have availed of nothing anyway. He's going to exchange Daisy. He says she's a good-for-nothing – won't come when she's called, kicks when she's milked. I think he exaggerates; and I'm sure if he were kinder to the beast it would be less defiant. But anyway, if we must lose a cow, it might as well be Daisy.

September 20 Ray is working on the Overland. My heart sank when I saw it. It is in shocking disrepair – worse than I had imagined. A cow and our cart for *that*! I thought; but I said nothing. To be fair, the motor does run. 'Like a clock,' Ray says. I think he is trying to comfort himself that he has done the right thing. He's working on it now, in the shade of the shed.

The crops won't be ready for a few weeks. The lull before the harvest provides no rest for Ray – though it could if he cared to avail himself of it. He has a passion for work. He never stops – or if he does, he's pining to be back at it.

September 22 I had an idea this morning, while I was bathing Cathy. (She's a good child and affords me no trouble, save the attention such a little one constantly needs.) I thought that perhaps we could use the Overland to go home to South Australia.

I am quite excited about the prospect. I can't wait for Ray to get in to ask what he thinks of the idea.

September 23 It was terrible. He was weary from working, so I should have put it off. But I was so excited I just had to ask. I don't know whether he was filled with fury or despair. I thought then it was anger; but this morning I think it was despair. 'Woman,' he said, 'we've not ten shillings to our name, and you want us to traipse half way across the country on a social call!'

It may have been a foolish idea, but I thought at least we would talk about it for a while. I remember when I was little how I used to talk about my childish dreams with mother: just to share them with her made them seem real. Well, I began to weep, and to speak wildly in my weeping. It went beyond anything I had intended. I said things I should never have said. I told him he was a brute and unfair. I told him he had promised that we would return home after the first harvest – as if he needed to be reminded. I didn't mean the half of them, and I should never have said the rest. By heaven! I wish God had sealed my mouth!

He went off this morning without breakfast. He's going to work on the car, then look over the crop. He said he'll not be back until evening. I have hurt him, and it breaks my heart.

September 29 I am cursed today. The cramps in my stomach are unbearable; and I am greatly depressed. Catherine is a burden to me, though she does not misbehave. God pity her, that she must grow to be a woman!

I can think of nothing but home today. I have been weeping all the morning for the loss of my mother. I pray that when Cathy grows up and marries she will not have to live far away. It is the curse that is making me feel so despondent; but knowing this does not help.

I started in on Ray again when he came in for lunch. 'When are we going home?' I said; and he could see that I had been crying. He tried to cuddle me, but that only made it worse, and I began to weep again. He could see I would not be comforted, so he left me to my tears and went out to work again. He had eaten nothing and took nothing with him.

October 6 I can think of nothing but home and mother. I am hard on Ray. I am wearing him down – like the nagging wife Solomon spoke of: a constant dripping upon the stone. I hate myself for it, but I can't seem to stop it. I am filled with longing for home, like the birds in Europe that feel the urge to fly south when the winter sets in. It has been four years since I have seen mother. I have a child that she has never seen.

Three crops have failed, and the fourth will probably be no better. We could not possibly have returned after the first harvest, nor the third, for that matter. It is not Ray's fault: he is not God to have power over the seasons. How we have prayed for this crop, though! But it will probably make no difference; it didn't with the last three.

Ray read from *Habakkuk* for our devotions last night: 'Although the fig tree shall not blossom, neither shall fruit be in the vines; the labour of the olive shall fail, and the fields shall yield no meat; the flock shall be cut off from the fold, and there shall be no herd in the stalls; yet will I rejoice in the Lord ...' You could tell by the way he read it that he meant it. I wanted it to be real for me, too. In my mind I said, 'I will rejoice in the Lord no matter what.' But in my heart I knew I couldn't. I wish my faith was like Ray's ...

I left off writing to pray the Lord's forgiveness for the way I have been despairing and hurting Ray over the past week or two. I feel better. He may not give us a good harvest, but He has made me clean.

October 11 Ray was nearly killed today. He was over by the shed working on the car when he saw a dingo at the sheep in the near paddock. He came running to the house, shouting for his gun. I got his shot-gun from the cupboard while he snatched a handful of shells from the drawer. He loaded it as he ran out the door. Alice, our sulky horse, was the only horse in the yard. He jumped on her back and was off. She is not a good horse for riding – though she is certainly the best we have for that purpose. As a sulky horse you couldn't do better, but she's not a rider. Ray had her heading towards the paddock at a gallop before she knew what was happening; but she shied when they reached the creek bed and threw him. The gun discharged, like thunder. Alice screamed. If you have ever heard a horse scream in pain or terror – even from a distance as I did then – you will know how it makes your scalp crawl. I snatched at Catherine and started to run; I felt sure Ray was dead. But then Alice fell down, kicking; and Ray got up, shaking. I stopped running and turned back to the house. Cathy was crying, almost screaming. She had sensed my terror and responded to it in her own way. The second shot came before we reached the house. It gave me a head-ache which has dogged me all day, even as I write.

Ray was ashen-grey when he came in. 'I had the hammers back. I should have known better.' That was all he said. I made him a cup of tea, but he didn't drink it, just stared into it until it was cold and had to be thrown out.

October 15 We didn't hear about it until this morning: the Dawsons lost their horses yesterday. Six of them dead! Nobody can say why. We lost one because of a snake bite a year ago. But six? Nobody can say why. We are all fearful for our own. We went over to see them, to offer our help. But Dawson says he's leaving – going tomorrow if he can pack everything in time.

It is a serious thing to lose a team just before harvest – or any time, for that matter. But I think Dawson is taking it too hard. Ray offered to help with our team when our work is done, and I believe some of the others have, too. And, as Ray pointed out, he could catch some brumbies and break them in time for ploughing next autumn. And besides, it might not even come to that. He might have enough money from the harvest to buy another team. But Dawson was implacable. He just cursed and said that it had been coming to this for a long time, and it was no use putting it off any longer. Ray said it was worse in the city. But Dawson said, 'We'll see.' And that was it.

October 16 We drove across in the Overland to see the Dawsons off this morning. Wilsons have lent them their bullock drays to cart their belongings into town to the railway siding. Dawson says they are going to his brother's place in Perth. The whole district came to see them off. Everyone tries not to be too grim; but Dawson's is the fourth farm in the district to be deserted. It's worse in other areas. We all wonder who will be next.

October 25 Ray finally finished the Overland today. He has cut off part of the body and fixed a cart top to the back of it to make it into a sort of truck, or ute. I don't know how he managed it; but he did. He has a genius for improvising. It runs well, and the back seems to be fixed firmly in place. I wonder if Gallaghers are as pleased with Daisy.

November 1 It is unbearably hot. How we will survive the summer when spring is like this I'm at a loss to say. You can see the heat lifting off the plains. Nothing moves bar the rising air, which makes everything – the trees, the out-buildings – contort and shimmer. The dogs lie under the house; the hens pant on their roosts – some have died; our few sheep huddle under a tree for shade. Poor, silly beasts! The heat of their bodies as they pack together must surely counteract a thousand times the coolness of the shade! Cathy is listless and doesn't want to play. I am worried about her, and try to make her drink as often as possible.

I said that nothing is moving. Well, I was mistaken. The crows are out, cawing in the heat. A murder has just settled in the gums over by the shed. They've come to steal eggs again, no doubt. They always come when Ray is away from the house and there is no fear of being shot. I can hear some of them down at the pen now. I'd best go and fetch the eggs. Heaven knows we've had precious few lately – with some hens dying and the remainder off the lay for the heat.

I hope Ray comes in for lunch. He is in the top paddock poisoning rabbits – the paddock is riddled with warrens. I hope he is careful with the cyanide. How he can do anything in this heat! I haven't his will; even to fetch the eggs seems to require too much effort!

November 18 Les arrived today. I had quite forgotten he was coming. When he knocked on the back-door I started and almost dropped the plate I was drying. There have been a lot of swagmen lately, looking for work or just passing through. We haven't had any because we are off the main road, but others have had trouble with them. I have been dreading the possibility of one coming to the house while Ray is away. Catherine screamed. The knock doubtless scared her; but I think she sensed my fear and it made her panic. It was pathetic and horrible to see her so frightened. She ran around and to and fro within the space of about a yard in the middle of the kitchen floor, quite bewildered with terror. I snatched her up quickly, and she clung like a barnacle while the waves of fear washed over her. I didn't want to answer the door. But he knocked again, this time harder, and the knocking was frightening Cathy further, so I had to go. I half laughed, half cried when I saw that it was Les. I hugged him and kissed him, quite beside myself with relief – much to his surprise and embarrassment.

Les is several years younger than Ray, but they look alike – almost as if they were twins. He came last year, up from Perth, to help with the harvest, too. Ray is grateful for the help, but more so for the company of another man, I think. It is hard on him out here in the middle of nowhere with only a woman and a child to talk to. But then, I suppose it is much the same for me. But I must be careful now, or else I might start pining again.

Ray and Les are in the kitchen, talking, as I sit in the bedroom writing this. I don't know what they are talking about – and I'll probably never know – but they'll be at it for hours, so I will go to bed by myself.

November 20 The Government has announced a subsidy for the farmers. Gallagher brought the news over this morning. They are going to give a bonus of fourpence ha'penny per bushel in the hope that it will enable the farmers to buy supplies enough for the coming year and stop them from leaving the land. Things must be getting to their lowest ebb if even the Government is moved to action. Ray was wild with joy. He shouted and leapt about like a schoolboy, and slapped Gallagher on the back. It is the first time I have seen him lightened from care for months. He was so pleased that he told Les to fetch the horses, and they started the harvest at once. I was left to entertain Mr Gallagher, who having brought good news was forsaken because of it.

December 2 Every day is much the same, which is a blessing in many ways. The men get up at sunrise each morning and tend to the horses – groom them, water them, feed them, harness them. They load the dray with the supplies for the day – mostly chaff and water for the horses, though various odds and ends are also thrown on. Then they come in for breakfast. They have a large bowl of porridge each and a half a dozen eggs between them; then some toast and tea. Then they go out and hitch up the cart horse and the team. It is lovely to see the team hitched up and moving out. They are yoked three and three in tandem to the bin side of the harvester. They are always in high spirits in the morning, and seem almost to frolic in their eagerness to be off – if you can imagine the large, regal draught-horses doing anything so undignified and 'small' as frolicking! An occasional whinny, the chink of chains, the creak and strain of leather, the rattle and rumble of the harvester, the dogs barking and yapping at the horses' heels, the sun catching golden in the dust! It is glorious!

I take them out some lunch at mid-day. I go out in the ute. Since we lost Alice, we can't use the sulky; so Ray has taught me to drive. I must confess a certain excitement as I sit behind the wheel.

They do another four hours in the afternoon after lunch, then bring the team in. Ray unhitches and waters them, then stalls and feeds them before he comes in for tea. And after tea he goes out again to groom them – to remove the dry sweat and dust. He replenishes the chaff in their mangers and strews some straw for their bedding and for hygiene. How he loves those horses! Then he comes in and has supper with Les and myself. He and Les talk a little about the day's work, and sometimes plan certain aspects of the following days. Then we have devotions and go to bed. Though Ray is tired, he usually is awake enough for me.

December 14 The harvest is going well, though Ray is having trouble with the team. One of the mares is in heat – which shouldn't be too much of a problem seeing there are only mares and geldings in the team. But one of the geldings, Darky, is playing to her. He must have been gelded late – doctored proud, as they say. Well, anyway, the whole team is agitated because of them. Ray comes in every evening with some new grumble about the team's misbehaviour because of 'that damned gelding'. 'Could be worse, Ray,' Les said this evening in his usual, dry way, 'he could have been a stallion.' I had to laugh.

Christmas Day It is hard to remember that Christmas is the celebration of the coming of the Saviour. I tried to keep this in mind, but succeeded only once or twice for a few moments during the whole day. Perhaps it would have been different if we could have gone to a church service.

We had no presents to speak of. Catherine seemed to like the rag doll which I made for her over the past few weeks. Ray gave me a small piece of lace which he must have bought with I-don't-know-what at the oddments-cum-haberdashery store. It is lovely lace, but not large enough to do anything major with. I think I will edge the collar and the sleeves of my best dress with it; and then if there is any left, I will edge a handkerchief or two. I had nothing to give to Ray. And Les received and gave nothing.

We had a splendid meal. Ray had managed to get a small turkey from Mr Gallagher; and I baked it with potatoes and carrots. I made a rich fruit pudding, which we had with custard. Ray gave me a threepenny piece to hide in Catherine's slice. She was delighted by the unexpected treasure.

But it was a depressing day, really. I thought constantly of mother, and missed her more than ever. I said nothing of this to Ray, though; he tried so hard to make the day go well.

1 January 1932 1932 has begun. I am wearied just thinking of it.

January 11 Ray was livid when he returned home from Burracoppin this evening. I knew something was wrong before he said a word because he came straight in without unhitching and feeding the horses. He and Les spent the morning topping up and sewing the bags they harvested over the past week. Then they loaded the waggon, and Ray took it into town while Les returned home (there is no need for both of them to go, as the Lumper does most of the unloading). Well, Ray had delivered the load to the siding – weighed and unloaded it – and was about to collect his weigh-chit from the weigh-bridge hut when the team bolted. Some, or all, of them decided that it was time to be off home and, as there is no breaching horse in the team to hold them back, they started off at a gallop. The Lumper cranked his car and was off after them like a shot – with Ray balancing on the front mudguard. They caught up with the team about half a mile down the road, and Ray jumped on the waggon and took control. He kept them going until they tired, and even then he forced them to canter the rest of the way home. You could see his anger ebbing as he told us all this; and though he had sworn earlier that he would not tend to them until after he had had his tea, by the time I had set the table he had recanted and was taking them in for feed and grooming.

When he came back he was in love with them again. He praised William, our only pure Clydesdale, for his strength and steadiness. It seems that the team came to a halt on a slight sandy grading at one point; and when Ray tried to move them they simply pranced about and wouldn't pull. William alone set to and almost moved the load by himself, and then the other horses fell in and got it moving again ('William shamed them into action,' is the way Ray put it).

Ray said the bags were a good weight. Fifty came to a little over five ton. You can't complain about that.

January 30 Though we have had a good crop, it will avail us nothing. As it turns out, the prices are so low this year that they cover only about half our production costs. Our agents advanced us three hundred pounds to put in the crop; but we will receive only one hundred and eighty pounds for it. So we still owe them one hundred and twenty pounds. We are thankful, though, that the Government is going to pay a sustenance bonus of fourpence ha'penny per bushel. This money is for our use, and the creditors cannot touch it. We expect that our bonus will come to forty pounds. It should come through in a week or two. It will be heaven to have money again.

February 23 Our money came through today! Forty-one pounds and six shillings!! Ray bought a dress for me, some liquorice for Cathy, and some lump sugar for the horses. The dress is lovely, though a little large around the bust. I will take it in tomorrow. It is a light cotton material, pale blue with an even paler floral design. It tapers tightly to my waist, then falls loosely over my hips and down to my ankles. It has a thin belt which accentuates the narrowness of my waist and the flare of my hips. 'Like a skittle!' Ray said when I came out to show him; and he ran his hands down my sides. Les was watching. I felt so embarrassed!

It is a funny thing, but I could never understand the way Ray sees me – I still can't, for that matter, though I've learned to accept and appreciate it. I am no belle – though I would simply be fishing for compliments if I were to say I am ugly. Yet Ray takes great pleasure in me. He makes of me the Shulammite that Solomon wooed; and I have come to feel lovely because he has loved me.

Les and Ray are still talking in the kitchen – planning what to do with the money, no doubt. I can't sleep. I wish Ray would come to bed.

February 24 Even to write it makes the joy of it seem unreal. We are going home! Ray told me this morning at breakfast. Les is coming with us. We are going to use the sustenance money to pay for the journey. That is what he and Les were talking about last night. We are going home! I will see mother again! We are going home! If I write it a thousand times, perhaps it will seem real. We are going home!

February 28 Les took the waggon into Burracoppin and bought the supplies we will need for the journey. He also paid off the debts we have run up at the general store over the past year. He didn't get back until late.

Ray spent the whole day going over the ute. He seems to be satisfied with it.

March 2 A man from the Agricultural Bank came to see us today. He had a lot of papers and things for Ray to sign. We won't have any debts it seems – something to do with the Government's Debts Adjustment Act – but we will be left with nothing. After all the work Ray has done, and all the money we put into the property when we first arrived, we will be leaving with nothing. The joy of our homing is dampened by this. If we stayed, we might battle through. Things surely could not get any worse. I know Ray would have stayed – at least until next year's harvest – if it weren't for me. But he is set on going, now; and I am too relieved to try and dissuade him.

March 4 We loaded everything today. A 44-gallon drum of petrol and half a dozen 4-gallon drums of water took up half of the back of the ute. We packed the food, bedding, clothes, and the rifles and ammunition in the remaining space. Ray put extra springs in the back to help take the strain. And he has fixed a box to the running-board on the passenger's side, in which he has placed all the tinned meat.

March 5 Ray spent a long time with the horses before we left this morning. Like the rest of the stock, they came with the property, so they must be left with it. His eyes were red when he came back. Les and I looked away, and said silly, awkward things, trying to pretend we hadn't noticed.

We stopped at Gallagher's on the way out. They have been good neighbours and friends, and our farewells were not easy.

What do you say to people you love when you are leaving them and will probably never see them again?

We left our two dogs with them. As we were driving away, I could see them barking and pulling frantically at their chains to be after us. To know that they will be well cared for will hardly make up for the loss of them . . .

We passed a camel train just out of town. Cathy was most excited. Burracoppin is a staging for the camel teams that service the Number One rabbit-proof fence which runs from Hopetoun on the south coast to Pardoo on the north. Why they bother to maintain it now, I don't know. 'Typical governmental affair,' Ray says. 'Slow to take up an idea, and slower still to abandon it once its usefulness is spent.' It is a standing joke here that the fence keeps the rabbits in rather than out.

Now that we are on our way, our spirits are higher. Ray is whistling – at least, he appears to be – I can't hear a thing above the sound of the engine.

We are going in to Kalgoorlie. From there we will travel east along the transcontinental railway line to Cook, then down to Nullarbor Station, and then east again along the main overland route. Ray said that we can be assured of plenty of water this way as we will be able to use the fettlers' tanks which are situated about every sixty miles along the railway track.

March 6 Kangaroo shooters have been working the part of the country we passed through earlier today. We saw several heaps of kangaroo carcasses. The hillocks of raw flesh were grotesque; and the stench was nauseating. The shooters are supposed to burn the bodies after they have skinned them, but they rarely do. The kangaroo heaps were the only things that broke the monotony of today's travelling. I think I would have preferred total monotony.

Cathy finds it hard to keep still: she fidgets and grizzles continuously. We have set up camp about twenty miles short of Coolgardie. I ache all over because of the long sitting and the constant bumping.

March 7 We have been travelling along the track made by the camel waggons since we left Kalgoorlie. We will have to use this track until we reach the fettlers' camp at Rawlinna, some one hundred and eighty miles on. The track is terrible. It is simply

one mass of limestone lumps and protrusions. We clatter and jar
along at a snail's pace. To ride bareback on a brumby would seem
like heaven by comparison! And to add to this, the car is constantly swaying, for the track curves every couple of chains or
so. I asked Ray why the track snaked like this instead of running
straight. He replied that camel teams never pull straight: the
camels in the middle of the team pull to the side to increase the
leverage against the load. In this way they are able to move the
heavy waggons of wool or railway material. So in following their
track, we sway to and fro, as if we were in a small boat rocked
by a huge, persistent swell.

March 8 I didn't sleep well last night. I was too sore from the jarring and jolting of yesterday's journey. Ray thinks that we have
another one hundred miles to go to Rawlinna. I am dreading
today's travel; but we must begin again in a few minutes, as soon
as we've finished our cups of tea.

It is only early afternoon, but we have had to stop. Ray had
a premonition that something was wrong, and stopped to check
over the ute. It is well that he did because several of the spokes
on the right rear wheel have broken. The weight of the load and
the constant swaying and jarring has proved too much for them.
Ray has jacked the ute up and taken the wheel off. He is going
to remove the broken spokes and space the rest out so that they
will take the strain equally. He and Les are working in the hot
sun. There are no trees to provide shade. The only vegetation
is low salt-bush and spinifex grass. I have unloaded the things
and Cathy is gathering sticks for the fire. We will be going no
further today.

March 9 The wheel has held up; and we are in Rawlinna. Thank
heavens that that part of the journey is over! Ray was hoping
to be able to buy a spare wheel here, but there are none to be
had. The men in the fettlers' camp seem pleased to see us. They
have given Ray a few odds and ends that might come in handy
for the ute, and me several pounds of flour to bolster our dwin-
dling supplies. We have filled our water drums; and I was even
able to have a bath, and to bathe Cathy. They offered Ray and
I a tent for the night, which we gratefully accepted.

March 10 We travelled well today. We have made camp beside
the railway line not far short of Forrest. Les is off with the rifle

in the hope of rabbits. Ray is tinkering with the ute. Cathy is running around and screaming. She is like a little animal let loose from a cage when we stop. She rushes about pulling at the salt-bushes, throwing sand and sticks, growling and screaming, and generally doing anything that enters her head to release the excitements she feels at being free. How she can have so much energy after nearly ten hours of travelling, I've no idea. I wish she would give me the secret.

March 11 This morning we are tired and short with each other. We lost much sleep last night because of the train. One minute we were asleep on the silent plain, the next we were wakened by the roar of iron on iron and the whirl and rush of wind. It startled us all, but it terrified Cathy. She could not comprehend what it was. She screamed and screamed; and even when we had quietened her down she would not sleep.

We will camp further away from the railway track tonight.

March 12 We reached Cook last night, and slept there. Today we travelled down to Nullarbor Station, near the coast, and on along the main overland route towards Ceduna, which is still about one hundred and twenty miles on. We have stopped at some water tanks, but there is no water. Someone has stolen the taps – for the brass, presumably. Fortunately, we filled our drums at the Station: we would be in real trouble if we hadn't. I think Ray had forebodings of this kind of thing, and that is why he chose the railway route.

The ute has run well today – though Ray is always on tenterhooks concerning it – and we have covered a reasonable distance. Yet, in spite of the eight days we have been travelling, we still have a great distance to go. I sometimes find myself wondering if it is all worth the effort. I try to comfort myself that at the end we will see mother; and this knowledge is a comfort of sorts, though it does not stop Cathy's whingeing or soften the bumps or diminish the days we've yet to endure before our arrival.

March 13 We have reached Ceduna, despite delays to change a tyre and, later, to mend a pipe which came adrift from the carburettor.

March 14 We were able to buy a second-hand Chevrolet wheel in Ceduna this morning. It cost us five shillings – a sum which we can ill afford now. Ray has used the spokes from it to replace those broken or weakened earlier in the trip.

March 15 We have come to within one hundred miles of Port Augusta today. When we made camp tonight, Les went off, as usual, to hunt for rabbits. As usual, he returned with nothing. To lift our spirits, I decided to cut into the fruit cake I cooked before we left, and which I had been saving for such a time as this. But when I went to get it from the box in which it was packed, I found to my dismay that some Lifebuoy soap had been packed in with it. The smell of carbolic had permeated it – and the flour which was also stored in the box – and it was inedible. I sat down in the dust and wept, I was so depressed.

March 16 By the time we reached Port Augusta late this after-noon we were almost out of petrol. We were in a dilemma. We hardly had enough money to buy petrol, and yet we had to buy some food, too. Ray decided that we would have to buy power kerosene for the ute instead of petrol, which would leave a little money over to buy several loaves of bread, some flour, a few veg-etables, and a jar of vegemite.

March 17 We were a sight this morning when we left Port Augusta! I've never seen so much smoke! Ray had to fill the bowl of the carburettor with petrol and run the car until it was hot before turning on the kerosene. Then we set off with the engine roaring and smoke belching out behind us.

We are camped half way between Port Augusta and Adelaide. We had hoped to be much closer to Adelaide by now. The prob-lem is the kerosene: it clogs up the engine with soft carbon, so Ray has to stop every so often to clean the spark plugs and what not.

Ray says we will go on tomorrow until we reach mother's. The hardships of the journey seem to take on meaning now: the past fourteen days have been steps towards tomorrow, when we will see mother. Now that we are so close, I am impatient to be off. I wish we didn't have to stop for the night. I don't feel weary at all. How pleased mother will be to see us again! And Catherine for the first time!

March 18 Mother is gravely ill. The first sight of her was an inde-scribable shock – like when the train started us from our sleep.

It is hard, it is bitterly hard to think we have left everything and endured so much only to arrive at this: mother dying and a deep darkness in our hearts. Yet I must at least be thankful that we have come in time to see her – and for her to see Cathy. She was propped up in bed like a pathetic rag-doll. She groaned, almost wailed, when she saw us – as if her heart were torn, as if to be surprised by joy at a time like this somehow heightened her decrepitude and despair – and rolled her head to the wall so we wouldn't see the tears streaming down her dear, wizened face.

Gerard Windsor

VIRGINS, WIDOWS AND PENITENTS

The old doctor finished the last spoonful of his baked custard, pushed his plate away brusquely, and wiped his moustache with his serviette. 'Thank-you, dear, thank-you, dear,' he said to the housekeeper opposite him. He rose, went into the bathroom and expectorated, then clumped his way, splay-footed, into the lounge-room and sank into his easy chair. He looked out over the colourless desert of his night and steeled himself for the passage. He lit a cigarette, smoked it evenly, with satisfaction but without greed, and stared high at the opposite wall, blankly amongst photos of his dead wife and family brides. It was two hours till the woman brought him tea, and joined him, on request. It was a gesture; normally other people were too much trouble for him now. Sometimes he wondered whether he didn't actually fret for a body going through its normal paces more or less beside him. Even with the woman the notion assailed him that the correct thing to do would be to reach out and caress her hand or tap her lightly on the shoulder. Sometimes. At appropriate times. Whenever that was. But the thought sounded suspicious. And then only at times could it in any case be called a temptation. At other moments quite the opposite. He could not yet deliver his summing-up on women. Or perhaps on himself faced with the ebb and flow of their pull on him.

He lifted the peg-board from beside his chair, adjusted the wad of unruled paper, and began to write generously across it with a blue felt pen.

My personal wisdom is meagre. That, however, is not a remark-ably humble claim. I stand by it, but eighty-seven years, more or less, of sermon attendance have convinced me that wisdom anywhere tends to be thin. I was in fact three when I was judged fit to attend Mass weekly. I have heard little over the subsequent years that I could say has struck me. The clergy have been parsi-monious with truly instructive thoughts. Their line of work is unfortunately wisdom, but in all charity I cannot give a high rating to their professional standards. Unless they have some-thing to offer I feel they should be silent. Of course there is no profundity in that, but the depressing fact is that very few human beings believe they have no right to preach. Give some of them a black suit and a collar and there's no calling them back. But in a lifetime of wheedling, cajoling, admonishing and fulminat-ing they hand out very little that's well-baked and nutritious. I do say this more in sorrow than in anger. Partly out of chagrin at my loss I admit; why should I have heard some five thousand two hundred and twenty-four sermons, to date, and have carried away so little spiritual baggage? Why should I have lost some one thousand seven hundred and forty hours, seventy-two and a half days of my life with virtually nothing to quicken my soul? In the not infrequent moments in which I succumb to rash judge-ment I consider that the priests will have much to answer for. They have demanded so much yet given so little. I wander. There is no point, as well as no justice, in condemning. Rather, I have been asking myself – naturally enough at my time of life – whether sermons are possible without preaching. Or perhaps preaching without sermonizing? Words fail me, but the meaning is obvious. Personally I have always been most affected – I realize that is not identical with most enlightened but the latter if it comes at all comes through the former – I have been most affec-ted by the saints. I mean not so much the élite group, as all those who are about to from their labours rest, go marching in and the rest of it. The living more or less. Those I have encountered at close quarters.

So I should like to try my hand at a panegyric. The preacher need not be too prominent. Besides, the clergy's monopoly of the medium has always made me particularly envious.

Thy beauty now is all for the king's delight. (Common of Virgins.)

This is a most embarrassing text. It was chosen, I imagine, some thousand years ago at least. He was a bold sort of lad that dug it out and got it through. It must all have been the most extreme piece of luck. For the life of me I can't see it being passed by any of the churchmen I know. And to be honest with you I wouldn't blame them. Metaphors for divine love are all very well, but to pay honour to a virgin by the public announcement that her beauty now is all for the king's delight, strikes me as really a gross piece of irony. But if you've no sense of irony and even less sense of sexual matters, you might find it wholly appropriate. There are such people, and at least once I have found nothing ridiculous about them. About her to be precise.

When the Japanese took over the islands, a convent of Carmelite nuns was evacuated south to Brisbane and set up out at Auchenflower. Australians, Frenchwomen, others too I imagine. Not long after they arrived I was called out to see one old nun, the oldest there I believe, something over eighty. She was a Frenchwoman, from the same area and much the same age as Thérèse of the Child Jesus, though of course Thérèse was dead over fifty years by then. Never an especial object of my devotion I must admit. Whether the two had ever met or lived together I don't know. I rang the bell as usual, the extern nun came and let me in, then bobbed ahead of me along the dark panelled corridor, ringing her tocsin to warn the intern nuns to avoid my sight. The Reverend Mother informed me about the patient: never had a day's illness in her life, but the fear of war and the sudden uprooting after fifty-odd years in the one building had proved too much. Reverend Mother didn't specify the illness – not that it was her business. War and transplantation had nothing to do with the ailment as it turned out. I followed Reverend Mother to the old Frenchwoman's cell. She knocked, opened the door without waiting for an answer, spoke a few words that I missed, then withdrew, motioned me in and shut the door. Diagnosis was immediate. The patient stood back against the opposite wall, her hands clasped under her scapular and her head bent forward so that her eyes would not have taken in even my feet. The only part of her body exposed was the shadowed oval of her face, framed by her wimple. But the cell was noisome, nothing less. Reverend Mother, I am sure, had called me in on the strength of nothing more than that. I had come across enough similar cases – old biddies living alone or, a couple of times, with an equally aged brother too far gone in manners or prudery or necrosis of the senses to notice. Prolapses of the uterus. A degree of incontinence is only one of the manifestations. Female tissue of that area is of course rich in secretions; they are best kept internal.

I told the old nun I would have to examine her, and asked her to take off what was necessary and lie down under the coverlet on her bed while I waited just outside. She didn't move, in fact gave no sign that she'd even heard. Imagining she was deaf I repeated the instruction more loudly but she still gave no sign at all of having heard. Then I remembered she was French and probably, over a lifetime of silence, would never have had occasion to learn English. I went to take her by the elbow and get her to lie on the bed, but her arm tightened and she moved back right against the wall. I had to be firm and make myself understood – it shouldn't have been hard; she must have known why I was there. But the instant I made to grasp her firmly by the arm she wrenched herself away, and her arms flew up, crossed over her bosom in the manner in which the artists always portray Agnes, Cecilia and the rest of those girl martyrs. I pulled at her, but those crossed arms were immoveable. For an ailing woman in her eighties the strength was unnatural, and she made it all the worse by throwing up her head, looking high on the wall above me and beginning to scream. Not just a shriek, but words, the same phrase over and over again. My French was rusty: I couldn't understand her.

I stood back and left her alone. But she didn't let up. Just hugged herself and screamed and screamed with a passion and grief that I now, looking back, find awesome. At the time I was simply annoyed, and, I suppose, a little self-concerned. I went straight out of the cell and tackled the Reverend Mother who was standing a few yards along the corridor in the usual posture of piety. I was offensively aggressive. 'What's the woman saying?'

She sounded apologetic as she articulated, in the whisper that was probably the only voice she'd used for the last sixty years, '*Il m'a vu*, Doctor. He has seen me,' she explained.

'Well I damn well haven't,' I came back at her. 'Bloody waste of time. I don't expect any patient to behave like that, least of all you people.' And I started ahead of her down the corridor, and she began to ring her tocsin with a shade more urgency than on my arrival.

Four days later she rang me. 'Sister will see you, Doctor, if you could be so kind as to come out again.' When I arrived just before their dinner, the Reverend Mother said, 'I've had a word with sister. I think she understands everything now.'

And of course there was no trouble. She was the most charming and gracious old lady. By then I was humbled a bit myself and was conscious of trying to make it as easy for her as possible. Over the intervening days that act of hers had taken something of a hold on me. It'd be ridiculous of me to get too melodramatic about it all, I don't want to do that, but I began to get a sense of the passion behind that scream, and I admit that with time it echoes even more inside me. 'He has seen me.' Of course I hadn't, at that time. But the sense of violation was so overwhelming that the future came at her in a rush and blotted out the present. All those years, eighty-odd of them, barely even spoken to a man, except I suppose her father and various anonymous priests through the confessional grille. They were the full extent of her sexual dealings, the bride of Christ through and through. And then suddenly, when she had almost made it, some rough foreigner of a fellow breaks in and tries to make her lie down and submit to him – and what would be the difference to her between that sort of examination and the gross activity she had forsworn and so decisively risen above? She must have wondered where her God was, maybe even wondered what sort of a sick, cruel lad he was at all.

It jolts me even now, a bit. 'He has seen me.' I was he, representative man I suppose. Man finally had seen her, got at her, and it makes me feel a terrible, awful inadequate blunderer. I hope it was the worst of what she meant, for I sometimes imagine she meant the devil more than man, or at least that she made no distinction between the two. To this day I am sure I did nothing at all reprehensible, but to her I was the devil himself; and she was the most charming old lady and in the end, by an exertion of obedience I don't like to think of, she submitted herself to me.

In the corridor beyond the door the housekeeper passed and repassed. The old man took no notice of the momentary shadows. He began on a new page.

Honour widows that are widows indeed. (Mass of a Widow.) I'd have thought it was a straightforward, yea or nay matter, like virgins and the dead. Either you are or you aren't. But on reflection I concede it's a title that you've got to earn. Twenty-six, twenty-seven years ago I thought I'd qualified automatically, but I don't know now whether I really rank. Further on in the book the apostle says a widow has to be desolate. Now that's a strong word, and hard as I've found it to be alone, and vehemently as I would urge seventy as the age at which a man really needs to marry, I still would feel a wee bit of a Pharisee, a wee bit of a fraud if I told you I was desolate. I've no idea how many fit the bill, but I've seen one case that does, and I know for certain that I don't.

I arrived in the hospital one morning just after eight. It must have been September or thereabouts; the early morning Brisbane warmth was getting into its stride again. The Matron, not a woman for leisure at all, was waiting about the desk for me. 'We've an urgent, Doctor,' she said. 'Up in the convent.' The second phrase was as we swung off into the corridor, and she said no more till we were upstairs and on the walkway leading across to the nuns' own quarters. And all she did then was mention the nun's name. I was surprised, though only as much as professional experience allowed me; the woman mentioned was young enough still, had always looked healthy enough, and I'd no recollection of her having been seriously ill. At the door of the patient's room the Matron took a key from somewhere in the white folds of her habit. I frowned; sick rooms are never locked. I felt a spurt of irritated censoriousness against the Matron. Why? Why should I have reacted that way? I had always had the utmost professional respect for the woman – and I liked her, too, I should add, in case the assessment sounds begrudging. Why should I spontaneously have jumped to condemnation? I don't know. The trait is not unusual but it's depressing to dwell on for all that.

At all events annoyance was still distracting me as I entered the room, when I should really have been warned by the locked door to expect something unusual. As it was I was still aware of the Matron locking the door behind us as I approached the bed. Then, at least, my professional machinery showed its condition and allowed me to process a rush of reactions quite instan-

taneously. For the nun in the bed had ceased being a patient and
was emphatically dead. I went through the routine of pulse and
forehead, although the Matron needed that act even less than I
did. There was nothing remarkable about the dead nun; at the
most her body was slightly clenched. She wore all her regulation
issue, cap and modest cotton nightdress, and her arms lay by her
sides under the bedclothes. I looked up at the Matron. She said,
'I'd be glad if you'd write us the death certificate and look after
the autopsy,' and her eyes held mine just enough to draw them
across the bedside table. On it lay a syringe and several
ampoules, their necks broken off. I could not, at the distance, see
their labels.

Naturally I did what was required. On several previous
occasions where the discretion of a good Catholic practitioner
was needed I had been involved. I officially confirmed the death
then and there so that the Matron was free to disarrange the
corpse. I didn't ask whether it had been previously tampered
with. She did little more than fold the hands across the chest in
the approved manner, and after a noticeably long search for the
objects she entwined the dead nun's rosary and metal crucifix
around her fingers. I didn't like to question the appropriateness
of this gesture although the irony of it was brought home force-
fully to me later on.

Briefly, the subsequent history of this case was as follows. The
nun had died from a solid, but economical injection of morphine;
she was a fine nurse and knew her pharmacology; she did not
believe in waste. My personal knowledge of the woman was
slight, and it was the business of her religious superiors, not me,
to go into the question of motivation. I don't know what happened about the funeral; I hardly made any effort to gather
details, before or after. This was in the days when suicides were
not allowed burial in consecrated ground. I imagine, in fact hope,
that the nuns found for their sister a way round that rule. Probably along the lines of avoiding scandal in the faithful. Just like
the old rule about mortal sin and communion; no one is obliged,
given certain circumstances, to shun going to communion and
thereby betray that he or she is in mortal sin. One of the Church's
moments of eminent good sense, that. And I imagine the convent
would have a similar feeling for its own. But the girl's, woman's
death had its full impact on me when I discovered, in the course

of my autopsy, that she was three months pregnant. The Matron was assisting me, no one else was present, and the moment I realized the cadaver's condition I passed on with as much affected professional equilibrium as I could muster to the next item on the routine agenda. I said nothing to the Matron, nor she to me. She may have missed it, but to this day I can't be sure. Given the woman's shrewdness and medical knowledge I suppose it's wishful thinking to hope that she did.

Whatever of that, it was the existence of the foetus that let me see into the desolation of that one-time bride of Christ. I cannot imagine a more complete widowhood than that. I've no idea what led her into the arms of some altogether more human male, but patently there was something wrong with the original marriage. She'd lost that husband somewhere, and just moved further away from him, down towards the centre of the Chinese boxes. There can't even have been a shadow of him by the time she pulled the last five walls down on herself, and it was then that she discovered that she had the child with her. Yet, she was absolutely alone, in a way that could evoke, even in someone who had never formed any bond at all, the most chilling desolation.

The housekeeper put down the coffee table, then returned with the tea tray. The old man watched her with a dull dispassion as she poured his milk, his tea, added his sugar and stirred it. When she handed it to him he laid it on the armrest, and lit a second cigarette. When he had drawn his first puff he looked at the food on the tray and gestured towards it with the cigarette, saying, 'What's that?'

She lifted the plate to him. 'Shortbread. It's nice and fresh.'

'Hey?' he asked. 'Speak up, woman.'

'Fresh shortbread,' she repeated.

'No thanks,' he said, and waved it away.

They sat and drank in silence. He stared at the brides and the dead on the far wall and shot out his smoke towards them. The woman looked towards her knees and several times brushed and smoothed down her lap. Once he made an effort and said, 'Have you enough for the weekend?' 'Plenty, plenty,' she shouted mildly. Otherwise he was silent, distracted by the saints. When he had finished both cigarette and tea the woman lifted his cup and saucer on to the tray, removed them, replaced the coffee table and disappeared.

As he reached to pick up his board the old man noted her absence. He held his bent pose an instant and murmured, 'Thank you, dear, thank you.' But for a moment, before he started on the clean sheet of paper, he gazed through it, distractedly.

Blessed are the undefiled in the way. (Mass of a Penitent.) This, to my encouragement but still to my bewilderment, is how they choose to sing the praises of a penitent. Who they are defeats me. I would never have imagined myself a Platonist, but such surprising wisdom seems to have an existence of its own quite apart from any mind I have encountered. Not the most idolatrous devotee of paradox would label our perennial soiled goods as undefiled. Repentance may well be a saving grace, but it hardly seems to warrant such generosity.

God knows how sin affects the soul. Chemical reactions are complicated enough; moral corrosion mocks any analysis. Set the process in reverse, try the catalyst of repentance, and the result must be profoundly incalculable. The text, in its wisdom, comments, 'I have seen an end of all perfection; thy commandment is exceedingly broad.' Make of that what you can. But it's wise, I'd bet on that. The language itself is too fine to allow any admixture of rubbish. But it sounds as though the penitent might be the daddy of them all. And I'm mystified by this notion of latitude; an infinity of ways of making good, I imagine.

I could never put a finger to all the skeins by which we lower ourselves down to vice any more than those by which we haul ourselves up. I couldn't even mark the turning point of the pulley.

Some years ago I was in my rooms when four of the hospital nuns called in to see me. It was Christmas time; they had been doing their shopping and merely called because they knew I'd be going over to the hospital in the afternoon. They'd catch their breath in the rooms, they said, and then we could all go back to work together. I knew all of them, but one not much more than by sight and by name. She was a stout girl about forty from somewhere up near Innisfail. She worked in the Children's. We had a bit to eat, or at least I did; somehow nuns still tend to be unobtrusive at such activities.

We found a cab at the rank on the corner of the Terrace. The women put me in the back, seemed to think my age warranted it. Two of them in with me, two in the front. The lady I didn't know opened the front door and got straight in. It was the others insisting on my welfare or what have you. Yet the comparative stranger was by far the youngest, and the discourtesy was all the starker contrast. To tell you the truth I couldn't swear I did consciously notice this at the time, but it rose up and fitted a pattern just a few minutes later. Heaven knows what the conversation was as we swung around and accelerated up the Terrace – family, other nuns, gallantries and teasing of one kind or another. You don't see much from the middle of the back seat of a taxi; not with five other people in it. You keep your eyes to the front and rest your attention on things other than the sights. So I don't know how long it took for me to become aware of the central object of my field of vision – the head and shoulders of the Innisfail woman. But they were shaking, or rather convulsing, shivering, and then I heard her breath too, distinctly louder than normal, a variety of gasping, but uneven and staccato as though some effort were being made to control it. It was a normal December mid-day, there was no air-conditioning in the cab, the woman had not been in this condition as late as our standing together on the footpath. My hand reached out, as an instinctive gesture to the driver, the natural, split-second forerunner of a call for him to pull over because the poor woman was having a fit. What stopped me I don't know. But I didn't call. I just let my hand rest on the back of the seat, and, as we were swinging left away from the Normanby turn-off, I hope the gesture looked natural enough. I'm not a man of the world – for good or ill. Some of those women in the cab with me had much more claim to the title, and any insight I had must have come to them far sooner and with much greater clarity. I am not sure that I had ever actually seen a woman in that condition. The admission perhaps damages me. Perhaps it exalts me. I've no idea and in any case it's not relevant. Neither had the other nuns ever seen it, I imagined, but I'd lay odds they knew exactly what was going on. My evidence for that was circumstantial but foolproof; all three of them redoubled the pace and the volume of their conversation. The woman next to the driver stayed in much the same condition until we all got out; she didn't seem in the least embarrassed when she said goodbye to me and went inside.

One of the others – I'd prefer not to name her – stayed behind. We knew one another well enough. 'It happens every time,' she said. 'She always makes sure she sits next to the driver. We all notice it, but I suppose we don't like to admit it to one another. I'm sure she's no idea what she's doing.'

I felt in no position to comment on that. I believed it. Riding, chaperoned, in a cab is an abnormal occasion of sin. So I simply said, 'You can hardly confine her. But you can't have a perform-ance like that taxiing round the town. One of you should have a word to her. It's a woman's problem.'

No, I wasn't buying out of it. I had dealt with the husbands of too many women like that, and I knew it was no man's busi-ness to admonish or even advise a woman that nature had afflic-ted with such a condition. For it to be a nun made it no worse. In fact I imagine it was what they call a dispensation of providence; God saved some poor fellow from her. And they are pitiable fellows too; no manhood left at all the way they are forced to come to me for advice, any magic word that might get them a moment's peace. But that's neither here nor there. The point is this. From that day to this that nun, the Innisfail woman, has never, to the best of my knowledge, taken the front seat in a cab. On the few occasions I've been present she's been more discourteous than ever on getting in. Into the back. But I have seen that it's almost a terror about being left to take the front seat. She cannot afford womanly modesty and reticence; they are luxuries that the healthy and unthreatened can indulge. But she has a devil to torment her and a justifiable savagery has entered her soul. I only know that she was never given any order, at least not by any human Superior. It was her own war entirely and the difficulty of it must be appalling. Whether and where she believes sin enters it I've no idea. But there is a threat to her soul for which she can allow no tolerance. Call her simple, call her neurotic, call her the washed-out victim of scruple and authority – and I would have no vehemence in denying any of the epithets – but I can't get past the fact that she has set her hand to the plough and will, at any cost, subdue the stubborn earth, dust, clay, that is herself. Beside a cause like that all other devotions and crusades have a quality of histrionic self-indulgence. Whereas constant evulsion, at one's own hands, from the front seat of a cab, sounds more the stuff of farce than of heroism and that very token assures its purity. That's enough. I'm going beyond my own guidelines. I am pontificating. While the light, if any, is supposed to be on the woman. And the point is that the stout lass from Innisfail, with the degrading affliction and the discourteous manner, is storming the kingdom of heaven by violence.

The old man dropped his pen and hoisted himself up by the arms of his chair. He stood some seconds to let the blood circulate, breathed deeply ten times, ran the same number of paces on the spot, then strode across the room and picked up a box of chocolates from the polished top of the dead television. He slid the lid off and held back the enveloping folds of paper to look at the selection. He plucked out four empty mahogany-brown paper cups and screwed them up into his pocket. He rearranged the selection so that the surviving chocolates were spread evenly across the cardboard surface, the hard centres grouped at one end, the soft at the other. Then, holding the box far out in front of him and intent on the stability of its contents, he moved out through the breakfast room and the kitchen. At the opening into the verandah alcove that was his own bedroom, and the annexe to the housekeeper's room, he paused and called through. 'Hello there, dear?' he said. Then he passed straight through.

'What is it, Doctor?' she answered, but the words were indistinct for her teeth were already in the glass.

'Would you have a chocolate for me, dear?' he asked her.

Neither of them looked at one another.

'I couldn't . . . deal with it properly, at the moment.'

'They're very soft, down the end. Take one of those now.' He stabbed a finger towards the selection.

'It's a bit late to be eating,' but she gave a quick laugh, part pleasure part tolerance.

'I'd have been here earlier, dear, if I'd had my wits about me. I'll come earlier in the future. But you'd still be able for a chocolate now, surely?'

'It's terrible the sweet tooth I've got,' she conceded. 'They're no good for me, I know.'

'One cigarette at my age does no harm to the body, but there's a lot to be said for its good to the soul. Have a chocolate for me, dear.'

There was a pause. She repeated her quick laugh. 'You choose one for me, Doctor.'

His fingers hovered above the box, unable to make any decisive distinction. They plunged in blindly, raised a chocolate and thrust it towards her.

Again she laughed and let it suffice for her thanks.

He went out and stood in the kitchen, trembling from the act, staring through the half-open window on the Tower Mill Motel. It was, they told him, a favourite first night stopover for honeymooning couples. It looked an uneven, unfinished patchwork of light and darkness. As he gazed, his nerves still open, he clearly beheld the young things rising in continuous procession, through the lights and shadows, through the ecstasy and fading of their passion, up towards the dome of the pointing tower. And he saw himself with them. And the tower was a ladder set up on the earth, reaching into the heavens, and he saw the couples, all angels, ascending and descending upon it.

V.M.H.Angus

THE LAST PADDOCK

At five o'clock Bill opened his eyes, reached out, and switched on the bedside light. He stared for a second at the red and green lampshade hanging from the centre of the high ceiling, then climbed out of bed. The boards under the mattress rattled and Doris stirred.

'Go back to sleep old girl,' Bill said. Doris lifted her head off the pillow and looked at him. Saliva trickled down the side of her mouth. She picked up the edge of the sheet and wiped it dry. 'Go back to sleep. No need you getting up.' Doris turned her head to look at the clock, then lowered it back to the wet patch on her pillow. Bill glanced down at the sleeping face. 'You look like a dried up old prune lying there. How many years have I been telling you to wear a hat in the sun?' He turned away from her. Picking up a bundle of clothes that lay on the floor, he started to dress.

In the kitchen he glanced down at the empty wood basket next to the stove and frowned. He hesitated for a few moments then walked over to a cupboard and removed a bright stainless steel electric kettle. A faint smile moved over his face as he walked towards the back door.

'What the eye don't see,' he said aloud. The two dogs chained behind the outhouse started to bark. 'Shut up y' bloody mongrels. If you wake the old woman up you'll get m' boot.' Bill filled the kettle at the water tank and returned to the kitchen. He buttered two thick slices of bread and waited for the tea to brew.

He emptied the kettle, swilling his mug out with its contents, then carefully replaced it in the cupboard. Taking a faded hat from a hook behind the door he put it on his head and pulled the brim down over his eyes. As soon as he opened the door the dogs began to bark again. 'I've warned you, I'll wrap the chain round your bleeding necks.' The barks turned to whimpers as the dogs settled down again. A rooster crowed in the distance and a tabby cat ran out from under the tank stand. Bill sat down on the step and put on his boots. The cat jumped onto his knee and rhythmically treddled his thighs with its front paws. 'How are you Mr Puss?' Bill ran his hand up the arched back then placed the cat on the ground. 'Go and earn your living. There's a rat in the feed shed.' The cat stalked off in the direction of the wood pile.

Bill tied up his boots and walked towards the dogs. Hearing his footsteps they crawled forward on their bellies and, straining on their chains, started to whimper. As he appeared around the corner of the outhouse their whimpers turned to yelps and they plunged forward, pawing the air with their front legs. The star picket that held the chains moved in the earth. 'Shut up y'curs.' Bill hit the smaller of the kelpies with the back of his hand. The dog yelped then sat down, her head hung close to the ground. The larger dog, seeing her master's displeasure, sat in silence. 'Away y'go.' Bill unhooked the dogs from their chain. They ran round and round sniffing the earth, then back to Bill. 'Heel,' he shouted. The dogs fell back immediately and walked either side of his boots. Over the surrounding hills the dawn was breaking.

They walked round the far side of the house to where a few rose bushes grew, their blooms full blown. The soil round their roots was still moist. Bill turned on a tap and water spurted out of the holes pierced through the length of plastic hose which ran between the bushes. The dogs had stayed close to him waiting for the water to flow, but then ran forward, each to a spray, and drank. 'The old girl thinks more of these roses than she does of me,' Bill said, addressing his words to the drinking dogs. 'Come on you idle curs. We haven't all day. The sun's nearly up.' The dogs took off after him.

Bill walked down the dirt track. The dogs ran in the erosion gullies, sniffing the earth. The smaller kelpie picked up a scent and ran off down the track. Under a pine tree a rabbit froze, sniffing the air. The dog caught sight of it and gave chase. The rabbit hesitated for a moment, then scurried under the wire into the open paddock, the dog close behind. The rabbit let out a faint

scream as the dog's jaws encircled it. 'Come back y' mongrel,'
Bill shouted, then whistled. The dog, catching the whistle on the
air, turned with the rabbit in it mouth and bounded back. Her
jaws relaxed as Bill took the prey. The rabbit's limbs twitched
and its eyes flickered. Holding it upside down he gave a quick
tug at its neck. Bill hung the carcass over the barb of the fence.
The dogs jumped up at it, barking. 'Get away,' Bill said, pushing
them down. 'You'll be good for nothing with your bellies full.'
Nearby a bloom of wattle quivered under the weight of a honey
eater.

Bill stopped at a gate made from an old bed base. Taking its
weight with the toe of his boot, he lifted the loop of wire off the
strainer post. The paddock was parched. Large patches of bare
earth lay exposed between the rank tussocks. The sheep drinking
at the dam stood still, their noses wrinkled, sniffing the air. On
the dam wall a group of lambs played, oblivious to his presence.
Their mothers bleated deeply and they ran back to the security
of the ewes' udders. The dogs ran towards the sheep, wagging
their tails. 'Heel,' Bill yelled. 'We've some bloody work to do.' The
dogs returned to his feet and walked quietly towards the flock.
The sun stood peeping over the hills, brilliant orange.

Slowly the sheep gathered under a dead ghost gum. Bill waited
for a while and then gave orders to the kelpies. 'Get way over.'
The dogs ran off either side of the flock. 'You silly curs – way
out.' The dogs ran further out. Bill watched their progress as he
brushed away the gathering flies. He whistled. The dogs turned
to face the flock and fell on their bellies; their eyes bright and
their ears pricked. The sheep stared silently back. On the dam
a lone drake called to a flock of wild duck.

The peace was broken by a flock of sulphur crested cockatoos
screeching overhead. The sheep stirred. The birds circled the
flock twice and landed in the ghost gum. A ewe stamped her foot.
Another bolted, jumping high in the air as she went. Others followed. 'Go Meg,' Bill shouted to the dog on the left. She leapt
over the ground, cutting off their retreat. The sheep froze in their
tracks as the bitch flung herself on the earth in front of them.
'Y'bloody vermin,' Bill shouted in the direction of the tree. From
its bare branches the cockatoos watched and cackled their
response.

'Get 'm up – move 'm up,' Bill shouted to the kelpie waiting by the tree. She ran forward, nipping at the ewes' heels, forcing them to join the renegades. Bill followed, his arms held wide. 'Hurry them up; move them up,' Bill shouted. The dogs started pushing the sheep up faster. The ewes bleated to their lambs. Meg ran to the head to keep the flock in line with the far gate. Through the gate they went and through the adjoining paddocks. In the last paddock before the escarpment they stopped. The panting sheep sniffed the air and headed towards a water hole. In the east the sun climbed; a ball of fire.

Bill leant against the gate post looking at the dry grass. 'Eat slowly,' he shouted in the direction of the flock, 'that's your last feed till the rains come.'

A tiger snake that had been basking in the sun slid down from the fork of a box gum and disappeared into its hollow trunk. Bill bent down and looked at his dogs. Their tongues hung out; pink and rough. 'You've done a good job.' He patted their heads and walked them slowly over to the water hole. The sheep backed off and the dogs drank. He bent down and filled his hat with water and poured it over his head.

The water flowed down his face and mingled with the perspiration.

The sun was overhead when Bill walked through the home paddock. Doris, kneeling on the earth talking to her roses, heard him call. She turned at the sound of his voice and looked around. He waved. 'My shiny kettle was used,' she said, staring in his direction. Her words were lost amongst the hum of insects and the song of the cicadas. Bill walked to the carcass hanging on the fence. The flies rose in a black cloud. From his pocket he took a pen knife and slit the rabbit down its belly and limbs, and peeled off the skin. He threw it to the waiting dogs who tore at its flesh. Doris stood up and walked towards the gate, her nightdress stained with wet earth. 'No wonder you look like an old prune,' Bill said, guiding her back in the direction she had come, 'you never wear a bloody hat.'

Doris knelt down at the rose bushes and continued her conversation. Bill leant over and turned off the tap. He stood for a while looking at her. At the back door he sat down and removed his boots. 'The cricket season's nearly over in England,' he said, and walked in out of the sun.

Olga Masters

YOU'LL LIKE IT THERE

The child came into the room bending her body towards the old woman in bed. The room was actually the child's and the old woman's, but the latter's illness made it necessary for the child to sleep on the lounge.

The lounge was the old-fashioned kind, eventually to be discarded, and the sloping back caused the child to wake up when she turned over and hit her face against it.

She dreamed once she was being crushed by a hill caving in but she did not tell her mother because she knew what the reaction would be.

'Hear that, Barry!' the mother would have said to her husband, the old woman's son. 'She can't get a proper night's rest. She needs her own bed!'

Her husband would twitch his body, indicating he had heard (and agreed) and would pull his face in. He was a slight man with skin and hair of a washed-out colour, like separated milk.

'Barry looks like the milk at that factory where he works,' the old woman often said to herself. 'Drained of all its strength.'

So the child very quietly would fold her blanket and sheet each morning and put them under the loose cushions on the lounge and put her nightdress in a drawer in her room.

She had the nightdress now to put away before she left for school.

'Can I bring you anything, Granma?' she said.

The old woman moved her head on the pillow. The bedclothes were tight across her except for a little hollow where her mouth was. The child moved closer and peered into the hollow to judge better how ill the old woman was.

'Granma?' said the child.

'Nothing,' the old woman said. 'I'll be better soon and you can come back to your own little bed again. I only put the light on twice last night.'

'Only twice!' the child marvelled as if she were the adult and the old woman the child.

'Once to take a pill, and once for a drink of water. I knocked the glass over, but it dried up I think. Take a little look and see if it dried up, will you?' The old woman's whispering voice lost its strength, like wind passing through dried grass.

The child felt the table and moved a package containing the old woman's pension card, and covered some dampness with it.

'Are you going to school now?' the old woman said. The child was in her check dress with her hair newly done and the ribbons pulling it upwards from her ears so it was obvious she was.

But the two talked to each other this way.

'You've got your brown cardigan on, Granma,' the child would say. The old woman's frame had shrunk since she bought the cardigan ten years before, and wearing it now she had the appearance of a peg doll dressed in something too big for it.

'Ah, stupid!' the child's brother would say, lunging out a leg and kicking her, and the mother's face would tighten and her eyes flash, agreeing that she was.

Embarrassed, the child would raise her rump higher and lower her head over her book on the floor and colour in with more vigour. The old woman's hand crunched on her knee would want to reach out and touch the child's hair.

Now the old woman wanted to take hold of the child's hand hanging loose with the nightdress under one arm.

But her own arms were bound to her sides in bed.

The way she makes a bed, the old woman thought shutting her eyes against a picture of her daughter-in-law stretching and tugging and tightening the covers, so the old woman had to wriggle her way into bed leaving her nightdress well above her waist.

'Grandma?' the child said again.

'Nothing,' whispered the old woman and struggled in her mind to find something to share with the child. Without looking she knew the bright blue of the child's eyes would be distinct from the white.

'Put your nightie away,' the old woman said glad to have thought of that.

The child was crunching it into a drawer when the mother came into the room.

'Don't do it that way!' she cried. 'Don't squash and wrinkle up everything!' She snatched up the nightie, rearranged the other clothing, and folding the nightie flat, laid it down one end. She slammed the drawer shut going 'tch tch' with her tongue as if to say here was something else disrupting the place.

She lingered at the dressing-table, changing expression at the sight of herself in the mirror. Few would guess to look at her that she worked on a delicatessen counter, discarding her out-door clothing when she arrived at work for a white overall and cap. She wore a long black skirt that swished about the top of her black boots, an imitation fur jacket and cap to match. Her hair had a red rinse which she was sure no one detected, and it was cut in such a way that two ends lay in spikes on her cheeks, matching her spiky fringe.

She turned her head admiring her profile but frowned when her eyes met the eyes of the old woman reflected in the glass.

She can't escape me, the old woman thought, turning away.

'Get your schoolcase and things,' the mother said to the child, not looking at her but pinching and plucking her coat about the shoulders and stroking and twisting the hair spikes.

'Well, go on,' she said with irritation, and the child scuttled ahead of her out of the room.

'I'll shut this,' the mother said loudly as if the old woman was deaf.

The child's eyes, like a piece of blue sky, showed briefly in the crack before the door closed with a snap.

The old woman heard the mother's boots and the child's school shoes tap down the steps and quicken on the footpath then become lost in the noise of the traffic.

Peace fell on the old woman's face like pale sun, but there was no sun. She ran her tongue inside her dry mouth.

'I'll get up and move around and get my sweat going,' she said, feeling an itch of her dry skin.

The wardrobe door was closed on her dressing-gown. Her daughter-in-law could not bear the sight of anything scattered on the floors so her slippers were out of sight too.

'Bugger me. I haven't got the strength to get them,' she said.

'But I'm not laying here. You rot in bed.'

She got her feet out and swung them above a small bedside mat.

'Japanese rubbish,' she said looking down at it.

She stood up gingerly.

'Weak as a cat,' she whispered, staring at the door, willing it to come closer.

Pins and needles raced up her legs. But she trotted forward and opened the door onto the carpet in the hall. The carpet was an off-white colour put down from earnings at the delicatessen. The daughter-in-law treated it with reverence. Coming home each day her eyes fell on it for marks. Leaving each morning she sometimes took a brush and kneeling in her good clothes brushed the pile upright. Now the old woman wished she could avoid walking on it. She felt so heavy she was sure every footstep would flatten it. But she was so light she wafted across it like thistledown in her billowing flannelette nightgown.

In the living-room she took hold of two chair arms, turned herself around and sat down.

'Ah,' she said, pleased at the achievement and putting her head back. It rested on one of the daughter-in-law's cushions and immediately she snapped her head forward. She had heard the daughter-in-law's boots pummelling the floor that morning as she went through the ritual of straightening mats, fixing cushions and pulling chairs to the angle she wanted them.

The old woman crossed her legs and began to rock a foot. The foot was a purplish brown colour like her leg, covered with hundreds of little criss-cross lines. She thought of the child's legs as she saw them that morning above her white school socks. Like fawn satin, she thought holding the memory under her shut eyes. She slept a little because she opened her eyes surprised at the sight of the living-room furniture.

All those sharp edges, she thought, feeling as if they were cutting her. The daughter-in-law always rubbed fiercely at the edges of tables and chairs with her polishing cloth as if she wanted to turn them into weapons. The old woman remembered the furniture at the old place. There was the fat old sideboard crowded with sepia pictures, the cruet set, water jug and glasses.

'Damn rubbish,' Barry had said for his wife who looked sharp and ferret-like on that last day.

There was a little tapping noise and the old woman opened her eyes. The venetian blind had swung around in a small wind from the window and speared at the air with its slats.

'Those things,' the old woman said with scorn.

'Give me my old red curtains any day.'

She saw them burning in the backyard and Barry walking around throwing sticks and leaves on the fire to make them go faster. One of the tassels had blown away and burned out lying a little away from the fire. She remembered it shaped like a little bell in ashes on the green grass.

'Pretty,' she said, wondering why she hadn't shown it to the child.

Why hadn't she? Where was the child that day? Had she been born then? Agitated she rocked her foot harder, plucking through loose ends in her brain to get events in order.

'You went to Hilda straight after the old place was sold,' she said stern with her muddled brain.

She saw them together, two old bandy-legged women struggling up a hill in the wind to buy cat food and indigestion powder (Hilda really had cancer and died, and it was decided then that the old woman's two sons should have her turn about for six months).

She saw herself waiting with Barry for a train to take her to Corrimal where she was to spend the first six months with Percy, the other son.

'You'll like it there,' Barry said when a great hiss and puff from the engine had died away.

'You can go and sit on the beach whenever you want to.'

The old woman remembered the wind lifting the sand and flinging it against her face. She saw Percy's wife making ridges in it with her hands. The two boys, blue like skinned rabbits in wet trunks, were hunched over sniffing in the cold. All of them were set apart reminding the old woman of gnomes in a garden.

They all looked out to sea as if to find the answers there.

Five months and four days after going to Percy she came to Barry because Percy had been given his holidays (he said) and her time was nearly up anyway.

She saw herself waiting with Percy for the train to Sydney. His wife was already getting the room ready for the younger of the boys.

'You're only a spit from all the shops,' Percy said. 'You'll like it there.'

She looked down remembering how she stood with only one case. When she went to Hilda she had three. What happened to the other two?

'Bugger me. They must have got lost somewhere,' the old woman said.

She rocked her foot and dozed. She must have dozed because she opened her eyes and Barry was there rolling a cigarette between his blue-white fingers. In his job he started at dawn and came home at midday.

Licking the cigarette paper Barry saw a picture crooked and went and straightened it.

'Damn kids,' he said. 'Jumpin' about the way they do. Wreck a place.'

He sat on a chair well forward to smoke.

The old woman with her head forward to avoid touching the cushion was so still she might have been a drawing.

'You still crook?' Barry said.

'Not too bad,' the old woman said.

She rocked her foot and Barry smoked. Then he screwed his rump around to put his tobacco in a back pocket.

'You ought to go into one of them places,' he said.

The old woman halted her rocking foot. She took hold of the two chair arms. She had a vision of a row of beds with grey-haired women in them. The floor was a vast slippery sea. She was struggling from one of the beds, made tight like the daughter-in-law's beds, to look for a lavatory.

'I'd need more strength,' the old woman said.

'They take you sick,' Barry said. 'Sick or well they take you. We've seen one. Clean. God, it's clean.'

Now? wondered the old woman and didn't know whether she spoke or not.

She thought of the child running home. Her shoes on the steps, tap, tap, tap. Her schoolcase banging the rails in her haste. She thought of all the child, her blocky little shape and those legs and arms and that fair, springy hair.

But not the eyes, bright blue inside all that white.

She dropped her head back on the daughter-in-law's cushion.

'Well, bugger me if I care,' the old woman said.

ACKNOWLEDGEMENTS

The following stories have been published previously in the sources mentioned:

'Young Father', *Meanjin*, No 3, 1979; 'Eclipsed', *Bulletin* Centenary Issue, 29 January 1980; 'Reunion in Gunyah Creek', *Southerly*, No 3 1980; 'The Courts of the Lord', Fay Zwicky, *Canberra Times*, 23 October 1982; 'Games My Parents Played', *Southerly*, No 1, 1980; 'Sunday Session', *Westerly*, No 1, 1980; 'Uncle Games', *Bulletin* Centenary Issue, 29 January 1980; 'Did He Pay', *Tabloid Story, Nation Review*; 'Reading the Signs' *New Yorker*; 'Graffito Spy', *Southerly* 1981; 'Speedie Lady', *Pink Cakes*, an anthology of short fiction and poetry published by the students of the NSW Institute of Technology, 1979; 'The Prince Philip Blues', *Versions*, 1981; 'Parting', *Pink Cakes*, an anthology of short fiction and poetry published by the students of the NSW Institute of Technology, 1979; 'Hospital', *Going Down Swinging*, 1981; 'Having a Wonderful Time', *Southerly*, No 4, 1980; 'Movements Before Falling', *Meanjin*, No 1, 1981; 'Chicken Street', *Island*, No 8, 1981; 'The House on Lafayette Street', *Inprint*, No 2, 1980; 'Young Man in Paddy Pallin Walking Boots', *Inprint*, No 2, 1980; 'Three Into Four', *Westerly*, 'The Bay of Islands', *Morning Parrot Trees*, Brian Cole, Red Press, 1979; 'The Codpiece and the Diary Entry', *Meanjin*, No 1, 1981; 'Working Hot', *Frictions*, Anna Gibbs and Alison Tilson (eds), Sybylla Cooperative Press, 1982; 'And She Gave One Twirl', *Jetaway* inflight magazine, Air New Zealand, 1981; 'Oh I Do Love to be Beside the Seaside', *Inprint*, No 1, 1980; 'Healing' *New Yorker*; 'Untitled', *Neos: Young*

Writers, No 1, 1982; 'Skinning Peaches', *Bulletin* Literary Supplement, December 1982; 'From A Bush Logbook: Going Into the Heartlands With the Wrong Person At Christmas', *Meanjin*, No 1, 1981; 'The Swallows Returning', *Southerly*, No 3 1982; 'The Arrival', *Inprint*, No 4, 1980; 'Virgins, Widows and Penitents', *Quadrant*, December 1980.

The editor and the publisher would like to thank the publishers of the following stories for permission to include them in this collection:
'Life and Death in the South Side Pavilion', from *The Fat Man in History*, Peter Carey, UQP, 1975; 'You'll Like it There', from *Home Girls*, Olga Masters, UQP, 1982; 'Dreaming of Glory', from *Whoring Around*, John Bryson, Penguin Books, 1981.

Every effort has been made by the editor, Frank Moorhouse, to contact the authors of the stories in this collection. He would be pleased to hear from those authors whom he was unable to contact.